THE
SUMMER
GIRL

ALSO BY ELLE KENNEDY

Good Girl Complex
Bad Girl Reputation

THE SUMMER GIRL

An Avalon Bay Novel

Elle Kennedy

ST. MARTIN'S
GRIFFIN
NEW YORK

First published in the United States by St. Martin's Griffin, an imprint of St. Martin's Publishing Group

www.stmartins.com

Designed by Steven Seighman

Library of Congress Cataloging-in-Publication Data

Names: Kennedy, Elle, author.
Title: The summer girl / Elle Kennedy.
Description: First edition. | New York : St. Martin's Griffin, 2023. |
    Series: Avalon Bay ; 3
Identifiers: LCCN 2023009381 | ISBN 9781250863874 (trade paperback) |
    ISBN 9781250863881 (ebook)
Subjects: LCGFT: Romance fiction. | Novels.
Classification: LCC PS3611.E55857 S86 2023 | DDC 813/.6—dc23/
    eng/20230227
LC record available at https://lccn.loc.gov/2023009381

Our books may be purchased in bulk for promotional, educational, or business use. Please contact your local bookseller or the Macmillan Corporate and Premium Sales Department at 1-800-221-7945, extension 5442, or by email at MacmillanSpecialMarkets@macmillan.com.

First Edition: 2023

10 9 8 7 6 5 4 3 2 1

THE
SUMMER
GIRL

CHAPTER 1

CASSIE

July

"I don't think we should hook up anymore."

Oh my God.

No.

No no no no no.

See, this is why parties should be banned. I'm not even joking. We need to go back to the prohibition days, except we outlaw social events instead of alcohol. It's the only way to avoid this level of embarrassment. Or rather, secondhand embarrassment, because *I'm* not even the one getting dumped.

That honor is bestowed upon the guy with the deep, playful voice, who hasn't caught up to the fact that his dumper is dead serious. "Is this some weird sort of foreplay? I don't get it, but, sure, I'm down."

The girl's voice is flat, lined with dry humor. "I'm being serious."

She pauses for a long beat, during which I consider whether I can make a run for it without the couple noticing.

No more than ten feet away from them, I'm sitting against a driftwood log, concealed by shadows. But a clean getaway is difficult because they chose to break up in the worst possible location—

right where the beach grass thins and the dunes flatten into a stretch of packed sand. My mind has been *Mission: Impossible*–ing escape routes since The Dumping commenced. The couple is facing the dark ocean, which means if I attempt to take the beach route back to the party, they'll see me. But if I try to sneak behind them, they'll hear me. Have you ever tried walking silently in beach grass? You might as well attach a bell around your neck.

My only option is to remain hidden until it's over. The conversation *and* the relationship. Because while nobody wants to get dumped, having it happen in front of an audience is a hundred times worse, so I'm officially trapped here. Held hostage by social etiquette.

Of *all* the times to wander away from the bonfire and look at the stupid stars.

"I think this has run its course," the dumper says.

I can't tell what either of them look like. They're mere shadows. A tall shadow and a shorter one. I think the short one has long hair; I glimpse wispy strands blowing in the night breeze.

From the other end of the beach, the hum of voices, laughter, and faint hip-hop music travels along the water, triggering the desperate urge to be back at the party. I don't know a single person there, yet I don't think I've ever longed for the company of total strangers more than I do in this moment. The party is at some local named Luke's house. I was supposed to meet my friend Joy, who bailed at the last second. I was literally getting out of my car when her text popped up; otherwise, I would've just stayed home. But I figured, hey, I'm already here. Might as well mingle, maybe meet some people.

I should've hopped right back in the car and escaped when I had the chance.

The guy is finally catching on that this isn't a joke. "Wait, really? I thought we were still having a good time."

"Honestly? Not so much lately."

Ouch. Sorry, bro.

"Oh, don't look at me like that. I don't mean the sex. That's always good. But we've been doing this friends-with-benefits arrangement for almost a year now. Yeah, it's been on and off, but I think the longer we keep it up, the greater the risk that one of us catches feelings. We said from the start that we didn't want anything serious, remember?"

"Yeah, I remember."

The tall shadow lifts a hand and drags it through his hair. Either that, or he's petting a tiny cat that's sitting atop his head.

I truly can't see a damn thing out here.

"I'm not interested in getting into a relationship anytime soon," she adds. "I don't want a boyfriend."

There's a pause. "What about Wyatt?"

"What about him? Like I keep telling him, he and I are just friends. And I just want to be alone for a while." She chuckles. "Look, we both know you'll have no trouble finding a new friend with bennies, Tate. And if you want more than that, you'll have no trouble finding a girlfriend either. It's just not going to be me."

Double ouch.

I appreciate her candor, though. She's not wasting any time. Not leading this guy around by the nose. I mean, it does sound like this was more of a casual FWB situationship, but that might actually be the worst kind of breakup. Being friends with the person before the sexy stuff and wanting to remain friends *after* it? That's a tricky needle to thread.

I haven't been officially dumped before—that would require being in an actual relationship—but if I were to ever be the recipient of a breakup speech, I'd want it to sound like this one. Quick and to the point. Just snuff out the candle so there's not even a glimmer of light left. It's over. Move on.

Granted, I say that now. But considering I bawl at those courier commercials where the lonely grandmother receives a holiday card from her grandkids, I'd probably collapse in a pool of tears at my dumper's feet and then promptly check myself into a posh wellness facility for melancholia.

"Okay. Cool." He chuckles too, albeit wryly. "I guess that's that, then."

"That's that," she echoes. "Are we good?"

"Of course. We've known each other since we were thirteen. We're not going to stop talking just because we've stopped banging."

"I'm holding you to that," she warns.

Finally, blessedly, miraculously—they're done. The interaction ends. Her flip-flops smack loudly against the sand as she walks away, taking the beach route toward the party.

One down.

One to go.

To my dismay, the guy moves closer to the water, where he proceeds to stand like a statue, staring out. The new position places him closer to a shard of moonlight, providing a better view of him. He's tall. Muscular. Wearing board shorts and a T-shirt, although I can't tell what color they are because it's too dark. I think his hair might be blond. And he's got a great butt. I don't tend to notice butts—didn't think I was a butt girl, in fact—but this one really draws the eye.

With his back to me, this is my chance to creep away. I slowly rise to my feet and wipe my clammy hands on the front of my denim shorts. Man, I hadn't realized how wrought with tension I was. My palms only get sweaty before a first kiss and a particularly harrowing situation. Aka every conversation with my mother. Ergo, my palms are perpetually damp.

I take a deep breath, and then a small step.

Relief flutters through me when the guy doesn't turn my way.

Yes. I can totally do this. Hell, I only need to make it to that dune ten feet away. If he notices me after that, I can pretend I came from the grass. Oh sorry! Just taking a walk, didn't see you there!

Escape is within reach. I can taste it. So, of course, I make it about five feet before my phone decides to thwart my efforts by loudly alerting an incoming text.

And then another one.

And another one.

The guy spins around, startled.

"Hey." His deep, suspicious voice travels toward me in the night breeze. "Where the hell d'you come from?"

I feel my cheeks heat up. I'm grateful it's too dark for him to see the blush. "I'm sorry," I blurt out. "I, um . . ." My brain scrambles for a suitable reason for my presence. It fails. "I didn't hear a single second of your breakup, I swear."

Oh, fucking hell. Brilliant, Cassandra.

That gets me a faint laugh. "Not a single second, huh?"

"Nope, not a one. Seriously, I can assure you I most certainly did *not* just sit here and listen to you get dumped." My mouth has run away from me. It's in charge. It's the captain now. Another thing that happens when I'm nervous: I tend to babble. "For what it's worth, you handled it well. I mean, you didn't drop to your knees and cling to her legs and beg her not to go. So I'm grateful for that. Spared us both more embarrassment, you know? It's almost as if you knew I was trapped behind that log over there."

"Trust me, if I knew you were sitting there, I would've upped the sadness factor by like two hundred percent. Thrown in some tears, maybe cursed at the heavens and bemoaned my poor broken heart."

He saunters closer, and when I get a better look at his face, my heart instantly speeds up. Holy shit, he's gorgeous. What on earth was that girl thinking letting him get away?

I sweep my gaze over his classically handsome features. I wish I could discern what color his eyes are, but it's too dark out here. I was right about the blond hair, though, so I assume he has light-colored eyes. Blue. Maybe green. In those board shorts and slightly rumpled tee, he looks like the quintessential beach boy.

"And why would you have done that?" I ask.

"You know, just to make you extra uncomfortable. As punishment for your eavesdropping."

"*Involuntary* eavesdropping."

"That's what they all say." His mouth curves into a mischievous smile, which I think might be his default expression. He tips his head thoughtfully. "But you know what, I'll let it slide. I can never hold a grudge against a cute girl."

My cheeks get hotter.

Oh my God.

He thinks I'm cute?

I mean, I did select tonight's outfit with the end goal being cuteness. Short shorts that give my legs a deceptively longer look, paired with a tight tank top. Black, because that's the only color with the ability to make my boobs appear smaller. In light colors, they're bouncing around like two uncontained beach balls, even with a super supportive bra.

I realize his gaze hasn't once drifted to my chest, though. Or if it has, he's done it so smoothly and discreetly that I hadn't noticed. His eyes remain fixed on my face, and for a moment I'm tongue-tied. I see attractive guys back in Boston all the time. My college campus is practically crawling with them. But something about this one is making me wobbly in the knees.

Before I can think of a witty response to his *cute girl* remark—or any response at all, really—my phone dings again. I glance down. Another text from Peyton. Followed by another one.

"Someone's popular," he teases.

"Um, yeah. I mean, no. It's just my friend." I grit my teeth. "She's one of those annoying people who send, like, ten one-line messages instead of a single paragraph, so they just keep popping up and the phone dings over and over again until you want to smash it over their head. I hate that—don't you hate that?"

His jaw drops. "*Yes,*" he says, with such sincerity I have to grin. He shakes his head. "I fucking *hate* that."

"Right?"

A final ding sounds, bringing us to a total of six Peyton messages.

When I skim the notifications, I'm once again thankful to be in the dark, because I'm certain my face is even redder.

Peyton: *How's the party?*
Peyton: *Any cute guys?*
Peyton: *Who are we going to fling with?*
Peyton: *Try to snap some pictures of the candidates!*
Peyton: *I really want to be part of this process.*
Peyton: *I wish I was there!*

I want to say that Peyton is joking. Alas, she is not. My main purpose for coming to the party tonight was to find a worthy candidate for my summer fling.

It's been a while since I spent an entire summer in Avalon Bay, but I still remember watching various friends over the years fall headfirst into summer romances. Those passionate, giddy, exhilarating love affairs where you can't keep your hands off each other and everything feels so urgent and intense because you know it's only temporary. Every moment is precious because come September, it's goodbye. I'd been so jealous of those girls, longing for a summertime love of my own, but it was hard to focus on boys and romance when my family was in constant turmoil.

After my parents divorced when I was eleven, Mom and I continued returning for the summers, at least at first. Mom's side of the family, the Tanners, has a long history with Avalon Bay. My grandparents own a beach house in the more affluent part of town, and they expected us to make the yearly trip to visit them. Back then, Mom and Dad were still putting on the cordial pretense for my sake. Once Dad remarried, however, all bets were off. Mom's anger and disdain toward him was out in the open now, and vice versa, which made coming back to the Bay an exercise in psychological warfare.

Fortunately, Mom remarried shortly after and announced we would no longer be spending our summers in the South Carolina beach town where I'd been born and raised. I can't say I wasn't relieved. It meant that when I did come back to visit, I could see Dad in peace and enjoy myself. Of course, then I'd return to Boston where Mom would interrogate me and demand to know every word my father uttered about her. Which was annoying and unfair, but still better than being trapped in the same town with both of them.

"Are you going to text her back?"

The guy's voice jolts me from my thoughts. "Oh. No. I'll answer her later."

I hastily tuck the phone into my back pocket. If I thought hearing him get dumped had been uncomfortable, it's nothing compared to the mortification I'd feel if he saw Peyton's message thread.

He watches me for a moment. "I'm Tate," he finally says.

I hesitate. "Cassie."

"Are you here for the summer?"

I nod. "I'm staying with my grandmother—she has a house over on the south end. But I actually grew up in Avalon Bay."

"You did?"

"Uh-huh. I moved to Boston with my mom after my parents' divorce, but my dad still lives here, so I basically became a summer girl. Well, maybe not an official summer girl, since I usually only come back for a week or two every July. Except this year I'm staying till after Labor Day, so I guess I'm a real summer girl now."

Stop babbling! I order myself.

"What about you?" I ask, desperate to take the focus off me and the fact that I must've used the phrase *summer girl* about four million times in one sentence.

"The opposite of you. I moved to the Bay at the start of junior high. Before that we lived in Georgia. St. Simon's Island." Tate sounds a bit glum. "I envy the Boston thing, to be honest. I kind of wish we moved to a city instead of trading one beach town for another. Do you go to school up there?"

"Yes. I go to Briar University."

"An Ivy girl, huh?"

We fall into step with each other, headed in the direction of the party. It's not a discussed course of action, just instinctive.

"I'm going into my senior year," I add.

"Cool. What are you studying?"

"English Lit." I glance over wryly. "I know. Totally useless unless I want to be a teacher."

"Do you want to be a teacher?"

"Nope."

He grins, and I catch a glimpse of straight white teeth in the moonlight. His smile is perfection. A girl could get lost in it.

I force myself to look forward, shoving my hands in my pockets as we walk. "You know what pisses me off, Tate?"

"What pisses you off, Cassie?" I can still feel him smiling at me.

"Everyone says you find yourself when you're in college, right? But from what I've seen, it's just a bunch of lame parties and all-night study sessions and listening to some blowhard drone on and on in a lecture hall. And meanwhile you sit there pretending you enjoyed the boring-ass book you were assigned to read, when in reality it's more enjoyable watching water boil than reading most classic literature. There—I said it. The classics suck, okay? And college is boring."

Tate chuckles. "Maybe you're not going to the right parties."

He's right. I'm not. Because I've never, ever attended a party where I've spoken at length with a guy who looks like Tate.

As we near the bonfire, our path is now clearly illuminated. Music continues to blast, a slow reggae song that has several couples wrapped around each other, moving to the sultry beat. The crowd seems to be comprised entirely of locals. At least, if there's anyone here from the country club, I don't recognize them. The summer set doesn't typically socialize with the year-round folks. Joy thinks the only reason she was invited tonight was because that Luke guy was hoping to hook up. "Those local boys get a kick out of seducing the rich girls," she'd laughed over lunch earlier.

Not that I would know. I've never been seduced by a local. I also don't consider myself a *rich girl,* although I suppose I am one. My mother's side of the family has money. A fair amount of it. But I'll always view myself as the girl who grew up on Sycamore Way, in a cozy house in the suburbs not far from this section of the Bay.

With the light of the bonfire making it easier to see each other, Tate eyes the ponytail I'm fiddling with and lets out a groan. "You're a ginger," he accuses, his eyes twinkling. They're a light blue, just as I suspected.

"Don't paint me with that ginger brush," I protest. "I'm a *copper.*"

"That's not a real thing."

"I'm a copper," I insist. I grip my ponytail and hold it closer to his face. "See? Dark red. It's practically brown!"

"Mmm-hmm. Keep telling yourself that, ginger."

He seems distracted now. His gaze drifts across the fire and my gaze follows, coming to rest on a girl with bright red hair. A true ginger. Unlike me, who is a *copper,* thank you very much.

The ginger is chatting with two other young women, and all three are drop-dead gorgeous. Shiny hair and pretty faces. Skimpy clothes. And they've got those perfect beach bodies that trigger a pang of insecurity in me. I've always wondered what it's like to have normal proportions. It's probably awesome.

Tate's expression grows pained for a moment before he wrenches his eyes off the girl.

Understanding dawns on me. "Oh my God. Is that her? The dumper?"

He slides out a laugh. "It wasn't a dumping. And we're still friends—that's not going to change. She just caught me off guard, is all. I'm usually the one who ends those types of things."

"Do you want me to go beat her up for you?" I offer.

Pursing his lips, he assesses my frame. I'm five-three and kind of scrawny. Slender, except for my huge chest. Really, my boobs are probably more effective weapons than my fists.

"Nah," he answers, lips twitching. "I don't think I'd feel right being responsible for your death."

"That's really sweet."

He snorts.

"Tate!" someone calls, and we both turn toward the shout.

A very tall guy with a reddish beard stands nearby, holding up a joint. He waves it enticingly at Tate and arches a brow. An invitation. Tate nods at the guy, indicating with his hand that he'll be right there.

"Why are there so many redheads here?" I demand. "Is this a convention?"

"You tell me. These are your people, after all."

I growl at him, and he just laughs again. I like the sound of his laughter.

"Want me to introduce you around?" Tate offers.

Hesitation grips me. I'm torn. On one hand, it would be fun to stay and hang out. But the redheaded girl is watching us now, a slightly bemused look on her gorgeous face. In fact, *a lot* of eyes are on us, I realize. I get the feeling a guy like Tate invites this kind of attention, and I suddenly wish we were still shrouded in the darkness of the beach, just he and I. I hate being the center of attention. And I can't imagine how much nervous babbling I'll do with each new person I meet.

So I shake my head and say, "Actually, I'm heading out. Got somewhere else to be."

He grins. "Fine. Be that way, Ms. Popular."

Hardly. The only place I'm going after this is home. But it's probably better to let him believe I'm fluttering from party to party on Friday nights like some elusive social butterfly. Peyton would approve of that plan. *Always leave 'em wanting more* is my best friend's motto.

"You're here till September, you said?"

"Yup," I say lightly.

"Cool. Then I'm sure we'll see each other around."

"Yeah, maybe."

Shit. That sounded far too noncommittal. What I *should* have said is something coy and flirty, like, *I hope so . . .* and then asked for his number. I inwardly smack myself, scrambling for a way to fix the error, but it's too late. Tate is already sauntering off toward his friends.

If they look back, it's a good sign. That's what Peyton always says.

Swallowing hard, I stare at his retreating back, his long stride making tracks in the sand.

And then.

He looks back.

I breathe in relief and offer him an awkward wave before turning away. My heart's beating fast as I head up the grassy path toward the road, where I parked my grandmother's Land Rover. I pull my phone out of my pocket just as another text lights up the screen.

Peyton: *So??? Have we found the lucky guy?*

I bite my lip and glance back in the direction of the party.

Yes.

Yes, I think we have.

CHAPTER 2

CASSIE

I find my grandmother in the kitchen the next morning, pulling a muffin pan out of the oven. She moves it to the cooling rack on the counter, next to the three other trays already sitting there.

"Morning, dear. Pick your poison," Grandma chirps, glancing at me over her shoulder. "We've got banana nut, bran, carrot, and the blueberry just came out so it needs some time to cool."

No doubt she's been up since 7 A.M. baking up a storm. For a woman in her seventies, she's still remarkably spry. Which is funny, because on the outside she appears so fragile. She's got a slender build, delicate hands, and her skin is thinning in her old age so you can always see bluish veins rippling beneath it.

And yet Lydia Tanner is a force of nature. She and my grandpa Wally ran a hotel for fifty years. They bought the beachfront lot for a song in the late sixties, after Grandpa was injured in Vietnam and discharged from the military. Even wilder is that they were my age when they built the Beacon Hotel from the ground up. I can't imagine building and then operating a hotel at twenty, especially one as grand as the Beacon. And up until two years ago, the waterfront property was my grandparents' pride and joy.

But then Grandpa passed, and the hotel was nearly gutted by the last hurricane to ravage the coast. It wasn't the first time the

Beacon fell victim to a storm—it's happened twice before—but unlike the previous times, nobody in the family wanted to renovate and restore it this time. Grandma was too old and tired to do the job herself, especially without Grandpa Wally by her side, and I know she's secretly disappointed none of her kids chose to take up that mantle. But my mom and her siblings weren't interested in salvaging the Beacon, so Grandma finally made the decision to sell. Not just the hotel, but her house too.

The house sale closes in two months, and the Beacon is being reopened in September under its new ownership, which is why we're back. Grandma wanted to spend one last summer in Avalon Bay before she moves up north to be closer to her kids and grandkids.

"How was the party?" she asks as she settles into a chair at the kitchen table.

"It was okay." I shrug. "I didn't really know anyone there."

"Who was hosting it?"

"Some guy named Luke. He's a sailing instructor at the club. That's how Joy met him. And speaking of Joy, she didn't even show up! She invites me to a party and then deserts me. I felt like a random interloper."

Grandma smiles. "Sometimes that's more fun. Going someplace where nobody knows you . . ." She arches a thin eyebrow. "It can be exciting to reinvent yourself and play a role for the night."

I grimace. "Please don't tell me you and Grandpa used to meet at hotel bars back in the day and pretend to be other people in some weird role-play to spice up the marriage."

"All right, dear. I won't tell you that."

Her brown eyes sparkle, giving her a youthful air. It's funny, Grandma comes off as so elegant and unapproachable in public. Always dressed like she stepped off a yacht, sporting these preppy little outfits more suited for posh Nantucket than laid-back Avalon Bay. I swear she owns a thousand Hermès scarves. Yet when she's around family the icy exterior melts and she's the warmest woman you'll ever meet. I love hanging out with her. And she's hilarious. Sometimes she'll drop a dirty joke out of nowhere at a big family dinner. It's jarring when spoken in her delicate southern accent, and it puts us all in hysterics. My mother hates it. Then again, my mother doesn't have a sense of humor. Never has.

"Did you make any new friends?" Grandma prompts.

"No. But that's okay. I'll see Joy while in town, and Peyton might come visit for a week or two in August." I wander over to the baking trays and study the muffin selections. "I still wish I didn't let you talk me out of getting a job this summer."

Grandma plucks off a small piece of her bran muffin. As long as I've known her, her breakfast has consisted of a muffin and a cup of tea. That's probably how she's maintained her figure all these years.

"Cass, sweetheart, if you'd gotten a job, well, then you wouldn't be able to have breakfast with me, would you?"

"That's a good point." I select a banana nut muffin and grab a small glass plate from the cupboard, then join her at the table. A little walnut falls off my muffin, and I pop it into my mouth. "So what are we doing today?"

"I thought we'd go into town and browse some of the new shops that have opened up? Levi Hartley has taken it upon himself to revamp the entire boardwalk. His construction company has been making its way through all the establishments hurt by the hurricane, fixing them up one by one. There's a very nice hat shop I passed the other day that I wouldn't mind visiting."

Only Grandma Lydia would want to go to a *hat* shop. The only hat I've ever worn is the Briar U baseball cap they handed out at freshman orientation, and that's because they forced us to put them on in order to swear fealty to our new school. I think it's somewhere in the back of my closet now.

"Hat shopping. I can't wait."

She snorts softly.

"And I need to find a present for the girls' birthday, so I wouldn't mind peeking into a couple of those kid stores. Oh! Any chance we can pop into the hotel too? I really want to see what they did inside."

"So do I," Grandma says, a slight frown touching her lips. "The young woman who bought it—Mackenzie Cabot—promised she would preserve your grandfather's and my intent for the property, maintain its charm and character. She sent me the drawings of the upgrades they'd be doing, along with pictures of her progress. They indeed showed her commitment to restoring everything as close to the original as possible. But I haven't received an update since early June."

Her concern is evident. I know that was Grandma's biggest fear—the Beacon becoming completely unrecognizable. The hotel was her legacy. It survived three hurricanes, was lovingly rebuilt by my grandparents twice. They put everything they had into it. Their blood, sweat, and tears. Their love. And it irks me, just a bit, that not a single one of their four children fought to keep it in the family.

My two uncles, Will and Max, live in Boston with their wives, and they each have three young kids. Both were adamant they weren't going to relocate to the South to renovate a hotel they didn't care about. Aunt Jacqueline and her husband, Charlie, have a house in Connecticut, three kids, and zero interest in dipping their toes in the hospitality industry. And then there's Mom, who has a full social calendar in Boston and is busy spending her ex-husband's money, which at this point is out of pure spite because she went into the marriage independently wealthy; the Tanners are worth millions. But my former stepdad Stuart made the mistake of being the one to ask for a divorce, and my mother is nothing if not petty.

I scarf down the rest of my muffin before hopping out of my chair.

"Okay, if we're going into town, let me change into something a little more presentable," I say, gesturing to my ratty shorts and loose T-shirt. "I can't be going hat shopping in this." I aim a pointed glare at Grandma's impeccably pressed chinos, sleeveless shirt, and striped silk scarf. "Especially next to you. Like, jeez, lady. You look like you're going to a luncheon with a Kennedy."

She chuckles. "Have you forgotten my most important rule of life, dear? *Always leave the house dressed as if you're going to—*"

"*—be murdered,*" I finish, rolling my eyes. "Oh, I remember."

I tell ya, Grandma can get dark sometimes. But it's good advice. I think about it often, in fact. One time I accidentally left my dorm wearing my must-do-laundry panties, the neon-orange ones with the huge hole in the crotch. When I realized it, I almost broke out in hives at the thought that if I were to be killed today, the coroner would undress me on that metal slab and my crotch hole would be the first thing they saw. I'd be the only blushing dead body in the morgue.

Upstairs, I find a pink sundress and slip it on, then braid my hair. My phone rings as I'm slapping an elastic band around the end of the braid. It's Peyton. I didn't call her back when I got home last night, but I did send an intentionally cryptic text I knew would drive her nuts.

"Who is he?" she demands when I put her on speakerphone. "Tell me everything."

"Nothing to tell." I wander over to the vanity table and examine my chin. I feel a zit coming on, but my reflection says otherwise. "I met a hot guy, turned down his invitation to hang out with him at the party, and went home instead."

"Cassandra." Peyton is aghast.

"I know."

"What the hell is wrong with you? The *whole point* of going last night was to meet a dude! And you found one! And you said he's hot?"

"Hottest guy I've ever seen," I moan.

"Then why did you leave?" Her confusion might as well be an accusation.

"I chickened out," I confess. "He was too intimidating! And you should've seen the girls he was with—they were these perfect, tall, fit goddesses. With perfectly proportioned boobs . . . unlike someone you know."

"Oh my God, Cass. Stop. You know how I feel about you beating up on yourself."

"Yeah, yeah, you want to punch me in the face. I can't help it, though. Seriously, those girls were gorgeous."

"And so are you." A frazzled sound echoes over the speaker. "You know, I really hate your mother."

"What does my mother have to do with this?" I snicker.

"Are you kidding me? I've been to your house. I hear how she talks to you. I was actually speaking to my mom about it the other day, and she was saying all that hurtful shit is bound to affect your self-esteem."

"Why are you speaking to your mom about me?" I demand, embarrassment climbing up my throat.

Having a best friend whose mother is a clinical psychologist is definitely a pain in the ass sometimes. I've known Peyton since we were eleven—we met not long after Mom and I moved to Boston—and Peyton's mother would constantly pry into my psyche when I was a kid. She always tried getting me to talk about my parents' divorce, how it made me feel, how my mother's criticism affected me. Blah, blah, and blah. I don't need a shrink to tell me there's a direct correlation between my insecurities and my mother's verbal attacks. Or that my mother is a raging bitch. I know it all too well.

On the rare occasions Dad and I have spoken about her, he's admitted that Mom has always skewed more toward *me me me* on the altruism scale. But the divorce really twisted something inside her. Made her worse. It certainly didn't help that he remarried within a year and a half and now has two other daughters.

"Mom thinks we need to silence your inner critic. Aka your mother's horrible voice in your head."

"I shut my inner critic up all the time. Silver lining, remember?" Because while my grandmother's life rule is to make sure you get murdered in your Sunday best, mine has always been to look on the bright side. Find the silver lining in every situation, because the alternative—wallowing in the darkness—is bound to destroy you.

"Of course, Little Miss Sunshine," Peyton says mockingly. "Always looking for the silver lining—how could I forget?" Her voice takes on a note of challenge. "Okay, fine. So tell me, what's the silver lining in letting Hottie slip away?"

I mull it over. "He's too hot," I finally answer.

Laughter bursts out of the phone. "That would be the reason *not* to let him slip away." She makes a loud buzzing sound. "Try again."

"No, that's really it," I insist. "Imagine if the first guy I ever sleep with is at *that* level of hotness? It'll spoil all future men for me! I'll expect every man who comes afterward to be a perfect ten, and when nobody measures up I'm just going to be devastated."

"You're impossible. Did you get his number at least?"

"No, I told you, I ran away like a nervous babbling bunny."

She lets out a loud, heavy sigh. "This is unacceptable to me, Cassandra Elise."

"My deepest apologies, Peyton Marie."

"If you see him again, you're asking him out, understood?" My best friend has snapped into totalitarian mode. "No babbling. No excuses. Promise me you'll ask him out next time you see him."

"I will. I promise," I say lightly, but only because I'm confident I'll never see him again.

Joke's on me, though.

The moment Grandma and I step outside five minutes later, I find none other than Tate standing in our driveway.

CHAPTER 3

TATE

It takes a second to realize the cute redhead on the porch is the same one from the party last night. She was right—her hair is more copper than ginger. I guess the bonfire made it appear lighter. My gaze then darts to her chest, just a quick peek to confirm I hadn't fallen into some teenage-boy fantasy yesterday. But nope, didn't dream it. Her rack is objectively spectacular. Sue me for noticing. I'm a man. I always notice a great rack.

She's wearing a short sundress that falls mid-thigh and clashes with the red-painted toenails poking out of her strappy sandals. And she's staring at me as if she's not quite sure what to make of my presence.

"Mr. Bartlett, what brings you here this morning?"

My gaze shifts to the older woman next to Cassie. "Morning, Mrs. Tanner." I flash an easy smile that my friends tell me could disarm a dictator. Not that Lydia Tanner is a dictator. She's a perfectly nice lady, based on the interactions we've had when I was housesitting the place next door. This is my fourth summer staying at Gil and Shirley Jackson's luxury waterfront property. I've been looking forward to it for weeks.

"Just wanted to stop by and let you know I'm watching the Jackson place again for the summer," I tell her. "So if you see lights on at random hours, or, you know, handsome guys walking around in the nude, don't be alarmed . . . and feel free to keep looking." I wink.

Cassie snorts out a sarcastic laugh.

"Cassandra," Lydia chides. "Let the boy think he's charming us."

"Think?" I mock good-naturedly. "You know you love me, Mrs. Tanner."

"As I told you last year, you can call me Lydia. This is my granddaughter, Cassandra."

"Cassie," she corrects.

"Actually, we met last night," I inform Lydia. "Ran into each other at a party. How's it going, ginger?"

"Do not call me that." Cassie glowers at me.

Lydia turns to her granddaughter. "Well, there you go, dear. We were just discussing your lack of friend options, and look, now you'll have a friend right next door. And he's already given you an amusing nickname! This is wonderful." She reaches out and pats Cassie on the arm, as if placating a distressed puppy.

Cassie's cheeks redden. "You are the worst," she grumbles at her grandmother.

Chuckling, Lydia descends the steps of the wraparound porch. "I'll go start the car."

"She said that on purpose just to embarrass me," Cassie mutters. She narrows her eyes at me. "I have friends."

I blink innocently. "Sure sounds like it."

"*I have friends,*" she insists, a growl coming from the back of her throat.

I choke down a laugh. Fuck, she's cute. Like, ridiculously cute. I have a thing for chicks with freckles. And ones who blush when I smile at them.

"Does that mean you don't want to be my friend?" I ask, eyeing Cassie in amusement.

"Friendship is a huge commitment. We should probably just

stick to being neighbors. But you're in luck, because that means we can do lots of fun neighborly things." She pauses. "I'm not quite sure what. Maybe stand at two windows that face each other and use flashlights to send Morse code messages?"

"Is that what you think neighbors do?"

"I don't know. My dorm window looks out at a brick wall, so nobody's sending any covert messages to me, unless you count the drunk frat boy who always gets lost on his way to Greek Row and stumbles around shouting that the moon isn't real. And I'm not friends with any of the neighbors at Mom's house in Boston. Not that you and I are friends. I mean, I don't even know you. We're total strangers. Although, I *did* see you get dumped, which was equally upsetting for both of us, and that kind of shared humiliation leads to a forced kind of intimacy that nobody should ever have to experience—" She cuts herself off. "You know what? I'm just gonna go. Grandma and I are going into town. Goodbye, Tate."

My lips twitch in a difficult attempt to suppress a grin. "Uh-huh. Cool. See you later, neighbor."

She huffs, and my smile springs loose as I watch her march off. My gaze lowers, resting briefly on her ass. Damn, a great rack *and* a great ass. She's on the shorter side, though. I've always been drawn to taller girls. At six-one, I don't want to break my neck bending down to kiss someone. Cassie's five-two, five-three tops, but something about the set of her shoulders and the way she walks gives her more stature. And she's funny. A little strange. But funny. I was already looking forward to these next eight weeks at the Jackson house. Having Cassie next door for the summer is the icing on an already delicious cake.

The white Range Rover heads for the end of the circular driveway with Mrs. Tanner behind the wheel. I watch it disappear, then head next door. Because the homes on this stretch of the waterfront are situated on a slope, there isn't a lot of space between the houses, at least not on the street-facing side, which means you're always seeing your neighbors. But the high, westerly location also means spectacular views of Avalon Bay, and unparalleled sunsets.

The Jackson house took a few hits in the last storm, but Gil instantly hired a contractor to fix it up and a landscaper to haul out all the fallen trees and debris. All that remains now are the moss-draped oaks and other mature trees that have stood strong and proud for decades. The property is loaded with charm. It blows me away every time I stay here.

I step through the graceful white columns onto the covered porch and let myself in through the front door. Inside, I give the immaculate main floor a long once-over. I always get paranoid housesitting this place, afraid of breaking something priceless or spilling beer all over their expensive rugs. I wander into the chef's kitchen toward the longest island I've ever seen. My fingertips skim sleek oak, painted a nautical blue. The housekeeper, Mary, was here yesterday, so everything is clean and dust-free. The smell of lemon and pine mingles with the familiar salty scent wafting in from the back doors. The first thing I did when I got here was open the three sets of French doors that make up the entire rear wall of the living room. My mood is always a thousand times better when I can smell the ocean.

My phone buzzes and I pull it out of my pocket to see a message from my mother.

Mom: *All settled in?*

I tap out a quick response.

Me: *Yup. Unpacked and ready for two months of freedom. You guys were really cramping my style.*

Mom: *Yes, I'm sure all that home cooking was a real drag.*

Me: *Shit. Fine. I'll miss that part. But Gil added a Fountain Lightning to his private fleet, so I think that might make up for all the greasy takeout I'll be eating.*

Mom: *I'll drop off some frozen lasagnas. Grease poisoning is no joke.*

Me: *How are my children? Do they miss me?*

Mom: *Well . . . Fudge just took a four-hour nap, and Polly just ate a bug. So I'm gonna say . . . no?*

Me: *Nah, sounds like coping mechanisms for missing me. You should let them sleep in your bed while I'm gone so they don't feel lonely.*

Mom: *Sure won't!*

I grin at the phone. My parents are sadists who refuse to let our family dogs sleep in their bed. I'll never understand it.

Me: *Anyway, I gotta go. I'll message you tomorrow.*

Mom: *Love you.*

Me: *Love you too.*

I don't care if it makes me the biggest loser on the planet, but sometimes I think my mom is my best friend. Hands down, she's the coolest chick I know. And I tell her nearly everything. I mean, sure, I keep my sex life to myself, but there's very little else I won't confide in Mom about. Dad, too. In fact, I think he might also be my best friend.

Christ, maybe I *am* a huge loser.

Leaving my phone on the counter, I amble toward the French doors and peer outside. Beyond the stone dining patio, grill, and outdoor fireplace is a short wooden staircase leading to the upper deck. Beyond *that* is the path that takes you to the lower deck and the Jacksons' long, private dock, complete with an electric boat lift and a covered pierhead. I focus my gaze on the end of the dock, admiring the two boats currently moored there. Gil's prized Hallberg-Rassy, the *Surely Perfect*, is moored at the yacht club marina, but he keeps his high-performance powerboat and Boston Whaler Sport Fisherman at the house for the season.

A shiver runs through me as I gawk at the red-and-white powerboat. The Lightning. Christ, I'd kill to take her out, but she's ludicrously expensive and I'd never dream of asking Gil if I could use her.

I seriously envy this man's life. A real estate developer who's worth millions, Gil owns several properties around the globe and pretty much an entire fleet of boats. He and Shirley are spending the next two months in New Zealand, where they're looking to add another house to their portfolio. And, knowing Gil, another sailboat. Lucky assholes. Their life sounds like pure heaven to me—sailing around the world, exploring new places . . .

The sailing part, in particular, is what really gets my blood going. Being a part-time sailing instructor at the club doesn't feel like enough to me; for years I've longed to be out on the water full-time, but that's simply not feasible, not when I also need to put in the hours at Bartlett Marine, the family business. Don't get me wrong, it's not a bad gig. And it's always astonishing to see how much money people are willing to drop on their boats. But still, I'd rather be *on* a boat than hand over her keys to somebody else.

Since I have the day off—and Gil's permission to use the Whaler and the Sea-Doos—I grab my phone from the kitchen counter. The weather's perfect for a day on the water, and I scroll through my message threads trying to decide which one of my boys to text.

I'm pretty sure Danny, a fellow instructor at the club, is working today.

Luke should be home, but I have a feeling he'll be too hungover from the party last night. When I left around 2 A.M., he was still doing tequila shots with our friends Steph and Heidi.

I'd ask my buddy Wyatt, our local tattoo artist, but things are kind of weird between us. Not on my account, though. I was just going about my business, hanging out with Alana here and there, when Wyatt broke up with his longtime girlfriend and suddenly decided he had a thing for Alana too. Next thing I know, I'm in a love triangle I never wanted to be part of, over a woman who doesn't actually want either one of us.

I text Luke first, who responds without mincing words.

Luke: *Bro, I'm so hungover. If I go out on the water I'll puke all over your ugly face.*

I try Evan Hartley next, though I'm pretty sure he told me last night that he and his brother Cooper were at one of their construction sites today. I message him anyway, because he's the twin more likely to shirk his responsibilities and go day-drinking on a boat with me.

Evan: *Can't. We're so fucking behind on this stupid job.*

Damn. Guess I'm on my own today.

Evan: *But we're grabbing beers with Danny later. Rip Tide. Around 7. You in?*

I quickly shoot off a response.

Me: *I'm down. See you there.*

CHAPTER 4

CASSIE

"Do you think a six-year-old would like this?" I hold up a red T-shirt that features a purple unicorn riding a surfboard. "What are kids into these days? I have no idea what's age appropriate."

My grandmother's laughter echoes between us. "And I do? I just turned seventy-four, dear. When I was six years old, dinosaurs still roamed the earth."

I snort. "Seventy-four is not old. And you don't look it anyway."

I put the shirt back on the rack. I feel like the colors are too loud. When I saw the girls at Easter, they were both clad in pale pastels. Hmmm. But that could have just been an Easter thing. I know my stepmother, Nia, likes to dress them up for holidays. When I visited this past Christmas, they were in matching red dresses and cute mistletoe headbands.

Ugh. This is way too hard, which only highlights how little I know my half sisters. But I suppose that's bound to be the result when their mother makes sure I spend as little time as possible with them. Hell, I bet if it were up to her, I wouldn't even be joining them for the birthday celebrations next month. Poor Nia. She was probably secretly furious when her twin girls were born on my birthday. And, God, the irony of that . . . Dad's new daughters born on the same day as his old one, effectively erasing me from his life and—

Silver lining! the voice in my head shouts before I sink any deeper.

Right. I draw an even breath. The silver lining of sharing a birthday with my sisters . . . One party instead of two. Consolidation is always a plus.

"I don't know." My gaze conducts another sweep of the rack of children's clothing. "Maybe we can go to the board game store instead? The one next to the smoothie place?" Shopping for this gift has become surprisingly daunting.

Grandma and I exit the store and step into the oppressive July heat. I forgot how hot it gets down here in the summer. And what a total madhouse the main strip becomes. But I'm unbothered by both the sweltering air and the crowds. Avalon Bay isn't just the quintessential beach town with its boardwalk, tourist shops, and annual carnival—it's my home. I was born here. All my childhood memories are tied to this town. I could be gone for fifty years and that sense of familiarity, of belonging, would still be right here when I returned.

"When are you seeing your father?" Grandma asks as we head down the sidewalk. The air is so hot and humid that the pavement beneath our feet is practically hissing from the heat.

"Friday," I answer. "I'm going over there for dinner. And then Saturday evening we might take the girls out somewhere. Maybe mini golf."

"That will be fun. He wasn't able to see you this weekend?"

Although there's no judgment in her voice, I can't help but come to Dad's defense. "The girls had a whole bunch of birthday parties to attend. I guess their entire social circle is a bunch of July babies."

And he couldn't step away for an hour or so and take you to lunch? Dinner?

Do the girls not have a mother who can watch them for a while?

Isn't their bedtime eight o'clock?

All valid questions if she'd asked, but Grandma has more tact than that and knows my relationship with Dad is complicated.

In all honesty, I'm used to being an afterthought to him. For years now he's made a concerted effort to avoid being alone with me if he can help it, grasping on to any opportunity to ensure Nia and the twins are there to serve as a buffer. I'm sure he knows I notice, but he doesn't acknowledge what he's doing and neither do I. And so it just keeps growing between us, this mountain of words I can't say to him. It started off as a tiny little word hill and now it's a peak of unspoken proportions. Thick with emotion and riddled with obstacles. Little accusations I'll never say out loud.

Why didn't you fight for custody?

Why didn't you want me?

"Are you looking forward to seeing your sisters?"

I push the bleak thoughts away and paste on a sunny smile for Grandma. "I'm always excited to see the twins. They're so cute."

"Are they still fluent in French?" she asks curiously.

"Yup. Fluent in French and English." My stepmother is Haitian and grew up speaking French, so she was adamant that her kids know her native tongue. It's fun watching Roxanne and Monique converse in French. Sometimes, it's Roxy speaking French and Mo answering in English, or vice versa, which makes for some hilarious one-sided conversations. I really do adore my sisters. I wish I got to spend more time with them.

Grandma seems to be slowing down, so I match my gait to hers. "You okay?" I ask.

We've been shopping for two hours. Not the longest time, but it's also a hundred degrees out and she's dressed in silk from head to toe. I'm surprised her clothing isn't plastered to her body. I would be a sweaty mess. But Grandma is perpetually put-together, even when baking under the sun.

"I am feeling the heat," she admits. She uncurls the scarf from around her neck and uses a pale hand to fan the exposed flesh. The sun continues to beat down on us. She's wearing a wide-brimmed hat, but I'm hat-free despite our visit to the hat shop.

"Let's just hit the board game place and then head home," I suggest.

She nods. "That's a good idea."

We're nearing the smoothie shop when a traitor appears at the storefront window. Joy taps on the window and waves at me. She holds up a finger to signal she'll be one second.

"Oh, Joy's coming out," I tell my grandmother.

I take her arm and move away from the sidewalk to let a group of pedestrians pass. It's a never-ending stream of people, Avalon Bay at its prime tourist peak. Families, couples, and groups of rowdy teens are already swarming the streets and filling the beach, and with the carnival having just been set up at the end of the board-walk, it's going to be even more packed in the coming weeks. I really missed this place.

Joy exits the shop sucking on the straw of her smoothie. She's wearing a white minidress that complements her dark complexion, wedge sandals, and oversized sunglasses. Gucci, her go-to designer.

"I'm so glad I bumped into you," she chirps, brown eyes shining happily. "I was literally about to text and see if you wanted to go out tonight."

I mock glare at her. "Why? So you can bail on me again?"

She groans repentantly. "Argh, I know, I'm so sorry about last night."

"What the hell was that about? You twist my arm into going to some townie's party and then don't even show?" I grumble.

"I'm sorry," she says again, but her tone is breezier now, her re-morse all but gone. Joy's been flighty for as long as I've known her, and she doesn't waste much time groveling. Once she apologizes for a sin, she moves on from it with lightning speed. "I left the club and was going home to change for the party, just like I texted, but then I pulled into the drive to find Isaiah waiting on my doorstep."

Isaiah is the guy she's been on and off with since we were sixteen. Last time she and I spoke, though, she swore she was done with that. I *tsk* with disappointment. "Please don't tell me you got back together with him."

"No, no. He was just dropping off a box of stuff I left at his place. And there were some photos in there that I'd printed out, so we started going through them, and one thing led to another and—cover your ears, Mrs. Tanner—we fucked."

My grandmother barks out a laugh. "It's lovely to see you too, Joy," Grandma says, before reaching over to lightly pat my arm. "Cass, why don't I drive back to the house and Joy can take over as your shopping companion?"

"Are you sure?" My brow creases. "You're okay driving on your own?"

"I drove us here," she reminds me, offering that dignified one-raised-eyebrow look that translates to *don't question your elders, dear*.

I question her anyway. "Yes, but you said you were feeling the heat. What if you have sunstroke—"

"I'll be fine. Go. You girls have fun. Sounds like you have a lot to chat about." Eyes twinkling, Grandma leaves us to our own devices.

I watch her go, and her strong gait and straight shoulders ease my concerns. Sometimes it's hard to remember what a tough broad she is when it looks like the merest breeze could knock her over.

"So what are we buying?" Joy asks.

"I wanted to pop into the board game store to find something for Roxy and Mo's birthdays."

"Wow, Nia's letting you see her precious progeny on their special day?"

"Be nice."

"Nah, that's your job. You're the nice one. I'm the raging bitch in this friendship, remember? That's why we make a good team."

It's an interesting friendship, I'll give her that. Whereas I met Peyton when I moved to Boston, I've known Joy since we were five. She was a summer girl, her family coming down from Manhattan every year to spend June till August in the Bay. We were inseparable as kids, but eventually drifted apart, not reconnecting until I was sixteen and visiting my dad for a few weeks. My sisters were barely two at that point, so Dad had his hands full and very little time for me. I ended up spending most of the vacation hanging out by the country club pool, where I bumped into Joy one morning and the friendship got a reboot.

"Yeah, and where was my teammate last night?" I demand. "I still can't believe you ditched me. I didn't know a single person there." Which isn't surprising, considering I could probably count the number of townies I know by name on one hand.

The summer kids don't usually socialize with the locals. They travel in different circles, spending most of their time on expensive family yachts or at the country club, where I anticipate passing the bulk of my time this summer. In my future I predict a lot of lying around on lounge chairs and checking out all the hot preppy boys.

Don't get me wrong, I'm not one of those rich girls who refuses to work. I've had part-time jobs since I was sixteen and just spent the last three years of college working as a barista. My work ethic comes solely from my father. Dad, who didn't come from a filthy-rich family like Mom, always hammered the importance of good, honest work into my head. Grandma, however, refuses to let me get a job while I'm in the Bay this summer, determined to force daily quality time on me. I'm certainly not complaining, though. I prefer Grandma's company to most.

"I heard it was a good time," Joy says as we fall into step with each other. She sips her smoothie. "The guy who invited me—Luke? He texted earlier asking why I didn't show. Poor boy was devastated." She grins. "I totally would've hooked up with him too. He's cute. But stupid Isaiah. I just can't stay away from that asshole."

"It's a real problem," I agree solemnly.

"You didn't talk to anyone at all?" she pushes. "Not even the infamous Hartley twins? I think one of them was there."

Okay, so I can name *those* locals. I'm pretty sure everyone, local and summer kid alike, has heard of the Hartleys. The two sinfully hot twins who used to raise hell around town. There was one rumor going around back in the day about a stolen goat, a stolen police car, and a joyride around the Bay that ended with one of the twins in the hospital for a concussion. But that sounds too ludicrous to be true. The tales of their numerous hookups, particularly with the Garnet College girls who arrive every September . . . well, those rumors I tend to believe.

"I didn't see them," I say, searching my memory. I vaguely remember a tall dude with dark hair and tattoos, but, really, that could have been anyone. "I did talk to one guy, though."

"Ahh! Yes! That's my girl. Who?"

"Tate." I try to recall what Grandma called him this morning. Mr. . . . "Bartlett. Tate Bartlett?"

Joy's jaw falls open. "Really? Oh, I know *all* about him."

"You do?" I'm surprised. Like I said, aside from the occasional illicit tryst, summer kids and locals aren't too socially compatible.

"Oh yeah, he hooked up with my sister last summer."

"No! Shut up! Louisa?" For the sheer life of me, I cannot envision Joy's older sister hooking up with anybody, let alone Tate.

Louisa is as prim and proper as they come. I always assumed she was waiting for marriage. "What about her chastity belt?"

My friend snorts. "Someone found the key, and his name was Tate Bartlett. He's an instructor at the yacht club, like that Luke guy. They're friends."

I still can't wrap my head around Louisa and Tate. "How did that even happen? Him and Louisa."

"She was feeling adventurous last year. Remember she was going through her awful platinum-blond phase? I texted you a pic of it."

I nod gravely. "That did not look good."

"No, it didn't." Joy twists the smoothie straw around with her fingers. "So, anyway, they met at the club, he asked her out, and they hooked up. Just third base, I think. Because, you know, it's my sister. But I'm told he's a major playboy."

Not exactly a shock. Guys that good-looking usually have their pick of women.

Hearing he's a player, though, does dull some of the Tate shine. "So he's got a rep for being a sleaze?"

"Actually, it's the opposite. Like, this man hooks up more than a celebrity, yet you won't hear a bad word about him. Everyone who knows him or who's been with him gets all starry-eyed when you bring him up. Starts gushing about how sweet and wonderful he is. And great in bed, of course."

"Of course," I echo, rolling my eyes. Inside, I'm a bit relieved to hear he doesn't have a slimy reputation.

"How did you meet him? What did you talk about?" She links her arm through mine. "I want all the details."

We spend the next hour in town, where I strike out on the girls' birthday presents. I realize I'm going to have to ask Dad for suggestions, which feels like defeat. Joy drops me off at home and we make plans to return to the boardwalk later to catch some live music. She leaves me with the promise that she'll grab me at eight and absolutely, one hundred percent *not* bail on me this time.

At home, I pass the rest of the day reading by the pool and texting with Peyton, then eat dinner with Grandma on the back deck overlooking the quiet bay. I offer to play cards with her afterward, but she wants to turn in early, so we part ways at the top of the staircase, Grandma heading to her room and me ducking into mine.

I always stay in the same room when I visit. Decorated in shades of white and yellow, the bedroom is spacious and airy, with hardwood flooring, a private en suite bath, and a big bay window with a built-in reading bench. Other than the antique desk and armoire, the main piece of furniture is the huge four-post bed that I toss my phone onto.

I need to take a shower, wash my hair, and find something cute to wear into town tonight. Operation Fling may have hit a snag last night, but if I'm serious about finding myself a passionate summer affair—and I am—then it's time to kick that plan into gear.

Ideally, my super-hot and apparently very-open-to-hookups neighbor would be the one to have a fling with, but I've already had two opportunities to make a move, or at least ask for his number, and I've blown it both times. Therefore, putting all my eggs in the Tate basket probably isn't a smart move. I need to be open to meeting other guys. Broadening my fling horizons.

And no better time to start than tonight.

I pull the elastic off and begin undoing my braid, wandering toward the window to preemptively close the curtains before my shower.

Then I freeze. My fingers go motionless, my half-undone braid forgotten.

From my window, I have a clear view of the house next door.

And the window next door. The one that faces mine. And since the two houses are separated by mere yards, and there aren't any trees on the side path that cuts between the homes, I am provided with a clear, unobstructed, perfect, glorious view of Tate as he undresses in the bedroom across the way.

My breath lodges in my throat.

He's facing away from me, and I practically drool while I watch the sinewy muscles of his back ripple as he tosses his shirt aside. His shoulders are broad, arms well-sculpted. He reaches for the waistband of his swim trunks.

His shorts drop to the floor and I almost choke on my tongue.

Holy fuck. I knew he had a nice butt, but seeing it in all its bare glory is . . . otherworldly. I can't take my eyes off it. I feel like a total perv, and I know if the situation was reversed and he was watching me change from his window, I'd be reporting him to the cops. But I'm frozen in place, unable to tear my gaze away.

Turn away, Cassandra.

Turn away.

Stop it.

My mouth has gone completely dry. His body is spectacular. Hard planes and lean muscles and long, tanned limbs all joining together to form one outrageously sexy specimen of a man. I'm breathing hard now. Heart pounding. Tate drags one hand through hair that appears a bit windblown, wandering around the room as if in search of something. Completely naked. Completely oblivious to the fact that his next-door neighbor is ogling him.

Then he turns toward the window.

And he's not so oblivious anymore.

He's visibly startled when our eyes lock. His brow furrows. Lips part, just slightly. I catch one brief glimpse of the full-frontal experience before I spin on my heel and dart away from the window. My heart rate is officially in cardiac arrest territory. He *caught* me looking. What the hell do I do now? What if he reports me or tells my grandmother—

My phone lights up.

"Oh my God," I moan out loud.

I can barely walk over to the bed, that's how weak my legs feel. My hand trembles as I reach for the phone. I grab it and dive into the bathroom, as far away from that damned window as possible.

On the screen, someone is trying to AirDrop me a note.

Tate B.

With a shaky finger I hit *accept,* and the note pops up.

I think we need to talk about this. —Tate

Underneath the message is his phone number.

I'm mortified. But I'm also not dumb enough to think we can sweep this under the rug and pretend I wasn't watching him undress. And while I'm normally the type of person who runs screaming from all confrontations, this needs to be dealt with ASAP. Otherwise we're in for a long, awkward summer.

I click on Tate's number to pull up a new message thread.

Me: *I AM SO SO SORRY. I swear I wasn't spying on you. I was just standing at my window when you walked by and started stripping.*

Tate: *Uh-huh. I'm sure that's exactly what happened.*

Me: *It's true! I only saw you naked for like three seconds, max.*

There's a short beat.

Tate: *Did you enjoy the show?*

Me: *Ew. No.*

Ew no?

What the hell is wrong with me? *This* is why I'm single. Some-one tries to flirt with me, and I respond with *ew no*. Clearly I have issues.

Me: *I mean, I barely saw anything.*
Tate: *Come back to the window.*

My pulse quickens again.

Me: *No.*
Tate: *Just come back. I promise I'm not standing here with my hand on my dick or something creepy.*

Wary, I exit the bathroom. As promised, Tate is not being creepy. He's at the window, a towel wrapped around his waist, a phone in his hand. When he sees me, he gives a cheeky smile and raises his other hand. He's holding a flashlight.

I narrow my eyes, which prompts him to start typing one-handed.

Tate: *What's Morse code for "peeping Tom"?*
Me: *OMG stop. I'm already embarrassed enough.*

It occurs to me that instead of texting, we could just open our respective windows and call out to each other. Then again, sound travels on the water and I don't want my grandmother hearing a second of this conversation.

Tate: *Look. Cassie. I'll be honest. You saw my ass. I think it's only fair that I see yours.*

I squawk in outrage. He can't hear it, but he must know I made some sort of indignant sound because he grins widely.

Me: *Absolutely not.*
Tate: *One cheek?*
Me: *No!*
Tate: *Fine. You drive a hard bargain. I'll settle for your tits.*

I know he's joking. And I think if anyone else had said that to me they'd come off as a total perv. But there's just something about this guy's good looks and dazzling smile. No part of him gives off perverted vibes.

Still, I can't reward him for that kind of talk. Don't want to set a precedent or anything. So I walk to the window while typing a final message.

Me: *You'll just have to use your imagination.*

Then I close the curtains.

CHAPTER 5

TATE

My dad calls when I'm on my way to meet the boys at the Rip Tide. The Bluetooth kicks in and I answer with a quick, "Hey, Dad, what's up?" Since I've got the top down on the Jeep, I ease up on the gas, driving slower so the wind doesn't drown out his voice.

"Can you do me a solid tomorrow, kid?"

I can't help rolling my eyes. I'm twenty-three and he still calls me *kid*. Meanwhile, if anyone is a kid, it's Gavin Bartlett. My dad is basically an overgrown boy, so full of energy and life it honestly gets overwhelming sometimes. He was a big baseball hero back in Georgia, so I grew up hearing from everyone on the island how awesome my father was. Then we moved to Avalon Bay, a place where he didn't know a soul, and within a year he had the entire bay singing his praises too. Everywhere he goes, people love him. He's just one of those universally likable dudes. Doesn't possess a shred of arrogance. Always puts his family first. He's humble. Hilarious. And other than his occasional grumbling when I was a teenager about me not being interested in following in his athletic footsteps, he's a pretty great dad. Luckily, our shared love of the water made up for my disinterest in baseball, so we still had plenty to bond over.

"Depends," I tell him, since I know better than to blindly agree to favors. "What's up?"

"Can you come into work tomorrow morning for a couple hours? I want to take your mom to Starfish Cove."

"What's the occasion?"

"Does there need to be one? A man can't take his wife on a spontaneous Sunday picnic? It's romantic!"

"Dude. I don't want to think about my parents making out at a romantic picnic, please and thank you."

"Making out? We're going to third base at least, kid."

I make a loud gagging noise, mostly for his benefit. Truthfully, there are worse things in this world than having parents who are still madly in love after twenty-five years of marriage.

I'm one of the rare members of my friend group whose family is wholly, disgustingly normal. I'm an only child, so I never had to deal with any of that sibling rivalry shit. Mom loves to garden and Dad still plays baseball with a men's league in town. When people ask me why I'm so laid-back and take everything in stride, it's because, well, I haven't encountered many hardships in my life. The closest thing to turmoil we experienced as a family was a brief rough period when we moved from St. Simon's to Avalon Bay. The stress of the move, combined with Dad changing careers, caused some arguing between my parents, a bit of friction around the house. And then it passed.

I've been lucky, I guess.

"Sure, I can do that," I relent. As much as I hate the idea of working two jobs tomorrow—morning at the dealership and then afternoon at the yacht club—I know Mom would enjoy a picnic at Starfish Cove. And I'm one of those assholes who likes making my parents happy.

"Thanks, kid. I owe you one. Oh, and keep an eye out for a man named Alfred. Or Albert? Can't remember. Anyway, he's coming in around nine to look at the fifty-foot Beneteau that Sam Powell just brought in."

"What? Sam's selling the Beneteau?" I ask in dismay.

"Already did. We closed the deal on Friday."

"Shit, really? Didn't he just do a refit in 2019? And he spent a chunk on that new teak deck, no?"

"That's why he's selling now—the refit upped the value. This is the time to sell."

"But Sam loves that boat."

"Loves his kid more. And she got into Harvard. Gotta pay for that Ivy League tuition somehow, right?"

"That's rough."

We chat for a few more minutes before hanging up. As I turn left onto the main road leading downtown, my mind is still on Sam Powell parting with his beloved sailboat. Man, I never want to be in the position where I need to choose between my kid and my boat. Not that I have either one of those yet, but my goal is to at least start working toward securing the latter. I could probably buy a used forty-foot Bristol, maybe even a Beneteau Oceanis in the next couple years if I'm able to save more money.

After that, well, ideally I'd be sailing her around the world, although that's more a dream than a goal. A pipe dream, at that, because there's no way I can just fuck off for months on end. Dad already has it all planned out—he wants to retire early, and once he does, I'll be taking over Bartlett Marine, selling other people their dream boats rather than sailing my own. And while I can't deny the dealership turns a serious profit, it hasn't exactly been my lifelong dream to run it.

Main Street is already packed with cars, not an open space to be found. I end up having to pull into one of the gravel beach-access lots and hoof it half a mile to the Rip Tide, where I find my friends gathered around a high-top table near the stage. Our buddy Jordy and his reggae band play this venue most weekends, but they're not here tonight. In their place is a metal outfit with a lead singer who's scream-singing unintelligible lyrics as I sidle up to the boys.

Cooper, clad in a black T-shirt and ripped jeans, is sipping on a beer and wincing at the ungodly noises coming from the stage. His other half is nowhere to be found, and by that I mean Evan, his twin. Mackenzie would be his *better* half, the chick who got Cooper to smile more times in the last year than in all the years I've known him combined. Genuine smiles, too, and not the cocky smirks he'd flash right before we used to fuck shit up.

Chase is next to Coop, engrossed with his phone, while Danny listens to the band with a pained expression.

"These guys are awful," I say, wondering who the hell decided to book them. The singer is now making strange breathing noises while the two guitarists whisper into their microphones. "Why are they whispering now?"

"Is he saying *my skull is weeping*?" Cooper demands, wrinkling his brow.

"No. It's *my soul is sleeping*," Danny tells him.

"It's both," Chase says without looking up from his phone. "My skull is weeping/my soul is sleeping. Those are the lyrics."

"Deep," I say dryly, and my own skull nearly weeps with relief when the song—if you could call it that—ends, and the singer—if you could call him that—announces they're taking a ten-minute break.

"Oh thank fuck," Danny breathes.

My peripheral vision catches the blur of a waitress, and I twist around to signal her before she can disappear. "Becca," I call, because everyone knows everyone in this town.

"Tate! Hey! What can I get ya?"

"Could I trouble you for a Good Boy?" I ask, naming one of our locally brewed beers.

"You got it. A Good Boy for a good boy." She winks and hurries off.

Cooper sighs. "Between you and my brother, I don't think there's a waitress in town who hasn't seen your dicks."

"And?" I counter, grinning. "Are waitresses off-limits now?"

"Only if you break their hearts. I don't need anyone spitting in our drinks."

"Ha, talk to your brother then. I've never had a hookup end on anything other than good terms. Can't say the same for Evan. And speaking of Evan—where is he? Wasn't it his idea to come here tonight?"

"Yup." Cooper rolls his eyes. "But then he got the better idea of locking Genevieve in their bedroom after we got home from work, and nobody's seen him since."

I have to laugh. Evan had been itching to get back together with Genevieve West since she moved back to the Bay after a year away in Charleston. Not only did he win her back, but they're now engaged. Good for Evan, though. He's loved the girl since the eighth grade, for fuck's sake. He deserves the win.

"I can't believe they're actually getting married," Chase says, shaking his head.

"It's wild," I concur.

"I hear you're next," Danny pipes up, elbowing me in the arm. "When do you plan on proposing to Alana?"

I pretend to think it over. "I'm gonna have to go with . . . never. I don't think I've met anyone less interested in marriage than Alana. Besides, that's not happening anymore."

Coop glances over, intrigued. "No?"

"No more friends with benefits," I tell him, shrugging. "We're back to being regular old friends."

Danny hoots. "She dump you?"

"Dumping would imply being in a relationship, and we definitely weren't in one."

"Did you break the news to Steph yet?" Cooper snickers. "I think the girls had a bet going that you would fall in love with Alana. Pretty sure Steph staked her life savings on yes."

"Love?" I raise a brow. "Dude, I can't be held responsible for Steph's irresponsible gambling choices. Has she *met* me?"

What the hell is love, anyway? It's one of those words that gets thrown around so haphazardly, like grains of rice at a wedding. *I love this. I love that. Love you. Love you too.* I've experienced platonic love, sure. I love my family, my friends. But romantic love? The kind of love that runs so deep you feel the other person in your soul? My only real relationship was with a girl I dated in high school for a year. We had a good time together. The sex was phenomenal. But was I in love with her?

When it boils down to it, I suspect it was just lust. Same as the rest of my encounters with the opposite sex. The string of hookups, the flings . . . love didn't play a role in any of those, and that includes my arrangement with Alana.

"Yo. Tate." A coaster nails me in the forehead.

I blink back to reality and hear the boys chortling. "What the hell was that?" I growl, rubbing my forehead.

"You literally zoned out for ten minutes," Danny informs me.

"Ten minutes?" I challenge.

"Okay, maybe, like, ten seconds, but still. Becca dropped off your beer and you didn't even say thanks."

Oh shit. I look over my shoulder, but Becca is already serving another table. I reach for my Good Boy and take a sip, just as the flinch-inducing shriek of microphone feedback fills the bar.

"No," Danny blurts out. "Fuck, no. They're back."

Unenthused, the four of us turn toward the stage, where the

band has indeed returned. They waste no time bursting into a song that starts with an inexplicable surf riff that's completely incongruous to the plaintive wails leaving the lead singer's mouth.

"Yeah, no," Cooper says. He slams his bottle down and glances at me. "Chug that beer so we can get the hell out of here. I can't listen to this all night."

"Joe's has half-price shots tonight," Chase says, already sliding off his stool. "I vote we go there."

Danny frowns when he notices I'm not drinking. "Didn't you hear the man? Chug," he orders, pointing to my bottle. "My ears are rebelling, bro."

"Fine." I grimace, then tip my head back and drain about two-thirds of my Good Boy before calling it quits.

While the band continues to assault the eardrums of the Rip Tide's patrons, my friends and I bail, hurriedly climbing the narrow staircase up to the street. We emerge into the night a moment later, the balmy heat warming my face. It's just as noisy out here on the main strip, but I prefer loud voices, raucous laughter, and faint carnival noises to the torture chamber we left behind.

We've made it about three steps down the sidewalk when a familiar face enters my line of sight.

Well, look at that. My new temporary neighbor. She's with a friend, a tall chick with flat-ironed hair and flawless skin. Both girls wear short dresses, although the friend's is much tighter than Cassie's.

"Seriously, ginger?" I call out, grinning. "You've been in town, what, less than a week and somehow I've run into you eighty-nine times already? If I didn't know any better, I'd think you were stalking me."

Cassie's jaw drops. "I am not. And stop calling me *ginger*. I told you I'm not a ginger, I'm a copper." She crosses her arms as if to emphasize her outrage, but all it does is emphasize her chest, pressing her tits together in a seriously appealing way.

Fuck. That rack. I can't handle it. It doesn't go unmissed by the others, either. Even Cooper, who has a girlfriend with whom he's nauseatingly smitten, briefly flicks his dark eyes toward Cassie's chest. She notices the attention, because her faces flushes and her arms drop to her sides.

The friend looks highly amused. "Don't deny it, Cass." She winks at me. "We totally followed you here."

"We did not," Cassie insists, poking her friend in the side. Then she gestures to the door of the Rip Tide. "We're just here to see the band."

"Oh, you don't want to do that," I warn. "Trust me. They're total shit."

"Aw, no, really?" Her expression conveys disappointment. "This is one of the only places that's featuring a live band tonight. Why are they shit? What kind of music is it?"

Cooper snorts. "Fucked if I know."

Danny thinks it over. "All right. If I had to pin down a genre, I'd say it was, like . . . rockabilly surf emo metal."

My gaze swivels to him. "Dude. That's actually pretty fucking accurate."

Cassie and her friend make identical faces, scrunching up their noses. "That sounds awful," Cassie complains.

"I think Sharkey's has a band playing tonight," Chase says helpfully.

The friend shakes her head. "Yeah, we can't go there," she answers, pouting. "It's the one place we always get carded."

Cooper spins toward me. "Bro, we're making friends with underage girls now?" He sighs.

"Hey. I'm twenty-one," protests the friend. She jabs a French-tipped fingernail at Cassie. "She's the one holding us back."

"Gee, thanks," Cassie says, her voice dry.

"But don't you worry," the friend assures Cooper, clearly having set her sights on him. "Cassie's birthday is next month, so she and I will be happy to meet you two"—that bossy fingernail snaps the air between me and Coop—"at Sharkey's once my girl is legal. How does that sound? One month from now. Eight o'clock. Sharkey's. It's a date."

"Joy," Cassie chides. She looks back at me. "She's just joking."

I raise a brow. "So it's not your birthday next month?"

"No, it is. That's not the part she's joking about. We're not going on a double date, I promise."

"I would've been up for a double date," Danny proclaims with a sad moan, pretending to be wounded. "But *I* wasn't invited."

"I'm gay, so I don't care," Chase tells the women.

Cooper lets out another snort.

"Anyway, it was nice seeing you again," Cassie tells me, already edging away. She glances at my friends. "I'm Cassie, by the way. This is Joy. And I'm not a stalker, no matter what your stupid friend says. I've never stalked anyone in my life. Well, unless you count that one week in high school when I kept refreshing this guy's Facebook page hoping his relationship status would change because I heard he and his girlfriend were having problems, but that's more cyberstalking, I guess, and I'm not sure that actually counts—" She stops abruptly when she realizes she's babbling.

Openly grinning, Joy doesn't come to her friend's aid. I suspect she's used to Cassie's blabbering, and I kind of love that she doesn't jump in and rescue her. Just lets her dig that hole deeper.

"Tate," I introduce myself to Joy, and she smirks in a way that tells me she knows who I am. Reputation precedes me, I guess. I introduce the others, ending with Cooper, and it turns out both girls know exactly who he is too.

"You're one of the bad-boy twins," Joy says with barely disguised glee.

He offers a faint smile. "Everything you've heard about us is a lie."

"Excellent," she says, flashing a sassy smile. "Because I heard you have a girlfriend. Now that I know you don't . . ."

I smother a laugh. She's got him there.

"Okay, that one is true," he amends, laughing softly.

"He's very much spoken for," I confirm. "Living happily ever after and building a hotel empire with his girl."

"Oh, right," Joy exclaims. "I heard about that." She looks at Cassie. "His girlfriend is the new owner of the Beacon."

That captures Cassie's interest. She instantly focuses on Cooper. "Your girlfriend is the one who bought the Beacon?"

He nods. "We've spent the past year restoring the place. The grand reopening is in September."

"I know. That's why I'm here. My grandmother was the seller. The Beacon was in my family for more than fifty years before she sold."

Coop is startled. "No shit? Lydia Tanner is your grandmother?"

"She is," Cassie confirms. "I'm staying with her for the summer. We sold her house here, too. It closes in October and then she's moving up north to be near family. My whole family is coming to the reopening. Grandma's really excited for it."

"Damn, don't tell my girlfriend that." Coop grins. "Mac is stressing so hard about it. She doesn't want to let your grandmother down."

"I'm sure she won't. Honestly, Grandma is just happy the new owner is dedicated to preserving her original vision for the place."

"We did our best," he says, his tone sincere. And now that he's realized these chicks are more than just thirsty boardwalk tourists looking to hook up, he's a lot more amenable to their plight. "Go to Big Molly's instead of Sharkey's," he advises. "They've got a band tonight too, and I have it on good authority the bartender there isn't above serving a cocktail or two to a twenty-year-old." He winks. "Tell Jesse that Coop says hi."

"Thanks for the tip," Cassie says, flashing a grateful smile.

Danny steps in, clearly bored with all the chitchat. "All right, ladies. Nice running into you, but we've got some alcohol to consume, fellas."

We say goodbye and part ways, moving in opposite directions. From behind me I hear Cassie tell Joy she needs to use the restroom before they hit Big Molly's. "I'll wait out here" is Joy's faint response, and the guys and I are almost a block away when I hear high heels on the pavement.

"Tate," a voice hisses. "Wait."

I look over my shoulder to find Joy barreling our way, heels clicking and slinky red dress swirling around her toned thighs.

"Interesting," Cooper murmurs, clearly amused.

"One second," I tell the boys. I break off from the group and meet Joy about ten feet away.

She's breathless from running in heels. "I gotta be quick," she blurts out. "Before Cass comes out."

Shit. Is she hitting on me? I hope not, because that feels kind of shady, doing it behind Cassie's back like that.

But she surprises me by asking, "What do you think of Cassie?"

I furrow my brow. "In what way?"

"In all ways. Think she's cute?"

"Smoking hot," I correct, a grin springing up.

Joy brightens. "Oh. Perfect. That was easy. And you're okay with all the nervous babbling?"

"In what way?" I echo. "What do you mean by okay with it? What's happening right now?" I feel stupid. Sometimes it feels like women are speaking an entirely different language from me.

My mom does it all the time, carrying on these conversations she must have started in her head, because I have no clue what she's saying, and Dad and I will constantly lock gazes over her head, like, *what the fuck?*

"Listen," Joy says in a serious tone. "Cass and I are fling shopping."

"I'm sorry, what?"

"Well, *she's* fling shopping. I may or may not be back together with my selfish ass of an ex Isaiah, but that's a whole other drama." She waves a manicured hand. "Anyway, Cassie's looking for a summer fling, and I think you'd be the perfect candidate."

I'm having trouble containing my amusement, biting my lip to keep from laughing. "Is that so?"

"Oh, it's so. But she's never going to ask you out, so I've taken it upon myself to intervene. Especially after I saw you two interact. It seemed like, I don't know, there was a little banter happening? From where I was standing, it looked like you might be interested in . . . dot dot dot . . ."

"I might," I say slowly. "I mean, I'm always up for . . . dot dot dot . . ."

She beams at me. "Excellent. Then I'm giving you her number."

I offer a smug look. "Already have it."

Her jaw drops. "Seriously? That sneaky little . . ." She shakes her head. "Well, okay then. That was supposed to be my role in this whole transaction. You know, putting the idea out there in the universe, that if you were to be into her, she might be into you too. I'm the sexual communications facilitator."

"Of course. Because that's a real job." I tip my head. "Are we at the part where you hand me the note that says *Do you like Cassie?* and I have to check the yes or no box?"

"Oh, honey, we're in the era of dick pics and *u up?* texts," she replies, rolling her eyes. "You can figure it out from here."

CHAPTER 6

CASSIE

On Thursday morning, Grandma and I finally get that tour of the Beacon Hotel, an experience that is paradoxically like stepping into a time capsule while also taking a time machine into the future. Mackenzie Cabot chose an aesthetic that somehow managed to preserve the original look of the Beacon while modernizing it. It's amazing to see. She knocked down walls I never would've thought of knocking down, brightening the main building with natural light and adding a dozen more ocean-view rooms.

Even with all the changes, I'm still overcome with nostalgia. Everything I see triggers a new memory. In the lobby, as we ascend the grand staircase, I run my fingertips along the intricately carved banister and remember hearing Grandpa Wally boast, *See this banister, kiddo? I sanded it all by myself. And your grandma, she helped me paint it.*

When Mackenzie shows us how she managed to replicate many of the old brass fixtures in the bathrooms, Grandpa Wally's excited voice is in my head, explaining, *These nifty towel hooks? They were specifically designed for passenger ships. Ocean liners. Grandma saw them in a nautical magazine and said,* Wallace, we need these for the Beacon!

His memory was so sharp, every detail etched into his brain.

That's probably what made it all the more heartbreaking when he started to forget everything in his later years. It was devastating to watch. He forgot our names first, the grandchildren. Then his own kids—my mom, her sister and brothers. Even Uncle Will, who'd been Grandpa's firstborn and favorite, was eventually lost to the jumbled sea that had become Grandpa's brain. And then, finally, he no longer recognized Grandma when she came to visit, and that's when we knew it was over. Mentally, he was gone. Physically, it took another year for his body to catch up. Sometimes I think the dementia was worse than his actual death.

Mackenzie radiates pride as she takes us around, pointing out various upgrades. They redid the electrical. All new plumbing. Installed two elevators. Constructed an addition in the back, moving the restaurant so that half of it is now an outdoor patio that overlooks the sprawling pool grounds. We visit the spa, which is no longer housed on the third floor, but in a newly built adjoining building connected to the hotel via winding palm-lined paths, with a gorgeous white stone fountain in the center of the main path.

Whoa. This chick has sunk a lot of money into this. And she's so young. Mackenzie can't be older than twenty-two or twenty-three, yet somehow she owns a beachfront hotel in South Carolina. I think I know who I want to be when I grow up.

"You did a stunning job," Grandma Lydia tells the young woman. "Simply exquisite." My grandmother can be hard to read when she's in public, but right now there's no mistaking her pleasure, the deep glow of approval in her eyes.

Mackenzie releases a breath heavy with relief. "You have no idea how happy I am to hear that. I swear, every design change I made, I was so conscious of trying to stay true to your original vision."

"You did, dear. This is . . ." Grandma looks around. We've ended our tour in the small café off the lobby. It used to be the gift shop, but Mackenzie moved that to another wing. "It's perfect."

A broad smile fills Mackenzie's face. "Thank you. I'm so thrilled you like it." She gestures behind us. "Can I get you two a coffee or anything?" she offers. Technically, the hotel isn't open yet, but she told us the café has been up and running the past few weeks to accommodate the workers who are still making finishing touches on the place.

"A tea would be wonderful," Grandma tells her.

"I'll take a coffee," I say. "Cream, no sugar. Thanks."

Mackenzie nods and goes to the counter, where she exchanges words with the barista, a man in a navy-blue polo with THE BEA-CON stitched in gold thread over the left breast.

"This is amazing," I whisper to Grandma as I lead her to a table outside.

The café offers a small patio with a smattering of tables. To our right is a white-painted staircase that leads down to a wide veranda with handmade rocking chairs, a cozy spot to sit and watch the waves.

Grandma adjusts her sunhat to better secure it to her head. She's always been incredibly protective of her skin. *Sun damage is no joke, Cassandra,* I grew up hearing. It's the one thing she and my mom agree on; Mom's always harping about sunscreen and hats too. Although in my mother's case, it's less about getting cancer and more about maintaining youthful-looking skin. Appearance trumps everything in my mother's world.

"Mackenzie is cool," I admit, sitting down. "Oh, and I met her boyfriend on the boardwalk this weekend."

"Is that so?"

"Yeah. Joy and I ran into Tate. The guy who's housesitting next door. He was with some of his friends, and one of them was Mackenzie's boyfriend, Cooper."

Grandma looks pleased. "That's wonderful you're making friends."

"I mean, I wouldn't say I'm making friends. I spoke to our neighbor on the boardwalk and consequently met his friends. That's about it." I chuckle at her. "Stop trying to force friendships on me. I'm good. I have Joy."

"I know, but it would be nice if you could find yourself a nice big group to spend time with this summer." She takes on a far-away tone. "When I was younger, all the young people in the Bay socialized together. There were about fifteen, twenty of us. We would take the boats out and spend hours on the water, or the girls would lie on the beach watching all the oiled-up boys play sports." She chuckles. "There might have been plenty of alcohol involved too."

I snicker, trying to picture my grandmother in a tiny bikini and oversized hat, cruising the Bay with a bunch of rowdy teenagers. But it's impossible. Whenever I try to imagine Grandma at my age, my brain can't compute. Same goes for my mother. It's even harder to imagine her as young and carefree. I refuse to believe Mom was ever anything other than a haughty, designer-clad woman in her midforties.

As if on cue, my phone buzzes. Mom has the unsettling habit of always calling just as I'm thinking about her.

"Ugh. It's Mom. I have to take this." I glimpse Mackenzie heading toward us with a tray of beverages, so I stand up. "I'll be right back."

Grandma nods. "Tell her I said hello. Take your time."

In the quiet lobby, I answer the call. "Hey, Mom," I say, and then I brace myself. You never know which side of my mother's personality you're going to get on any given day. But I'm an old pro at dealing with her now, always prepared for whatever attack she throws my way. Sometimes, it's instant criticism, or a huffy demand to explain why I committed one perceived crime or another. Other times she starts off sweet, complimentary even, encouraging you to lower your guard, and then bang! Goes in for the kill.

But I'm not a naïve little girl anymore. I know all my mother's tricks and what tactic is required to deal with each one.

So when she says, "I'm hurt, sweetie! Why has it been three days since I've heard your lovely voice?" in that light, teasing tone, I know it's a trap. She's not hurt, she's pissed. And she's not teasing, which means I can't counter with a joking response.

"I'm sorry," I tell her, with just the proper amount of grovel in my voice. Too apologetic and she becomes suspicious. "You're right. I should have called sooner. It's been chaotic here."

My strategy works. Nothing elates my mother more than hearing those two words: *You're right*.

"I suppose your grandmother is keeping you very busy," she says, which is her way of "forgiving" me for my sin.

And although it's clearly an opening to shift the blame from me to her own mother, I'm not going to throw Grandma under the bus.

"Not really. We went shopping on the weekend, but mostly I've been catching up with Joy. How's Boston?"

"The whole city? What kind of question is that?"

I smother a sigh and quickly switch tacks, letting out a fake laugh. "Ha, ha, you're right, that was a stupid question. I'm so dumb sometimes. I just meant, how are you doing? Are you enjoying the city or are you looking forward to coming down—"

Abort!

I rue the question the second it slips out. Shit, maybe I'm off my game.

Sometimes it's so hard to forget you're not dealing with a normal human. Narcissists are a whole other breed.

Her bitterness practically permeates the line. "There is nothing I'd like to do less than spend time in that town." She snorts humorlessly. "But we owe a duty to our family."

It infuriates her that she can't back out, I know that. But my two uncles and my aunt committed to making the trip to say goodbye to the Beacon, and if there's one thing my mother can't allow, it's looking like the bad guy.

The ingratitude, though, is kind of incredible. The Beacon belonged to our family for decades. It's the reason for all that wealth my mother sure enjoys taking advantage of. The least she can do is give it a proper farewell. It's the Tanner family's final hurrah. Like giving away a treasured ship and watching the new owners christen it with a champagne bottle before they sail away forever.

"I'm actually at the hotel right now," I say, hoping to mollify her with one of her favorite topics: money. "The new owner poured buckets of money into it, and it has absolutely paid off. It's gorgeous. I swear, you're going to love it. We just finished the tour of the spa—all the products there were custom made in Italy. An exclusive brand just for the Beacon."

That piques her interest. "Well, that sounds promising!"

"Right?" Then, although I'd rather gnaw my own tongue off than speak the words, I know the script and force myself to speak it. "We should do a mother/daughter spa day," I suggest, injecting as much fake enthusiasm into my voice as possible.

The silver lining when talking to narcissists is they assume everyone adores them and is dying to spend time with them, which means they rarely stop to wonder if you're being disingenuous. In their minds, *of course* we want to hang out with them. Because they're perfect and remarkable and a credit to all of humanity.

The worst part is, most people don't see through their bullshit. At least not at first. I can't even count how many times over the years I'd been told how wonderful my mother is. Or accused of being "too sensitive." Of reading too much into her veiled—and sometimes not at all veiled—barbs. *Oh, that Cassie, so insecure that she imagines disparaging subtext with every word.*

Eventually, though, most people see the light. I still remember the first time Peyton had her epiphany after my mother took us out to dinner during a sleepover. We were thirteen and, wide-eyed and shaking her head, she announced, "I just realized—your mom is a real bitch."

There is nothing more liberating than having your traumatic experiences validated like that.

"What a lovely idea!" Mom says in response to my suggestion. "Also, I just thought of it, but while you're there you should ask for a tour of the fitness center too."

My jaw tightens. I know where this is going.

"Yeah, we peeked into it," I answer carefully. "It's attached to the spa, but it's closed off because none of the equipment has been delivered yet."

"You should use the gym at the club, then. I saw on Joy's Instagram that she's been going there every morning. She's looking very fit these days."

I smother an inward scream. I hate that Mom follows my friends on social media. Joy even has a private account, but she confessed she would've felt like an asshole if she hadn't accepted my mother's request.

"Maybe she can give you some fitness tips," Mom adds, because no conversation with my mother is complete without her advising me on all the ways I can better myself.

"Yeah, I'll ask her," I say obediently.

"Oh, and speaking of Instagram, I was on your page this morning too and saw the picture you posted. The one of you in the pink top and denim shorts? Those shorts were adorable!"

I wait for the next sniper's bullet.

"But the top . . . you know I mean well when I say this, but maybe you should consider taking the photo down. That cropped style isn't the most flattering on you, Cass. With your proportions, you know. Oh! We should also go shopping when I'm here, how does that sound? Maybe drive into Charleston?"

"Sounds great! I'd love that, actually. I always appreciate your opinion."

There's a short beat, and I know that in her judgmental, self-absorbed brain, she's wondering, *was that sarcasm?*

But that would be too detrimental to her ego, so rather than question me, she does her trademark subject switcheroo. "Have you seen your father yet? And his nurse?"

I hold the phone away from my ear for a second and scream silent obscenities at it, making faces at the screen.

As is my luck, a passing man in work boots and a tool belt enters the lobby at that moment. He looks startled by my antics at first, then barks out a laugh before walking on.

I bring the phone back to my ear. "Not yet. I'm seeing them tomorrow for dinner."

"He's waited an entire week to see his child?" she says indignantly. "That's selfish, even for Clayton."

You wrote the book on selfish, lady.

Although for once, she's not entirely wrong. I've been thinking the same thing since I arrived in Avalon Bay. So what if the twins go to day camp and Dad and Nia have work? They still eat dinner together every weeknight, do they not? Is it that difficult to invite me to join them?

On the other hand, when her husband's bitter ex-wife refers to her as his *nurse,* maybe it's understandable Nia doesn't want that bitter woman's daughter around her house. The nurse comments grate on me too, especially since it's total nonsense. Nia was never Dad's nurse. She was his physical therapist after he got in a car accident not long after his and Mom's divorce. He required surgery for a torn bicep, and Nia was in charge of his rehab. That's how they met and fell in love.

"Mom, I gotta go," I say, done with this entire conversation. "Grandma's waiting for me to drive her home." In reality, Grandma's deep in conversation with Mackenzie, the two of them leaning forward, animated about whatever they're discussing.

"All right, sweetie. I'll see you next month."

"Can't wait."

I'm exhausted when I return to the table. Talking to Mom really does feel like I've just fought a war. Grandma eyes me with a flicker of concern. "Is everything all right?"

"All good," I lie. Because that's what I do. I plaster on sunny smiles and pretend the attacks on my appearance, my father, my entire life have zero effect on me.

"I was just telling your grandmother there's a bonfire tonight at my place," Mackenzie says, giving me a warm smile. "Having a few friends over. If you'd like to join?"

My first instinct is to beg off and say thank you but I'm busy. I'm so awkward around strangers. But then it occurs to me that Mackenzie's boyfriend is friends with Tate. Which means Tate might be there. Which means maybe I can work up the nerve to . . . to what?

Ask him out, I guess.

Proposition him.

Rip my clothes off and order him to rock my world.

Okay, maybe not the last one. But I've been back in town for a week now, and Tate is the only guy I've met who makes my heart pound. I feel like I'd regret it if I didn't at least *try* to stop babbling and ask him to hang out. And I suppose there's no better time than tonight.

CHAPTER 7

CASSIE

The Hartley twins live in a Low Country–style beach house with a huge front porch and not a neighbor in sight. It isn't at all like my grandparents' house, which was built in the last couple decades and has a more modern feel. This is a house that's been in someone's family for a hundred years. Old, rambling, and oozing charm, a testament to time and the elements. The roof looks new, however, and the covered porch has clearly been painted recently, hinting that the residents are in the process of upgrading.

The front door creaks loudly when Mackenzie opens it to let me in. "Hey!" She looks delighted to see me. "You made it!"

"Thanks for having me." I awkwardly fiddle with the belt loops of my denim shorts. Despite my mother's negging earlier, I'm wearing a cropped T-shirt that shows a sliver of midriff, and black flip-flops that Mackenzie tells me to leave on.

"We're going out back," she says, leading me through the living room and country-style kitchen toward a set of glass sliding doors.

Out back is a massive deck that overlooks the ocean, with a winding, wooden staircase that goes down to the sand. The view alone is worth a million dollars, and my eyebrows soar as we step onto the deck.

"Whoa," I remark. "That view is *sick*. I'm surprised developers haven't tried to snatch this place up. Build a little condo community or something."

"Oh, they've tried, but we're never selling," Cooper Hartley says, appearing behind us. He steps out of the kitchen, shirtless, barefoot, and clad in red swim trunks. He's sporting two full sleeves of tattoos and rock-hard abs, and I get a little starry-eyed just looking at him.

Then I blink and a second Cooper appears to my left from the rickety stairs. Also shirtless, except this Cooper is wet, as if he'd just come from the ocean. His tall, muscular body drips seawater all over the deck floor as he strides up.

"Oh wow." I glance at Cooper, then his twin. "You guys really are identical."

"Nah," the twin says. "I'm way better looking."

"Bullshit," Cooper argues.

Rolling her eyes, Mackenzie introduces me to Evan, Cooper's twin, who flashes a sexy grin before disappearing into the house.

"Come on," she says, touching my arm. "Everyone's already on the beach."

We head down to the sand, where several loungers and Adirondack chairs are arranged in a haphazard circle around the fire pit. The fire's not yet lit since the sun hasn't set, and it's still so hot out that a bonfire feels almost redundant.

On one of the loungers, a platinum blonde sits in the lap of a guy who, even sitting down, looks massive. Six-five at least, with huge muscular arms that could probably bench-press everyone here. A gorgeous brunette in a black string bikini is sprawled on the neighboring lounger, scrolling on her phone, while another girl with a high ponytail and dusky complexion stands at a plastic table laden with drinks, pouring liquor into a tall plastic cup.

Mackenzie quickly runs through some more introductions.

Table girl is Steph. The couple on the chair are Heidi and her boyfriend, Jay. The brunette is Jay's sister, Genevieve, who also happens to be Evan Hartley's fiancée.

That startles me. "You guys are engaged?"

"Sure are," Genevieve answers. She narrows her eyes at me in a challenge. "And don't give me that *you're too young* BS. I hear it from my brothers on a daily basis."

"You're too young," her brother grumbles as if on cue.

"I wasn't going to say that," I assure her. "It's just so rare to find people who want to get married in their early twenties."

"Well, I mean, we gotta tie that knot ASAP if we're going to start pumping out kids. We've decided we want at least six. Isn't that right, Hartley?" she calls up at the deck.

Evan appears at the railing above us. "Seven," he calls back. "That's my lucky number."

"Do you want a drink?" Mackenzie heads over to the table, where I greet Steph with a tentative smile.

"Here, let me make you what I'm having," Steph says, reaching for another plastic cup. "I'm experimenting with a new recipe. I picked up some of that vanilla-flavored vodka and I'm mixing it with raspberry lemonade. It's either going to be vomit-inducingly sweet or the most delicious thing you've ever tasted."

"Can't wait to find out," I say with a snicker.

As I wait for her to mix the drink, I glance toward the deck, where the twins are laughing about something at the railing. I guess Tate isn't here. Neither is the redhead from the party last week, I note. Alana. For some reason that triggers a tiny prickle of jealousy. What if they're both gone because they're hooking up again?

I ignore the tight knot in my belly and accept the drink Steph hands me. I'm thirsty, so I take a big gulp and it isn't until after I've swallowed that I realize what I'm in for. The liquid burns a fiery path to my stomach and induces a bout of coughing.

"Too sweet?" she frets.

I gape at her. My eyes water as I let out a final cough. "I can barely taste the lemonade," I squawk. "This is, like, ninety percent vodka."

Steph grins. "So?"

"So I wasn't expecting that. Jeez. Warn a girl next time."

We rejoin the others around the unlit fire pit. Steph settles in one of the chairs, while Mackenzie and I share a lounger. I take a teeny sip of my potent cocktail. This time I anticipate the vodka burn and make a conscious decision to pace myself. One cup of this stuff is liable to get me sloppy drunk.

Mackenzie and her friends aren't much older than me, yet for some reason I feel like a kid next to them. Maybe it's because they're all so gorgeous. Genevieve is basically a supermodel— long legs, toned body slick with tanning oil, sunglasses resting on her pert nose. Beside me, Mackenzie looks like she stepped off a yacht, a striped T-shirt hanging off one tanned shoulder and dark hair loose and cascading down her back.

Mackenzie glances at Genevieve. "Gen, so Cassie is Lydia Tanner's granddaughter."

"Oh, are you?" Gen exclaims. "I was *obsessed* with your grand-mother when I was a teenager."

"Really?" I laugh.

"Oh yeah. I used to see her around town all the time in those big sunglasses and silk scarves. She always wore a scarf, even in the summer."

"She still does. It's her trademark."

"She was the most elegant woman I'd ever seen in my life," Gen says wistfully. "I wanted to be her when I grew up, and it was my dream to work for her at the Beacon one day. Joke's on me. Now I'm stuck working for this one." She jerks a thumb at Mackenzie, but her sparkling eyes tell me she's joking.

"You work at the Beacon?" I ask.

"I will be when we open in September. I'm going to be the general manager."

"Wow. That's a lot of responsibility," I tell her. "I remember our old manager, this British guy. James De Vries. Grandma flew him in from London, after poaching him from some five-star hotel near Buckingham Palace. He always wore this navy-blue blazer with a gold—"

"—bowtie," Genevieve finishes, snickering loudly. "Oh, I remember the man. Remember him, Heidi? Mr. De Vries?"

"Oh my God. Yes." Heidi's laugh is a bit evil. "We used to hop the fence into the pool area and try to steal people's cabanas, and De Vries would appear out of fucking nowhere."

"And every time," Gen picks up the story, "every damn time he'd greet us with this bland smile and politely ask if we were guests of his fine establishment, even though he clearly knew we were a bunch of delinquent teenagers breaking the rules."

"He never chased us out, though," Steph pipes up. "Dude was classy. He'd escort us out through the front doors, then watch us leave while giving one of those stiff Queen of England waves, all distinguished like."

I laugh, totally picturing what they're describing. James was the epitome of a well-mannered Brit.

"Meanwhile," Genevieve says to me, snorting in amusement, "you were probably there legally, sunbathing poolside and watching us being marched past your lounge chair."

"Actually, we never stayed at the hotel," I admit. "Before my parents got divorced, we lived in a house on Sycamore. And after that, we stayed at Grandma's house whenever we were in town for a visit. I would've killed to spend an entire summer at the Beacon."

"Well, you're in luck," Mackenzie says cheerfully, "because you now have a room there for life. Free of charge."

"No way," I protest. "I could never accept that offer."

"Seriously? *I* can," Genevieve declares. "I totally want the free room." She shouts up at the deck again. "Hey, Evan, we have a permanent suite at the hotel."

"Nice," he shouts back.

"Oh," Mackenzie says suddenly, glancing at me. "I forgot, I wanted to ask you something."

"Yeah?" I shift self-consciously and take another sip of my vodka lemonade, aka vodka and a teaspoon of lemonade. I'm already feeling the alcohol, my blood buzzing from it.

"Beach Games is next month," she says. "You've heard of it, right?"

"Yeah, of course. It's a tradition."

Beach Games is an annual event in Avalon Bay, where teams representing local businesses compete in, well, beach games. It's a two-day affair, and I think there're gift certificates and trophies in it for the winners, but most of the competitors do it for the glory. The honor of being dubbed *Best Business on the Bay*.

Last time I attended a Beach Games celebration was a few years ago, right before freshman year of college. I went with my dad, and we had a blast watching the various activities. The tug-of-war event that year got real ugly. I remember the old ladies from the bakery brutally heckling the dudes from the mechanic shop. I believe the phrase *You're going down, motherfuckers* was uttered more than once. Afterward, Dad and I got ice cream and walked along the boardwalk. It was nice. Maybe he'll want to go again this year.

"We missed out last year," Mackenzie says, "but now that the Beacon is back in business we need to put together a team. Your grandmother and I were talking about it this morning and she mentioned nobody in your family ever competed in the Games. She thought you might like joining us on Team Beacon."

"Me?" I say, startled.

She nods. "You'd be our fourth. Right now it's me, Gen, and our activities director, Zale."

"I'm sorry—Zale?" Genevieve's brother guffaws. "That's gotta be a fake name."

"It's not," Gen says with a grin. "I questioned it too, so he showed me his birth certificate."

"Those can be forged," Jay insists.

"Zale is hilarious," Mackenzie tells me. "You'll love him."

I'm still trying to wrap my head around the offer. "You really want me to be your fourth? Did my grandmother force you into this?" I ask suspiciously.

"Not at all. Like I said, she just mentioned it's something you might enjoy."

Apparently Grandma's going to foist a friend group on me come hell or high water. It's baffling. I mean, seriously. Why does she believe I'm an antisocial loser? I don't know what signals I'm giving off to make her think I'm some tragic shut-in, but I might need to have a talk with the lady.

"All right. Then, sure," I relent, because even if it *was* my grandmother's idea, it does sound like fun. "I'm down for Beach Games."

"How are your sandcastle-building skills?" Gen demands.

I mull it over. "Above par?"

She nods, pleased. "I'll take it. Mac and I have a little wager going with the twins."

"You mean the *winners,*" comes Evan's smug voice, and he's projecting some serious swagger as he descends the deck steps. Scampering at his feet is an eager golden retriever with a bright orange ball in its mouth.

Evan hurls the ball down the beach and the dog takes off like a rocket, paws kicking up sand.

"You haven't won a damn thing yet," Gen retorts.

"But we will." He offers a broad smile. "Aka you will lose. Badly, and with no mercy from us."

Laughing, I glance between them. "What are the stakes?"

"Well, I'm glad you asked, Cassie," Evan says solemnly. "*When* we win, my beautiful fiancée here, along with my brother's okay-looking girlfriend—"

Mackenzie gives him the finger.

"—will be serving us a home-cooked dinner . . ."

"That's not so bad," I tell the girls.

But Evan isn't finished. ". . . in French maid uniforms."

I bite back a laugh. The others do not display such tact. Jay, Heidi, and Steph are doubled over, practically howling.

"Nah," Gen argues. "When *we* win, my smartass fiancé here, along with his obnoxious brother, will proudly be holding up signs advertising the Beacon Hotel on the boardwalk . . ."

"That's not bad," I say to Evan.

". . . in neon-pink G-strings."

I sigh.

"Yeah, no. Never gonna happen," Cooper announces as he joins the group. He's put on a shirt and is holding a beer.

Someone else follows him down the steps, and my heart skips when I realize it's Tate. He's wearing a white T-shirt, khaki shorts, and a pair of aviator sunglasses. For some reason his hair always looks a little windblown, pushed away from his face to emphasize his cheekbones. He's so good-looking it makes my throat run dry. I try to remedy that by gulping my drink, remembering only at the last second that it's basically pure vodka.

My coughing draws Tate's attention. An easy smile curves his lips. "Ginger," he drawls. "I didn't know you were going to be here tonight."

I respond with a self-conscious shrug. "Uh, yeah. Mackenzie invited me. And stop calling me *ginger*."

"I will when your hair is no longer ginger."

"It's copper," I growl.

"You two know each other?" Mac's wary green eyes shift from me to Tate.

"We're neighbors," I explain.

"Just for the summer," Tate adds. He grabs one of the Adirondack chairs and drags it closer to our lounger.

"Oh right. You're housesitting for the Jacksons," Evan pipes up. "Fuck, I love that house. Remember the rager we threw there a couple summers ago?"

Tate makes a sardonic noise. "Oh, you mean the night you did body shots off Gen's ass on the custom-made hand-carved coffee table Shirley Jackson had specially shipped from Denmark?"

Evan's eyes glimmer as he winks at his fiancée. "That was a good night."

Genevieve's eyes are equally ablaze. "Such a good night," she echoes, and the two exchange a sultry look loaded with so much heat I have to turn away. They might as well be having sex in front of everybody—that's how potent their chemistry is.

"Yeah, well, there won't be any repeat performances of that," Tate warns his friends. "I had to pay for an army of cleaners to come deal with the mess you guys left behind. Never again." He sips his beer, watching me over the lip of the bottle. "Has Mac given you a tour of the hotel yet?"

"Did that today," I confirm.

"And Cassie just agreed to join our team for Beach Games," Gen tells him.

"Oh yeah?" He cocks his head at me. "That officially makes us archenemies, then."

"You're competing?" I demand.

"Of course. Someone's got to represent the yacht club. Plus, this is the twins' first year competing, and I never miss an opportunity to kick their asses at something."

"Is your uncle going to be on your team?" Steph asks the Hartleys. "Because I'd pay to see that."

"We asked him, but he said no way in hell," Cooper says. "So we're using our foreman, Alex, and this guy Spencer who's on the crew." From his chair across the pit from us, he flashes a cocky smile at his girlfriend. "Be prepared to get murdered, princess."

She presses one hand to her heart. "You're so romantic."

Cooper just chuckles.

The rest of the evening flies by, much to my surprise. But the conversation is lively and the various personalities are so entertaining that three hours pass before I know it. I'm having a great time. Mac's cool. Gen's hilarious. Heidi's kind of bitchy, but after a while you get used to it. At some point Steph plants a fresh cup of vodka lemonade in my hand, while Evan and Cooper, who are literally identical from head to toe, start arguing about which one of them is better looking. And the entire time, I'm shooting sidelong looks at Tate and wondering how it's possible for someone to be so hot. Like, criminally hot. Every now and then my gaze flicks toward his abdomen, because whenever he runs a hand through his hair, the bottom of his shirt shifts upward and I catch a flash of his abs.

God, I just want to lick him.

Annnd the second vodka lemonade has officially gone to my head.

In fact, my knees are a bit wobbly as I stand up and head for the drinks table. I rummage around in one of the mini coolers in search of water. I need to hydrate. My mind is too foggy with thoughts of Tate's abs.

"Hey, neighbor."

I jump at the sound of his deep voice. I didn't even notice him come up beside me, but here he is, less than two feet away, a hint of a smile on his face.

"Sorry, didn't mean to startle you," he says. He brings his beer to his lips, taking a long swig. "You having a good time?"

Before I can answer, Steph shouts, "There she is!"

"Finally! Bitch, where've you been?" Heidi now.

I turn to check out the newcomer, faltering when I realize it's Alana. She saunters up to the group, bright red hair loose around her shoulders, eyes gleaming from the light of the fire that Cooper lit about an hour ago. I don't miss the way her gaze flicks toward me and Tate before focusing on her friends.

Gulping down some water, I move away from the table. Tate follows along beside me.

"Should I go introduce myself?" I ask, giving a discreet nod in Alana's direction. I feel like I should, but she's chatting with her friends and, what, I'm going to interrupt them just to say, *Hello, my name is Cassandra, what's your name,* like some awkward fool?

"Nah," Tate says to my relief. "She'll make her way over here eventually."

"Or she'll avoid you because she thinks you're pining over her."

He rolls his eyes. "I'm not pining. And she knows me better than that."

"So you're over it?"

"I'm over it," he confirms.

"Come on, you must still be a *little* into it," I push, sneaking another peek at Alana. "She's gorgeous."

"The view's not bad," he agrees, nodding. "But neither is *this* view." He slowly rakes his gaze down my body. Not even trying to hide the fact that he's checking me out.

A part of me is now like, *fuck,* because I'd debated this crop top earlier and now I'm doing it again. Not only does it cling to my boobs, but it shows a lot more skin than I'm used to.

But another part of me really, really enjoys having those appreciative blue eyes on me.

"You're staring," I accuse.

"Yes." He takes another sip of his beer. I wonder if he's drunk. His eyes have a hazy shine to them that tells me he might be. But he's not slurring or stumbling.

Still, I say, "You're drunk."

"No. Just buzzed." He shrugs, a lazy smile tugging on the corners of his mouth. "I feel good. You look good. Life's good right now, Cass."

I laugh. And then, because they've gone dry all of a sudden, I lick my lips.

He doesn't miss that. "Fuck." He groans softly.

My forehead creases. "What?"

"You licked your lips."

"Yeah, and? They were dry. So I licked them and now they're moist—oh my God, what a horrible word. *Moist.* Isn't it horrible?" I shake my head in dismay. "I'm sorry I said the word *moist.*"

Tate chokes out a noise. A cross between a laugh and a sigh. "Man, I swear, it's like you go out of your way to kill a mood."

"What mood?" I ask, and my lips are suddenly bone-dry again. "Was there a mood?"

His shoulders quake with laughter. "Yes, Cassie, there was a mood. We were having a moment."

I blink. "We were?"

"Well, *I* thought so." Now he sounds exasperated. "In case you didn't notice, I was about to kiss you."

CHAPTER 8

TATE

"Seriously?" Cassie stares at me with narrowed eyes, as if she can't possibly fathom why I would be interested in kissing her.

"Seriously," I say, fighting a laugh. This chick is such a confusing puzzle to me. She must know she's gorgeous, right? Unless she's lived her entire life without looking in a mirror or seeing herself naked, I can't imagine she's unaware of her appeal.

"You said you were about to . . . Does that mean now you're not going to?" The groove in her forehead deepens.

"That's up to you." I lift a brow. "Do you want me to?"

She hesitates, and once again I'm thrown for a loop. Her friend Joy seemed real confident last weekend when she cornered me on the street and informed me that Cassie was down for a summer hookup. If I hadn't been swamped at work, I would've called Cassie earlier in the week. Tonight was my first opportunity to be social. In fact, I was planning on asking her to hang out this weekend, but that was before she hesitated at the thought of kissing me.

Maybe her friend was just fucking with me.

My gaze rests on her lips. Goddamn, she's licking them again. She has no idea what that does to me.

"Or do you want to keep dissecting the word *moist*?" I prompt.

She gives a weak laugh. "No. I'm sorry. I'm just . . . I'm not good at this stuff. Like, I'm standing here with the hottest guy I've ever seen and he just told me he wants to kiss me, and my first instinct is to interrogate him because I'm so awkward when it comes to—" She cuts herself off, as I'm noticing she's prone to do when she catches herself babbling.

Then she shocks the hell out of me. On an impatient groan, she mumbles, "Screw it," and the next thing I know, her soft lips are pressed against mine.

Christ. *Yes*.

My surprise quickly turns to hunger, a jolt of heat going right to my dick when Cassie's tongue finds mine and she makes a tiny whimpering sound. Nothing gets me harder than a really good kiss. Sure, I love the feel of a woman's mouth on my cock. The sensation of sliding in and out of a hot, tight pussy. But nothing beats a kiss. Especially one of those kisses where your mouths melt together, tongues teasing while your hands drift downward to find a firm, supple ass in your palms.

Cassie moans when I squeeze her ass over her shorts. Her lower body shifts closer, straining against my groin. She tastes like vodka and raspberries and feels like absolute heaven. I drive the kiss deeper, groaning against her lips, completely forgetting my surroundings until a voice shouts my name.

"Tate!"

Cassie and I jerk apart. I glance over my shoulder to find Mackenzie waving at me from the deck. There's no mistaking her slight frown.

"I need your help carrying some beer cases," she calls out.

Bullshit. Ten feet away, she's got Jay West, a dude who can lift a mountain, not to mention her own boyfriend who works construction. And she's targeting me for help-me-carry-something duty?

Cabot's cockblocking me and it's intentional.

But regardless of Mac's motives, she's succeeded in ruining the moment. Cassie is hastily taking a step back, shoving errant strands of hair behind her ear. Her cheeks are flushed. A moment ago, that was because she was turned on. Now it's from her visible embarrassment that all eyes are on us.

"Uh. Yeah." My voice sounds like gravel. I clear my throat. "Hold that thought. I'll be back in a minute."

As I turn away, I do some discreet rearranging beneath my shorts. Damn, that kiss got me rock hard. My pulse is still racing, too. On my way to the deck, I catch Alana watching me. I nod in greeting, and she rolls her eyes as I walk past her. It's funny. Any other girl would probably display at least a trace of jealousy at watching a former fling make out with someone else, but Alana's expression is wholly indifferent.

I didn't kiss Cassie to make Alana jealous, though. It's been a while since I met someone who makes me laugh as much as Cassie does. And she's goddamn edible. That body does something to me. Turns me on something fierce. Alana was the furthest thing from my mind just now. The moment Cassie's friend told me she was in the market for a summer hookup, my dick got on board faster than you can say *hell yeah.*

On the deck, Mackenzie fixes a bemused look on me but doesn't speak as she gestures for me to follow her.

Annoyed, I trail after her. "What the fuck was that?"

"What?" She spares me a glance before stalking forward again, crossing the living room toward the front door.

"What do you mean, *what*? I was clearly indisposed," I grouse.

"Yeah, I noticed." Her tone is unapologetic, which confirms my suspicion she broke up that kiss on purpose. Yet I'm still oblivious as to why.

Mac and I aren't joined at the hip or anything, but I thought we were good friends. And I've always thought she was cool, especially for a rich girl. Around here we call them clones, but while the women I encounter at the country club literally came off a clone conveyer belt, with their stuck-up personalities and yoga instructors on retainer, it didn't take long to realize Mackenzie Cabot was one of a kind. I'm starting to wonder if us locals might be rushing to judgment when it comes to clones, because Cassie doesn't fit that mold either. Her family is loaded, but she's one of the most down-to-earth people I've ever met.

It isn't until we step into the twins' garage that Mac makes her reasons known. "Why do you have to make a move on everything with a pulse?" she asks with a sigh.

I blink. Flabbergasted. "I don't," I protest.

"Bullshit. Every time a new girl comes around, it takes all of five seconds before you're sticking your tongue down her throat."

My surprise gives way to indignation. I don't know where this is coming from, and I don't like it.

"Were you trying to get Alana's attention or something?"

"Not in the slightest," I reply, which startles her. I roll my eyes at her reaction. "Come on, Mac. We both know Alana and I were just killing time. We were just bored." I shrug. "I like Cassie, so I kissed her. Big deal."

"I like Cassie too. And what if it is a big deal?"

"What do you mean?"

"I mean, she's really sweet. I don't want to see her get hurt."

I swallow my irritation. Why must women always jump directly to the worst-case scenario? And why do they always assume one measly kiss will lead to a trip to the altar? Like, damn. Slow down, ladies. Sometimes we kiss because it feels good.

"I don't plan on hurting her," I answer with a frown. "I like her. And all we did was make out."

"Then maybe you should leave it at that. Just be her friend."

I bristle. "You in charge of my dick now, Mac?"

"No, but . . ." She pauses, then voices a sheepish confession. "This morning when her grandmother and I had a moment alone at the Beacon, Lydia asked me to watch out for her. I don't know . . . I guess I'm a bit worried. You're the king of hookups. Which is fine," she adds hastily. "No judgment. That's probably why your arrangement with Alana worked so well. Neither of you have ever been interested in relationships. But Cassie is one hundred percent girlfriend material—you get that, right? She seems a lot more serious than your usual type."

I feel a deep groove form in my forehead. She's not entirely wrong. Cassie *is* different. Sweeter, as Mac had said. And not as confident or outwardly experienced as women I've been with in the past.

"I just figured I'd point all this out before things out there got . . . un-take-back-able."

I draw a troubled breath. The more I'm thinking with my upstairs head, the more I'm realizing Mac's cockblocking might have been for the best.

"Unless you're in the market for a girlfriend now, which I don't think you are. I mean, you just spent months seeing Alana, who we both know is the safest choice for someone actively *not* looking to settle down. She'd be the first person to say she's not interested in a commitment. She's constantly referring to herself as emotionally unavailable."

I go silent. In all honesty, I never gave much thought to why I spent so much time with Alana. But my gut tells me Mac isn't completely off-base. For as long as I've known her, Alana has been aloof, untouchable. The woman locks her emotions behind a steel wall. I never had any illusions about breaking down that wall.

"Anyway, I'll stop meddling now. But I made a promise to Lydia, and I just wanted to make sure you're going into this with your eyes wide open."

"Noted."

"Okay, good." She heads for the door, adding over her shoulder, "Oh, and I do need you to bring out a couple cases of beer."

"Yes, Mom."

I'm grumbling under my breath as I cross the garage toward the drinks fridge. Despite my lingering aggravation, I can't quite bring myself to hate on Mac for interrupting. Now that the buzz is wearing off and my head is clearing, it's easy to see the mistake I almost made.

Hooking up with Cassie is a disaster waiting to happen. First off, we're neighbors. What if we sleep together and things go south? I'd still have to live next door to her until September, and that could get mighty awkward.

And then there's the fact that I like her a hell of a lot. She's fun to talk to, and I can envision us building a genuine friendship this summer. To some people that might seem more like a perk than a disadvantage, but I know how fragile male/female friendships can be. After Cooper and Heidi hooked up a couple years ago, their friendship almost didn't recover. Yes, Alana was my friend when we started sleeping together, but like Mac said, Alana isn't Cassie.

I'm not sure whether Cassie can keep things casual. Sure, one conversation could clear all that up—but that's based on the assumption she's being honest with herself. In my experience, plenty of women *say* they're down for no-strings sex. And maybe they mean it in the moment. Maybe they think they'll be okay keeping it strictly physical. But more often than not, the strings form before you can blink, and suddenly you're accused of being a selfish prick. It's a frequent occurrence for my more promiscuous friends, but to me it only happened once.

Last year of high school, I slept with a cute girl on the yearbook committee, not realizing that one—she was a virgin, and two—

she'd had a crush on me for years. Lindsey assured me she just wanted a hookup before she left for college. Next thing I know, I have her entire friend group screaming at me in the school corridor accusing me of breaking her heart and ruining her life. To this day, I feel goddamn awful about it. I never meant to hurt Lindsey, but I'd made it clear I didn't want a relationship.

Well, I still don't want that relationship, and I really don't want to hurt Cassie either.

Sometimes, having a good friend in your life is more rewarding than a few nights of hot, sweaty sex.

Except Cassie has other ideas. When I return, she's standing by the water, her back to the fire. She hears my footsteps and turns toward me, a soft smile curving her lips.

Man, she's pretty. She took her hair out of its ponytail, and the copper-colored strands are loose around her shoulders, once again appearing bright orange in the firelight.

"Hey," she says.

"Hey. Sorry about that."

"No worries."

"So . . ." I step closer but maintain a few feet of distance.

She notices, because her eyes drop to the gaping space between us. "So . . ." she mimics. She bites her bottom lip and studies me for a moment.

Damn it. I don't know if I should bring up the kiss and let her know it can't happen again, or just pretend it never happened. I shove my hands in my pockets, shifting in discomfort. I'm still trying to decide what to say when Cassie beats me to it.

"Will you fling me?" she blurts out.

I blink. "Sorry, what?" I blink again. "You want me to throw you? Like, into the water?"

At that, she bursts out laughing. "No! Why would I want you to throw me into the water?"

I snicker. "I don't know! It's a crazy request. That's why I clar-ified."

Still giggling, she offers her own clarification. "I'm asking if you want to have a fling with me. A summer fling."

Shit.

She went there.

And here her pal Joy thought Cassie would never have the balls to ask me.

I sort of wish she hadn't found the courage. Because I'm about to look like a total asshole by saying no to a hookup ten minutes after I made a move on her. If that's not liable to give a woman whiplash, I don't know what will.

"Uh. Cass." I scrub a hand over my forehead then drag it through my hair. I'm stalling. But that means I'm also prolonging the agony and that's even worse. I let out a breath and say, "So, listen, I was actually just thinking that I . . . well, that I was sort of glad for the interruption."

"Oh." Her eyes instantly go shuttered, but not before I catch a flash of hurt.

"It's good we got interrupted before things went any further, you know? I like you, and I think you're awesome, but I'm not sure it's a good idea for us to get involved. Like, sexually." Christ, this is torture. "It's better if we keep things platonic."

"Okay." She studies me for a moment, her expression unread-able. "Can I ask why?"

I shrug lamely. "I just don't think it's a good idea, especially with you being next door. I'm going to be busy this summer. I work two jobs, you know? I won't have a lot of free time to spend with you, and even if we agreed to no expectations, that never actually pans out. This kind of arrangement always leads to conflict, and, honestly, I like you too much to screw up this friendship thing we've got going—"

"All right, I get it," she cuts in. "It's cool."

"Are you sure?" I still can't gauge her expression.

"Yeah, it's fine. This town is full of suitable candidates for a fling, right?"

"Right," I say, nodding in relief. "And you're smoking hot. You'll have no trouble finding someone. I can help you scope out potential candidates if you want."

Seriously?! shouts the incredulous voice in my head.

I wish you could un-say words the way some platforms let you un-send messages, but nope. I said what I said and there's no taking it back.

Man. I basically friend-zoned her and now I'm offering to be her *wingman*? Way to twist the knife in deeper. I'm a fucking asshole.

Clearly, she agrees, because she eyes me in disbelief before letting out a sarcastic laugh. "Um, yeah . . . I don't know about that." Rolling her eyes, she steps away from the water's edge. "Come on, friend, let's go back to the party. I desperately need another drink."

CHAPTER 9

CASSIE

Freshman year of college, I was plagued by a recurring anxiety dream. The damn thing tortured my sleeping brain at least once a week and it always went the same way. I'm staring at a small suitcase; behind it, there's an entire wall with stacks and stacks of test answer booklets. Those thin, lined notebooks the profs hand out when you write exams. My task? I need to put the notebooks in the suitcase. All of them. I must make them all fit, no matter what. It is imperative they fit.

And somehow, by some miracle, I manage to jam all the booklets into the suitcase. The anxiety would then lift, my subconscious breathing a sigh of relief, and I'd think, *Thank God, I've done it.*

All good, right?

No. I then cart the suitcase into my English Lit lecture hall, where I need to give a presentation on a Brontë book. Not one written by Charlotte or Emily, but Anne. The lesser-known Brontë. I haven't read the book—and yet *that's* not what I'm stressed about? Go figure. Despite that, I nail the presentation.

All good, right?

No. Now I'm supposed to hand the suitcase to my professor. I pick it up and carry it toward him, and just as I reach the center of the room, the overstuffed case bursts open and its contents spill out. Except, for some inexplicable reason, all the notebooks are gone.

They've been replaced with naked pictures of me.

Now the entire floor of the lecture hall is covered in eight-by-ten photographs of my bare boobs and ass and lady bits. A sea of nudes.

And then I wake up.

I don't know what that says about my psyche—or what I was watching on TV the first time I dreamed it—but that nightmare became imbedded in my subconsciousness like a rusty nail. I could expect it every week like clockwork, and I'd wake up every time feeling the burn of humiliation and a potent rush of insecurity.

I can honestly say that what I felt last night was a hundred times worse.

I have never propositioned a guy in my life.

And I never intend to do it again.

Because rejection is a bitch. It's soul-sucking. Confidence-crushing. I cannot erase from my mind that uneasy look on Tate's face. The flicker of panic in his eyes when I suggested a fling. The way he fidgeted when he told me he just wants to be friends.

Brutal.

Fucking brutal.

If I'd had a shovel on me, I would've dug a huge hole in the ground, gotten into it, and buried myself alive. Knowing my luck, though, the afterlife would end up being that nightmare lecture hall full of my nudes.

Now, I'm forced to repeat the whole story to Peyton, whose voice blares out of the car speakers as I drive over to my dad's house for dinner.

"There's no way it was the kiss," Peyton insists.

She's responding to the suspicion I'd just voiced: that Tate had kissed me, almost threw up in his mouth, and promptly decided he could never do it again.

"What other explanation is there?" I counter. "One minute we're making out. Then he leaves for a few minutes and when he comes back, he tells me he wants to be platonic. That absolutely means he hated the kiss."

"Not necessarily." She pauses. "But if we were to play that theory out . . . were there any signs he didn't like it? Did he try to pull away at any point?"

"No," I groan. "If anything, he just came closer! And I swear he was hard. I felt him against my leg."

"Hmmm. Okay?" She mulls it over. "Maybe he was drunker than you thought?"

"Gee, thanks, Peyton. So what you're saying is, a man needs to be completely wasted to kiss me?"

"That's not what I'm saying! *But.* Maybe he was drunk when he kissed you, and we both know people do impulsive things when they're drinking, right? So hooking up could've seemed like a good idea to him in the moment, but then he sobered up a bit and everything he said afterward wasn't some elaborate excuse. He really *does* want to do his own thing this summer and not hook up with anyone. And he really *does* think you're awesome, is attracted to you, but doesn't want to do anything to jeopardize the friendship. All of those things can be true at once."

She's right. But the bottom line remains the same: I propositioned Tate Bartlett and he said no.

"Honestly, it's probably for the better. Remember my silver lining? Don't spoil all subsequent prospects by flinging with a guy that's too attractive. I shouldn't have let myself forget that." I purse my lips. "What I need to do is find myself, like, a seven. Maybe a six."

"You are *not* flinging with a six." She is utterly aghast. "Over my dead body. I'm willing to compromise and settle halfway between a six and a ten—Tate's a ten, right?"

"Oh yeah," I say miserably.

"Fine, then we're aiming for an eight. Go out with Joy tomorrow to try to meet someone else and send pics so I can verify his eight-ness."

"We'll see. I might need to nurse this rejection for a little while first." I turn onto Sycamore Way and slow down. "Anyway, just got to my dad's. I'll text you later."

"All right. Love you, babe," she chirps before disconnecting.

It's so strange returning to my childhood home when I don't even have my own bedroom there anymore. The twins usurped it because it's larger than the other option, which Dad and Nia use as a guest room now. That's where I sleep when I come to visit, ensuring my old house never quite feels like home anymore. Also, Nia redecorated the entire place not long after she moved in. Where my mom's design eye lends itself to grays, creams, and whites and modern furnishings, Nia is all about bright colors. She loves mismatched furniture, pieces that offer a cozy rather than museum-like feel. I can't deny I like Nia's décor better.

I also can't deny it stings that Dad's new daughters sleep in my room.

Excited shrieks greet me in the front hall. Two dark-haired tornadoes spiral toward me, and then two sets of arms curl around my legs like greedy tentacles.

"Cassie!"

They're both screaming my name as if they didn't just see me in the spring. Honestly, it's great for my ego. I give them an enthusiastic bear hug, but Monique is hopping around, so excited to see me, that she loses her footing and ends up teetering out of the three-way hug, falling to the floor onto her butt. Her sister Roxanne starts hooting with laughter.

I tug Mo to her feet. "Hey, squirts," I say. "How's life?"

"Life. Is. Awful," announces Roxy, the ringleader of the two. Both my sisters possess sweet, lovable temperaments, but Roxanne is definitely bossier, always speaking in a more authoritative tone. She's the elder by two minutes and takes that role very seriously. Even if she didn't have that tiny birthmark on her left cheekbone that allows me to tell them apart, I'd know Roxy just based on her tone of voice.

"And why is it awful?" I ask, fighting a smile.

"You tell her," Mo says, as if Roxy wasn't going to do it anyway.

"Mama won't get us a turtle."

I stare at them. "A turtle?"

"Yes!" Roxy huffs loudly. "They *promised* we could have a turtle when we turned six and now we're turning six and there's no turtle."

"There's no turtle!" Monique echoes.

They're wearing identical looks of outrage, and since their features are identical to begin with, their thunderous expressions give off some serious *redrum* vibes, a la *The Shining*.

"Like, a pet turtle?" I'm still perplexed. "Wait a second. You guys are campaigning for a pet and you chose a *turtle*? Man, I would've killed for a dog growing up."

"We don't care for dogs," Roxy says, sniffing. "They're waaay too much work."

"And we'd have to pick up *poo*," Mo adds. "That is so gross."

"*So* gross." Roxy peers up at me, her brown eyes twinkling impishly. "Did you know the French word for poo is *merde*?"

I smother a laugh. I'm pretty sure the correct translation is *shit*. Either way there's something hilarious about hearing the word *merde* exit the mouth of a six-year-old.

The most delicious smells float out of the kitchen, so I wander toward it with the twins scampering at my heels. Neither Dad nor Nia is anywhere to be found, but I notice there's something baking in the oven, and several pots and pans simmering on the stove.

The big, airy kitchen was the first room Nia renovated when she moved in, changing the tiled floor to hardwood, painting the white cabinets a bright eggshell blue. She replaced the marble island for a cedar one, claiming she didn't like the way marble feels beneath her hands. She told Dad the counters were cold and unfeeling and made her sad. I didn't know counters could have that much of an impact on a person, but I suppose she's not wrong. Mom's aesthetic did lean toward cold and unfeeling.

Beyond the kitchen is the sunroom, which also doubles as the dining room, its entire wall of windows overlooking the spacious backyard. I peer into it, but it's empty.

"Where are the folks?" I ask, just as footsteps thud behind us.

"There's my girl!" Dad appears in the kitchen doorway, wearing khakis and a flannel shirt. "All my girls!" he adds, noticing the twins who are still bouncing around me. "C'mere, Cass. Give your old man a hug."

I go over and let him envelop me with his arms. Dad's not a tall man, but he's stocky and has some bulk, so his hugs always make you feel safe and warm.

His eyes shine behind his wire-rimmed glasses when he releases me. "Sorry I didn't get to see you this week. Just been busy around here."

"No worries. You know I love spending time with Grandma."

"Well, I'm glad you're here tonight. And I know you're excited to spend the summer with Lydia, but we were hoping you'd come stay here too."

"Yes!" Roxy says happily, throwing her arms around my legs again. "Then you can tell us bedtime stories every night."

"Every single night!" Mo gives an enthusiastic nod.

"I want one now," Roxy begs. "I wanna know what happens to Kit!"

"Me too!"

The request makes me smile. It's become sort of a tradition that I read the girls a bedtime story whenever I'm here, but these last couple years I've been entertaining them with an ongoing original tale. I pulled it out of my ass one time when we couldn't pick a book they both agreed on, and before I knew it I'd created an entire imaginary world for them, in which a little girl named McKenna finds a dragon egg in her backyard and proceeds to raise a pet dragon she names Kit, without anyone in her family catching on.

"What do you say?" Dad presses. "Can you swing a longer visit this summer? Stay for a week? Or maybe a weekend here and there?" he trails off, a bit uncertain.

"Definitely," I assure him. "Nia's okay with that?"

"Of course she is. She loves having you here."

Doubtful. But I never voice my suspicions about Nia's level of enthusiasm toward me, especially not to Dad. Peyton's psychiatrist mother would call it a coping mechanism, and I suppose it is. Whether I'm talking to my mom or my dad, I always put on that bright, sunny show. It's not just because I hate conflict—I've been burned too many times in the past with Dad shutting down. The brunt of it happened right after the divorce, whenever I tried talking to him about my feelings. He didn't even fight for joint custody of me, for Pete's sake. He let Mom have it all. And I never got answers for that, only uncomfortable silences and stilted smiles as he changed the subject.

As the memories surface before I can stop them, I swallow the lump clogging my throat and then take a breath, firmly banishing the resentment to that place inside of me where all the dark thoughts go.

My father is a good guy, he truly is. I know he loves me. But sometimes it feels like he wanted to wash his hands of everything after the divorce. He wanted zero reminders of my mother, and, unfortunately, I was the biggest reminder of all. Hence, I became collateral damage.

And to Nia, I'm a reminder of her husband's bitchy ex-wife, which is why her smile seems forced and her hug lacks warmth when she greets me a few minutes later.

"Cassandra," she says, her dark eyes guarded. "It's so good to see you."

"Good to see you too. Can I help with dinner?"

"*Non, non.*" She still has a noticeable French accent despite all her years living in the US. "Why don't you go sit at the table and catch up with your father and sisters? I have it handled."

"Are you sure?"

"Yes."

She's practically shoving me out of the kitchen. Not exactly the actions of a woman who's desperate to spend time with her stepdaughter.

In the sunroom, Dad and I settle at the dining table while the twins wander around us, running their little fingers over the backs of all the chairs. Those two can't sit still to save their lives.

"We told Cassie about the turtle," Roxy informs Dad.

He's clearly fighting a smile. "Oh, did you now? Why am I not surprised?" He glances at me. "The girls have alerted every single human they've encountered this past month to their desperate need for a turtle."

"Because we need a turtle!" Roxy complains.

"And it's not fair," Mo chimes in.

I arch a brow at Dad. "Just out of curiosity, why are we anti-turtle?"

"We're not," he answers, shrugging. "But pets are a lot of work.

We're not convinced the girls are grown up enough to handle all the responsibility that comes with it."

"Yes, we are!" they both shriek, and stomp their feet, basically proving the point he's trying to make.

Dad and I wince. "Indoor voices," he chides. "And we're going to table this turtle discussion for now, all right? Your mama and I said no turtle. We can revisit it next year."

Their faces collapse.

Knowing that tears are imminent, Dad snaps into action. He glances around the table with an exaggerated look of dismay and proceeds to do that thing I've seen him do a thousand times before, where he pretends there's a critical task that needs undertaking. Usually it's a pretty impressive trick, but tonight he's reaching.

"Oh no!" he exclaims. "We only put out the red napkins. We also need the white ones!"

"Oh, do we?" I say innocently.

He shoots me a look. "Yes, Cassandra. You know this. We must always dine with both red and white," he says poetically, laying it on thick. "To go with the wine."

I choke down a laugh. "Right. How could I forget that."

"We'll get them!" Roxy offers, just as Dad had intended for her to do. The girls are in that phase where they must be involved in *all* household matters.

"I'll help!" Mo chimes in.

"Oh wonderful. Thanks, girls." His tone oozes gratitude, as if he didn't just con them into doing his bidding.

The moment the sliding door closes, I stare at my father. "One: That was really smooth."

"Thank you."

"Two: You realize next to a goldfish, a turtle is the easiest pet you can have, right? And those things never die, so there's no risk of you flushing it down the toilet and replacing it with a thousand other goldfish like you did with mine."

Dad chortles. "Man, you were a clueless kid, Cass. I think we were on Rocky Fifteen before you figured it out?"

"Why would my child brain ever immediately go to *my fish died, so my parents drowned his corpse and keep replacing him with impostors?*" I glare in accusation. "Parents who do that are sociopaths."

"Sure, come talk to me when you have kids and your hamster accidentally gets eaten by a red-tailed hawk. Would you rather your child live in ignorance and love an impostor hamster, or do you plan on sharing all the gory details? And I'm talking *gory.*"

"Oh my God, Dad, did that happen to you? Did a hawk eat your hamster?"

"Yes." He sounds glum. "And Grandpa Lou sat me down and gave me a play-by-play of his death. I'm sure if he'd taken pictures of the carnage, he would've showed them to me."

I bust out laughing. Oh man. Dad's father was the greatest. It honestly sucks that I lost both my grandfathers within a couple years of each other. But at least my grandmothers are still alive and kicking.

"Can I tell you a secret?" Dad says. His gaze flicks toward the kitchen. "I wouldn't mind getting a turtle. I think they're cool. But Nia isn't having it. She insists they're a lot more work than we think."

"Maybe there's a certain breed that's easier to own than others," I point out. "Did you even research it?"

"No."

"Did Nia?"

"I don't think so. She just shot down the idea point-blank. Told the girls we'll talk about it next year." Dad purses his lips for a moment. Mulling. "You think I should get them one?"

"Not necessarily. But I don't think it hurts researching the pros and cons." Crap. This isn't going to endear me in Nia's eyes. She already doesn't like me. But I feel like I owe it to my sisters to advocate for their dreams of turtle ownership. "I mean, it can't hurt, right? The least you can do is go to a pet store and talk to someone about it."

"Yeah. I suppose we could do that." One corner of his mouth quirks up, and then his eyes start twinkling. "Whatcha doing tomorrow morning?"

"Um." I offer a pointed look. "Potential turtle shopping?"

"Damn right."

We both snicker, exchanging secretive smiles when Nia and the twins return and we all settle around the table for dinner. It makes me feel like a little kid again, sharing a secret with my father. It's rare to have these bonding opportunities with him, where we're truly connecting without the heavy pall of my mother or Nia hanging over us. Those rare times when it's just us, me and him. The way it used to be when I was a child and he was my dad. When he didn't have two other kids, or two different wives who both can't stand to be around me.

I cling to those moments, because they're so few and far between.

CHAPTER 10

CASSIE

"I can't believe we're doing this," Dad whispers the next morning.

"I can't believe you're wearing a disguise," I respond in a normal speaking volume, for there is absolutely no reason for us to be whispering.

"I told you, Nia's friend works at the bakery over there," Dad protests, nodding toward a storefront on the other end of the strip mall. He glowers. "Chandra. One of the nosy PTA moms. I don't want her to notice me."

"Dad. You're wearing a hot-pink adventure hat with a purple string. She is absolutely going to notice you. In fact, you had a better chance of her not caring what your face looks like *without* the hat. Now she's going to *want* to see your face in order to understand what sort of person would ever choose to wear that hat."

"All I'm hearing is, you love my hat."

"That's not what I'm saying at all."

He just grins. We're a few feet from the entrance of the pet store when he says, "The girls loved seeing you last night, by the way. They were going on and on over breakfast about that bedtime story you told them, the one about the purple dragon? You need to start writing some of those down, Cass. I bet if you compiled all the stories in one file, you could have an entire—"

I suddenly gasp.

"What? What is it?" he demands, looking around in a panic. "Have we been compromised?"

"Oh my God, no. Dad, the baker lady doesn't give a shit about you." I'm practically bouncing with glee. "But you just gave me the best idea for the girls' birthday present. I can take one of the Kit 'n McKenna stories and create a children's book for them. I'm sure I could find a place to print a hardcover version of it." I pause. "I just wish I could draw. It would be cool to have illustrations to go with the story."

My mind snaps into troubleshooting mode, scanning through every person I've ever met in my life while I try to recall if they possess any artistic talent.

Robb! I remember in triumph. Robb Sheffield was my stepbrother for five years during Mom's marriage to his dad, Stuart. He was always doodling in his sketchpad when we watched TV together, mostly drawing fantasy-type stuff, like freaky-looking monsters and warriors with deadly weapons. He works in videogame design now, creating the kind of imagery that's a lot grislier than a tale of a little girl and a purple dragon, but maybe he'd be willing to do me this favor.

"That's a terrific idea," Dad tells me. "The girls would love that. And if the final product turns out well, you should try to sell it."

"What do you mean? Like, self-publish a children's book?"

"Or submit it to a publishing house."

My brow furrows. "Really?"

"Sure. Why not? Aren't you majoring in literature?" he teases.

"Yes, but . . . I mean, I never really thought about going into a creative field. I only picked English Lit because I couldn't think of anything better to major in."

Truth be told, I have no clue what career path to take after graduation. So many people just *know*. They have that one skill, that one field they've always been passionate about. I'm not one of those people. I was hoping by the time graduation rolled around, I'd have landed on something, anything, but I'm going into my senior year and remain completely stumped as to what job I'll end up in.

"Could I even make a career out of that?" I ask, chewing on my lip. "It's just a bunch of silly bedtime stories for my sisters. It's not like I've been writing forever."

"Do you need to have been writing forever to start doing it now?"

"I guess not." I glare at him. "Ugh. You've given me a bunch of stuff to think about now."

"God forbid my daughter thinks!" Snorting, he reaches for the door handle. "Ready to turtle down?"

"Please don't ever say that."

When we enter the store, Dad pushes the pink hat off his head so it's dangling at his back by its purple string. He looks like a lost adventurer who stopped to ask for directions. We find ourselves surrounded by rows and rows of tanks, each housing various aquatic creatures.

I approach a fish tank full of fat orange goldfish and raise a brow. "I had no idea goldfish could get this big. If you tried to flush one of these guys, you'd clog the toilet."

"Welcome to AquaPets," a bored voice says from behind us. "Can I help you find something? You looking for a goldfish?"

A teenager in a store uniform sidles up to us. His name tag reads JOEL, and he's got shoulder-length black hair, acne-riddled skin, and he reeks of pot. The skunky odor practically radiates from his pores.

"We're considering buying a turtle for my six-year-old daughters," Dad explains. "But we're hoping for some more information before we commit."

"Yeah, yeah, that's cool," Joel says. The kid is clearly stoned. "I can help you with that. I've got three loggerheads at home. Those little dudes are rad."

"Loggerheads?" I echo.

"Loggerhead musk turtle," he says briskly, and, stoned or not, we discover the kid knows his stuff. For the next twenty minutes, he dumps an obscene amount of information on us, ushering us from tank to tank while spitting out reptilian facts.

"These guys? Smallest species of turtle you're allowed to keep in captivity. So if you got limited space, this is your dude. And they're so cute, man. Like, look." Leaning closer to the glass, he proceeds to make cooing noises at the spotted turtle. "You doing okay in there, Marshall? I named him Marshall. After Eminem."

I press my lips together. "Cool."

"The problem is, Marshall can't swim too good. See? That's why his water isn't very deep. And let's be honest—he's kind of a dick. The spotted ones get cranky sometimes. You want a social one, I'll show you my man Jay-Z. He's what we call a Reeve's turtle. Come. You'll love him."

Dad and I exchange a look that loosely translates to *why is this happening to us?*

But we're committed now, so we follow Joel the Turtle Whisperer to see his man Jay-Z.

"Best thing about this breed is they like being stroked," he tells us, so animated I'm having a hard time reconciling him with the pothead who greeted us at the door. "Most turtles don't enjoy being handled. It's stressful for them, you know? But if you're patient with him, Jay-Z might let you hold him sometimes."

He stares longingly at the tank. "The downside is," he says, and his expression collapses, "they've got a shorter life expectancy. Fifteen years, maybe twenty? If you're looking for a little dude who'll live longer, I'd go with the common musk. We're talking a ripe old age of fifty years. Just don't handle them roughly. They're feisty, man. If they feel threatened, they skunk you out."

"Skunk you out?" Dad echoes blankly. He looks as over-whelmed as I feel. Who knew turtle ownership was so intensive?

"Yeah, like, they release a foul odor. It stinks." Joel guffaws. "We call 'em *stinkpots*."

I don't ask who *we* is, but I'm definitely curious.

"They're not strong swimmers either," he adds. "But they've got pretty basic care requirements compared to other breeds."

"Wow," I say. "This is a lot of information."

So much, in fact, that eventually Dad and I beg off and tell Joel we need to think about it. Then we make our escape and step outside, breathing in the non-marijuana-infused air.

Dad sags against the concrete wall separating AquaPets from the pool equipment shop next door. He heaves a massive sigh of relief. "That was . . ."

"Intense," I supply.

"Very." He pulls his glasses off and cleans them with the hem of his T-shirt before popping them back on his face. "Thoughts?"

I join him at the wall, shoving my hands in the pockets of my denim shorts. "That Keanu Reeves turtle sounded promising."

Dad snickers. "Really? I'm leaning toward the musk."

"But Keanu Reeves has a shorter life expectancy," I argue. "Do you seriously want a pet that lives for fifty years?"

"What do I care? I'll probably be dead."

"Don't say that."

"Come on, there's no way I'll be alive to experience that turtle's entire life."

"But the musks don't like it when you touch them. They lose their shit and skunk you out, remember? Meanwhile, we were told on the good authority of Joel the Pothead that Keanu Reeves enjoys being stroked."

"Ahem."

Dad and I jump in surprise. Our heads swivel in the direction of the throat clearing, and at this point I'm not even surprised when I lay eyes on Tate. Since I arrived in Avalon Bay, it seems like everywhere I go, Tate Bartlett is there.

"Hi," he says in amusement, giving a nonchalant wave.

"You know," I say solemnly, "I long for the days of yore when I turned my head and didn't always find you standing there in front of me." It's meant to be a joke, but it then occurs to me that after last night's mortifying exchange, he might think I'm being serious. So I quickly add, "Kidding. But really, why are you here?"

He gestures toward a storefront on the other side of the parking lot. "I work at the boat dealership. Saw you from the window and came over to say hi—a decision I deeply regret because I'm not sure I want to know why you're discussing Keanu Reeves's love of handjobs and how you stumbled upon that information."

I can't stop the laugh that pops out. "You know what, not even going to explain it. I'm going to let it haunt you forever." I notice my father sporting a questioning expression, and gesture toward Tate. "Dad, this is Tate. He's housesitting the place next door to Grandma's."

Tate extends a hand. "Nice to meet you, Mr. Tanner."

Dad blanches.

"Oh no, no," I hastily intervene. "He's not a Tanner. My mom's side is the Tanners."

"Clayton Soul," Dad corrects, stepping forward to shake Tate's hand.

"Soul?" Tate turns to me in surprise. "Your name is Cassie Soul?"

"Yeah." I frown. "Is that bad?"

"Bad? Try bad-*ass*. That's a solid name."

"I guess? I never really thought that much about it. It's just my name."

There's a long beat during which we both start fidgeting with random sections of our clothing. I toy with the hem of my tank top. Tate pretends to pick at some lint on his shirt sleeve. Damn it. Things are awkward between us now. I knew this would happen.

"Turtles!" I blurt out.

Tate startles. "What?"

"Um, my sisters demanded a pet turtle for their birthday. That's why we're here. Doing some research. But it sounds like turtles are kind of jerks."

"Nah," he disagrees. "They're the easiest of pets. I had one when I was a kid and all it did was laze around in his tank all day. They pretty much entertain themselves." He shrugs. "My dogs, on the other hand . . . needy as fuck. Dogs require attention pretty much twenty-four-seven."

Dad chuckles. "You're making a good case for turtles."

"I'm telling you, they're great."

Another silence falls.

Tate fiddles with his other sleeve. I play with a frayed thread on my shorts. It's unbearable. This is what rejection does to people.

"Bye!" I blurt out.

Tate blinks at the sudden dismissal. "Oh. All right. Bye."

"I mean, we have to go now," I amend lamely. "So, ah, good-bye. See you around."

"Sure." His forehead creases. "See you around."

I practically drag Dad to the car, where I hurl myself into the passenger seat and pretend not to see Tate walking past the wind-shield on his way back to work.

"So," Dad says cheerfully, "do we have a crush on that boy, or is this how you interact with all your peers? Because I remember you used to be a lot less . . . weird."

"That was weird, wasn't it?" I moan. "Do you think he noticed?"

"Yes."

"Damn it." My face is on fire, and I refuse to look in the side mirror because I'm certain I'm redder than a lobster. "He and I are just friends." I pause. "I think." Pause again. "It's complicated."

"It always is." Dad suddenly jolts in his seat before reaching into his pocket to retrieve his buzzing phone. He checks the screen and balks. "Son of a bitch."

"What is it?" I ask immediately, concern washing over me.

Without a word, he hands over the phone to show me the text from Nia.

Nia: *Chandra said she just saw you at a pet store. Explain yourself!*

My eyebrows greet my hairline. "Wow. Fuckin' Chandra did us dirty."

"Did I not tell you?" Dad grumbles. Sighing, he starts the engine and puts the car in drive. "Time to go home and face the music."

* * *

Later that night, I walk up to my window just as a familiar figure enters my line of vision. It's becoming routine now. Grabbing something from my room? Tate's doing the same. Getting ready for bed? Tate's doing the same. This time, we're both reaching to close the curtains, almost in perfect sync. We stop, look at each other, then start to laugh. He disappears for a moment and returns holding his phone.

A message pops up on mine.

Tate: *Are we good?*

I stifle a sigh. I guess I knew that was coming. I meet his eyes briefly, then type a response.

Me: *Yeah, we're fine.*
Tate: *You sure? Because you were babbling more than usual when I saw you this morning.*

I don't have an excuse for that, so I just repeat myself.

Me: *We're fine.*
Tate: *I know last night was kind of awkward and I'm sorry about that. I really didn't want to embarrass you or anything. But I do think we're better as friends.*
Me: *OMG you're embarrassing me NOW by talking about it. We're cool, I promise. And we are friends, okay?*
Tate: *Yeah?*
Me: *Yeah.*
Tate: *Good.*

Rather than end the conversation there, he remains at the window, still typing, and I do my best not to stare at his bare chest. His abs look like they were chiseled out of stone and his pecs are stupidly defined and—damn it. I'm failing at not staring. I swear, would it kill him to throw on a shirt? He rarely wears shirts when he's inside the house. Doesn't he ever get cold? Here, we've always got the AC blasting. I'm wearing a sweater right now, for Pete's sake.

Tate: *I'm still waiting for deets on that Keanu Reeves handjob . . .*

I grin at the phone. Really? That's what took him so long to type? I wonder how many messages he deleted before he settled on that one.

Me: *I'm taking it to the grave.*
Tate: *You're a cruel woman, ginger.*
Me: *Copper!*
Tate: *It's really cute you actually believe that. What are you up to this weekend?*
Me: *I'm spending the day at the club tomorrow with Joy. We're going guy shopping.*
Tate: *You realize if any man said something like that he'd be labeled as the biggest douchebag in the Bay?*
Me: *Double standards, you gotta love them!*
Tate: *Sure don't!*
Me: *What are your plans this weekend?*
Tate: *Working, working, and working. Tomorrow I'm at the club too. Teaching a beginner dinghies class for kids. If I run into you, I'll make sure to say hi. You know, just to make it awkward again.*
Me: *Perfect. I'll pencil you in.*

At least we can joke about it.

CHAPTER 11

CASSIE

"Okay, don't kill me. But I like him. He's funny." Joy reaches across her lounger and hands me back my phone. I showed her last night's text exchange with Tate with the goal of highlighting how embarrassing it was. Instead, she goes and declares her love for the guy who rejected me.

Not that I disagree with her assessment.

"He *is* funny," I sigh. "And I like him too."

As the memory of his rejection pricks at my skin, I order myself to conduct a silver-lining check. Shockingly, I land on something genuine.

"You know what, though? Maybe it's a good thing he turned me down. I can see myself catching feelings," I admit.

Joy gives me a somber look. "Oh boy. Yeah. That's no good. You can't fall for your summer fling. Well, unless you plan on moving to Avalon Bay and living happily ever after with a local."

I muse on that for a moment. "I don't know if I could live here. I enjoy the energy of the city. The Bay is nice to visit, but I think I prefer a faster pace."

"Exactly. I wouldn't live here full-time either," Joy says, leaning back in her chair. She readjusts her sunglasses and gazes up at the cloudless sky. It's a perfect day for sunbathing. "And from what I've seen, the townies don't tend to leave this place. If you fell for the guy, you'd be stuck here forever."

"There you go," I say wryly. "One more item in the plus column for getting friend-zoned."

Joy smiles. "For what it's worth, it sounds like he really does like you and want to hang out with you. Maybe being friend-zoned isn't the end of the world."

"Maybe not," I agree, and while I half mean it this time, it doesn't exactly change my current situation. I'm still left in the same fling-less predicament.

I want my fling, damn it. I was genuinely looking forward to finding someone to spend the next couple of months with. Finally experiencing that summer romance I've always envied my friends for. I'd hoped to go into my final year of college with a fresh dose of confidence and some experience under my belt. My entire collegiate dating experience consists of the six months I spent with a guy in junior year, Mike. He was funny and interesting, but we didn't sleep together because I wasn't ready, and eventually he got bored of third base and bailed. This year I want a relationship that actually lasts, one that's chock-full of passion and chemistry. I'm craving passion.

"We should pick you up someone at the bachelor auction," Joy suggests while applying some moisturizing lip balm. She always complains that the sun dries out her lips.

"Are they seriously still doing that?"

"Oh yeah. You should go check out the events desk. I peeked at the calendar when I got here to see what's coming up this summer, and I swear there are *so* many events."

"Like what?" From the table sandwiched between our chairs, I grab the aerosol can of sunscreen and spray some on my legs. Either my sunglasses are warping the colors around me, or I'm starting to burn a little. I lift my shades and wince. Yup, burning.

I can practically hear Grandma's voice in my head lecturing me for not consistently reapplying my sunscreen.

"We just missed the regatta—that was last week. Next weekend is the charity gala, which features the bachelor auction. First week of August is the golf tournament. Beach Games at the end of the month."

"Did I tell you I'm competing this year? Mackenzie Cabot asked me to join Team Beacon."

"That sounds like my worst nightmare," Joy informs me. I'm not surprised, seeing as how she's the least athletic person I know.

"Nah, it'll be fun. And then the grand reopening of the Beacon is the weekend after that," I remind her. That's the only event I'm truly excited about, although I know it'll be bittersweet. "Grandma and I will be at the charity thing this weekend. She likes bidding in the silent auction. She's giving me some cash to bid with since it's for a good cause, but I doubt I'll attend the bachelor event. It's always a bunch of old dudes with very noticeable hair plugs."

She laughs. "Nuh-uh, last year there were some young'uns in the mix." She waggles her eyebrows at me. "Including your best friend Tate."

"Really?" I ignore the way my heart skips a beat. "You think he signed up again?"

"No idea. But I vote we check it out regardless. Maybe we'll find you a cute guy to fling with."

"Wasn't that today's goal?"

"Well, yeah, but I haven't seen any suitable candidates yet. Have you?"

"No," I say glumly.

She slides up in her chair, readjusting her sunglasses. "Let's take another look."

Weekends at the Manor are always busy, so the pool area is packed, every single lounger occupied. We had to reserve ours in advance, and Joy had grumbled up a storm when she was informed there were no available cabanas to book for the day. Her family usually reserves one for three full months, but this year her parents opted out because her mom got a promotion at work and will be spending the bulk of the summer in Manhattan.

"Oooh," she suddenly says. "I got one. Eleven o'clock, end of the bar."

I pop my sunglasses back on to make it less obvious that we're staring. The guy she's homed in on does look promising. Average height, dark hair, chiseled profile. He's decked out in shorts, a green polo, and brown Sperrys. When he turns slightly, angling away from us, my gaze lowers to his butt, because apparently I'm a butt girl now. It's decent. And he's at least an eight, which ought to satisfy Peyton.

"I sure could use a refill of this piña colada," Joy says. With a grin, she waves her empty glass around.

"You're really going to make me go up there? Haven't we established I'm terrible at asking guys out?"

"Who's asking him out? Just go and talk to him. See if you like him. Then you can decide if you even want to ask him out. You always make yourself needlessly anxious by assuming the outcome."

Good point. I do tend to jump the gun a lot, assuming every cute guy I speak to is my potential boyfriend when really it's just a person to say hello to.

"Fine." With a brisk nod, I slide off the striped towel draped over my chair and get to my feet. I don't bother with my shorts, just slip into my flip-flops and saunter across the pool deck. There are women here walking around in string bikinis; my one-piece is hardly scandalous. It's high-cut and does show quite a lot of thigh, but it supports my boobs well, a rare feat for a Cassie Soul bathing suit.

When I approach, the guy is sitting on a stool laughing at something the bartender just said. The second bartender, a curly-haired woman with a deep tan, greets me with a smile. "What can I do you for?"

"Two piña coladas, please. Virgin." I blush at the word, but it sounds less dorky than *nonalcoholic*. Joy and I decided against day drinking today, even though I'd probably be served here. Most of the bars in the country club turn the other way when it comes to underage clientele, provided their families are rich enough. And my family passes the wealth test, apparently.

The sound of my voice catches the guy's attention. He gives me a sidelong look.

I crack a half smile, one of those teeny quirks of the lips that says I acknowledge his presence.

He smiles back.

And as always, his eyes drop to my chest. The curse of owning double Ds.

His gaze lingers, and now I feel self-conscious standing there in nothing but a bathing suit and pink flip-flops. There's nowhere for me to hide. No clothing to burrow under. His perusal doesn't feel overly creepy, only a glimmer of appreciation, but I'm still relieved when he raises his eyes.

"Hey," he says easily. "I'm Ben."

"Cassie."

"Are you new here?" He flashes another smile, a tad bashful. "You must be, 'cause I thought I knew all the pretty members in this club."

"Uh, no. I'm not new. I'm here a lot. I mean, I don't visit for the whole summer often, but I have been here before."

The bartender approaches with an apologetic look. "It'll just be a few more minutes. We ran out of coconut milk. Someone's running over to grab a fresh case from the restaurant bar."

"That's fine. I can wait." I glance over my shoulder to find Joy watching us intently. Grinning impishly, she gives a little wave.

"Sit," Ben urges, gesturing to the stool beside him. "Take a load off."

We chat for a while, the coconut milk taking longer than a few minutes to arrive. Ben tells me he's originally from New York but goes to Yale. He's in his first year of law school and loving it. His family recently bought a vacation home in the Bay and this is his second summer here. When I tell him my grandparents were the previous owners of the Beacon Hotel and built it from the ground up, he's suitably impressed. He's got a bland sort of humor but the conversation flows easily, and when two piña coladas are finally slid in front of me, I decide I don't want the conversation to end yet.

I lean toward an approaching waitress and ask, "Do you mind dropping this drink off to my friend? I don't want it to get all melty." I point across the pool deck at Joy's lounger. "She's the one in the red bikini."

"No problem," the blonde chirps, taking the tall glass, which is already dripping with condensation. Before she steps away, she gives me a warning look. Or at least I think it's a warning? I'm not entirely sure.

When I wrinkle my forehead, her head moves, almost imperceptibly, toward my companion, who's checking something on his phone. Is she warning me away from Ben? I must be misreading the look, but she hurries off before I can figure it out.

A few minutes later, I figure it out.

"You want to get out of here?" he suggests with a devilish gleam in his eyes, twisting his body so that our knees are now touching.

I shift in my seat, easing my knee away. "And go where?" I ask uneasily.

"My family booked a cabana here for the summer. We can hang out there. Lots of privacy . . ." He raises an enticing brow.

"Oh. No, it's fine. Let's just stay out here." I lift my drink and take a sip. "I'm good."

"Really? 'Cause I think you'd feel a lot better if we had some privacy."

It's funny how fast they transform from cool guy I'm talking to, to *run, girl, run.*

"Yeah, no. Like I said, I'm good. But my friend's probably getting bored sitting there all alone. I think I'll head back." I start to slide off the stool.

Ben stops me by reaching out and placing a hand on my bare thigh.

Instantly, my cheeks are scorching and my palms feel damp. This stupid bathing suit. Why didn't I put my shorts on?

Clenching my teeth, I shove his hand off and say, "Don't."

"What?" he protests. "I thought we were getting along." When he notices my dark expression, he leans closer. Lowers his voice. "Look, I'm going to be honest. I think you're hot. From the second you walked up here, I've been fantasizing about pulling that bathing suit off you and feasting my eyes on those tits. They're gorgeous."

My eyes become hot, stinging wildly, which is stupid because there's no reason for me to cry. I've been objectified before, and I'll be objectified again. That's just the reality of it. And yet shame clamps around my throat, squeezing my windpipe so tight I have a hard time choking out words.

Luckily, someone else does it for me.

"She said no."

Tate appears behind us. He's wearing his club uniform, khaki shorts and a white polo with the name of the club embroidered in gold, Tate's name stitched beneath it. His hair is tousled, probably from being out on the water all morning.

Relief trickles through me as I meet Tate's hard blue eyes.

"Uh, yeah, get lost, Bartlett," Ben says snidely, which tells me the two of them are already acquainted. "This is a private conversation."

"I don't think I'm the one Cassie would like to see go." Tate tips his head toward me. "Isn't that right, Cass?"

I finally find my voice. "That's right."

A scowl darkens Ben's face. "Are you fucking serious right now? *You're* the one who came over here, smiled at me, sat down beside me. And I'm the bad guy? Clearly you started this."

"And I'm about to finish it if you don't leave," Tate snaps. "Seriously, dude. I'm getting sick of having to pry you off women who clearly don't want you around."

"Fuck off." But he does get up. Ben throws a hundred-dollar bill on the bar and then stalks off without a backward look. Asshole.

"Thanks," I tell Tate, letting out the breath I'd been holding.

"You okay?"

"I'm fine. He didn't do anything, really. Just put his hand on my leg and told me how much he loves my boobs." I shrug, my tone flat. "They always love my boobs."

"Don't do that," Tate says softly.

"Do what?"

"Try to make light of it. Look, yes, men enjoy a nice rack. But that doesn't give them the right to objectify you or make you feel uncomfortable. Or to lay a fucking hand on you."

I chew the inside of my cheek. The truth is, I have a very complicated relationship with my breasts. When I was younger, they made me so self-conscious, which led to some seriously bad posture thanks to my attempts to make them appear smaller by hunching. Eventually I grew to accept my chest, although I'm still not entirely comfortable that it tends to be the first thing most people notice about me. It's embarrassing. I mean, I get it—humans are visual creatures. It's hard not to stare when someone has huge tits. Sometimes I even like showing mine off, wearing a tight top or a sexy dress. But Tate is right. Being objectified isn't a joke. I shouldn't make light of it, no matter how immune I've gotten over the years.

"You're right. That wasn't okay." I release another breath. "He seemed really cool at the beginning."

"I know. I've seen him pull the Mr. Charming act all summer. Usually he keeps it going for at least a few dates, though. I think you caught him when he was drunker than usual. The lowered inhibitions make it harder to hide the sleaze."

"He didn't seem that drunk," I start, but then remember the waitress's warning look. She'd probably been serving him all afternoon. Both bartenders had seemed well acquainted with him too. I pick up my drink and chug the rest of it. "Oh well. Another fling bites the dust."

"Nah, ginger, you don't want that loser. There are a million better candidates."

I roll my eyes. "Is this the part where you offer to be my wingman again?"

"You know what? Yes. Let's do this shit." He flashes that dimpled smile.

"Do what?" I find myself laughing. It's amazing how fast he's able to cheer me up. I'm not even thinking about creepy Ben anymore.

"Let's go out tomorrow night," Tate urges. "I'm done at the dealership at five and then having dinner with my mom, but I can come grab you afterward. We'll hit Joe's Beach Bar. It's got a balanced combo of locals and your crowd."

"My crowd?"

"Yeah, the clones. The rich folks. There'll be a good variety at

Joe's. I'll help you scope out the candidates. I know practically everyone in town, so I can tell you which ones to stay away from."

"Really. You're going to help me find a fling." I remain reluctant. "I don't know."

"Come on, what do you have to lose?"

My dignity.

My self-esteem.

"I don't know," I say again.

"C'mon."

"Ugh . . ."

"C'mon."

"Are you just going to keep pestering me until I agree?"

"Pretty much." His dimples make another appearance. "C'mon."

"Oh my God. Fine."

*　*　*

And that's how the following night I find myself waiting outside Joe's Beach Bar while Tate searches for a parking spot. The boardwalk is packed, even on a Monday night. And Joe's is situated in a prime location, its beachfront patio a major draw for the tourist crowd. Six steps off the patio and literally you're on the sand. I've always liked this place. The food is great. Super laid-back atmosphere.

"Ready?" Tate saunters up the sidewalk toward me.

"How far away did you have to park?"

"Not too bad. Beach access lot near the Soapery."

We step to the door as a group of loud, drunk young men are exiting, one of them stumbling into us before offering a slurred apology. Tate reaches out to steady me, which places his hand at the small of my back. And since I'm wearing a cropped tee, his palm meets my bare skin.

A hot shiver runs through me.

"You okay?" he says.

"Good." I swallow. Wishing my pulse still didn't careen whenever we accidentally touch.

But Tate made it clear he's not interested in flinging with me, and since I'd really like to find a cute guy to spend the summer with, I can either mope around during my remaining six weeks in the Bay and moon over Tate Bartlett—or I can try to meet someone who's equally cool.

As a woman who's trained herself to forever focus on the positive, I do what I always do and paste on a cheerful smile. "All right, Bartlett. The game's afoot."

"The game is gonna end in spectacular defeat if you keep using phrases like *the game's afoot*." He rolls his eyes. "Let's get us some drinks, Sherlock."

We order a couple of beers and migrate toward a standing table against the wall, which offers a view of the entire bar, including the patio. Sipping my beer, I scope out the room. Tate's doing the same.

"How about him?" he suggests. Gives a discreet nod to our right.

I follow his gaze to a dark-haired guy with a lean frame and an attractive face. Sadly, his good looks are eclipsed by his unfortunate choice of arm ink.

"Absolutely not," I retort.

"Is it the tattoo?"

"Of course it's the tattoo. I'm not sure I want to date someone who loves tacos so much they permanently etch one into their flesh. Imagine how often we'd have to eat tacos for dinner?" I shake my head. "No way."

Tate stares at me.

"What?"

His lips twitch with unrestrained laughter. "Cassie. Baby. Sweetie. I'm pretty sure that's not the kind of taco he's looking to commemorate."

"What do you mean? What else—" I gasp. "Oh. Ew. No." I glare at him. "Really? And you think *he's* a viable option?"

"Why not? Means he does oral . . ."

"Thank you, next."

"So picky. Won't even consider a man who wants to worship your taco."

I burst out laughing. He doubles over half a second later and then we're both in hysterics. Damn it, why do I have such a good time with this guy? You wouldn't expect Tate to be so funny. With his perpetually tousled hair and lazy smiles, that trace of a Georgia accent thrown into the mix, he gives off a slacker, surfer-boy vibe, when he's the total opposite of that. Tate is intelligent, hard-working. And I think it speaks volumes that every single person who knows him genuinely likes him. Not many people can say that.

"How about him?" I nod toward a cute guy by the dartboards.

The bar features an entire wall exclusively for darts. It's basically a huge wooden board riddled with so many dents, holes, and puncture marks it's clear many a projectile has been hurled at it by intoxicated hands. The guy I point out is in the process of aiming. He grips his dart, forehead lined with intensity, when his friend sidles up to him and breaks his concentration. The guy swivels his head and snaps something. The friend, taken aback, holds up both hands and backs away like he just confronted a territorial lion.

"Are you kidding me?" Tate says. "Mr. Angry over there?"

"He wasn't angry when I first noticed him," I protest.

"Well, he is now and that's a red flag. It's fucking darts. Nobody gets that invested in darts."

He's right. I can't date someone who's so passionate about *darts* they nearly bite someone's head off for interrupting.

Or is that too picky?

"Am I being too picky?" I ask in dismay.

"No. I mean, yes. *Must hate darts* is picky. But I also know those overcompetitive blowhard types. They're not fun to be around." He shrugs. "And they tend to be selfish in bed."

"Really? Had sex with a lot of overcompetitive men, have ya?"

"No, but I'm friends with a lot of girls. They spill the tea."

"I cannot believe you just used that expression."

"Why? It's legit."

I rib him with my elbow. "Maybe you're the one who needs pickup help if that's the kind of lingo you're dropping around the ladies."

"Trust me, I do just fine."

I have no doubt.

We spend the next little while people-watching and joking around. Despite his assurance that Joe's draws a diverse crowd, there aren't many prospects here for me. Mostly drunk tourists or couples. Tate goes to grab us another round of beers, and I take the opportunity to check my phone. My message thread with Peyton contains her customary one-line format.

Peyton: *How's it going?*
Peyton: *Is your wingman any good?*
Peyton: *Did we find somebody?*
Peyton: *They better not be a six.*
Peyton: *Well?*

Would it kill her to send one paragraph? I have an impossible time trying to locate the silver lining in Peyton's aggravating texting style.

Along with Peyton's messages, I find a response from my former stepbrother to my illustration request.

> Robb: *Sorry for the delay! Was trying to figure out if I could squeeze it in. I just wrapped up a project at work ahead of schedule, so I'm in! Send me the story and I can come up with some concepts this week.*

Yes! The children's book is a go. I give a mental fist pump. My sisters are going to love me forever.

Before I can reply to Robb, a shadow falls over the table. I look up . . . and then up . . . and up. Because the guy who's wandered up is a literal giant. He must be six-six, maybe even taller.

A hesitant smile touches his lips. He's got a sweet-looking face. "Hey," he says. "A pretty girl like you shouldn't be sitting all alone." Then he winces. "Shit. I'm sorry. That's a terrible line."

I can't help but laugh. "I mean, it's not the most original, but it does the job."

"Mind if I join you? My friend kind of ditched me." He gestures toward a booth across the room, where a young couple is eating each other's faces off. And I'm pretty sure she has her hand down his pants. They're either going to be kicked out any second, or soon the entire bar will witness an enthusiastic bout of public sex.

"Wow," I remark. "They're really going at it."

"Yeah. I know. He does this every weekend." The giant makes a face. "He's the worst person to go out with."

"And yet you keep doing it every weekend . . ."

"Maybe I'm hoping one day I'll find a cute girl to keep me company."

"Nice. That line was much better."

"Thank God." He gives a tentative smile and rests one forearm on the table. "I'm Landon."

"Cassie."

"It's nice to meet you, Cassie."

His shyness is slowly melting away, so of course my wingman chooses precisely that moment to return with our beers.

Landon takes one look at Tate and instantly goes on guard. "Oh. I'm sorry. I didn't know you were with someone."

"No, no, we're not together," I say. "This is my friend Tate."

"I'm her wingman," Tate supplies.

Landon laughs, but the sound is laced with discomfort. "That's, um, cool."

Tate flicks up an eyebrow. "I'm also her gatekeeper."

"You are not." I turn to reassure Landon. "He's not, I swear."

"Of course I am. I'm not letting my friend leave here with anyone unless I know their intentions." Tate crosses his arms in some macho posturing move that makes me roll my eyes. "So." He pins Landon with a stern stare-down. "Please state your intentions."

"Oh my God," I groan. "Just ignore him."

"I'm serious. Intentions. State 'em. I'm waiting."

Landon shifts awkwardly, and he's so big that he can't help jarring the table. I'm surprised the liquid in our bottles doesn't start rippling like in Jurassic Park when the T. rex walks up. With an uncertain expression, he finally pieces together a response.

"Um. I don't know. I thought I'd buy her a drink. Is that okay? I think she's cute, and, um . . ." I don't know if it's the word *cute* that causes him to lower his eyes to my boobs, or if he's simply trying to avoid Tate's death glare and it's pure coincidence where his gaze lands.

Either way, it earns him a warning growl from Tate. "Eyes on me." He points two fingers at his own eyes as if to punctuate that.

"I'm sorry." Landon's panicking. "I . . ." He takes a step away. "You know what? I think my friend's calling me."

Nobody is calling him, but my poor sweet giant has apparently decided that watching his friend grope some chick is better than being subjected to Tate's outrageous interrogation.

"Cockblock," I accuse, scowling at my wingman.

"Nah. Trust me, that's not our guy."

"Why not?"

"He kept apologizing for everything. And he was too nervous."

I object to the latter. "Nervous can be endearing."

Tate is quick to disagree. "He asked if it was okay to buy you a drink. Is that really what we want? No. We want someone who's proactive. Someone with confidence. Dude over there is the kind of guy who asks for permission to hold your hand." He pauses. "If you were only allowed to use one word to describe what you want from your fling this summer, what would it be?"

"Passion," I answer without thinking, and immediately regret that decision.

The air between us shifts, growing thicker, headier. Or maybe it's only happening on my end. Maybe I'm only imagining that his lips are slightly parted, that his blue eyes suddenly appear darker, loaded with heat. There's no way those eyes are smoldering at me right now.

"Passion," he echoes, his voice a bit raspy. I swear I see him gulp. Then he clears his throat and shrugs. "Are you telling me you think *that* guy actually fits the passion bill?"

"No," I admit.

"Then I've done my wingman duty."

We finish our second beers and order a third round, eventually drifting over to the dartboard wall to play a couple of games. After Tate beats me for a second time, the guys next to us, a pair of brothers visiting from New York, challenge us to a game. Two on two. I'm downright terrible, but luckily my counterpart is equally atrocious. Tate and *his* counterpart are stupidly good, hitting bullseye after bullseye while the other guy and I glumly watch our teammates outshoot us. At this point, we're completely inconsequential to the outcome of the game. Those two are basically battling it out alone.

"We suck," the guy informs me. They introduced themselves earlier. I can't remember his brother's name, but his name is Aaron. He's tall and lean, with bright brown eyes, a great smile, and not a single pink taco tattoo.

"Oh, big time," I agree.

Tate scores another bullseye, prompting Aaron's brother to rub his forehead and marvel, "Damn, bro. You're like some darts whiz kid. How often do you play?"

"Hardly ever," Tate replies proudly. "I was born with this gift."

I snicker from our spot on the sidelines, prompting Tate to turn and flash me a grin.

"How long have you two been together?" Aaron asks.

"Oh, we're not together," I reply, and I don't miss the flicker of interest in his eyes. He really is cute. And I'm definitely picking up on some chemistry between us while we've been chatting.

Once he knows Tate and I aren't a couple, Aaron gets even flirtier. After three beers, I'm feeling loose and relaxed, and find myself flirting back with very minimal nervous babbling. It's going well, at least until Aaron's brother takes a bathroom break and Tate comes over and interrupts us. He looks Aaron up and down, then shifts his gaze to me and lifts a brow, as if to ask, *Do we like this guy?*

I nod slightly, then curse myself for it because Tate views that as permission to interrogate.

"All right," he says cheerfully, planting himself in front of Aaron. "Let's hear it. What are your intentions with my friend?"

A faint grin appears on Aaron's face. He dons a thoughtful look. Goes quiet for several seconds. "Hmmm. Alright. Tough question. At the moment, I'm torn between inviting her to accompany me to the carnival tomorrow night—or, and hear me out, asking her to partner up for a darts tournament, except instead of playing to see who's best, we'd be vying for the title of America's Worst."

Tate nods his approval. "Two solid options. Okay. Permission granted. Carry on." He claps Aaron on the shoulder and wanders off.

"Well?" Aaron says, directing that appealing smile my way. "You, me, and a carnival? Tomorrow night?"

"Sure," I say shyly. "I'd love to."

CHAPTER 12

TATE

Tuesday is a slow day at Bartlett Marine, so Dad and I spend half the morning looking at boat porn. He's hoping to replace our ancient thirty-seven-foot Hatteras with a newer model, maybe one with built-in GPS and a few more bells and whistles. But while I keep trying to steer him toward more practical options, Dad keeps clicking on shit that in no way meets our criteria.

"Dude," I chastise. "We don't need a high-performance speedboat."

"Everyone needs a high-performance speedboat."

"Well, yeah." I sigh. "But we're looking for something suitable for deep-sea fishing, remember?"

"I know, but . . ." Dad groans happily. "Look at this one, kid. Check out the design of her V-bottom hull . . . aw, man, she's so sexy I can't take it."

A dry laugh echoes from the door. We both look up to see Mom standing there. We were so engrossed with the computer screen we didn't even hear her come in.

"What's her model number?" Mom asks.

I snicker. Most people would hear *she's so sexy I can't take it* and assume we're ogling photos of women. "What makes you think we're not looking at human porn?" I challenge.

"Because I know you boys better than that." She strides toward us, an oversized wicker tote slung over her shoulder. With her yellow dress, flip-flops, and blond hair in a ponytail, she could easily pass for one of the college girls who'll be swarming the Bay in September.

"Hi, sweetie." She plants a kiss on my cheek.

"Hey, Mom."

She turns to greet Dad, except when her lips near his cheek he pulls a sly switcheroo and plants his mouth on hers instead. I glimpse a slip of tongue, and cringe.

"You guys are repulsive," I say, pretending to gag.

I don't really mean it, though. Because all that stuff Mackenzie said last week about me never showing much interest in girlfriends? I suspect my parents' relationship has a lot to do with that. When you grow up witnessing that sort of love, you start to believe that's how all relationships are supposed to feel. And then you wait. You hold out for that feeling. It's obscure, impossible to describe, but you know it exists. *I* know it exists because I see it with my folks.

I've been with many women, fucked a lot of them, dated a few, but I've yet to experience a deep connection with anyone. It might be cheesy and embarrassing and I'd never say it out loud, but I think I'm waiting for that feeling. And unless I feel it, there's no point falling into a relationship with anyone.

Dad says he knew Mom was the one the moment he met her. She tells it a little differently, always teasing him that *technically* they met in high school and clearly he had no clue she was the one, otherwise they would've been dating back then. Dad was a big baseball star, dated cheerleaders and didn't know Mom existed, according to her. After graduation, he left Georgia for St. Louis to play in the minors, while Mom stayed in St. Simon's and started dating an accountant named Brad. A year into his ball career, Dad got injured and returned to the island, where he quickly reconnected with an old cheerleader flame. Which means they were both otherwise involved when they bumped into each other in the grocery store one afternoon. Despite that, Dad claims he took one look at her and knew he was going to marry her.

Mom ditched Brad, Dad ditched the cheerleader, and they've been blissfully married for twenty-five years.

Dad calls it their origin story. He gets a kick out of telling it. But Mom . . . it's weird. Sometimes when she talks about it, she still wears this odd expression of disbelief. As if she can't fathom how Gavin Bartlett could have chosen *her,* Gemma McCleary, over some cheerleader he dated in high school. I don't get why she's so stumped. Of course he chose her. Mom's the coolest person I know.

With a curious expression, she peers closer at the computer screen, then lifts her head to narrow her eyes at Dad. "You can't fish in that, Gavin."

"But isn't she beautiful?"

"Can you fish in her?"

"Well, no, but—"

"Then she's ugly," Mom declares. "Utterly hideous."

Dad pouts. "Spoilsport." He leans back in his rolling chair. "What brings you here, darlin'?"

"I took a half day at work today, so I decided to drop off some lunch for my boys."

She reaches into her bag and pulls out a pair of sandwiches wrapped in foil. They're *man-sized,* as she calls it. Meaning each sandwich is about the size of a shoebox.

"The vegetable garden is growing out of control, so I'm trying to use everything I can from it. Picked some fresh tomatoes, lettuce, peppers. And I grabbed some of that deli meat from the butcher in town. The roast ham you like."

Dad's eyes light up. "Oh man, yes. Thanks, Gem."

"How are my children?" I ask Mom. "You're not sending me enough pics of them."

"Because I have more pressing matters to attend to than taking pictures of your dogs, sweetheart. You know, like go to work every day?"

"The kids are great," Dad assures me. "Polly killed a rabbit last week and brought us its severed head as a token of her love."

I guffaw.

"And Fudge got into the pantry yesterday and ate half a box of cookies, so he was farting all night. Around ten he was in a dead sleep and ripped one out so loud he woke himself up. Got so freaked out he was barking for a solid five minutes."

Now I can't stop laughing. "Shit, I can't believe I missed that."

Leaning against the side of the desk, Mom glances at Dad and nods toward me. "Did you ask him yet?"

I eye them both. "Ask me what?"

"No, I didn't get a chance to yet," he tells her. "Got distracted looking at boat pics." He spins around in his chair, hands propped behind his neck. "It's a big ask, but we were hoping you could do us a favor, kid. You know how we planned to take a trip in the fall?"

I nod. "A week in California."

"Right. Well, we're hoping to be gone a little longer than a week. We figured if we're already on the west coast, we should make a real holiday out of it. Add Hawaii to the itinerary."

"Hawaii!" Mom claps excitedly.

I rise from my chair and head for the water cooler to pour myself a cup. "So how long would you be gone?"

"If you're on board, it'd be a month," Dad says. "Your contract with the club is done in September, right?"

"Yeah." I don't teach sailing during the off season, working only from April to September. After that, I switch over to full-time shifts at the dealership. But I've never run the place on my own before. It's always Dad and me, so the responsibilities are split fairly evenly. Working solo for a month means much longer hours.

On the other hand, it also means much bigger paychecks. I could put all that extra money toward buying my own sailboat.

"I think I could manage it," I say slowly.

"Thanks, sweetie." Mom comes up and gives me a quick hug, resting her chin on my shoulder. "We really appreciate it."

"Told you we could count on him," Dad says with a pleased smile. "Family always takes care of family, right, kid?"

"Yup."

*   *   *

The rest of the workday flies by after Mom leaves. Around one o'clock we deal with a rush of tourists coming in to inquire about boat rentals, which we also provide. Dad and I are so busy we don't even have a chance to eat our sandwiches. I scarf mine down in the Jeep on the way home later.

As always, I conduct a quick visual sweep of the Jackson house when I walk in, just to make sure nothing bad happened when I was at work. No wild animals finding their way in, or greedy hooligans getting the bright idea to rob us. All is good, and I head upstairs to change into sweats.

My plan for the night is lazing on the couch and watching mindless TV, because tomorrow's going to be busy. Working with Dad till four, then speeding over to the yacht club to teach a five o'clock safety class to a group of teenagers who're hoping to get the certification required for them to compete in single-handed dinghy racing. I love that the Manor sponsors junior programs for young sailors—I found them so valuable when I was their age. I do wish we offered club races to prepare kids for national events, but at least they're able to compete at our sister club in Charleston.

I've just pulled a pair of gray sweatpants up my hips when I glimpse a flash of movement next door. It's messed up, this strange synchronization Cassie and I have going on. As she passes her window, I narrow my eyes, frown, then grab my phone to text her.

Me: *You're wearing pink to your carnival date? No.*
Cassie: *Why not??*
Me: *Because you'll get lost in a sea of cotton candy. You won't stand out.*
Cassie: *But I look cute in pink.*

I can't argue with that. As it happens, she looks cute in everything, but I keep that observation to myself. I insisted I only wanted to be friends. Telling her how hot she is would only send mixed signals and confuse us both. And to be honest, I'm enjoying the hell out of this friendship. Hanging out with Cassie feels so damn natural. We have fun together, and there's no pressure on my end to be on top of my game. I can be stupid and say whatever nonsense comes to mind, and, like a good friend, Cassie just laughs and doesn't judge.

At the window, Cassie toys with the edge of her side braid, clearly mulling it over. She types another message.

Cassie: *Okay. Stand by.*

The curtains shut. But I don't think she realizes they're kind of sheer, especially when the bedroom light is on. The gauzy white material does very little to conceal the silhouette of the pinup girl next door.

Don't look.

Too late.

Heat streaks through my bloodstream and settles in my balls, drawing them up tight. Oh fuck. I never knew a silhouette could turn me on so much. My throat is dryer than sawdust as I watch Cassie's delectable shape move around the room. She disappears for a moment. In the walk-in closet, I think. Then she's back and my dick weeps with joy. I'm semi-hard and unable to stop myself from staring. She's in profile now. Her arms raise as she slips a garment over her head. The move makes her chest jut out, offering a perfect side-boob view.

Sweet Jesus.

She's incredible.

Gulping rapidly, I wrest my pervy eyes away from her and make a mental note to jerk off next time before even *thinking* about stepping foot in my bedroom. It appears I need to curb all temptation before indulging in future window time.

The drapes part, and she reappears, clad in a white sundress. Instead of a bra, she's wearing a bikini top, or at least I think that's what those thin straps belong to. The pink strings peek out of her bodice, climbing up her collarbone to wind around her neck. The dress itself is knee-length, with a skirt that flutters around as she gives a little twirl before texting me.

> Cassie: *Now hear me out. Yes, I threw in a splash of pink with the bikini top. But that's because I think it's smart to color-coordinate with the cotton candy. We'll complement each other.*
>
> Me: *I'll allow it.*
>
> Cassie: *Do we like?*

She does another twirl and I pretend the glimpse of bare thigh doesn't do all sorts of things to my body.

I give her a thumbs-up, then type, *Go get 'em, tiger.*

* * *

Around midnight, I finally admit defeat and accept I can't sleep. It has nothing to do with the fact that I haven't heard a car engine next door or noticed her bedroom light flick on. She's still out with that Aaron dude, clearly. Good for her. She deserves to have fun. My inability to fall into slumber is not Cassie-related at all. Like, at all.

I make my way down to the dock and sit at the very end of it, dangling my bare feet over the edge. But let's say Cassie *is* the reason I'm still up. Obviously, this just means I'm a good friend. A friend who worries about the well-being of another friend. I mean, I know nothing about this Aaron kid. But I do know for a fact the carnival shuts down at eleven. So, really, she should've been home by now.

Unless she went back to his place.

My shoulders stiffen. His brother said they were staying in a rental on the north end, right on the water. The reminder makes me frown. I hope he doesn't convince her to take a late-night dip. The waters up there are choppier. It's where we usually go to surf. Swear to God, if fuckin' Aaron allows Cassie to get sucked into the sea by a freak midnight riptide . . .

I'm suddenly craving a cigarette. I only smoke if I'm drinking, and then maybe one or two max, but right now I could use some help easing the jittery sensations inside me. My smokes are in the house, though, so I debate going for a swim instead. I allow the toes of one foot to skim the water, finding it much warmer than expected. I'm about to strip off my shirt and dive in when my phone lights up.

Cassie: *You up?*

I laugh softly. Swim plan instantly abandoned, I reach for the phone.

Me: *Is this a booty call or a debriefing?*
Cassie: *Debriefing. I need my wingman ASAP.*
Me: *I'm on the dock.*
Cassie: *Be there in two.*

The heaviness in my chest lifts as if someone flicked a switch. I try not to question it too hard. It's crucial to this friendship that I don't.

The tall grass at the base of the slope rustles, and I turn to see Cassie emerge from the shadows. Her hair is no longer arranged in a side braid but falling around her shoulders. With her white dress, bare feet, and loose copper waves, she has an almost ethereal quality about her. Practically floating down the dock toward me.

She plops beside me, legs over the edge, and releases a moan of unhappiness. "Hi."

I grin. "That bad?"

"No. Not bad at all. We stayed out past midnight, so obviously there were lots of checks in the plus column." Yet she's visibly distressed.

"Okay, let's hear 'em. Give me the play by play."

"He's super funny. He's smart. He didn't monopolize the conversation. Asked me lots of questions, but it didn't feel like an interrogation. It was just, you know, a good conversation. Flowed easily."

"All pluses so far."

"He held my hand and didn't ask beforehand if he could. I figured you'd view the confident hand grab as a plus."

I snicker. "Oh, absolutely. What else?"

"He's scared of heights, but still rode the Ferris wheel after I said how much I love seeing the town from above. That was another plus."

"Agreed."

"The carnival grounds close at eleven, so we left and got slushies afterward. We sat in the parking lot and talked, and . . ." She pauses, and I notice a blush rising on her cheeks. "We were definitely feeling each other."

"This is all good so far," I point out, ignoring the weird clench in my chest. "How did he manage to fuck this up? What were the minuses?"

"Just one minus." She turns to me with a look of defeat. "The kissing. Oh my God, Tate."

"Aw, shit. Our boy Aaron can't bring it home? What was the issue? Saliva? Because that might not be his fault. My friend Chase dated a guy once who had something called hypersalivation and—"

"It wasn't the saliva," she interjects. "It was the tongue."

"Too much of it?"

"Too much is an understatement. And it was right from the get-go. I'm talking even *before* our mouths actually touched. He came at me tongue first, eyes closed. Want me to demonstrate?"

"No, I think I get—"

Cassie ignores my objection and demonstrates anyway. "It was like this." She squeezes her eyes shut, sticks her tongue straight out, and comes barreling toward my face.

It's so unsettling I instinctively rear back.

"Holy shit. He didn't."

"He did. It was terrible."

I try to control the laughter bubbling in my throat, but it's difficult. "Okay," I say carefully. "That sounds . . . unpleasant. But once the lips made contact, did it get better?"

"It did not," she groans. "It was just too much. He was trying so hard to be passionate, I guess, but it wasn't working in the slightest. When it finally ended I felt like I'd run a marathon. Or worse. Like . . . like I'd just changed a duvet cover."

"Did you ask him to slow down at any point?"

"No."

I roll my eyes. "Why the hell not?"

"I don't know." She offers a self-conscious shrug, her fingers toying with the hem of her dress. "I'm not that person."

"You're not the person who asks a dude not to shove his tongue halfway down your throat and pretend you're sword-fighting during a make-out session?"

"I'm not the person who tells someone they're a bad kisser," she corrects.

"Requesting to go slower isn't telling him he's a bad kisser," I argue. "You're just vocalizing your needs."

"Vocalizing my needs? What are you, a self-help guru?"

"Apparently you need one," I say in accusation, flashing a smile so she knows I'm half kidding.

"Why, because I'm too polite to tell a guy he's doing it all wrong?"

"Would you rather be polite, or would you rather enjoy a kiss? And anyway, you don't go about it that way, like *he's* doing something wrong. You make it about *you*. You pull away and say something like . . ." I ponder. "*I like it slow*. And make sure to sound all breathy, even apologetic, as if it's a *you* problem. Know what I mean?"

Wariness flickers through her expression.

"Or you could pull back and whisper something like, *I like being teased*. Then flutter your eyelashes and give him that hot-girl look and order him to tease you for a bit."

Now she looks fascinated. "Okay, you're not bad at this."

"I know," I say smugly.

"But it's easier said than done. It's easy to imagine myself saying and doing all those things *after* the fact. In the moment, though, I know I'll freeze. People are so vulnerable when they're kissing. It's like this super precarious state of being. When he's kissing me, his self-esteem hangs in the balance. One negative word from me, and it's an embarrassment he'll carry with him forever." She heaves a sigh. "Plus I don't like conflict."

"One, you're giving yourself way too much importance in this dude's life if you believe your criticism will haunt him forever. Either that, or *you* hang on to embarrassing shit a lot longer than most people, which is a whole other conversation altogether. And two, I'm pretty sure nearly everyone is conflict averse. Conflict fucking sucks." I cock my head. "Do you want to practice on me?"

"Practice what?" She wrinkles her forehead.

"Being assertive." I angle myself so I'm facing her. She's blushing again, a deep, noticeable red. "C'mon, I think this'll be good for you. I'll come at you tongue first and let's see how you handle it."

Cassie spits out an unequivocal, "No!"

"Nah, this is an excellent idea. It'll be an exercise in self-assertion and conflict mitigation." I roll my neck around my shoulders, stretching it out. When Cassie sighs at me, I lift a brow. "What? I need to be limber for this. Ready?"

"No."

"Great. Here I come!"

I shoot forward with my eyes closed and tongue spearing the air.

Cassie shrieks and pushes my chest, nearly knocking me off the dock. She doubles over in laughter, which makes me chuckle as I regain my balance. Her spirits are lifting, so that's good, at least.

"Oh my God. Are you sure you're twenty-three and not an overgrown child?"

"I've been informed by my mother that all men are overgrown children until the age of thirty." I snort. "Or in my dad's case, still a child in his midforties."

"So that's where you get it from."

"My dashing good looks? Yes."

"I meant your antics."

"Antics? I'm trying to help you here, ginger. You need to learn to speak up. Vocalize your needs. Don't tell me you're not sitting here wishing you handled tonight differently." I meet her suddenly troubled eyes. "You regret not saying something, don't you?"

"Yes," she confesses. "I wish I said something."

"Good. Then I'm serious—practice on me. Let's try again."

She eyes me suspiciously. "Are you going to launch yourself at me with your tongue again?"

"Nah." I wink. "But get ready for the worst kiss of your life."

CHAPTER 13

TATE

A few hours ago, I was ordering myself to sustain a platonic friendship at all costs. I guess that plan went by the wayside because, and I could be wrong, I don't think kissing falls under the *platonic* category.

In my defense, *this* can't be classified as kissing. At least not enjoyable or acceptable kissing. When our mouths collide, it's pure disaster. Nothing like the hot kiss we shared at the Hartley house, when the feel of Cassie's soft, warm lips got me so hard I had trouble walking afterward. This kiss is overbearing and sloppy. We're both having trouble breathing and not in a sexy way. My tongue is like an action star, kicking and punching around in her mouth as if we're dueling for dominance. It's actually exhausting.

Her outraged squeal vibrates against my lips. "Ahhh, stop! This is awful!" She shoves me.

I laugh, wiping the excess saliva off my chin. "Nope. We both know you'd never actually say that to him. Try again. Redirect the negative into a positive request. Make it a *you* issue, remember?"

She's instantly shamefaced. "Right. I forgot." Her lips press together in humor. "Sorry I pushed you."

"All good." I draw a deep breath to stock up on oxygen, then dive in for round two.

This time, when my tongue pillages its way through her parted lips, I feel a firm touch on the center of my chest. Then she awkwardly eases her mouth away and orders, "Slow!"

I narrow my eyes.

She softens her tone. "I mean, I like it slower." Then, as if struck by inspiration, a naughty smile tugs on her lips. "I love being teased. Slow kissing is *such* a turn-on for me . . ."

Oh man. Those words do something to *me*. My sweatpants suddenly feel too tight.

"Excellent ad-libbing," I tell her, my voice coming out a bit husky.

She brightens. "Thank you. What now?"

"Okay." I clear my throat. "I think we practice an even more proactive approach—this one deals with the aggressive entry. When he comes at you tongue first, this is what you do. You touch his cheek to stop him, stare at him, and give him a compliment."

"About what?"

"Anything. His eyes. His dimples. Anything on his face. Just slow it down before he even gets the chance to Hulk-smash his mouth against yours. Now *you're* in the position to get the kiss going, and that means you pick the pace."

"Genius."

"I know. Ready?"

Her throat dips as she swallows. When she licks her lips in preparation, I almost groan out loud. Lip-licking is my goddamn kryptonite. I can't see a woman do that, especially this one, and *not* want to rip her clothes off.

Platonic, I remind myself. *You're just helping her out.*

With a gulp of my own, I adopt my ridiculous pose—eyelids shut, mouth gaping open like a trout's—and move my head toward hers.

A pro at following orders, Cassie intercepts the trajectory of my tongue by touching my cheek. My pulse kicks up a notch from the feel of her soft fingertips stroking the stubble on my jaw.

Her eyes slowly meet mine. Those bottomless brown depths glimmer with desire. Our faces are inches apart, her sweet breath tickling my chin.

"You have the sexiest lips," she whispers, brushing the pad of her thumb over my bottom lip. "I'm obsessed with them."

Our gazes remain locked. This late at night, the breeze traveling along the water tends to be cooler, but I'm burning up. My dick is hard and my skin is on fire. Her touch feels like heaven along my flesh, and I instinctively sag into it, forgetting I'm supposed to be playacting. That I'm simply helping her shore up her boundaries so they're nice and firm the next time she sees that Aaron kid. The next time she makes out with someone else.

I abruptly straighten out. "That was smooth. Nice job."

Her answering smile is so relaxed and careless I have to wonder if I imagined what just happened. If I was the only one to feel the surge of raw need that traveled between us.

"When are you seeing him again?" I ask lightly.

"Saturday night. I would've invited him to be my date for that charity gala on Friday, but I'm already going with Joy and my grandmother. This year's charity is Habitat for Humanity, Grandma's pet cause, so she's giving me five grand to spend on the auctions. Can you believe that? *Five* grand."

"Oh shit," I say, feeling my face go pale. "I forgot that was this weekend. I'm in the auction."

She grins at me. "Of course you are."

"Not by choice," I growl. "It's a job requirement. My boss at the club forces all the sailing guys to volunteer. I fucking hate it."

"Uh-huh. I'm sure it's *such* a chore to stand on a stage while women literally throw money at your feet for a chance to date you."

An idea strikes. I look over hopefully. "Will you bid on me?"

"I'd rather not," she replies in amusement.

"Please? I can't go on a date with another cougar, Cass. I just can't."

She snickers. "How many years have you done it?"

"This will be my third. Last year I went on a sunset cruise with a fifty-something-year-old broad who offered me my own boat and a weekly allowance if I came over every Sunday when her husband was playing golf."

"You turned down a sugar mama? Oh, Tate."

I glower at her. "I'm not for sale."

"You're literally putting yourself up for sale in an auction!"

"And I'm *trying* to rig it by asking my friend to bid on me." I give her my best puppy-dog eyes. "Come on, you just said your grandmother is giving you money to bid."

"Yeah, and I wanted to bid on the Charleston Sanctuary package for me and Joy," Cassie whines. "It's literally the best spa in the country."

"What's more important? The spa or my dignity?"

"The spa."

I flip up my middle finger. "Asshole. Come on, do me a solid. I think last year I only went for a couple grand."

Her mouth falls open. "You're asking me to spend two thousand dollars on you? On *this*?" She vaguely waves a hand at my body.

"Like you don't want to be all up in this business."

"For two grand I don't."

"You think I could twist Lydia's arm into bidding on me?"

"Doubtful. She's too classy to participate in what's basically the equivalent of *Magic Mike* for rich people."

"Hey, is your dad going to be there too this weekend? Both my folks are coming."

Cassie shakes her head. "I don't think so. The country club is a Tanner family thing. The Souls are much more laid-back."

"He does seem like a super laid-back dude," I remark, remembering Clayton Soul's relaxed demeanor and quick laughter. "You two are close?"

"Sometimes."

I chuckle. "What does that mean?"

"I don't know. I just don't see or talk to him as often as I'd like." She gazes up at the dark sky, and her hair falls down her back in waves. "It sucks, because we were practically inseparable when I was a kid. I was much closer to him than my mother."

"How'd that happen anyway? Your parents, I mean. Your mom's a clone and your dad's a local—how'd they get together in the first place?" I lean back on my elbows and make myself comfortable. Despite the fact it's nearly 1 A.M., it doesn't seem like Cassie's in any hurry to head inside. Neither am I. The stars are out and the water's calm. And I like talking to her. A lot.

She brings her legs up and sits cross-legged, arranging her dress so it covers her thighs. "They met when Mom was a junior in college. Before my grandparents decided to live in the Bay year-round, they'd split their time between here and Boston, but summers were always spent in the Bay, no exceptions. Mom was visiting and they met at a party, I think. Somehow they fell in love, despite being so different in every conceivable way." She shrugs. "Opposites really do attract, I guess. And she had to have loved him, right? Because she came to live here full-time after college, which would've been a major sacrifice for her."

"You sound like you're trying to convince yourself of that."

"Maybe I am. I mean, I know what my dad saw in her. She's gorgeous, obviously. And she's very charming when she wants to be. Funny, sociable. When she puts on her act, she's the most lovable person you'll ever meet. She'll be coming to town mid-August, so I'm sure you'll experience the act for yourself."

I wrinkle my brow. "What makes you think it's an act?"

"Because I've seen the person behind the mask. She's manipulative. Entitled. Hypercritical. She gets a kick out of putting you down, then plays the victim when you call her out on it. And don't get me started on the total lack of empathy. There isn't an empathetic bone in her body. She's the most self-centered person I've ever known."

"Man, that's rough. Has she always been like that?"

"I think so. For as long as I can remember, anyway. And although my grandmother would never say a bad word about her own children, I can tell she's disappointed with Mom's behavior. Especially when it comes to all the passive-aggressive bullshit, the scathing criticism. She wasn't too awful to me when I was little, but she was constantly snapping at Dad. I remember thinking he had the patience of a saint. It wasn't until after the divorce, once she and I were alone all the time, that she turned most of her vitriol toward me. Suddenly she always had something to bitch about, some element of my appearance to disparage, some immoral behavior to call out." Cassie offers a weak laugh. "Lucky me."

I study her face, my heart squeezing at the thought of a young Cassie having to endure her mother's vile bullshit. But her expression remains detached, accepting even, as if any past—or present—trauma is no big deal.

"You always do that," I tell her.

"Do what?" Her teeth dig into her lower lip. Finally revealing a trace of emotion.

"Downplay all the shit that hurts you."

"Because I'm an optimist." She tucks a section of reddish hair behind her ear, her eyes shining in the moonlight. "No situation is entirely bad. There's always a silver lining. Always. You just have to look for it."

"Really? So there's a silver lining in having your mother treat you like crap?" I say dubiously. "Or your parents getting divorced?"

"If it weren't for the divorce, I wouldn't have my little sisters," Cassie points out. "And I'm quite happy that my sisters exist."

"You can be happy they exist and still wish the divorce hadn't happened."

"True. But honestly, it was probably for the best. Nothing Dad did could ever make her happy. He's definitely better off without her." Cassie pushes more hair out of her eyes. It's getting breezier out, causing those long, wavy strands to fly into her face. "Let me guess—your parents are happily married?"

"Yeah, it's disgusting."

We both laugh.

"They've always been great role models," I admit, albeit grudgingly. "That's why I hate disappointing them. I swear, I'm the only kid who would willingly ground himself or demand extra chores after getting in trouble. This one time in high school, I stayed out all night with the twins. My parents were up till dawn, wearing holes in the carpet from fear I was dead in an alley somewhere. The next morning, I walked in, hungover as fuck, sat on the sofa in front of them, and was like, *I think you should ground me for two weeks and put me on permanent dog-poop duty.*"

Cassie peals out a laugh. "You are such a loser."

"First of all—I got laid that night. Losers don't get laid. Second—don't tell me you wouldn't have done the exact same thing, Ms. I Avoid Conflict."

"Fair. But," she adds smugly, "I never got in trouble. Ever."

"I don't know if that's something to brag about."

She starts to answer, then breaks off in a wide yawn. "Oh

man. I'm tired." She blinks a few times. "That just hit me out of nowhere." She yawns again. "I think it's time for bed."

When she unfolds her legs and gets to her feet, I can't stop a pang of disappointment. I'm working two different jobs tomorrow and yet I want nothing more than to stay up all night talking.

As friends, of course.

But she's already pulling me to my feet. "Come on, walk me up the path so I don't trip on a rock or something and crack my head open."

I offer my arm, then yank it away before she can take it. Her jaw drops, and I cock a brow. "On one condition—you bid on me this weekend."

"Nope."

"You're really going to throw me to the wolves like that? The cougar wolves?"

"Oh my God, drama queen. All right," she relents. "How about this? I'll bid—only if I see the cougars making their move."

"Thank you. You're the best."

Cassie grabs my arm and links hers through it. "No promises," she warns.

CHAPTER 14

CASSIE

"That dress is so hot." Joy's approving gaze travels over my knee-length pale green minidress. "Honestly, I should become a stylist. I'm so good at this."

"I like how not once in that series of compliments did you mention me. The *dress* is nice and *you're* a great stylist."

"I assumed the Cassie part of the equation was a given. You always look hot." She links her arm through mine as we glide toward the next table.

We're part of the crowd by the far wall of the Manor's grand ballroom, browsing the tables that make up the silent auction, while canned piano music blares out of the PA system. Much to my chagrin, I haven't found the Charleston Sanctuary package yet. They fucking better not have decided to skip the event this year. I love that place, and they're always booked solid. It's impossible to get an appointment. One time I even demeaned myself by name-dropping my grandmother and still couldn't get a slot.

"Ooh, how about this?" Joy suggests, picking up the sheet of crisp ivory-colored cardstock. "Six golf lessons with . . . drum roll, please . . . *Lorenzo!*" She dons an Italian accent when saying his name.

Lorenzo has been working as a golf coach at the club for about a hundred years. If you told me he was a ghost trapped between worlds and forced to roam the Manor for all of eternity, I'd have no trouble believing it. There are honest-to-God pictures of my mother holding me as an infant at the club, with Lorenzo lurking in the background sporting the same long ponytail and leathery skin as he has now. The man doesn't age. He also has no concept of personal space, always leaning in way too close when he's talking to you. As teenagers, Joy and I used to hide whenever we saw him strolling our way.

I blanch at the listing. "I'd rather eat my own hair. No joke."

She howls before clapping a hand over her mouth to stifle the outburst, which has drawn the disapproving stares of the older country-club set milling around us. Damn, and we're not even drunk yet. These folks are going to despise us by the end of the night.

I approach the adjacent table, where my grandmother is bent over, using a black felt-tip pen to scribble an amount on a small white card. She's bidding on a jumbo gift basket donated by the Soapery, one of the local artisan shops in town.

"Oh my God. No. Mrs. Tanner." Joy peeks at Grandma's bid. "You just bid *two grand* on a basket of soap. Soap!" She shakes her head in disbelief.

"It's very good soap," Grandma says primly, then slides the card into the slot of the cardboard box on the table. "Have you found anything to bid on?" The question is directed at me.

"I haven't seen the spa package yet. That's the only thing I want." I set my jaw in determination. "And I'll murder anyone who outbids me. I swear, I fantasize about their hot stone massage on a daily basis."

"Don't blow all your cash on it," Joy reminds me, dark eyes twinkling impishly. "Gotta make sure you have enough left over to bid on your friend Tate in the bachelor auction."

Grandma looks amused. "You're bidding on Mr. Bartlett?"

"Maybe," I say grudgingly. "He asked me to rescue him if the cougar crowd gets overzealous."

"I like that boy." Grandma chuckles softly.

So do I.

It's becoming a real problem, in fact. Particularly after what happened between us the other night. Joy maintains it wasn't a big deal. Even Peyton sort of dismissed its importance when I told her about it. But they're both dead wrong.

When you return home after real-kissing one guy and proceed to pretend-kiss another one, that's a problem.

And when the guy you're pretend-kissing is the one you wish you were real-kissing, except you can't because he's not into you like that . . . this is also a problem.

Before I can dwell on my thorny predicament, my phone beeps with a text from, ironically, the person who *is* into me.

Aaron: *How's it going at the charity thing?*
Me: *My grandmother just bid 2K on soap.*
Aaron: *Bold move.*
Me: *Right?*
Aaron: *Are we still on for dinner tomorrow night?*
Me: *Yup. Looking forward to it.*

I tuck the phone back into my silver clutch while assuring myself I *am* looking forward to seeing Aaron again. And, hey, maybe in the days since the carnival he's been honing his kissing skills. Practicing on a pillow or something. A girl can hope, right? Because the memory of his forceful tongue repeatedly plunging into my mouth like it was mining for tonsil treasure almost makes me gag. It's a shame, because he's such a cool guy otherwise. He's been texting me every day since we met. Memes, random thoughts. He's hilarious.

But . . .

I don't know if Aaron is the one.

Don't get me wrong, I certainly haven't been saving my virginity for my one true love. I'm not sitting at home waiting for Prince Charming to sweep me off my feet. But at the very least, I'd like to be wildly attracted to the man. I want to be unable to contain myself when he's around. I want to want him so badly that I can't wait to rip his clothes off. I want *that* level of chemistry.

Still, one date isn't enough to assess the full scope of chemistry. At least that's what Peyton always insists. According to my best friend, a date introduces you to the potential, the spark. And if the spark is there, however small it may be, you need to give it a chance, kindle it to discover how hot the fire can burn. The spark was there with Aaron, I can't deny that, so I suppose it's time to see if it develops into an inferno.

"Here's the spa package!" I exclaim, spotting it at the next table.

I practically bulldoze my grandmother over to grab a bid card and a green golf pencil from the basket. I wish I could see what other people have already bid, but the format of this auction is asinine. It's a silent, *secret* auction. The bids go into the box, someone flips through them to find the highest number, and that's the winner.

"This isn't rocket science," Joy says, grinning at my indecision.

"The next available appointment at this spa is next July. July, Joy! They're booking a *year* in advance. This is my one shot. My one opportunity."

"You have issues."

While she taps her foot with impatience, I mentally calculate what I think the package is worth, then double it. Then I cross out that amount and triple it instead.

"Pray for me," I declare. I slip the card into the box.

"I need new friends," Joy tells Grandma.

"Laaaadies and gentleeeemen," a male voice booms from the stage at the front of the room. "If we could have your attention over here!"

The noisy ballroom quiets, but only slightly. Most of the formal-wear-clad crowd continues whatever they were doing and ignores our hosts. The gala has two emcees this year—a former running back for the Panthers whose name I didn't catch, and a news anchor from the local network whose name I also didn't catch. Joy and I have just been calling them Big and Blonde, because he's big and she's blonde.

"The silent auction is now closed," Big announces. "Our wonderful staff will start tallying the bids, and winners will be announced after the bachelor auction. Until then—eat, drink, and be merry!"

Blond teeters up beside him on dangerously high heels to shout into the microphone. "Let's get our gala on!" As her shrill voice reverberates through the cavernous ballroom, I don't miss the way Grandma winces.

"Are you all right?" I ask, touching her arm.

"A bit tired," she admits. "And, if I'm being frank, I don't think my eardrums will survive listening to that woman for another hour."

"Do you want to leave?"

After a beat, she nods. "I think so, yes. Are you all right taking a car service home?"

"Yeah, that's no problem. But are you sure? It's only eight o'clock."

Grandma gives that prim smile of hers, the one that always holds a trace of mischief. "I made my appearance, dear. Nobody will notice if I slip away."

"I'll walk you out, then." I glance at Joy. "Meet you back at the table."

"'Night, Mrs. Tanner," Joy says, leaning down to kiss my grandmother's cheek.

"Good night, dear."

After I've seen Grandma off, I return to the ballroom, weaving my way through tables. The centerpieces this year are massive—fancy crystal monstrosities with tall feathers and sprigs of baby's breath. I think they're supposed to look like swans. Or horses. It's really a toss-up. The riser extending out from the stage is meant to serve as the runway for the bachelor auction, and as I pass it I smother a laugh. Poor Tate. I haven't spotted him yet tonight, so I assume he's cowering in a corner somewhere.

Or he's chatting with Joy, which is what I find when I reach the table Grandma sponsored.

He's wearing a dark gray suit, the wool jacket stretching deliciously across his broad shoulders. He has a white dress shirt underneath, no tie, top two buttons undone. With his handsome face clean-shaven and his golden hair styled, he looks like one of those preppy boys he likes to call *clones*.

"Someone busted out the hair products," I tease.

"Damn right." Those blue eyes sweep over my dress. "That's a great color on you."

"Thanks," Joy says. "I picked it out."

I snort. "Yes. Joy deserves all credit. You ready for your big moment?" I ask Tate.

He nods briskly. "I've covered all my bases. Lined up a plan A *and* a plan B."

I narrow my eyes at him. "Which one am I?"

"A, definitely. I mean, no man wants to win a date with his mother."

That makes me laugh. "Your mom's here?"

"Her and Dad are sitting over there." He points to a table to the right of the stage. "She promised she'd save the day if you bailed on me. Hey, you know what, come meet them."

"What?" I shift in discomfort, the heels of my pointy nude pumps sinking into the burgundy carpet. "Ah, that's not necessary."

"No, come. They'd love to meet you. I was telling them about you earlier."

He was?

I notice Joy giving me a look that says *he's talking you up to his parents?*

When I respond with a panicky look that says *help,* she throws me into the deep end as usual. "I'll stay here," she chirps, snagging a flute of champagne from one of the waiters. She takes a sip, smiling impishly around the edge of her glass. "Go meet his parents, Cass."

Traitor.

"What, is this weird?" Tate asks as he loosely holds my arm to escort me through the crowd.

"No," I lie. "Why would it be weird?"

"Joy's acting like meeting my parents is a big deal or something." He offers a flippant shrug. "It's just my folks. They're nothing special."

He's wrong. The moment I meet the Bartletts, I become a bit starry-eyed. I'm not the only one either. The couple holds court in the middle of a large group, clearly the center of attention. Tate's dad, tall, blond, and gregarious, is regaling everyone with a tale that's making them yowl with laughter. A gray-haired man wipes tears of mirth from his eyes, declaring, "Jesus Christ, Gavin, that's the craziest thing I've ever heard."

When they notice Tate approaching, the Bartletts break away

from their friends, greeting us with broad smiles. Tate had described his parents as being *disgustingly in love,* and I pick up on it instantly. They emit a distinctive aura that surrounds them, and everyone around them, in a loving cocoon of tenderness.

And they're always touching each other in some way. Even while Tate's dad holds out a hand toward me, one arm remains wrapped around his wife's shoulder. "Gavin," he introduces himself. "Nice to meet you."

When Tate's mom shakes my hand, her other one remains nestled in the crook of Gavin's arm. "Gemma," she says. She's a petite, curvy woman with dirty-blond hair and warm brown eyes, appearing much younger than her age. A white sheath dress fits her body like a glove.

"I'm Cassie." I return the handshake before glancing over at Tate. "Aw, man. They even have the same initials. Gavin and Gemma. I love it." I grin in delight. "You guys totally missed an opportunity to go all Kardashian and give Tate a G name."

"We were definitely considering Gate," Gavin replies earnestly, "but Tate had a better ring to it."

I snort out a laugh. "Hear that, Gate? You dodged a bullet."

"Tate says you're his auction backup?" Gemma prompts, smiling at me.

"I don't know . . . I *thought* I was. Now it sounds like it's going to be a bidding war between you and I . . ." I tip my chin in mock challenge.

Gemma feigns a glare. "Oh, it's on."

"Ladies, please. Don't fight over me." Tate grimaces. "Like, seriously, don't. I can't have my mother involved in any competition where I'm the prize."

Gavin booms with laughter. "Good point, kid." He claps Tate on the shoulder before focusing his attention on me. "Cassie, how are you enjoying the summer?"

"It's been nice. I've just been taking it easy."

"Tate says you grew up in the Bay?"

"I did. My dad and stepmom still live here, with my two half sisters, but I'm in Boston now. I go to college there."

"Did you tell her my news?" Gavin asks his son.

Tate is flabbergasted. "Of course not. Why would I do that?"

"Maybe because it's the most exciting thing that's ever happened to anybody?" his father shoots back.

Tate wasn't kidding about his dad being an overgrown child. And Tate is the spitting image of his father. The two of them are so similar in both looks and personality that I have to smile watching them interact.

"What's the news?" I ask curiously.

Gavin's entire face lights up, pride in his eyes. "Guess who's being featured in the newspaper."

Tate glances at me. "The *Avalon Bee* is doing a write-up on Dad," he explains. His voice lowers to a stage whisper. "He thinks this makes him special, but they run a profile on a local businessman every month. He's literally one of dozens."

"Front page?" challenges Gavin.

"Well, no," Tate relents. "But the only reason you're being featured on the front page is because you gave Harvey a deal on that speedboat. You basically bribed the guy."

"Me? You think *I'm* capable of bribing a journalist?"

"Yes," Tate and Gemma answer in unison.

I laugh, then dutifully *ooh* and *aah* as Gavin offers more details about the article. We chat for a few more minutes, until Big and Blonde return to the stage and ask everyone to take their seats. The bachelor auction is about to commence.

"Kill me now," Tate moans.

"You're going to do great," his mother assures him. "Everyone will bid on you, sweetie."

"Mom, no. You don't understand the assignment. We *don't* want everyone to bid on me. Just Cassie."

Gavin waggles his eyebrows at me. "Look at you, young lady. You seem to have captivated our son."

"Oh, we're just friends," I'm quick to protest.

"I'm just teasing," he says with a boisterous laugh.

I laugh awkwardly in response. "Oh. Anyway, it was nice meeting you guys. I should go join my friend, though."

"Wonderful to meet you, Cassie," Gemma says warmly.

"They're so normal," I hiss at Tate as he escorts me back to my table.

"I know. I told you."

Ten minutes later, the bachelor auction is in full swing. From the shiny podium at the head of the stage, Big clutches a stack of cue cards and introduces the first bachelor.

"Everyone, let's give a warm welcome to Morty!"

A tuxedo-clad man with glasses and a red bow tie takes the stage. He's pushing sixty, with an infectious smile he flashes to the entire room. He waves to the crowd and starts strutting.

"Oh, he's adorable," Joy exclaims.

"Morty is sixty-two years young, an accountant with a head for numbers and a love of pickles. And not just *eating* pickles! Creating them! In his spare time, Morty pickles anything he can get his hands on. Beets, peppers, tomatoes, peaches, squash, rhubarb— Farrah, did you know you can pickle rhubarb? I didn't!"

Right. Blonde's name is Farrah.

"Sounds yummy!" she chirps into her microphone.

"So how about it, folks? Who fancies a date with Morty? Bid high and maybe he'll pickle something for you! I'm told his entire garage features rows and rows of jars, all full of pickled delights . . ."

"I changed my mind," Joy whispers. "I think he might be a serial killer."

"The jars, right?"

"Oh yeah."

"We'll start the bidding at fifty dollars."

Three hands shoot up. "Fifty!"

"A hundred."

"A hundred and fifty!"

Before we know it, Morty the Pickler goes for six hundred dollars.

"That's about five hundred and fifty more dollars than I thought he'd go for," Joy whispers to me, and we nearly keel over in laughter. The champagne at this event has been free-flowing, and although I'm only on my first glass, I'm already feeling a buzz.

The next bachelor is a silver fox who causes a murmur to ripple through the crowd when he emerges from behind the black velvet curtains.

"Hot damn. Hello, Daddy," Joy coos.

"Oh gross. Don't say that."

"Come on, don't tell me you wouldn't hit that."

I study him. He's wearing a white linen shirt, fine-pressed gray trousers, and deck shoes. Sporting a deep summer tan. He's tall, handsome, and when it's revealed that he runs a hedge fund, the ladies are clamoring to bid.

Farrah the Blonde barely gets out his job title before a woman shouts, "Five hundred!"

"Six!"

"Seven!"

"Eight fifty!"

Joy looks over. "Can I borrow some of Grandma's money?"

I elbow her. "Absolutely not. You literally just got back together with Isaiah."

"Oh right. Fuck. I forgot."

After Silver Fox is taken for fifteen hundred smackeroos, several more bachelors grace the stage. The owner of the Good Boy brewery. A dog trainer. Two waiters from the club restaurant, then one of the golf instructors. Luckily, not Lorenzo.

When Tate's friend Danny is up, the winning bid for the attractive ginger is a staggering $2,300. Doesn't bode well for Tate if that's the going price for hot sailing instructors.

Danny's smile seems forced as he walks off the stage to greet his date. The pair isn't required to go out tonight, but it's customary to say hello to the person who "wins" you. Instantly, the woman's fingers curl around Danny's biceps and she peers up at him eagerly. Now I see why Tate was so worried. There are a lot of hungry women in this ballroom tonight.

"Our next bachelor is Tate!" Farrah announces.

"Here we go," I say.

Tate appears on the stage, hands loosely resting on his belt loops. His long stride eats up the runway, fair hair gleaming in the spotlight aimed at him.

"Tate is an avid sailor, splitting his workdays between the yacht club and Bartlett Marine, our number-one boat retailer in Avalon Bay."

"Yeahhhhh!" cheers a loud voice I recognize as Gavin Bartlett's.

"He loves being out on the water, any way he can. When he's not on a boat, you'll find him on a surfboard."

Tate reaches the end of the runway and stops to strike a cheesy pose. He seeks out my face in the crowd and winks before turning back.

"This golden boy is a romantic at heart. He enjoys long walks on the beach and stargazing with that special someone."

It's physically impossible for my eyes to roll any harder. I wonder if he wrote this himself.

Farrah sighs dreamily as Tate returns to stand beside her at the podium. "Oh, honey bear, I'll stargaze with you any day."

"Farrah," Big hisses into his mic to snap her out of it.

She blinks. "Right. We'll start the bidding at—"

"Five hundred," someone shouts instantly.

Joy snatches the flute out of my hand before I can drink. "Focus. It's your time to shine."

I swipe the flute back. "I'm waiting it out. Can't seem too eager." I grin over a gulp of champagne. "Plus, I want to make him sweat."

"Evil bitch."

"Six hundred!"

"Eight!"

"Nine fifty!"

From the stage, Tate's eyes implore me. His outward smile does nothing to conceal his agony. I tip my glass at him and take another dainty sip.

"One thousand dollars!"

"Eleven hundred!"

"Cassie," Joy warns.

"I've got a strategy," I insist. "Let them tire themselves out. That's what I do with my sisters when they're on a sugar high."

"Twelve hundred!" bids a nasally voice.

"Fifteen hundred." This voice is throaty.

Uh-oh. I turn to scope out the competition and raise an eyebrow. All right. Interesting. The current high bidder is a gorgeous brunette who doesn't seem as thirsty as the others. She's clearly in her late forties, though. So now I'm torn. Tate ordered me to not let any MILFs win. But maybe this is the kind of MILF he would like? She's a stunner and isn't giving off any predatory vibes.

"Going once—"

But I did make him a promise.

"Going twice—"

"Cassie," Joy hisses.

Shit.

Caught off guard, I end up blurting the first number that pops into my head because I wasn't paying attention.

"Three thousand!"

My friend gapes at me. "Dude. It was at fifteen. You just doubled it."

"Three thousand," Big crows. "Highest bid of the night! Someone sure wants to go stargazing!"

Farrah takes over. "Going once . . . going twice . . ."

The hot brunette on the other side of the room remains silent.

"Sold for three thousand dollars to the redhead in the green dress!"

On the stage, Tate beams at me.

I smother a sigh. Whatever. At least it's for a good cause.

CHAPTER 15

CASSIE

"Does this mean I get to order you around now?" I ask later. "Like for the rest of the summer?"

Tate snorts at the question. We walk down to the dock of the Jackson house, where the water laps quietly against the wooden pylons and the drone of insects buzzes in the air. It's eleven thirty and the night is calm and still. I'm in my minidress but abandoned the heels up on the lawn. He's taken off his suit jacket and rolled up his shirt sleeves.

"For the rest of the summer? Dream on."

"I just dropped three grand on you. Show me some respect, you ungrateful brat."

"Three grand of your grandmother's money."

"Which I stand to inherit one day. Well, along with my cousins, but still," I grumble under my breath. "So that's it? I don't get anything out of this deal? At the very least you should be my pool boy on the weekends or something. You know, wear a tiny Speedo and serve me drinks poolside."

"You donated money to a good cause. Isn't that enough?"

"No!"

He rolls his eyes. "Fine. I'll tell you what. I'll let you order me around for the rest of tonight."

"But I'll be going to bed in, like, an hour," I complain.

"Then you have one hour to call the shots."

I plant my hands on my hips. "Fine. Go get us some drinks." *Ugh.* Except, ordering someone around isn't in my nature, so I quickly add, "Please?"

He throws his head back and laughs. "You're terrible at this. But you're in luck—I'm already on top of the drink situation. Got a surprise for you."

That piques my interest.

"Get comfortable. I'll be right back."

I sink onto one of the loungers facing the water, twisting around to adjust the backrest. The weather is perfect tonight. Feels like room temperature outside, and I stretch my legs out in front of me and close my eyes, just savoring the night. My eyelids pop open at the sound of Tate's footsteps on the wood slats of the dock. He reappears holding two bottles of champagne.

I gasp. I recognize the gold label. These were the expensive bottles of bubbly they were serving at the Manor tonight.

"Did you steal those from the club?" I demand.

"Oh, I did."

"Oh God, you're a thief."

"Trust me, they owe me for all those safety classes they keep roping me in to doing without paying me overtime."

"I can't drink stolen contraband."

"You can and you will."

He sets the bottles on the small table between our loungers, then pulls two skinny glasses from his pocket, which he must have grabbed from Gil Jackson's kitchen. Picking up a bottle, he peels off the gold foil packaging around the lip.

Just as he's about to pop the cork, I balk, screeching loudly. "Don't aim it at the water!"

"I could aim it at your face," he offers.

I give him the finger. "Point it at the grass over there. But not the water. What if the cork lands in the bay and a fish eats it and chokes to death? Or a turtle? Oh my God, what if there's a Keanu Reeves turtle living under your dock and he thinks we're feeding him and then he *dies*—"

"The babbling never ends with you, does it, ginger?"

"Don't call me ginger, Gate."

He jabs the air with his finger. "No. Absolutely not. That is *not* becoming a thing."

"What's the matter, Gate?" I ask sweetly. "Did someone give you a nickname you don't enjoy?"

"Call me that again and I'll murder a turtle right in front of you."

"You wouldn't dare." I grin at him. "Oh! Speaking of turtles. My dad messaged earlier, and guess what—my stepmother agreed to the turtle. They're planning to give it to the girls after their birthday party in a couple weeks. The twins are going to die of excitement."

"Isn't your birthday coming up soon too?"

He remembered that?

My heart skips a beat, but I pretend to be unaffected. "Also in a couple weeks," I confirm. "My sisters and I share a birthday."

"Damn. Let me guess—somehow you've managed to find a silver lining for that too?"

"Yup." I nod at his hands. "You gonna open that bottle, Gate?"

"*Gate* is not becoming a thing," he growls, before turning in a safe direction to pop the cork. A moment later, he pours the bubbly liquid into our flutes, hands me one, and settles in the chair beside me.

As we sip our champagne, I try to ignore the pounding of my heart. The dampness of my palms. This feels like a date, even though I know it's not.

To hammer it home to my silly, smitten brain that such thoughts are counterintuitive, I force myself to say, "I'm going out with Aaron again tomorrow."

"Ah, right." Tate chuckles quietly. "Tongue battles part two."

"God, I hope not."

"We practiced for this. If it happens again, you're saying something," he warns.

"I will," I promise.

"And let's just hope kissing isn't the only activity he's bad at."

I straighten up in alarm. "Oh no. Oh *no*. I was planning to let him go to second base. Nobody can be bad at second base, can they?"

Tate drinks some more champagne, mulling it over. "He could be an aggressive tit squeezer."

I blanch. "If he is, I'll have no choice but to say something, because that'll earn him an involuntary scream of pain. The girls are sensitive."

Tate's eyes briefly flick my way. "Are they?" he drawls.

"Yes. Very." My throat is suddenly dry.

His must be too, because he chugs the rest of his glass and then pours himself another one.

"Easy, partner," I caution.

"Don't worry. Look how tiny these glasses are. It'll take a lot of refills to get me even close to drunk."

He has a point. So I hold out my own tiny glass, and he tops it off with that playful smile I'm beginning to crave on a daily basis. While we lie there on the dock, my gaze drifts up to the sky, sweeping over the twinkling carpet of lights.

"It's incredible how clear the sky is out here," I remark. "In Boston, the sky is different. All the pollution in the air, I guess. You hardly ever see any stars."

"I love it. Especially when you're on the open ocean. No land anywhere around you, this huge sky above you. That could freak anyone out, looking around and seeing nothing but water. But the stars, right? They're always there. They're fixed. You can't get lost when you can see the stars. Can't lose yourself."

"Holy shit," I accuse. "You're actually into stargazing? I assumed that bio they read at the auction was bogus." I snicker. "*He's a romantic at heart and enjoys long walks on the beach.*"

"Nah, that part was BS. Whoever wrote the intro decided to improvise." He shrugs. "I listed four interests on the questionnaire they emailed, and all of them started with an S. Maybe they didn't like that."

"Four S's . . ." I start to list them. "Sailing. Surfing. Stargazing. Wait—what was the fourth?"

"They didn't read it."

I eye him curiously. "Why? What was it?"

"Sex." He winks.

My face almost bursts into flames, which isn't a favorable thing because I was already burning up from the alcohol. I don't even want to know what color my cheeks are right now.

Between the two of us, we've officially polished off an entire bottle of champagne. He's ingested more, but my tolerance is shit and the champagne loosens my tongue.

"Yeah . . . I don't have much experience with that," I confess.

Tate is already removing the foil from the second bottle. He stops for a second and meets my eyes. "You're a virgin."

"Man, you drop it like a statement of fact," I say dryly. "Not even a question, huh? What, is it written on my forehead or something?"

"Nah. Just an educated guess."

I stick out my glass for another top-up. "Well, the answer to the non-question is yes, I'm a virgin. I've done other things, though."

"Is that right?" Eyes dancing, he cocks his head at me.

"Don't you dare tell me to spill the tea."

"C'mon, let's hear it, ginger. Whatcha done?" When I remain quiet, he chugs nearly half his fresh glass. "All right, then. I'm going to start guessing. Okay. So. I know you've made out."

I roll my eyes. "Yes."

"Handjobs," he guesses.

"Yes."

"Blowjobs?"

"Yes." I turn toward him. "And I even swallowed."

Tate, who was mid-sip, spit outs his drink at my proud response. Laughing, he pours himself more champagne. "You wild thing," he says in amusement.

"Anyway. That's it. Sexy times by Cassie Soul. HJs and BJs. The end."

"Nuh-uh," Tate argues. "That's what *he* got out of it. What about you? Did he go down on you?"

"This is not proper friend talk."

"Sure it is. I talk about sex with my friends all the time."

"Your *girl* friends?"

"Sure. You should hear some of Steph's stories. And she's bi, so it's, like, twice the dirty. Sometimes she talks about pussy, other times it's dick. Exciting times."

I laugh. "Sounds like it."

He eyes me over the rim of his glass. "You ever had an orgasm?"

Oh my God.

"Yes," I grumble. "Both solo and with a partner, before you ask."

"I don't think I've ever seen anyone's cheeks turn that shade of red before."

"I told you, this isn't appropriate subject matter."

"Why, is it turning you on?"

Yes!

"No," I lie.

He just grins. "So why haven't you had sex? Waiting for Mr. Right?"

"No." I sigh. "I'd settle for someone I'm madly attracted to, but I rarely come across that. I swear, my friends walk out their front doors and, bam, they're hooking up with someone they can't keep their hands off of. Meanwhile, I'm a total disaster when it comes to meeting men. I babble—have you noticed I babble? And if I do manage to overcome my nerves and actually interact with someone I'm attracted to, they end up not being attracted to me. And then the ones I *don't* want are all over me."

"That's how it usually goes."

"I was dating someone last year," I admit. "Lasted about six months, and there was chemistry, for sure. But something just didn't fully click. Didn't feel right. I wasn't entirely comfortable with him, I guess. And I couldn't pull the trigger."

"If you couldn't pull the trigger with a guy you were dating for six months, how do you expect to do it in one summer? July's almost over," Tate reminds me. "Doesn't leave you with much time to execute your fling plan."

"I mean, in my defense, I tried pulling the trigger three weeks ago." A case of the giggles suddenly hits me. "You realize you were literally the first guy I spoke to this summer? What are the odds? I *never* meet guys I'm attracted to, and I meet one the first night I go out." I double over laughing. "And you friend-zoned me."

"Doing okay over there, Soul?"

"I'm great," I croak between wheezy laughs. "This is hilarious. I've been in town almost a month and look what I've accomplished. First I go on a date with a dude who learned to kiss in a barnyard. And now I'm lying here stargazing with a hot guy and neither of us is naked because he's not into it."

"I never said I wasn't into it," he protests.

"Let's not rehash this," I say, reaching over to pat his knee. "Don't worry, I'm not mad or anything. Just stating how absurd this whole situation is."

Clearly flustered, Tate goes to pour another glass. Only a few drops trickle out of the bottle.

"Shit." He sounds amazed. "We just killed two bottles of champagne, Cassie. In an hour. We're fucking barbarians."

"I think that's our cue to say good night, then." My knees are wobbly as I rise from the chair. I scoop up the empty bottles. "Come on, Gate. Walk me home so I don't trip in the dark and break my neck."

"Gate ain't happening, ginger."

"Oh, it *so* is."

Tate rests his palm on my lower back to guide me, keeping me steady as we walk. I'm certain I feel his fingertips move in a light caress. But it's probably an accident, a result of the fact that we're stumbling up the path, both a little drunk. Still, there's something very intimate about the feel of his hand at my back.

I want it on other parts on me.

He wasn't wrong. I *am* turned on. Painfully so. I'm practically squeezing my thighs together, desperate to go inside, as we stop and say goodbye on the stretch of manicured grass between our two houses. I want nothing more than to lock myself in my room, slide my fingers in my panties, and bring myself to orgasm thinking about him.

Inside, I make sure all the lights are off because Grandma is forgetful sometimes. Then I enable the alarm and sprint upstairs as quietly as I can. The throbbing between my legs has become unbearable. I'm already unzipping my dress while I hurry down the hall. I enter my room and throw my phone on the bed, hands tugging my bodice down. I let my dress drop to the floor about half a second before remembering I haven't shut the curtains yet.

Tate is at his window.

My heart jumps to my throat. I'm wearing nothing but skimpy panties and a strapless bra. And he notices. Of course he notices. His eyes rake over my body, admiring, lingering, then moving up to my face. I expect him to reach for his phone and text a smart-ass remark.

Instead, he starts unbuttoning his shirt.

My breath hitches.

It's impossible to look away. I've seen his bare chest before, but the act of undressing . . . it's almost more intimate than nudity itself. I can scarcely breathe. Slowly, he parts the front of the white dress shirt and eases it off his shoulders. His gaze never leaves mine as he tosses the shirt away.

I step toward the window, but I don't draw the curtains. Not even a gun to my head could compel me to close these curtains right now. I swallow, trying to bring moisture to my throat. It remains bone-dry.

Tate unzips his pants.

I moan out loud, and even though he's twenty feet away, I swear I see the corners of his mouth quirk up.

He pushes his gray trousers down his legs. Kicks them away. My gaze involuntarily lowers to his groin. There's no mistaking the long ridge of arousal straining against his white boxer briefs. The material is stretched taut over his erection, leaving very little to the imagination. I'm mesmerized.

This is dangerous territory. We're on the edge of a cliff here. He just stripped down to his underwear and now it's my move. I can shut the drapes and pretend this never happened.

Or . . .

I hear a buzzing from the bed. I look over, expecting an incoming text. But it's a call. Gulping, I grab the phone with a shaky hand. I swipe to answer it.

"I'm not *not* into it." His raspy voice tickles my ear.

"W-what?" My mouth is so dry I can barely get that one word out.

"You said I friend-zoned you because I'm not into you. That's not true." He huffs out a breath. "I know it sounded like a bunch of excuses, but I meant it when I said it's easier to keep things platonic. But that's not to say I wasn't attracted to you. I was. I still am."

"Really?"

"Yeah." There's a beat. "You have no idea what you do to me."

"Show me."

The request slips out before I can stop it.

Forget the cliff. It's long gone. I've sailed over the edge and am basically free falling. My heart beats so hard and so fast that my ribs are sore. Every muscle in my body is tense, knees quaking as I move closer to the window.

Tate's got the phone to his ear. He's watching me. But he still hasn't responded.

And then his low voice slides into my ear.

"Are you calling the shots?"

This time there's no mistaking the naughty curve of his lips. And I realize this is the out we both require. A way to distance ourselves from the mistake we're probably about to make. He said I could order him around just for tonight. So why not. Let's treat it like a game. A fun little game without any consequences.

"Yeah." My voice is soft. "I'm calling the shots." I take a breath. "Show me how much you want me."

As I watch, he taps his phone and then sets it on the window ledge. He's put me on speaker. Three seconds later, he's naked. Naked and gorgeous and gloriously turned on. Long and hard, and bigger than I expected.

My mouth turns to sawdust again, and I gulp rapidly. Tate drifts a hand down his bare chest. Slow, leisurely. He wraps it around the thick shaft and gives a slow stroke. I bite back another moan.

"I'm drunk," I tell him.

"Me too."

I can't take my eyes off his hand. Those long fingers curled around his erection. "We're friends."

"We are," he agrees.

"Friends shouldn't do this."

"Probably not." He pauses. "See this?" Another long, deliberate stroke. "This is how hard you make me. Lately I've started jerking off before I know I'm going to see you, just to curb the temptation."

The filthy picture he paints makes my nipples tingle. "Are you serious?"

"Mmm-hmm. And I'm going to get myself off the moment you close those curtains."

My hand trembles so wildly I nearly drop the phone. "Who says I'm going to close them?"

From across the way, I glimpse the faint movement of his tongue, swiping across his bottom lip to moisten the corner of his mouth.

"You have no idea how good you look right now," he says roughly.

Clutching the phone to my ear, I bring my other hand behind my back, searching for the clasp of my bra. It's an easy one to undo single-handed. I flick it open and the bra flutters to the floor.

The moment my breasts are exposed, Tate makes a tortured sound. Husky and deep.

"How about now? How do I look?"

Oh my God, who is this woman? What are these words leaving my mouth? Whose throaty voice is that? I'm on display for him, and yet I'm not at all self-conscious.

"You look goddamn edible."

A smile flits over my lips, but dips into a slight frown when I realize his hand has gone still. "You're not touching yourself anymore."

"I'm waiting for your orders," is the gravelly response. "Tell me what you want."

I realize then, despite the bravado I just exhibited, I'm completely out of my depth here. I don't know how to direct an encounter like this. I don't know what to ask for. How to ask it. All I know is that my clit is throbbing and my nipples have never been harder.

"I want you to help me," I order. "I want you to take control and help me . . ." I trail off.

A strangled groan fills my ear. "Help you what? Help you come?"

"Yes."

"All right. Then I want you to slide your hand inside those panties for me. I want you to rub that hot pussy until you're coming for me. Can you do that for me?"

A wave of lust nearly knocks me off my feet. Sweet Lord.

"I don't know if I can," I confess. "Standing up, I mean." I'm certain my face is redder than it's ever been.

"Move closer." His voice is hypnotic. It's a lure and I'm drawn in like a fish, gliding beneath the surface toward it.

"Put me on speaker," he says when I'm a foot from the window. "Leave your phone on the windowsill."

My pulse is thudding, a rapid, rhythmic beat thrumming in my blood. He's touching himself again. A lazy stroke here and there. No rush at all. I admire the defined ridges of his abdomen, the sexy V of his oblique muscles. He's incredible. I wish he were here in my bedroom with me, that his warm, tanned flesh were pressed up against me.

I put him on speakerphone, grateful for the fact that my grandmother isn't a light sleeper.

"Good girl," he encourages when I set the phone down. "Now take your left hand and hold onto the ledge. Hold yourself steady."

I follow his instructions.

"I want to see your other hand inside your panties."

I slip the fingers of my right hand under my waistband, and the moment they collide with my clit, I almost keel over. "Fuck," I choke out, grateful to be holding on to something.

He chuckles. "Feel good?"

"Uh-huh."

We continue to watch each other. He's stroking a little faster now. I rub a little faster.

His gaze is fixed on me. I don't know if he's focused on my breasts or the motions of my hand, but either way his breathing is quickening. I can hear it over the speakerphone.

I'm starting to make breathy sounds too. I grind the heel of my palm over my core, rocking against it. Pinpricks of pleasure dance along my skin. My nipples are tight. Breasts tender.

I exhale slowly. "I wish you were here with me."

"Me too."

And yet neither of us take that thought to its logical conclusion. I don't ask him to come over. He doesn't offer. Instead, we continue to pleasure ourselves. Our eyes remain locked. My entire body is a live wire, desperately waiting for a spark to set it off.

"Do you wish my dick was inside you right now?"

A soft moan slips out. "I don't know," I answer truthfully. "I've never had a dick inside me before."

That summons a low groan from him. "Christ. Why is that the hottest thing I've ever heard?"

When I see his fist tighten around his erection, I rock faster against my hand. The tension is agonizing. I apply more pressure on the swollen nub that's hurting for release, and a shudder runs through me.

"I'm close." I barely hear my own voice over the persistent hammering of my heart.

"Yeah? Let me see it."

I bite my lip. My body feels heavy and weak, as if my limbs are about to give out on me. I grip the ledge, digging my fingernails into the white painted wood. I sag forward and lean my forehead against the window. My erratic breaths fog up the glass. A whimper escapes my lips as the pleasure mounts, gathering in my core. God. This is the most erotic experience of my life.

"Cass. *Yes*. You're gonna make me come."

Those husky words provide the spark. My body detonates. The orgasm surfaces in a flash of light, a surge of heat. A rush of bliss that sweeps me away, coursing through me in sweet, pulsing waves. When Tate grunts, my eyelids flutter open. I watch him climax, listening to the quiet noises he makes while he loses himself to release. Finally, his hand slows. His chest rises and falls with each shallow breath he sucks in.

"Holy hell," he curses, biting his lip as he meets my eyes.

Holy hell, indeed.

CHAPTER 16

CASSIE

The need to belong is deeply ingrained in us. I think it's because there's no worse feeling in the world than being on the outside looking in. Watching a group of friends laughing together in school and wishing you were in on the joke. Seeing your coworkers gathered around at the water cooler and longing to be part of the conversation. Or, in my case, desperately wanting to belong in my own family. From the moment Dad married Nia, I felt pushed aside. And then, when the twins were born two years later, I was more than pushed aside—I was pushed *out*. At least that's what it feels like. Nia never warmed up to me, and I'm constantly walking on eggshells with Dad, which in turn makes me all the more desperate for their approval.

That's probably why, when Dad calls thirty minutes before I'm supposed to meet Aaron for dinner and asks if I can babysit, I answer yes without hesitation.

"I thought Nia's friend's daughter was the best babysitter on the block," I joke, unable to stop from dropping a passive-aggressive jab under the guise of teasing. On past visits I offered to babysit numerous times so Dad and Nia could go on their monthly date nights, but they've always dismissed the offer, opting instead for some teenager on their street.

Dad chuckles. "Kendra's great. But she's no match for their big sister. Anyway, she sprained her ankle this afternoon, so she had to cancel. We hate to bug you on Saturday night, though. You didn't already have plans?"

"Well, I did. But I'm fine rescheduling. Unless . . . any chance I can invite a friend over? We had plans for dinner and a movie. Maybe I can talk him into coming by and watching Disney movies instead."

"Is this the friend from the fish store?"

"No, somebody else."

"Ms. Popularity over here! Sure, that won't be a problem. Go ahead and invite your friend. And thanks, Cass. I owe you one. We really didn't want to cancel date night—there's a CCR tribute band playing in the park tonight. I'm stoked."

"No worries. I've hardly seen the girls this month, so it'll be nice to spend some time with them."

After we hang up, I text Aaron.

Me: *I am SO sorry to do this, but there's been a last-minute change of plans. My dad's in a bind and needs me to babysit my sisters. Any chance you want to come by and keep me company? Their bedtime is nine, so we'll still have alone time. AND . . . there's a Disney movie in it for you . . .*

Aaron: *Make it Frozen 2 and you've got yourself a deal.*

Me: *I'm afraid you'll have to negotiate with two six-year-old girls on that. They run the show.*

Aaron: *Challenge accepted.*

Me: *I'll text you the address.*

An hour later, Nia opens the front door to let me into my childhood home, her reluctant expression telling me how little she's enjoying this change of plans.

"Thank you for babysitting, Cassandra." Her smile is a bit stiff. "I'm sure you have better things to do on a Saturday night."

"It's fine. I've barely seen the girls this summer."

It's not meant as an accusation, but I see a flicker of guilt in her eyes.

Before she can say anything, I change the subject. "Anything I need to know for tonight? Any new allergies since the last time I was here? Or still just coconut for Roxy?"

"Just the coconut." Nia leads me into the kitchen. "They already had their dinner, and they just finished their bath. Clayton is dressing them." When the faint sound of girlish shrieks rings out from upstairs, she gazes at the ceiling with amusement. "Or at least he should be. Your father always turns the simplest task into a game."

I grin. "He's always been like that."

She stops at the counter. "We went grocery shopping today, so there are plenty of snacks and drinks. But don't let them drink any soda. Not even a drop."

"I won't," I promise.

"Let me go upstairs and speed them up."

As Nia ducks out of the kitchen, I take off my jean jacket and drape it over the back of a breakfast stool. Setting my purse on the counter, I reach inside it for my phone and find a message from Tate.

Tate: *I've prayed to the kissing gods on your behalf. Good fortune be with you.*

I've been waiting for him to text all day. I hadn't wanted to do it first, and the longer today dragged on without a word from him, the more I worried just how badly last night had screwed things up between us. I'd passed out like a light after our mutual pleasure session, then woke up this morning wondering what the hell I'd done. A line had undeniably been crossed, but I didn't know how to address it. I figured when he got in touch and brought it up, I could blame it on all the champagne.

But this? This is the message I get?

We're just going to pretend it never happened? That I don't know what his face looks like when he ejaculates?

A warm flush spreads across my skin at the filthy memory. I'm never going to be able to erase that image from my mind. His teeth biting into his lip. Hand clenched around his cock. The husky noise he made. Watching Tate Bartlett shudder in orgasm was the hottest thing I've ever witnessed in my life.

But okay. I guess we're not going to talk about it.

> Me: *LOL thanks. Might be hard to get some kissing in, though. I got roped into babysitting, so Aaron's going to keep me company.*
> Tate: *Lame.*
> Me: *I know. Maybe we'll go out afterward if the folks don't get back too late.*
> Tate: *All right. Have fun.*

Sighing, I lay the phone down. Hell, maybe it's better we don't talk about it. Just forget it ever happened.

Only, as with most impossible tasks, forgetting last night is . . . well . . . impossible.

"Bedtime is nine," Nia is saying ten minutes later, as she and Dad slip into their shoes in the front hall. "They can watch one movie. Only one."

I watch as she secures the ankle strap of one gold sandal. She looks beautiful tonight. Her hair is loose, tight black curls framing her face and making her appear softer; usually it's pulled back in a low bun, giving her a more severe look. Her makeup is light, just the sweep of gold eyeshadow and a touch of mascara. She's clad in a flowy blue dress with a unique pattern on it, paired with those strappy gold sandals.

"You look gorgeous," I tell her, the compliment popping out before I can stop it. Experience has taught me that Nia is terrible at receiving compliments. Or at least ones that come from me. She typically dismisses them with a stiff wave of her hand.

Tonight, she surprises me. "Thank you." She smooths the front of her dress. "My mother sent me this dress last year, but this is my first opportunity to wear it."

"Care package from Haiti, huh? That's cool."

Nia smiles. "It's always a wonderful surprise. Makes me very homesick."

I'm pretty sure this is the first time she's shared something this personal with me. Holy shit. Are we bonding?

Dad ruins the moment by peering past my shoulder into the living room, where my sisters are on the couch babbling to each other in French.

"*Au revoir, mes petites chéries,*" he calls out.

"*Au revoir,* Daddy!"

"Don't give your sister too much trouble," he warns.

"We won't," Roxy promises.

Dad kisses my cheek and ducks out the door. Nia lingers, her expression taking on a glint of panic.

"No soda," she reminds me. "If they want a snack, there are rice cakes on the top shelf of the cabinet. Monique loves them, especially if you spread some peanut butter on them. Oh, and be sure to keep a close eye on her. She likes to climb the furniture."

"We'll be fine," I assure her. "I'll call you if I need anything. Go out and enjoy the concert."

"Thank you, Cassandra." Everyone else calls me Cassie or

Cass, but in the eight years I've known her, Nia's never called me anything but Cassandra.

I close the door behind them, lock it, and proceed to dance into the living room like a game show contestant who just got chosen to go onstage. "All right, the adults are gone!" I shout. "Let's party!"

The twins burst into giggles. I flop down on the couch between them and throw an arm around each girl.

"So, I should warn you," I say, "I invited a friend to hang out with us tonight."

Roxy squeals. "What's her name? How do you know her?"

"Well, firstly, it's a him—"

"Ewwwww," Mo says, making a face.

"What's his name? How do you know him?" Roxy demands.

"His name is Aaron. You'll like him. He's really funny. I told him he can watch a movie with us."

"I don't want a movie. I want a story," Monique whines. "I want Kit 'n McKenna!"

"We can do both," I tell her. "Movie now, and a story at bedtime."

At the reminder of their favorite bedtime story, I suddenly realize I haven't heard from Robb in a few days. I gave him the story line for our *Kit 'n McKenna* book last week, but he still hasn't sent back any concepts for the artwork. Since the printer I found takes about seven days to print the book, Robb and I need to finalize the illustrations by the end of next week if I want it to be ready in time for the girls' party.

As Roxy continues to interrogate me about Aaron, a message from him pops up, informing me he'll be here in forty minutes or so. When I told him we wouldn't be eating together, he ended up driving to Charleston with his brother for dinner, and they're on their way back now.

Me: *The girls are feeling very nosy today, so expect some grilling when you get here.*

Aaron: *Ha! I'm not worried. All kids love me.*

He's not lying. An hour later, we're watching *Moana,* and the twins are laughing their butts off while Aaron stands in front of the TV and belts out the entire number that The Rock sings in the movie. He knows every word, and when I demand an explanation afterward, he offers a sheepish smile and says, "My older sister has a four-year-old daughter. We watch a lot of movies together."

Halfway through the film, the girls declare they're bored and would rather play a game, so Mo brings out a ridiculous card game that Roxy tries valiantly to explain. It involves monsters and severed body parts and requires us to fight each other in weird card battles. I don't understand what the hell is going on, but Aaron picks it up fast, and the next thing I know he and Roxy are competing in a fierce monster battle rife with dark glares and very bad trash talk.

"Oh, you're going down," he warns my sister.

"Nuh-uh. You are."

"No, you are."

"No, YOU ARE!" Roxy sticks her tongue out at him.

Aaron sticks his tongue out right back at her.

I stare at him. "I'm dating a six-year-old."

"Dating, huh?" His eyes sparkle.

Smiling, I arch a brow. "I mean, yeah, isn't this a date?"

"Ewwww!" Monique cries.

"Cassie has a boyfriend!" Roxy yells.

I roll my eyes. "You guys are SO immature," I say haughtily, and Aaron snickers.

Eventually, I check the time and notice it's almost eight thirty, so I encourage everyone to wrap up the game. Roxy wins, but I think Aaron lets her, which is another check in his plus column. Not batting an eye about our change of date venue is another one. He really is a decent guy.

"You okay staying down here while I put them to bed?" I ask him.

He's already reaching for the TV remote. "I'm good," he assures me. "Preseason game is on. Gotta see how the Bills are looking so far."

I keep forgetting he's from New York. *Not that far from Boston,* a little voice in my head points out.

I suppose that's super convenient. If we keep dating, that is. Right now, though, while I'm having fun with him, it still feels very platonic. Our initial spark doesn't seem to be catching fire. I don't feel a sense of eagerness to kiss him, but I'm not sure if the lack of heat and passion is because of what happened last time we kissed, or if it's simply just not there with us.

I know I'm capable of feeling it. I felt it last night. I'm sure some of *that* had to do with the alcohol we'd consumed, but most of it had to do with Tate.

Upstairs, I tuck the girls in and switch on the little lamp atop the night table between their beds. When I turn off the main light, the lamp casts a yellow glow over the room and projects glowing mermaids on the walls. It's the coolest thing. I wish I'd had one of those growing up.

I drag a white-painted rocking chair closer to their beds. It's a remnant from when they were babies, and I suddenly have a memory of Nia sitting in this chair, rocking my tiny infant sisters to sleep.

"Okay," I say cheerfully. "Are we ready to find out what happens when McKenna's older brother finds Kit hiding in the garage?"

* * *

"Thanks for waiting." I come downstairs about thirty minutes later. Aaron's made himself comfortable in the living room. Feet up on the coffee table, leaning back against the couch cushions with one arm propped behind his head.

He looks kind of sexy in that position . . .

This is promising.

When his head turns toward the doorway and his eyes smolder at the sight of me, I feel a fluttering between my legs.

Promising, indeed.

"The girls asleep?" he asks.

I settle beside him on the couch. "Roxy's out like a light, but Mo will take a bit longer. She was drifting off when I left, though."

"They're cool kids. Half sisters, right?"

"Yeah. Their mom is Dad's second wife. Nia."

"And you don't have any other siblings?"

"Nope. I was an only child until I was fifteen, and then the twins came along."

We talk about families for a while, but I have to admit I'm not paying too much attention to what we're saying. Aaron's arm is around me now, and his fingertips are brushing my bare shoulder. Stroking lightly. It feels nice. I'm pleasantly surprised to find heat gathering in my belly. My heart beating faster. Okay, I can work with this.

"Cassie."

I look over to see him peering at me through heavy-lidded eyes.

"Yeah?" I swallow.

"I really want to kiss you."

I swallow again. "Good. So kiss me."

For all of Tate's advice about how to ward off the "aggressive entry," it happens so fast I barely have a chance to blink, let alone touch his face and compliment him. The speed with which his lips latch onto mine and his tongue is thrusting inside is almost remarkable. He's perfected the art of persistent passion with zero buildup. In fact, I've never met anyone who's *this* skilled at kissing *this* bad. Once again, I'm caught in the same predicament, a helpless participant in a kiss that makes my head spin, and not in a good way.

Tell him to slow down.

I hear Tate's voice in my head.

But I feel too awkward asking him to change gears. Not when he's moaning as if he's thoroughly enjoying this. His fingers are threaded through my hair. One hand strokes my thigh over my yoga pants. Fortunately, I'm granted a reprieve when he comes up for air. I suck in as much oxygen as my lungs will allow, while Aaron mumbles, "You're so fucking pretty," and abruptly starts "kissing" me again. At this point, I don't think it qualifies as actual kissing, so much as face banging.

Say something.

I say nothing.

Yup, I chicken out. I let him keep doing what he thinks of as sexy kissing for another solid minute. Until, to my sheer relief, a little voice interrupts us.

"Cassie?" Monique whines from the stairs.

Aaron and I break apart. "Hold that thought," I tell him, when inside I'm like, *please, forget that thought.*

I step into the hall and find Mo wobbling down the stairs in her PJs, wide awake.

"Hey, squirt." I frown. "Why aren't you in bed?"

"I can't sleep."

"Aww. Well, that's not good. How can we fix that?"

"Can you tell me another story?"

I glance at the clock hanging on the wall at the entrance to the kitchen. It's five past ten. An hour past her bedtime. And Nia and my dad should be home in the next hour or so. I bite my cheek. I can't have Monique up and about when they get back or Nia will never leave me alone with the girls again.

"All right." I let out a sigh. "Go up to bed and we'll do another story. Just give me a sec to say goodbye to Aaron."

"I'll wait here." With a stubborn jut of her chin, she plants her butt on the bottom step.

"Okay. But don't move."

When I reenter the living room, Aaron is already up, phone in hand. He swipes his keys off the coffee table.

"You heard that?" I say wryly.

"Yeah."

"I'm sorry. I need to go back upstairs and put her to sleep, and I feel bad making you sit and wait again." Monique's insomnia also happens to be the escape hatch I'd been praying for, but I keep that thought to myself.

"It's no problem," he says easily. "Why don't we meet again during the week? I heard there's a really good mini golf course on the south end of the boardwalk."

"Sure. Sounds good."

I walk him to the door, where he leans in to kiss me goodbye. Luckily, just a kiss on the cheek, his tongue remaining firmly in his own mouth.

"Good night, sexy," he says huskily, and I can't lie—it does nothing for me.

I close the door after him and lock it. Then I stand there for a moment, exhaling a long, tired breath when I hear his car driving away. I don't think this Aaron thing is going to work. A friendship, maybe, but I honestly can't envision anything more than that. Which means—

A resounding crash jolts me from my thoughts.

It sounded like it came from the kitchen.

A wave of fear slams into me, propelling me forward. "Monique?" I shout, running through the house.

I fly into the kitchen and my heart stops when I spot her small body sprawled by the tall cabinet where we keep the snacks. The bottom shelf has broken off, the splintered plank now lying on the floor. It's clear she tried to climb it, and it didn't hold her weight. Random items are strewn around her feet—bags of chips, a can of peanuts, an array of baking supplies. On the top shelf, another tin of nuts teeters on the edge before crashing down and missing Monique's head by mere inches. She screeches in surprise.

I dive onto the floor and help her into a sitting position. "Oh my God. Sweetheart. Are you okay? Where are you hurt?"

I snap into emergency mode and search her for injuries, the frigid chill of panic icing my veins when I notice the cut on her jaw. It's not bleeding, just a few red dots, but whatever hit her did break the skin and leave a small indentation.

Tears stream down Monique's face. "The thing fell on my face. That one." She points.

I follow her finger to a peanut can that's rolling toward the fridge. Okay. Thank God. It's a plastic container. Not glass. Although either way Nia is going to kill me.

"It broke my face," Mo sobs. "I just wanted the rice cakes."

"Come here, baby." I pick her up. She wraps her arms and legs around me and clings tight. Her wails begin to quiet, transforming into hiccups.

"Let's get you a Band-Aid."

"I don't want a Band-Aid," she cries, then hiccups again.

"Tough. I'm going to put you down now, okay?" I set her on the chair at the kitchen table. "Don't you move a muscle, you hear me? Not one muscle, Mo."

I duck into the hall bathroom, where I know Dad keeps a

mini first aid kit under the sink. I grab it and hoof it back to the kitchen, where this time Mo listened and didn't move from her chair.

Sinking to my knees in front of her, I tear open an antiseptic wipe. "This is going to sting just a little," I warn her. "Ready?"

She nods weakly.

When I swipe it over the tiny cut, her face scrunches up. "I don't like that!"

"I know, but it's over. See? It's over. All done." I check the wipe, gratified to find no blood on it. She might have a wee bruise, but that's it.

Once the Band-Aid is on, I scoop her up again and search her face. "Are you okay? Does it still hurt?"

She shakes her head. "No."

"Good. Come on, let's get you back to bed."

We reach the stairs as the front door opens.

Shit.

I hear Nia and Dad's voices. So does Mo, because she exclaims, "Mama! Daddy! I broke my face! Come see!"

I swallow a groan. "Monique," I chide.

It's too late. The adults are galloping in. Nia pries Monique from my arms, while Dad barks, "What happened? Is everything okay?"

"It's fine," I reassure them. "I promise. There's a broken shelf in the kitchen, but Mo is fine."

Eyes now completely dry, Mo shows off her Band-Aid. "Look! Maybe I'll have a scar."

"A scar?" Nia swivels on me in reproach. "What happened?" Her voice is sharp.

"I was walking Aaron to the door. Mo couldn't sleep and was alone in the kitchen—when she was *supposed* to be waiting for me in the hall." I frown at my sister.

"I'm sorry," she says meekly.

"She tried to climb the cabinet to get a snack—"

Nia's eyes blaze. "I told you not to let her climb anything, Cassandra."

"I know." Guilt jams in my throat. "I swear I only left her alone for thirty seconds. Aaron was just leaving."

"It's okay, sweetheart," Dad says gently.

"No, it's not." Nia's voice rises as she blasts Monique with a reprimand. "You're not supposed to be climbing the furniture!" Dad touches Nia's arm, but she pushes him away. "No. I'm taking Monique to bed. Say good night to your father and sister."

"Good night, Daddy. Good night, Cassie." Monique's face is forlorn as peers at me over her mother's shoulder. She knows she got me in trouble. *I'm sorry,* she mouths.

I flash a smile of assurance. *Love you,* I mouth back.

They disappear at the top of the stairs.

Dad observes my expression and sighs. "Don't worry. She'll be fine. Kids are resilient."

"I know," I moan. "It's just . . . Nia already doesn't like me."

His features soften. "What are you talking about? That's not true."

"You know it is."

"It's not," he insists. "She thinks you're wonderful. We both do."

Sure. If he says so.

His false assurances still echo in my head as I drive home ten minutes later. It's eleven o'clock and I'm exhausted. I was supposed to go on a fun date tonight, which somehow turned into my trying to prove to my stepmother that I can be a good big sister. Instead, I only validated her already low opinion of me. And I couldn't even be assertive with Aaron. Too afraid to hurt his feelings by asking him to slow things down.

God. I feel like shit. My self-esteem is in the toilet, and for the life of me I can't conjure up a silver lining for tonight. I simply want to go home and climb into bed and sleep the rest of this disastrous weekend away.

When I pull into the driveway of Grandma's house, I'm startled to find another car parked there.

A silver Mercedes.

Oh no.

No.

Please, don't let it be her.

Please.

My stomach churns as I shut off the engine. My mother's go-to rental car choice is a Mercedes. She hates driving Grandma's Range Rover when she's in town. Claims it's too clunky.

Only, Mom isn't due to arrive for another two weeks. She's scheduled to come on my birthday weekend, and there's no way she would show up in Avalon Bay early. Not willingly. Ever since the divorce, this town has become a source of deep hostility for her.

In the front hall, my worst fears are confirmed when I spy several Louis Vuitton cases stacked against the wall. She always leaves her bags down here. Waiting for poor Adelaide to cart them up the stairs as if it's our housekeeper's job to play bellhop.

I kick off my tennis shoes and swallow a sigh when I notice the light on in the kitchen. I reluctantly make my way toward it. Steeling myself. Because apparently only bad things happen in kitchens tonight.

I enter to see Mom at the kitchen table, sipping a glass of white wine.

Yup. Only bad things.

"Hey!" I exclaim, slapping on a cheerful smile. It's difficult, though. My spirits are already dismally low. And if there's one thing I know about my mother, it's that she has the power to drag me down even lower. "What are you doing here? You weren't due for two more weeks."

"I decided to come early," she replies. "Mother mentioned on the phone the other day that you two haven't even started going through the house to decide what she'll be shipping to the city next month. Clearly my presence is needed here more than in Boston, which, frankly, has been sweltering this summer. It will be nice to spend a month by the ocean." She takes another sip, then sets down the wineglass and rises from her chair. "Is that a problem?"

"No, of course not!" My voice sounds high, squeaky.

"Wonderful. Then come here and give your mother a hug."

I walk over and obediently step into her embrace.

"Ah, it's so good to see you," Mom says, planting a kiss on the top of my head. The reception is more genuine than I expect, her hug infused with more warmth than I'm accustomed to. "I missed you, sweetie."

"Oh. I missed you too." My guard drops a couple of feet. I seem to have caught her in a good mood tonight.

She squeezes me tighter. "I'm hoping we get a chance to spend a lot of time together this month."

Her brown eyes shine with what seems like sincerity as she releases me. Then they fix on my yoga pants and tight white tank, flicking briefly to the black bra straps peeking out of my top.

A frown twists her lips. "Is that what you wore out tonight?"

And so it begins.

CHAPTER 17

TATE

I don't know . . . I've never had a dick inside me before . . .

I thought I was cured of spontaneous boner syndrome once I turned fourteen. Turns out, my dick still has a mind of his own. Only, this time, I'm not in front of the class delivering a presentation on the founding fathers when I pitch a tent. I'm at the bar, standing up to greet Evan, whose gaze doesn't miss what's happening down below.

"Do you have a boner?" he demands.

"Say it louder for the people in the back," I grumble.

Luckily, I revert to a state of non-arousal the moment I'm presented with a distraction. Before Evan arrived, I was sitting alone with far too much time on my hands to ruminate over what happened with Cassie. Since the night of the charity gala, I've been playing it off like it's no big deal. Friends always masturbate in front of windows together. Like, come on, bro. It's just a cool thing platonic people do. But it's not working. She's not dumb and neither am I. A line had definitely been crossed. And every time I hear her breathy voice in my head, whispering those words—*I've never had a dick inside me before*—I get harder than granite.

"Seriously. Is that for me?" Evan sounds amused.

"You wish." I push the beer I ordered for him across the booth. "Here."

"Thanks."

It's Sunday night and I dragged Evan out for drinks because both Danny and Luke bailed on me after work. Pleading exhaustion after a long day on the water with a group of disastrous, albeit enthusiastic, would-be sailors. Me, I desperately need the diversion, so I pried Evan out of Gen's bed. At least that's what I assume he was doing when I called.

Evan raises the pint glass to his lips. "And you're still not answering the question. Clue me in already. I want to solve the case. The case of the mysterious boner."

"I have a sex problem," I confess.

His amusement grows. "Oh, I can't wait to hear this. Hold that thought." He waves at one of the waitresses, whose hips sway deliberately as she saunters over to us.

Her name is Nicole, and I'm pretty sure Evan hooked up with her during Genevieve's year in Charleston when she went radio silent on him. Dude attempted to cure his broken heart by sleeping his way through the Bay, hitting on any cute chick that crossed his path. Fortunately, like me, he's on good terms with most of his hookups.

"Hi, boys," Nicole chirps. She eyes me. "You look . . . flushed."

Evan snickers. "Could I grab an order of chicken wings? Hottest sauce you've got." He winks at her. "Please and thank you."

"Coming right up."

Once she's gone, Evan takes another swig of his beer. "Okay, what's the problem?"

"I think maybe I have a virgin fetish I didn't know about."

He almost chokes on his beer. "I'm sorry, what?" He coughs a few times.

"You know that chick Cassie who was at your place a couple weeks ago? Her grandmother used to own the Beacon?"

"Yes . . ." He shakes his head, sighing. "You stupid bastard. You took her virginity?"

"No, no. I mean, she did sort of proposition me. Asked if I was interested in a summer fling. But I said no."

Evan lifts a brow. "Since when do you turn down propositions like that?"

"Mac talked some sense into me," I admit. "And when I took a step back to really think about it, I realized it wouldn't be a smart idea. Cassie didn't strike me as the type who could keep things strictly physical. I don't want to hurt her."

"Worried she'll fall in love with you, huh?"

"Kind of, yeah. Do you remember what happened in high school with Lindsey Gerlach?"

"I'm pretty sure our entire graduating class remembers," he says dryly. "What did her friends spray-paint on your locker again? *Stupid asshole?*"

"*Selfish prick,*" I correct.

"Eh. I've been called worse."

I reach for my glass. "Anyway, I didn't want Cassie catching feelings. And now we're becoming good friends, and honestly, I kind of learned my lesson the last time I hooked up with a friend."

Alana and I haven't even spoken since she ended it. Granted, it hasn't made for any awkward group gatherings, but that's probably because I barely attended any parties this July. I've been too busy with work. Still, the idea of screwing up my friendship with Cassie bums me out. I don't want to lose her. I would miss talking to her.

"But—" I add.

He chuckles. "There's always a *but.*"

"The other night, we kind of had a moment . . ."

"Of course you did. What'd you do? Make out?"

"Nah, it was a phone sex thing." I omit the details, especially the window element of the scenario. He doesn't need to know all that. "But yeah . . . it came up a couple of times that night, the virginity thing, and now I can't stop thinking about it."

"About what? Popping her cherry?"

"Yes," I groan, then slug back nearly half my beer. It's so hard to articulate. I mean, I've watched porn. I'm sure some of that porn featured virgins, but the actual genre—virgin porn—isn't my thing. I prefer experienced women. I like women who know their way around a man's body.

And yet the idea of being the first guy inside of Cassie gets me going something fierce. I wonder if there's an anthropological reason behind it. Some recessive caveman instinct in us, a primal urge backed by science. Except this urge never existed in me before.

Another possibility occurs to me. Maybe it's not the fact she's a virgin that's making me crave her on such a deep level. Maybe it's because she's beautiful and funny and so damn easy to be around.

Maybe I just . . . like her.

Shit.

"I know it's not a good idea, though. It's a lot of pressure. I don't need that kind of pressure, right?"

"Christ, no. You never want to be a woman's first. You're literally going to be someone she remembers for the rest of her life. But what's your legacy gonna be? Best-case scenario, she's got you up on a pedestal because you rocked her world. Likely scenario? She'll be nervous, which'll make *you* nervous, and then you'll fuck it up and ruin the experience for her because you're both so uncomfortable. Either that, or you come too fast because she'll be so tight—" He breaks off abruptly. "Speaking of fast."

Our waitress is back, holding a platter of wings. "Do I even want to know?" Nicole asks politely.

Evan blinks. "Nope."

I offer an innocent smile. "Nothing to see here."

"Why do I get the feeling you're up to no good?" Her narrowed eyes shift between us.

"Who, us? We're choir boys," Evan says. "You know that."

"Yeah, sure." Snorting, she plants his chicken wings in front of him and wanders off.

Evan wastes no time pulling the plate closer and snatching up a sauce-drenched wing.

"So, now that we've discovered you have a deflowering kink," he says between bites. "What are you going to do about it?"

"Nothing," I say glumly.

"Nothing?" he echoes. "Well, that's no fun." He wipes his chin with a napkin, then slides out of the booth. "Be right back. Gotta hit the head."

He's only gone a minute before Nicole returns to check on our booth. She eyes Evan's empty side. "Where's Hartley? He abandon you?"

"Nah, he'll be right back."

"Pity. I'm almost done with my shift." One eyebrow flicks up. "I would've kept you company."

Well. This is interesting. Nicole and I haven't interacted much, but I've seen her around the Bay, and I can't deny I've always enjoyed the view. Tall. Curvy. Pouty lips and shoulder-length dark hair.

"Guess we need a raincheck," I say lightly.

"Yeah? How about Friday?"

"You asking me out, Nic?"

"Something like that. I've seen you around for years." She purses those full, red lips. "Maybe it's time we got to know each other better."

A faint smile tugs on my lips. Yeah. There's no mistaking her intentions. She's not asking me on a date—she's looking to hook up. And the more I think on it, the more I realize it's exactly what I need to clear my head. I haven't gotten laid since I met Cassie.

If I don't find an outlet soon, all that pent-up sexual energy will explode and push me right into Cassie's bed.

So, why not? Indulging in a no-strings hookup is a surefire way to stop myself from corrupting Cassie and blowing up our friendship. I can't keep jerking off before seeing her. That's not a viable long-term solution. Eventually my dick is going to require a lot more than my tired hand.

"I work until seven on Friday," I tell the smirking brunette. "Why don't you come by for a drink around eight? I'm staying at the Jackson place. Housesitting for the summer."

"Really? I pass that house on my dad's boat all the time. I've always wanted to see the inside."

"Is that a yes?"

"It's a yes." She licks her lips. "Sounds like fun."

"Great. See you then."

Evan returns as Nicole's sashaying off and doesn't miss the coy smile she tosses me over her shoulder. "Man, you move fast." He slides back into the booth. "Nic is good people, though."

"Yeah, she's cool." I steal a chicken wing off his plate. "She's coming by on Friday."

"I get it." He nods. "You need the distraction."

He does get it. "Yup."

Despite the plans I made with Nicole, I still have Cassie on the brain when I get home a couple hours later. I park my Jeep in the driveway and enter the house to conduct my usual security check. Everything looks good. Me, though, I'm still on edge. Restless. So after a quick shower, I head downstairs and grab the pack of smokes I stashed in the kitchen, along with a cheap plastic lighter.

I step onto the back deck, where I fish out a cigarette and pop it between my lips. It's nine thirty, and although the sun set not too long ago, the moon is high and shining bright, casting streaks of silver over the calm water of the bay. I flick my gaze toward Cassie's house. The patio light is on, but I don't see anybody out there. I approach the railing that overlooks the dock below and light my smoke. I inhale deeply. Let the nicotine lodge in my lungs until they feel like they're going to explode, and only then do I exhale, watching the thick cloud of smoke float away and dissipate.

I love this town, I truly do. But sometimes it's so damn oppressive. Especially when I look out at the water, when my gaze rests on that strip of land that curves at the very edge of the bay. Because I know beyond it is the open ocean, and every cell in my body cries out for me to go to it. I want to be navigating the ocean using the stars. I want to see new places, meet new people, experience things I know I'll never experience in Avalon Bay. Small towns are familiar. They're a comforting pair of arms that bring you close and keep you safe.

But those same arms hold you back. Keep you locked in place.

I'm feeling too introspective tonight. I should've stayed out with Evan, talked him into another round of beers, a game or two of pool.

I take another drag. Exhale again as I listen to the sounds of the night. Insects humming. Trees rustling. I hear a car drive by. A burst of laughter from the dock several houses down, where it sounds like they're hosting a small gathering. Then, another car engine, this one from the vicinity of the Tanner house. I hear a door shut. A flash of movement crosses my peripheral vision, and I realize the patio wasn't empty, after all. There's a woman on the deck, drinking a glass of wine. It doesn't appear to be Cassie's grandmother. Lydia Tanner has dark hair. This woman has red hair, several shades darker than Cassie's.

I furrow my brow. Is that her mother? I thought Cassie had said her mom wasn't arriving until mid-August.

The back door creaks open and another figure steps outside. The foliage shields her from view, but I recognize Cassie's voice.

"Hey, Mom. I just got back from dinner with Joy. Just wanted to say good night."

Okay, so it is her mother. I wonder when she got in. I've been at the yacht club all weekend, so I haven't paid much attention to the comings and goings next door. That, and I've been diligently avoiding Cassie since window sex.

"That's the outfit you wore to dinner?" her mother inquires.

"Yes. What's wrong with it?" Cassie's tone sounds strange to my ears. Forced, as if she's trying to remain neutral but can't quite master it. "We went to Joe's Beach Bar. Dress code is casual there."

"I thought we talked about the crop tops, Cass."

I crush my cigarette in the ashtray on the railing. Feels wrong eavesdropping. I don't mean to, but it's also hard not to, especially at night when there're no boats on the water. No shrieking children. No birds or seagulls squawking. Only the soft whine of mosquitoes, the occasional cricket, and the very clear voices of Cassie and her mother, who isn't letting up.

"It's really not a flattering look for you, sweetheart."

My body tenses up. Oh, screw that. Cassie looks good in everything. And as I recall, she was wearing a crop top the first time we kissed. I vividly remember the way it hugged her tits.

And now I also remember what she told me about her mother. The way she described the woman. Highly critical. Self-centered. Zero empathy.

Checks out so far.

"I don't know . . . I kind of like them." Cassie's flippant now, but the mere fact that she's defending her fashion choices makes me frown. She doesn't have to justify herself to anyone.

"I just think it's something you should leave to girls like Joy, or

Peyton. Girls with abs, you know?" Her mom gives an airy laugh, as if they're sharing some lighthearted joke. "You need to have a very flat, toned stomach to pull off that kind of top."

My eyebrows soar.

Fuck you. That's what Cassie ought to be saying. I get it, respect your elders, obey your parents and all that. But come on.

"Eh, abs are overrated." I have no clue how Cassie is managing to retain her composure. Somehow her voice remains calm and unruffled, when I suspect that inside she's anything but.

"Sweetie. You know I want you to always look and feel your best. And it's not only about showing the midriff. With your breast size? You need to choose your wardrobe carefully. I understand at your age you want to look sexy, but on your body type, most sexy outfits tend to have the opposite effect. There's looking sexy, and then there's looking like a bimbo."

Cassie remains silent.

"Large breasts are a curse and a blessing. Trust me, I know." Her mom laughs again, as if she hasn't just bullied her daughter to the point of silence. "I think right now you're seeing the curse aspect of it."

Finally, Cassie lets out an awkward laugh. "Well, I mean, it's not like I can get rid of these things, so . . ."

"*I* did it. There's no reason you can't either. We can talk to Dr. Bowers about doing a reduction."

"I don't want a reduction. I've already told you this."

"You said you were scared of the anesthesia, but—"

"It's not only that. I just don't want it."

"Cass—"

"I'm not doing a reduction," Cassie repeats. For the first time since she stepped outside, her tone brooks no argument.

There's a beat. Then her mother, totally unbothered, says, "You look tired. We probably shouldn't be talking about this when you're clearly exhausted. Let's discuss it another time. Why don't you head up to bed?"

"You're right. I *am* exhausted. Bed sounds like a wonderful idea."

"Good night, sweetheart. Love you."

"Love you, too."

After *that* conversation, it's hard to believe there's love on either end. Particularly Cassie's mother. What kind of parent talks like that to their kid? Hypercritical, Cassie said? Try downright cruel.

I'm startled by the torrent of anger that floods my gut. I remain on the deck and pull out another smoke, my fingers shaking when I flick the lighter. I lean into the flame, sucking hard on the cigarette. That dark, angry sensation inside me only heightens, forming a knot of tension between my shoulder blades.

A light turns on. A yellow glow radiating from the second floor of the Tanner house. I tip my head toward it. I don't have a direct view of Cassie's window from down here, but I catch a blur of motion and then a fleeting glimpse of her face. She's scrubbing two fists over her eyes.

Goddamn it. She's crying.

My jaw tightens to the point of pain. I force myself to relax it and take another deep drag.

No.

Fuck that.

I snuff out my cigarette and head next door.

CHAPTER 18

CASSIE

When the window rattles the first time, I assume it's the wind, though I was just outside and it wasn't windy at all. Nonetheless, that's the most logical assumption to reach when you hear your window shaking in its frame. But then it happens again. And again. And I realize I'm not hearing rattling. It's tapping.

God. I do not have the energy for this, whatever *this* is, right now.

Sniffling, I swipe at my wet eyes on my way to the window. I know I'm too old to be crying over my mother's veiled insults, and yet here I am. I think she just caught me off guard tonight.

I jump when a hand appears on the glass. Heart racing, I quickly lift the window open and see Tate's face.

"What the hell are you doing?" I whisper-shout.

He's literally clinging to the lattice like a monkey. And either I'm imagining it, or the delicate crisscross frame is beginning to bend under his weight. Everything about this situation seems extremely unstable.

Tate groans softly. "Can I come in or are you going to let me fall to my death? Because I'm pretty sure this thing is going to give out any second."

"Have you ever heard of a door? More specifically, a front

door? We've got one of those downstairs, and it has this little gizmo on it called a doorbell that you ring and then someone answers and—"

"This is not the time for your babbling, ginger. I'm about to plummet to my death."

Good point.

Sighing, I help him up, and a moment later he tumbles onto my floor. When he's standing, he runs both hands through his tousled blond hair to push it away from his face. He smooths out his T-shirt, which is rumpled from his climb, then fixes the waistband of his gray sweatpants. I notice he's barefoot and hope he didn't scratch his feet going up that lattice.

"To answer your question," he says, visibly frazzled, "I didn't use the front door because I was afraid I'd have to meet your mother, and I'm not her biggest fan right now."

I freeze. "Why do you say that?"

"I was outside having a smoke when you got home and—"

"You *smoke*?" I demand. "How come I didn't know—" I stop myself, because that is not the thing to focus on right now. "You heard us?"

He nods.

Oh God.

My eyes start to sting again. And now I feel like throwing up too, because the hottest guy in the world heard my mother disparage my body, insinuate I'm a slut, and encourage me to get a breast reduction.

I blink rapidly. Mortified.

Tate doesn't miss the way I hastily rub underneath my eyes with the pad of my thumb.

"No," he begs. "Please don't cry again."

Again?

He saw me crying?

I might actually be sick. I take a few breaths, attempting to keep the nausea at bay. My knees go weak, so I sink onto the edge of my bed, but because I'm wearing my bimbo crop top, it creates an inevitable roll in my stomach. Normally I wouldn't care about that—everyone gets it when they sit down—but after my mother's callous assessment of my figure, I'm now feeling extra self-conscious.

I shoot back up. "Look," I start, then trail off. I don't even know what to say. I draw another deep breath and opt for honesty. "I feel like throwing up knowing you heard all that."

His jaw ticks, as if he's clenching and unclenching his teeth. "You realize none of it's true, right? It was all bullshit. I almost stormed over there and gave her a piece of my mind. Does she always talk to you like that?"

"Pretty much. But she tries to disguise it as helpful advice, so most of her criticism falls under the *I just want you to look your best* umbrella." I shrug. "She's called me a lot of things over the years, but a bimbo? That's new. It's also extremely outdated, but I suppose *bimbo* is her generation's *slut*? And I guess I prefer *bimbo* to *slut*. It's more fun to say. Bim-bo."

"Stop it, Cass. It's not a joke."

I crack a half smile. "It is kind of funny."

Tate isn't amused. "Have you told her you don't like it when she says that shit?"

"I used to," I admit. "When I was younger. But it doesn't register. People like her only hear what they want to hear. Like I told you before, I eventually just gave up on . . ."

"Saying how you feel," he finishes, then shakes his head in disapproval. "You should never stop telling people how they make you feel."

"Doesn't make a difference, Tate. She'll never accept she did anything wrong, and she'll never apologize. That's not who my mother is." I smile sadly.

"You don't do it for an apology. You do it for yourself. Because when you don't release those dark emotions, you end up bottling them up. You let them consume you from the inside out until you're running upstairs in tears believing you're unworthy or unattractive or whatever other false ideas she planted in your mind—when in reality, you're the most beautiful woman I've ever fucking met."

My smile falters. "Okay, you're laying it on thick to make me feel better. I appreciate it, but—"

"You are. Christ. Just look at you."

He gestures toward me, his earnest gaze taking in the outfit I'd chosen for my boardwalk dinner with Joy. A wrap skirt, a burnt orange color, that swishes around my knees. The tight black top that shows off my abs-free but still decent (or so I thought) midriff. I left the house believing I looked nice, but now all I hear is my mother's voice in my head talking about girls with perfect abs and how big boobs will only ever look trashy. Never sexy.

"You're goddamn perfect, Cassie."

"Now you're just bullshitting." I start to turn away.

"I'm not." He grabs my hand, tugging me closer. "You didn't know I was listening earlier, right? Well, I could've gone inside and you would've been none the wiser. I didn't have to scale a tower tonight and stumble in through your window just to tell you how hot you look. Why would I do that, or say that, if I didn't mean it?"

Another good point. But . . . I still think he's bullshitting.

He notes my skepticism and chuckles. "Do you really not see what you do to me?"

Despite myself, my gaze lowers to his groin. And yeah, there does appear to be some . . . swelling . . . happening beneath his sweatpants.

The evidence of his arousal, however, only triggers a gust of frustration.

"What the hell!" I burst out.

Confusion creases his forehead. "What?"

"What do you mean, *what*? You're the king of mixed signals, Tate! Do you realize that?" I back away from him, aggravation rising inside me. "You can't do this shit, okay? It fucking confuses me. And it's fucking inconsiderate. And now look at how fucking much I'm swearing because that's how *fucking* frustrated I am with you!"

He takes a step forward. "Cass—"

"No." I whip up my hand to stop him from coming any closer. "You're confusing. And insensitive! First you kiss me—and then you tell me you want to be platonic. Fine. So now we're friends and suddenly you're my wingman, and I feel like, okay, things are moving in a platonic direction—and then you jerk off in front of me! Seriously, Tate. What am I supposed to think here?"

"I know." He releases an equally frustrated groan. He drags both hands though his hair, messing it up even more. "I'm sorry."

"Yes, you should be! I don't get it. If you're attracted to me like you insist you are, then why wouldn't you just agree to be my summer fling when I asked instead of feeding me a bunch of excuses and platitudes?"

His expression grows tortured. "I honestly thought it was the best idea at the time. I was worried I might hurt you if we got involved. That you might want something more. And I don't have a great track record with relationships. I'm sort of just the hookup guy."

"And I wanted a *hookup*! I literally approached the hookup guy for a hookup!" I realize I'm practically shouting at him and force myself to lower my voice.

"I know, but you said so yourself, you don't have a lot of expe-rience in this department. You've never even had sex before. I felt like I'd be taking advantage of your inexperience."

I'm so horrifically embarrassed that my entire face is on fire. I wish I had a cold glass of water to hurl at my cheeks. "My virginity freaks you out *this* much?"

He hesitates. "I'm not freaked out, not really. It's . . . the pressure, you know? Being your first puts a lot of pressure on me to make it good for you. To make it the best you've ever fucking had. Well, I suppose you wouldn't know if it was the best, since you've never done it before, but you know what I mean."

Kill me.

Kill me now.

This time, I all but collapse on the edge of the bed. I don't even care what my stomach does. I bury my face in my hands and moan. "Please leave, Tate. I've had enough humiliation for one night."

"Cassie." I feel the mattress dip under the weight of him. "Come on, look at me."

"No," I mumble into my palms.

"Look at me."

"No."

"Don't you want to know the silver lining here?"

"There is none. We finally found a situation without a hint of lining, silver or otherwise. It's all black. Just big, black thunderclouds."

I twitch when I feel his thumb on the side of my jaw. He gently pries my face out of my hands and cups my chin, forcing me to look at him.

"Let me tell you the silver lining," he says. Gruff and sincere.

"Can't wait to hear it," I grumble. And although he's trying to impose eye contact on me, I keep my gaze downcast. Focusing it on his thumbnail.

"The silver lining is, if I hadn't heard your mother calling you a bimbo and—hey, you're right, it *is* fun to say. Bimbo."

I laugh faintly and accidentally meet his eyes, which are twinkling.

"If she hadn't said that shit, I wouldn't be sitting here right now telling you how beautiful you are."

Despite myself, my pulse speeds up. Because hearing those words spoken in his deep, earnest voice does something to me. Hits me in a different way. Aaron had called me beautiful the other night, but it hadn't elicited this kind of response. Hadn't made my heart flutter or my hands shake so wildly that I have to place them on my knees to keep them still.

"And if I hadn't heard all that shit, I wouldn't be saying: Cassie Soul, I would like to fling you."

My jaw drops. "What? Oh no. No way. I don't need a pity hookup." I peel his fingers off my chin.

He captures my hand and brings it to his groin.

I give a sharp intake of breath at the feel of an unmistakable erection beneath my palm.

"There is zero pity involved here," he says. "Not even a shred of it. Seriously. Feel how hard you make me. I want you so bad it hurts."

"What about my virgin status?" I challenge.

He visibly gulps. "I mean, I won't lie. That part is kind of scary. The pressure—"

"Stop," I order with a choked laugh. "There's no pressure. I promise."

Tate seems unconvinced.

"I mean it. I don't expect rose petals and declarations of love. And I certainly don't expect a commitment. All I want out of this is to have fun. And to gain some experience," I admit, suddenly feeling a bit shy. "I'm heading back to school after Labor Day weekend. I know this won't lead to a relationship, and I'm fine with that. I'm also not naïve enough to think that the first time—or even the first couple of times—is going to be a perfect, magical moment of sexual delights. But." I shrug. "Based on our previous encounters, I suspect we're going to have fun." I eye him. Daring him to contradict that. He doesn't. "So, really, where's the pressure?"

It's only after I conclude my speech that it occurs to me my hand is still on his dick.

Classy.

Noticing where my gaze went, Tate flashes those playful dimples. "Well. This is awkward."

"I don't know about *awkward*." Before I can stop myself, I move my palm in a featherlight caress.

"Stop that. That was only intended to show you how on board I am." With a firm look, he pries my hand away from his crotch. "But I didn't come here for me. I came here for you."

My pulse quickens. "For me," I echo.

"Mmm-hmm." His blue eyes grow serious. "But if we do this, we take it slow. That means . . ." He raises a brow. "No sex. At least not tonight."

"Ugh," I say in mock disgust. "Then why are you even *here*? Jeez."

He lets out a laugh. "Slow," he repeats. "Deal?"

"Slow," I agree, nodding my assurance. I give him an expectant look. "So then what happens tonight?"

"Tonight . . . I want to make you feel good." He licks his lips, and I instinctively lick mine too. "I want to make you feel beautiful."

Our heads move closer, as if drawn together by a magnetic field. Then he kisses me. It's soft and gentle and almost too much of a tease. I make an anguished noise and deepen the kiss, clutching the back of his neck to keep him close. When our tongues meet with a teasing stroke, it's his turn to make noise, a hoarse groan that comes from deep in his chest and vibrates against my lips. *This* is what a passionate kiss is supposed to be like, I realize. You don't need your tongues to do all the heavy lifting. You don't need loud groans and grabby hands. Chemistry. That's all you need.

Despite his muttered objection, my hand seeks out his erection again. "You know what makes me feel beautiful?" I tell him. "*This.* Knowing I did this to you. Knowing you're so turned on you can't even think straight."

"Mission accomplished," he says wryly, then groans when my fingers dip beneath the waistband of his sweatpants.

He's not wearing underwear, and I find him hard and ready for me. I stroke him for a moment, enjoying the way his lips part, the way he breathes a little faster. Then I drop to my knees in front of him. I run my fingers along the heavy length of him. He's rock hard.

"I want you to tell me how good I make you feel."

His eyes are molten. Pure lust. "You mean you can't literally feel it?" He thrusts into my hand.

My thumb finds a streak of moisture at his tip and glides over it before my fingers curl around him again. When I stroke him, firmer this time, his expression burns hotter, a flash of pleasure bordering on pain. He wants me so bad it hurts, he said. I don't think he was kidding.

He continues gazing down at me as if I'm the most beautiful creature he's ever seen. It does wonders for my ego. Melts away that horrible lump of inadequacy that was jammed in my throat before.

When I bring my lips to his tip and place a soft kiss on it, his entire body jerks. "Tease," he growls.

Smiling, I plant another kiss on him, then swirl my tongue around the crown of his cock. Teasing again. His exhalations get heavier. Eyelids are heavy too. I peer up at him, loving the sight of his features stretched taut with need. How he looks like he's having trouble performing even the most basic task, like breathing.

My gaze locked with his, I take him fully into my mouth.

"Jesus," he swears, and I get a thrill knowing I'm responsible for the desperate groan that flies out of his mouth.

It's such a sexy sound that I proceed to do everything in my power to hear it again, to keep drawing those groans from his lips. I suck him deep, using my hand and tongue to drive him wild.

"Feels so good," he mumbles. Yet at the same time, he's suddenly trying to ease away from my hungry mouth. "I didn't come here for this."

I release him. "Well, this is what you're getting, so are we really going to complain about a blowjob, Gate?"

Tate shudders out a laugh. "I told you, that is not becoming a thing—" He halts when I take him in my mouth again. "Holy *hell*." A tortured moan escapes his throat. "I love this, I really do. I, ah—" Another moan. "I never want you to stop, but—ah, hell, that's good." He thrusts deeper. "But I want us to come together."

My nipples tighten at the lewd suggestion.

"Like, I'm right here. And you're right here. And I need you on me." He's basically fucking my mouth now, his hips moving in a restless, impatient rhythm as his long fingers tangle in my hair. "I need to touch you and see your face and hear that noise you make when you're getting close."

"What noise?" I lift my mouth off him, breathing hard.

"I can't describe it. It's just hot. Please," he begs.

I give him what he wants. Hell, what we *both* want. Because as fun as it is to tease him, my entire body is screaming for release. I climb onto the bed and we fall back on the mattress, his mouth instantly finding mine in a ravenous kiss. His hand fumbles to get under my skirt, where he pushes aside the crotch of my panties. I'm wet and ready, and he uses that wetness to stroke my clit, to drag a finger up and down my slit.

"Put your hand on me again," he whispers.

"Wait, I have an idea," I say.

He grunts in complaint when I roll over, but I'm not going far. Just reaching for the hand lotion I'd left out on the nightstand earlier. I squirt some on my palm and roll back toward him. That first smooth, wet glide of my fist along his shaft makes his eyes glaze over.

"Ah. Keep doing that."

I grin. "Good?"

"So good. Don't stop." His hips start rocking as he thrusts into my hand.

He props himself on his elbow and lifts my shirt, hurriedly undoing the front clasp. Then his mouth latches around one beaded nipple, while his fingers return between my thighs, rubbing, teasing, stroking my clit to bring me closer and closer to the edge.

When he pushes one finger inside me, his startled curse heats the air between us. "This is the tightest pussy I've ever fucking felt." He's practically moaning the words.

My breathing becomes labored as I strain against his skilled touch. "I'm getting close. Are you?"

"I was close before you even took off my pants." He raises his mouth from my breast to grin at me. "Just say when."

"Kiss me," I plead.

He does, and the moment our tongues meet, the orgasm breaks through the surface. My inner muscles clamp around his finger, and Tate groans and spills into my hand. We're both panting, hips moving as we lose ourselves in our respective bliss.

When my eyelids finally open, Tate is watching me. Pleased. "You made that noise." He sighs happily. "It's my favorite noise."

Our foreheads rest together, slightly damp with sweat.

"That was really good," I mumble with a satisfied sigh of my own. I try to nestle closer and realize my range of motion is constricted because my top is tangled around my collarbone. With a giggle, I attempt to free myself. "I'm stuck."

"Damn, ginger. You needed it so bad you forgot to take your clothes off?" Chuckling, he leans in to brush his lips over mine. "You're such a bimbo."

This time a whole slew of giggles shudders through me. "Shut up, Gate."

CHAPTER 19

CASSIE

I want my mother to go back to Boston. No, even better—let her go south. I want her to drive all the way down to Florida, find her way to Cape Canaveral, board a rocket ship, get launched into outer space, and make a new life for herself on a distant planet somewhere.

Ugh. All right. Maybe I'm being overdramatic.

Actually, no. You know what? I'm being a perfectly reasonable amount of dramatic.

Since she got here, Mom has been utterly insufferable. And maybe if she were behaving poorly toward only me, I'd have an easier time letting it slide off my shoulders. But she's been bitchier than usual to my grandmother, and that makes me see red. It's inexcusable and Grandma doesn't deserve it. Besides that, it's quite repulsive watching a woman in her forties act like a spoiled brat, which is what Mom is doing when I enter the kitchen for breakfast.

"Mother!" she snaps. "You *have* to give a speech. I'm not letting this go."

"It's no longer our establishment, Victoria. The new owner is the one who should deliver the speech."

"The new owner is a *child*," Mom retorts, lifting her nose up. "And she made the offer. She asked you to do it."

"And I declined."

"Mother."

"Victoria." Grandma's looking increasingly annoyed. "I already declined the offer. The subject is closed."

"This makes our family look bad." Mom, as usual, refuses to drop it. "The Tanners built the Beacon, and a Tanner should be the one to speak at the reopening. Say a proper goodbye. If we say nothing, it looks like we're just handing it over."

"We sold it, dear." Grandma gives her a pointed look. "Primarily because neither you nor your siblings wanted to take on the responsibility of renovating it. So, please, let the new owner reap the rewards of her efforts and enjoy her moment in the sun. I had nothing to do with this reopening and I wouldn't feel comfortable taking any credit for it."

I hide a smile. *Go, Grandma.*

"Good morning, dear." Grandma catches sight of me in the doorway. "Adelaide stopped by the bakery in town this morning and picked up some fresh croissants and pastries."

"Oh, nice." I feel my mother's eyes on me as I go to the counter to assess the goodies our housekeeper brought.

"Just take one," Mom warns. "We have a dress fitting today and you don't want to be bloated for it."

I resist the urge to roll my eyes. "I'll try my best not to eat this entire platter."

Grandma chuckles.

"You slept in," my mother says.

I don't miss her frown of reproach. Awesome. Now my sleeping habits are an issue. I genuinely can't do anything right in her eyes. Well, unless we're in public together. Then suddenly I'm the most wonderful, accomplished, thoughtful daughter in the world. That's the image Mom needs to project. That we're best friends. That my achievements, few as they are at this current time in my life, are all a credit to *her*.

"I had a late night." I duck my head and hope they don't notice my blush, aka the curse of the red hair.

Tate snuck into my bedroom again last night. We hooked up again, and it was better than the first time.

And the second time.

And the third, fourth, fifth . . .

I've seen him every night this week.

Last night, though, was one for the books. He went down on me for almost an hour, his mouth voracious, one hand squeezing and kneading my breasts while the other pushed two fingers inside me. I was biting my lip to stop from being too loud. Tate is very good at what he does.

Truthfully, his breadth of experience is overwhelming sometimes. He's so comfortable, not just with his own body, but mine. There's no hesitation when he touches me, only the confident hands of a man who knows what he's doing.

The one thing he refuses to do, however, is freaking *have sex with me*.

What? Who's bitter?

Okay, fine. I'm not actually bitter. I'm impatient. Tate keeps reminding me we're taking it slow, but part of me wonders if he's still too scared to be my first. Not just because of the supposed pressure, but for what it may mean for us. Peyton concurred with that suspicion when we texted about it earlier. She said men are terrified women will immediately expect promise rings and *I love you*s once they lose it to a guy. I told Tate I wasn't expecting a relationship out of this, but I have a feeling he doesn't trust that.

"Yes. It did sound like a late night for you." Grandma's voice interrupts my thoughts. "I heard you talking long past midnight. You had a friend over?" she prompts, looking like she's fighting a smile.

Shit. I thought we were being quiet, but evidently not.

"No, I didn't have anyone over," I lie. And there's no way Grandma could've seen him last night, since Tate still insists on climbing through the window when he comes over, claiming he doesn't want to bump into my family. I think he just enjoys the sneaky element to it. The excitement. What I'm learning about Tate, the more time I spend with him, is how much he loves leaning into his playful nature.

"I was just watching a movie," I add. "I didn't realize I had the volume on so loud. I'm sorry if it woke you."

Her eyes sparkle. I know she knows I'm lying. "My mistake. Well, then you really ought to lower that volume, dear."

Mom, of course, believes my lies. "Of course she didn't have anyone over, Mother. So late at night?"

In Mom's mind, there's no way her daughter could possibly have a guy over. Which is ironic since supposedly I look like a bimbo, soooo, apropos to *her* logic, there should be a line outside my bedroom door.

I grab a plate and a croissant, then reach for the butter. I expect a comment from Mom about going easy on the butter, but it doesn't come. She's busy checking her phone now.

I join them at the table, my own phone coming to life the moment I sit down. I peer at it, anticipation dancing through me when I notice the email subject line.

"Ahh! The printer sent me the digital proof!" I tell Grandma.

Mom looks up and asks, "What proof?" at which point I remember I hadn't told her about my foray into the world of children's book authorship. Wasn't planning on it, either.

But it's too late now.

"Oh, it's no big deal," I say, downplaying the project. "I put together a little illustrated book for Roxanne and Monique. You know, for their birthday." I shrug. "It's cute. I wrote the story, and asked Robb to do the illustrations—"

Shit.

What the hell is wrong with me? I'm two for two now with boneheaded slipups.

"Robb?" Mom is visibly displeased. "Robb Sheffield?"

"Yeah." I tear a piece off my croissant and shove it into my mouth. Maybe if I'm chewing she'll stop questioning me.

"I didn't realize you two kept in touch."

"Oh. Yes. Here and there."

"Here and there," she echoes.

"Uh-huh." I chew extra slowly. "We exchange the occasional message on social media, just to say what's up."

Her lips flatten as she picks up her coffee cup. "You know how I feel about that, Cassie."

Well, too frickin' bad. You can't give me a stepbrother for five years and then expect me to never speak to him again just because you got another divorce.

I don't say that out loud.

Honestly, though, I genuinely liked the man Mom remarried. Stuart Sheffield. Filthy rich, of course. I mean, with a name like that, of course he's wealthy. Stu was more serious than my dad, stricter as well, but he was kind. Sucks that he fell for my mother's Ms. Congeniality act, but I don't blame him for that. She's very skilled at charming people. And seeing as how the world revolves around her, the moment she decided Stu and Robb didn't exist, I was expected to follow suit.

"It's not a big deal," I repeat. "Not like Robb and I are vacationing together in the Hamptons. I just asked him to do a few drawings for me."

"And what's this, you're writing a children's book now?" She sounds irritated. "That's what my big, fancy college tuition check is going toward?"

"It's just a birthday present. The twins love the bedtime stories I make up for them. Dad suggested I put one in a book."

"Of course he did."

I grit my teeth, then force myself to release the tension in my jaw.

It tightens right back up when Mom coolly inquires, "And what is your father's nurse planning for the birthday celebrations?"

"Victoria," my grandmother snaps.

"What?" She flicks up an eyebrow.

"I thought I instilled better manners in you than that."

"Seriously, Mother? You're siding with Clayton's trophy wife?"

I swallow a laugh, because Nia is the furthest thing from a trophy wife. Nia doesn't care about image, about money, about clothes, about status. She's everything that my mother isn't.

"There's a party for the twins during the day," I say, ignoring the jab about Nia. "All their friends will be there. And afterward we're having dinner, just the five of us." Then, since I anticipate a bitchy comment about being left out of her own daughter's momentous twenty-first birthday, I add, "You and I are still going to Charleston that weekend, right? Spending all of Sunday there? I'm so excited for that."

Making it about her has the desired effect. She smiles warmly. "I'm looking forward to it too." She rises from her chair. "Anyway. We have the fitting in an hour, and I'd like to get there a bit early. Will you be ready to leave after you eat?"

"Yup."

"Okay, great. I need to make a phone call before we go." She saunters out of the kitchen.

I don't know why, but I have a feeling she's off to call my

former stepfather to gripe about the fact that their kids are still in contact.

And speaking of that . . . I quickly click on the email and open the attachment.

"Let me see too," Grandma urges, so I drag my chair closer to hers and together we *ooh* and *aah* over the final product. "Oh, Cassie, you did a tremendous job."

"It was a team effort." I'm not being humble—it really had been. I wrote the story. Robb did the drawings. And Peyton, who works for a graphic design firm in Boston, put together the layout that I sent to the printer.

I pinch the screen to zoom in on an illustration. Robb's creative interpretation of Kit the dragon is remarkable. Somehow, he found the perfect balance between scary and cutesy. He brought Kit to life.

"He is so talented," I marvel. "They look like real characters, don't they?"

"They are real characters. You created them, dear."

"I know, but now I can *see* them. This is so cool." I feel myself beaming.

"There's that smile." Grandma leans over and tucks a strand of hair behind my ear. "Cassandra . . ." Her voice softens. "I know your mother is . . . difficult. To say the least. I hope you don't hold some of the things she says too close to your heart. And I want you to know that I'm proud of you. I'm proud of the woman you're becoming and I think you are absolutely wonderful."

I blink back tears. I didn't know it, but that's exactly what I needed to hear this morning.

CHAPTER 20

TATE

"That was incredible!" Riley exclaims. The teenager's face is flushed with excitement as he helps me tie off the line. We just got back from a double-handed sail on the practice dinghy. It was windier than anticipated today, so we caught some major speed. Also ended up in the bay more times than I would've liked, but you've got to be prepared for that in competitive racing. That's why I love it so much. Always guaranteed a wild ride.

"I can't believe how fast we were going," the kid gushes.

"That was awesome," I agree, hopping onto the pier.

"When can we take the Optimist out?"

I snicker. "Yeah, hold your horses, kid. Not until you have a few more lessons under your belt." The boat we used today is far easier to handle. She's stable and basically unsinkable, whereas the Optimist dinghy capsizes easily.

"It's hard to right the Optimist," I remind him.

Riley's quick to protest. "I can handle it."

I study him for a moment. He looks back hopefully, shoving his blond shoulder-length surfer-boy hair behind his ear.

I shake my head. "No. You can't. Not yet. But soon."

"I'm telling Evan," he threatens with an evil grin. "I'll turn on the waterworks and cry about how sad I am that my Big Brother's best friend is depriving me of my dream of racing on an Optimist."

I respond with a loud snort. The kid's got balls, I'll give him that. Riley is the product of the soul-searching journey of reformation Evan decided to embark on a while ago. In other words, Evan needed to prove to Genevieve he was willing to stop being a boozing, brawling jackass and grow the fuck up. One way he did that was by enrolling in the local Big Brother program. He totally lucked out with Riley, who's a great kid.

"All right," I tell him. "Next lesson, we'll practice positioning at different angles, teach you some racing tactics. There're a couple different strategies you can use when rounding marks. And the next race you enter, don't partner with Evan. He's lousy."

Riley hoots. "No shit."

"If you're doing a double-handed race and need a partner, hit me up. I mean it—drop the zero and get with the hero." I wink at him.

I don't offer myself up like that to just anyone, but I like Riley. I like his enthusiasm. A lot of these kids who take dinghy lessons just want to go fast on the water. They don't want to think too deeply about the ins and outs of sailing. But Riley's different. He's thirsty for knowledge.

I clap him on the back. My favorite part of this job is working with the kids. The teens. Adults are fun too, but their eyes don't light up the same way.

"I'll see you next week."

"Cool. Later, Tate."

He dashes off, and I head back in the direction from which we came to double-check the boat is securely moored, as the wind's still blowing hard. Sometimes it sucks working on other people's boats; I'm always scared I'll fuck something up and be on the hook for it.

In the yacht club's employee quarters, I strip out of my damp uniform and change into my street clothes. A few minutes later, I cross the parking lot toward my Jeep, checking my phone while I walk. I find a couple messages from the twins. And one from Cassie.

> Cassie: *You, me, a bed covered in rose petals, and my virginity on a silver platter?*

I bust out laughing. I swear, this chick . . . Since the night we agreed to the fling, she's been persistently trying to get me to bang her.

> Me: *No.*

She instantly replies.

> Cassie: *You're mean.*
> Me: *Just taking it slow. Window time later?*
> Cassie: *Can't. You took too long to reply to my message, so I made plans with Joy. We're going to see a band at the Rip Tide. It'll probably be past your bedtime when I'm back.*
> Me: *Text me anyway. Maybe I'll still be up.*
> Cassie: *Only if you take the V-card.*
> Me: *Anyone ever tell you you've got a one-track mind, ginger?*
> Cassie: *Anyone ever tell you you're a tease?*
> Me: *Who's teasing? I'm pretty sure I made you come twice last night.*
> Cassie: *I was faking it, Gate.*

I grin at the phone and toss it on the passenger seat, then start the car. I can't believe I'm the one depriving someone of sex. Me, of all people. But despite Cassie's insistence that we don't need to make a big deal out of it, I feel like I should do something for her first time. Something special. Maybe not rose petals, but certainly not a quick bang while her family is right down the hall. That just feels wrong. It's all I would've been able to offer her this week, though. I've had early mornings, a packed sailing schedule, and late shifts at the dealership. Which means I'm always exhausted by the time I scale her wall and tumble through her window for an hour or so of mutual orgasms. Exhaustion is not conducive to good sex, and since I'm determined to make sure her first time is beyond good, I've been trying to stall her until the weekend.

Unbeknownst to Cassie, I took Saturday off. I'm planning to take her out on the water for the day. Anchor at my favorite cove. Spend the night . . .

My heart beats faster, and my palms suddenly feel slick around the steering wheel. Jeez. You'd think *I* was the virgin here.

At the Jackson house, I start prepping dinner. I throw a couple baked potatoes in the oven, then pop outside to turn on the barbecue. I'm doing shrimp skewers on the grill tonight. It's too bad Cassie's out with Joy. Would've been nice to cook dinner for her.

I falter, wondering where *that* thought came from. Cook dinner for her? I'm pretty sure I've never made dinner for a woman other than my mother. I force myself not to overthink it, though.

While the barbecue's heating up, I head to the dock to ensure the boats are secure because it's still so windy out. Then I walk back up to the house, reaching it just as Cassie's mother appears around the side of their house. She's clad in a long summer dress with sunglasses atop her head.

"Hi." I lift my hand in a wave. Honestly, I'm surprised it's taken this long for our paths to cross. It's been days since she arrived in town, but it seems she spends most of her time inside the house. Or shopping in Charleston, according to Cassie.

She startles at the sight of me. Eyes widening.

"Sorry, I didn't mean to scare you," I call out. "I'm Tate. I'm housesitting for the Jacksons. And I'm friends with your daughter."

Cassie's mom still hasn't spoken. Just keeps staring at me. I note the resemblance between her and Cassie, in their wide-set brown eyes and red hair, but while Cassie has a rounder face, her mother's is narrower, giving off a different vibe. Colder. Or maybe that's her personality.

She shakes herself out of her surprise and offers a smile far warmer than I expect. "Oh hello. I'm sorry. I was in my head. I'm Victoria." She stretches out an arm. "You can call me Tori."

I stride forward to shake her hand. "Nice to meet you."

"How long are you housesitting for?" Tori asks, her appreciative gaze still fixed on me.

Yeah. She's totally checking me out. Which is awkward as fuck, considering I'm hooking up with her daughter. "Gil and Shirley return Labor Day weekend, so I still have another month here."

"Lucky you."

"Yeah, it's not a bad gig," I admit. "It's my fourth summer doing it. I look forward to it every year now."

The Jacksons don't pay me much while I'm here— I'm responsible for my own food, gas, all the usual expenses—but I don't do it for the money. It's worth it to get out of my parents' house for a couple months. Living at home at the age of twenty-three cramps my style sometimes, but at the moment it's convenient, allowing me to save more money. Save up enough and eventually I can finance a boat that I'll probably call home.

"Anyway, I've got dinner going, so I need to check on it. Have a good evening, Mrs. Tanner."

"Tori," she corrects.

"Tori," I repeat clumsily.

She smiles. "It was nice to meet you, Tate. Don't be a stranger."

Inside, I find a missed call from Gil Jackson. Frowning, I quickly do the math, then realize it's not a cause for concern. With the time difference, he's sixteen hours ahead of me, making it 9 A.M. in Auckland.

I check on the baked potatoes, then return Gil's call.

"Hey, Gil," I say after he picks up. "Sorry I missed your call. I was outside chatting with the neighbor."

"Oh, how is Lydia?"

"She's good. But I was talking to her daughter. Tori?"

"You mean Victoria Tanner?" he asks in amusement.

"She said to call her Tori."

His laughter, a deep baritone, sounds in my ear. "Oh boy. I think someone has a crush on you," Gil jokes.

"No," I groan. "Don't even kid about that. Anyway, what's up? Everything okay?"

"Everything's great here. I wanted to check in and see how things are going on your end, discuss a couple matters. We haven't touched base in a few days."

"All good here too," I assure him. "I was just down at the dock securing the boats. The wind was really gusting on the bay today, and it's supposed to storm tonight."

"Thank you. Have you taken the Lightning out yet?"

My dick actually twitches. "What? Oh. No. I haven't even touched her."

"Are you crazy? Take her out for a ride!"

"Are you sure?" I gulp. "I mean, she's super expensive." Alarmingly expensive. The idea of anything happening to her makes me nauseous.

"Tate. Son. You can handle a boat better than anyone I know. Take her out. Enjoy yourself. I promise you, it's a thrill like nothing you've ever experienced."

I don't doubt it.

"In fact," he says, "your sailing expertise is the other reason I called."

I crinkle my forehead. "How's that?"

"Shirley and I just closed on a house down here."

"You did? Congratulations." My brain is scrambling to connect those two dots. What my sailing ability has to do with them purchasing a house in New Zealand. "Are you leaving the Bay?"

"No, no, but we will be splitting our time going forward. Half the year in Auckland, the other half in Avalon Bay. Shirley loves it down here, and the house we found is breathtaking. It's on a bluff overlooking the ocean. Just magnificent. We want to do some sailing while we're here. Cross the Tasman to Australia, explore the Gold Coast, see the Great Barrier Reef. Which means I need someone to bring the *Surely Perfect* over."

I'm startled. My gaze immediately travels beyond the French doors to the sailboat at the dock before I remember she's not the boat in question. The *Surely Perfect* is at the yacht club. And he wants someone to sail her?

"Bring her over?" I echo. "You mean to New Zealand?"

"Yes. Gotta hire someone to sail her. Shirley and I were discussing it last night, and she says, why not Tate, he has his captain's license. And I thought about it and realized, yes, why not? That boy could handle a solo voyage in his sleep."

I feel winded. I flop onto a kitchen stool, shrimp skewers forgotten on the counter. "I don't know about *in my sleep*," I say slowly. "But . . . yeah, I could probably manage it. How long would a journey like that take?" I'm playing it cool, but this would be a massive undertaking.

"It's a long way, no doubt. You'd be leaving from the Port of Miami, and according to the folks I consulted, if you're averaging eight to ten knots and the weather permits, you could do it in two months—I would help you chart out a course that makes the most sense for you. The wife and I are returning to the Bay next month and we'll be here through the holidays. Planning to return to Auckland in January," Gil continues, "which means we'd need her down here by New Year's. So, realistically, you could set sail in September if you wanted. Take three months. Four, even. It's entirely up to you."

I shake my head, dazed. "Are you serious right now?" I demand.

He laughs. "Quite serious. And, of course, you'll be paid accordingly." He proceeds to name a sum that makes my head spin. It's enough to put a down payment on a sailboat of my own. Not a Hallberg-Rassy, but definitely something higher end.

"You'll also have a credit card for expenses, so if you need to restock any supplies when you make port, it'll all be covered. Your only concern will be getting our girl from point A to point B."

"Can I think about it?" Obviously, I want nothing more than to shout out *yes*! But I can't just drop my entire life and sail to New Zealand. I have a job, responsibilities. Especially to my family. I hate letting Dad down. And I literally just agreed to run the dealership alone so my parents can take September off.

"Take your time," Gil says. "You can let me know the weekend we get back. If it's a no, that still leaves us plenty of time to hire somebody else. There's a company we can use that hooks you up with a captain. But we'd prefer to see you do it. I know you've always wanted to do a major crossing, and, selfishly, I'd rather pay someone I like and trust than a complete stranger."

"Wow. Thank you, Gil. I mean it. I really appreciate the opportunity."

"Of course, son. And don't forget to take the Lightning out for a spin." He chuckles. "You'll thank me for it later."

CHAPTER 21

CASSIE

Aaron: *Hey stranger.*

I stare at the screen, my stomach dropping. I'm parked in front of the post office and was about to get out of the Rover when his message came in. Aaron's been trying to get together all week. I keep turning him down, claiming to be busy with my mother. Which isn't exactly a lie; since she got in, she's monopolized all my time. Still, I can't deny it's been a relief to have a legitimate excuse to avoid hanging out with him. The moment Tate and I started hooking up, I all but forgot about Aaron. That makes me kind of a jerk, I know that. It's just so difficult to tell him I'm no longer interested.

But I also can't keep putting him off. He's going back to New York next week. I don't want him spending his last week sitting around waiting for me.

Unsure how best to phrase it, I text Peyton instead.

Me: *I need to tell Aaron I don't want to see him anymore, but I need to say it in a nice way. Suggestions?*

She must be right by her phone because her response is instantaneous. Or rather, her respons*es*. As usual, six messages pop up in quick succession.

> Peyton: *All right, this is what I always say:*
> Peyton: *Hey! I've had so much fun hanging out with you, but I kind of see this as more of a friendship thing.*
> Peyton: *I'm not really feeling a romantic spark.*
> Peyton: *You're so awesome, and I know you're going to find someone you totally click with.*
> Peyton: *I just don't think it's me.*
> Me: *Wow. Not bad. Thanks!*

I do a bit of tweaking, copy and paste, then take a deep breath and hit send. Instantly, I get that weak feeling in my stomach and my heart starts pounding. The idea of an impending confrontation makes me queasy, but at the same time I experience a pang of pride. I may not be able to tell Aaron he's a terrible kisser, or tell my mother how much I hate her sometimes, but at least I was able to accomplish this one teeny, tiny thing. There's the silver lining, I guess.

I try to focus on that feeling of pride, but the nervous energy doesn't abate. It continues to wreak havoc on my gut as I approach the pickup counter at the post office.

"Hi," I greet the elderly clerk. "I need to pick up a package for Cassie Soul? I got a notice on my door saying they dropped it off here because nobody was home to sign." I hand him the notice.

"Let me go check." The gray-haired man shuffles into the back room.

While I wait, my phone buzzes in my hand. Aaron's name appears on the lock screen. The nausea returns. All I can see from the notification preview is: *Thanks for being honest. I really—*

Then it cuts off.

Oh God. *I really* what? Optimism eludes me as my brain fills in the blanks with all the worst-case scenarios.

I really hate you.

I really think you're a bitch.

I really hate that you wasted my time.

I click the notification.

Aaron: *Thanks for being honest. I really appreciate it. So many people just ghost these days. Thanks for being so cool.*

Relief flitters through me. Wow. Okay. That went way better than expected.

Me: *Thanks for understanding. You're really cool too.*

Aaron: *Enjoy the rest of your summer, Cassie.*

Me: *You too.*

Just like that, I handled the confrontation with such ease I almost want to call Tate and brag. Then I realize how weird that would be, considering I haven't brought up Aaron since Tate and I got together. And I don't want him to think I'm still seeing other guys.

"Here you are!" The postal clerk returns with a thin cardboard box. "Sign here, please."

My entire body vibrates with excitement as I get back into the car, where I tear open the package. I reach inside. The next thing I know, I'm holding the physical manifestation of *Kit 'n McKenna*. It's a hardcover, the front image featuring the titular characters, and it looks and feels incredible. Even more astonishing is the byline at the top.

WRITTEN BY CASSANDRA SOUL

At the bottom is a second listing:

ILLUSTRATED BY ROBB SHEFFIELD

Squealing out loud, I quickly snap a picture and text it to my former stepbrother.

Me: *LOOK!!!!*
Robb: *Holy shit!*
Me: *I had a second copy printed and shipped to the penthouse. You should receive it end of day tomorrow.*
Robb: *This is so cool. Thanks for including me. Imagine this takes off??*
Me: *What do you mean? We're not actually selling it lol*
Robb: *Why the hell not?*
Me: *It's just a present for my sisters.*
Robb: *Umm . . . Okay, we need to get on a call to discuss it. This could be a missed opportunity, Cass.*
Robb: *I'm away this weekend, heading to the Montauk house, but how about Monday? You free to chat?*
Me: *Sure. Sounds good.*

My head is spinning like a carousel now. I didn't plan on selling this book at all. Dad made that throwaway comment about self-publishing or submitting it to a publisher, but I'd brushed it off. Becoming a children's book author was never at the top of my career choice list. But now I've got a hardback copy of *Kit 'n McKenna* in my hands, and it looks *real*. Sharp, professional. This printer did an exceptional job. The pages are glossy, and the interior illustrations are gorgeous. As I flip through and read lines from the story, I find myself grinning like a silly schoolgirl. This is good. It's really, really good.

So why not? Why not try to make something happen? Turn this project into something other children can enjoy, not just my sisters. I suppose next weekend's birthday unveiling will be the real test. If Roxy and Mo love the book, that bodes well for the prospective success of this venture.

My phone buzzes again while I'm reading.

Joy: *Is that you sitting in the Range Rover giggling to yourself like an escaped mental patient?*

I look up and spot her by the smoothie shop. She gives a nonchalant wave.

Rolling my eyes, I hop out of the Rover and dart over to my friend. "Check this out!" I shove the hardcover into her hand.

"Oooh!" Her eyes light up. "This is amazing!"

"Do you think the girls will like it?" I ask anxiously.

"Are you kidding? They're going to love it. I think a lot of kids would love it, actually." She flips through it, then stops on one page in particular. She giggles and twists it around to show me the visual of McKenna trying to jam her secret dragon into a too-small cupboard. In the next panel, the doors bust open and Kit bursts out in a flurry of purple scales. "This is great. I would read this to my little cousins."

"Robb wants to talk about publishing it properly—"

"Do it!" Joy says immediately.

I bite my lip as tiny ripples of excitement dance in my stomach. "I'll have to think about it."

"What's there to think about?"

"A lot. I'm about to start senior year of college. I don't have time to think about publishing children's books on the side." I shrug. "Anyway, what are you up to now? Want to grab lunch?"

"This is lunch." She holds up her gross-looking green juice. "But

I'll come and watch you eat." She waggles her eyebrows. "Sounds hot."

I snicker. "That's something Tate would say." I tuck the book under my arm and nod at the smoothie place. "I'll just grab a smoothie too. Treat me? I left my purse in the car."

"Jeez. So demanding."

We go in, and a moment later we're at the end of the counter, waiting for my order to be prepared.

"Did you see Tate when you got back last night?" she asks.

"Yes," I answer, thinking about the brief encounter. Joy and I left the Rip Tide around midnight, and despite needing to wake up early, Tate still snuck in through my window . . . to kiss me good night. Yup, just a kiss. I swear, he's the biggest tease I've ever met.

"I can't believe you still haven't been fully naked together," Joy says, marveling over what I told her last night at the show.

"It's weird, right? It's like he thinks if we have all our clothes off, his penis will accidently fall into my vagina."

She hoots. "Maybe he's a virgin too."

"Definitely not. Honestly, I think he's scared to deflower me. He's moving at a snail's pace. It's maddening."

"Then let's give him a nudge."

"What kind of nudge?"

"Um. Seduce the guy, Cass."

"How?"

"What do you mean, how?" She looks amused by my total lack of seduction proficiency. "There are *so* many options."

"Name one," I challenge. "Because it sounds like you don't actually know—"

"Sneak into his house and be naked in his bed when he comes back from work." Joy offers a self-satisfied smile. "There. That's one suggestion."

"I can't sneak into the house," I protest. I step up to the counter to take my banana-strawberry smoothie, courtesy of the teenage employee who just placed it on the counter. "There's an alarm."

"Really, that's what you're focused on?" she says as we step back onto the sidewalk. "You can find ways around it. Text him and say, *hey, where's your spare key? I need to pop over to your place to borrow some sugar.*" She tilts her head. "That's a neighbor thing, right? They always need sugar."

I snort. "Okay, I'll play. So I text him, tell him I need something from his house. And then?"

"You get naked. You lie on his bed. Instead of flowers, you cover yourself in a sea of condoms—"

"Oh my God." I start to laugh. "No."

"Fine, no condom décor. But I stand by the rest. Trust me, if he walks into his bedroom and finds you lying there naked? He won't be resisting you anymore."

I mull over the idea. Honestly, it does sound kind of hot. Exciting. And it'll be hot and exciting even if we don't end up having sex.

"I don't know if I can be naked," I admit, lifting my straw to my lips. I take a long sip of fruity goodness. "But maybe lingerie?"

"*Yes!* Even better! We need something positively slutty! Okay. Go get your purse." Joy has snapped into dictator mode. "We're going shopping."

* * *

Later that night, Grandma and Mom embark on a rare outing together, heading to Charleston for dinner. I think it was Grandma's idea, her attempt at giving me a reprieve.

Mom's been on my case all week, roping me into numerous shopping excursions, painful lunches, and constant criticism.

Mostly directed at my fashion choices, but she's also been throwing in complaints about Dad, Nia, and my friendship with Robb, just to keep me on my toes. The main reason she's bent out of shape, though, is because I refused to go along with her dress suggestion for the Beacon's reopening. I vetoed the floor-length gold gown on sight, which, in hindsight, may have been a mistake seeing as how it led to several more shopping trips to find another dress.

With my family gone the house is completely empty, so there's no reason Tate can't come over here, but the idea of him finding me in his own bed is a lot more appealing. More of a sexy shock for him. He's done working at seven today. He had to stay late so his dad could train him in some payroll matters, but said he'd be home by seven thirty. I told him I'd cook him dinner.

What he doesn't know is that we're having dessert first.

Me: *Hey. What's the keypad code to get in through your back door? I need to steal some spices. Can you believe we ran out of both salt and red pepper?*

Tate: *If I tell you the code, you can never share it with anyone.*

Me: *Of course not. I was only planning to post it on Twitter, not any of my other social media accounts. Keep it exclusive, you know?*

Tate: *Perfect. 25591. I'm on my way home now. Grabbing a quick shower and then I'll head over to you.*

Excellent.

I'm all ready to go. I shaved my entire body, so it's smoother and softer than a baby's bottom. I chose the color white for the lacy bra and matching thong I picked up in town earlier. According to the saleswoman, the official shade of it is honest-to-God called *virginal white*. Once I heard that, I would've bought the lingerie set for the comedy appeal alone. Thankfully, I look great in white. When I stepped out of the dressing room, Joy and the saleswoman assured me no man would be able to keep his hands off me.

There's really only one man I care about tonight.

I give my reflection one last inspection in the hall mirror. I've straightened my hair and am wearing it loose. No makeup, save for some lip gloss and light mascara. Definitely no blush, because I'll be doing that naturally anyway. It's my cross to bear. I don't even keep blush in my makeup case.

Since I can't strut next door in my underwear, I throw a loose tank dress over my head and slip my feet into a pair of flip-flops. I walk the path at the side of our houses toward the Jacksons' back deck, where I punch in the code on the door, and the lock releases.

Tate's been keeping the place super clean. I like that. I head for the wide spiral staircase in the front hall that's painted a nautical blue and features white wainscoting. At the top of the stairs, I get an idea. I dart back to the hall and kick one flip-flop off, leaving it on the hardwood floor. I leave the other flip-flop on the first step. My dress halfway up the stairs. Grinning at the little trail I've created, I head for the guest room where Tate's been staying.

His bed is made and the duvet smells good, like fabric softener and Tate's unique, masculine scent, which always makes me think of the ocean. I'm not surprised everything is so neat and tidy. He told me he picked up the habit at Scouts' camp. Because of course he was a Boy Scout. Apparently his dad was his troop leader, which also doesn't surprise me. Gavin Bartlett is the epitome of *fun dad*.

Speaking of Gavin, Tate said his parents had invited me over for dinner. So far, I've been putting it off. Dinner with his parents would make it feel like we're seriously dating, and I'm trying to keep a proper distance there. I know this is just a fling. I'm returning to Boston at the end of the summer, and it's not like long-distance relationships ever work. Besides, I already told him I don't want a relationship, and Tate doesn't want one either. He's simply having fun. We both are.

My heart rate spikes when I finally hear the front door open. The alarm beeps a few times, then stops once Tate arms it.

His muffled voice says, "What the . . ." and I smother a grin. Someone's spotted my abandoned flip-flops and dress.

"Cassie?" he calls warily.

Footsteps approach the stairs.

"Up here!" I tell him.

"Oh, thank God." His voice gets louder. "I was worried I was going to find you murdered up there."

I choke out a laugh. "Why would a murderer take the time to arrange my clothing in a trail?"

I hear him approaching the bedroom door. "I don't know. To fuck with my head and—" Tate halts in the doorway. His Adam's apple bobs when he spots me. Eyes instantly blazing. "Holy hell." He shakes his head. "Wow."

"What?" I ask innocently.

"Don't *what* me. You look . . ." He swallows again. "So . . . fucking . . . good."

His hungry eyes devour my body, which I've posed pinup style just for him. One knee propped. Head resting on his pillows and back arched, a position that makes my boobs jut out enticingly. It's rare for me to put the girls on display like this, but I love the way he's looking at them right now.

A cheeky smile springs free. "Are you just going to stand there and stare, or are you going to take your clothes off?" I inquire.

Without a word, Tate reaches for the hem of his shirt.

"Good choice."

Chuckling, he pulls his shirt off, revealing that tanned, muscular chest. "What did I do to deserve this?" he asks, and I don't know if it's a rhetorical question.

"Do you like?" I toy with the tiny lace bow on my bra, flashing a coy smile.

"I love."

He undoes his pants, shoving the material down. Boxers disappear next. Now he's naked, his erection out and proud.

He takes a step forward.

"Still want to take it slow?" I taunt.

"Don't know if that's possible," he growls, and then he's on the bed, covering my body with his.

Our lips meet, and it gets hot and dirty real fast. Greedy kissing and impatient hands running over each other's bodies. Tate makes no effort to remove my lingerie. He lifts his head, breathing hard, then kisses my breast over my bra.

"This is so sexy," he groans. His fingertips slim over the lacy edge. "Solid choice with white."

I'm pleased he approves.

Slowly, his hand glides along my stomach toward the delicate straps of my thong. "Goddamn," he croaks. "I don't even want to take these off you. The bra too. I want to fuck you while you're wearing them." He strokes my clit over the panties, and a rush of pleasure skitters through me.

His erection is heavy against my thigh, an erotic reminder of what I'm about to experience. I can't wait. Swallowing through my dry throat, I reach for him, circling his shaft with my fingers and—

The doorbell rings.

We both jump in surprise. "Are you expecting someone?" I ask him.

"No, not that I—" He cuts off. His face, which only a second ago was flushed, suddenly pales.

Then his phone chimes.

"Shit," Tate curses. He practically dives off the bed and grabs the phone from his pants pocket. He lets out another expletive when he reads the text.

"What's going on?" I sit up. For some reason, I instinctively lower one arm to cover my breasts, which are nearly overflowing from my skimpy bra cups.

The doorbell rings again.

"Who is that?" I demand.

He raises his head from his phone, features pained. "My date."

CHAPTER 22

TATE

Before I can blink, Cassie is off the bed and sprinting to the door.

"Cass, wait."

"Are you fucking kidding me?" she shouts back without turning around.

I grab my discarded boxers and hurriedly pull them on. I reach the doorway just as she makes it to the top of the staircase. Christ, her ass looks phenomenal in those cheeky panties. Her tits are practically spilling out of that bra, more so now that she's breathing so hard. A moment ago, I was about to devour her. Now I'm chasing after her to keep her from leaving.

She picks up the dress that's lying on the stairs, slipping it over her head as she descends. I hurry after her.

The doorbell rings again, making me wince.

I totally forgot about Nicole. I'm an asshole, I know. But I made the date last Sunday while I was trying not to think about Cassie and then forgot to call it off because I've had a busy week.

"I cannot believe you have another woman coming over tonight!" Cassie's murderous gaze eviscerates me. "What was the plan, exactly? You were going to meet her first, and me right after? Or go back and forth between the houses like Hannah fucking

Montana pretending to be in two places at once? Did I spoil your little plot by coming over here instead?"

"No, not at all," I say, reaching the bottom of the staircase.

She puts on her flip-flops and marches to the front door.

"Cassie, come on, wait. Can I please explain?"

"No," she barks, then flings the door open to reveal the startled face of Nicole.

"Oh, I'm sorry," Nicole hedges in. "Am I interrupting . . . ?"

"Nope," Cassie replies as she storms past. "He's all yours," she calls over her shoulder.

In completely misery, I watch her go.

"Fuck!" I groan, scrubbing my hands over my face. I briefly close my eyes, sucking in a frustrated breath. Then my eyes open, only to be confronted with the cloud of displeasure darkening Nicole's face.

"Uh, yeah, it's pretty obvious I did interrupt something. What the hell, Tate?"

"I'm sorry." I exhale a heavy breath. "I forgot you were coming over."

"Are you fucking serious?"

"I'm sorry." Shame now pours off me by the bucketload. "I started seeing someone this week—"

"Clearly," Nicole interrupts, jaw tightening.

"She and I were just friends when I asked you out, but then it turned into something more and I forgot to cancel with you. I'm sorry. I'm such an asshole. Honestly, I need you to hit me right now. Just clock me in the jaw. Please." I groan again. "You know I don't do this. I never play around with women. Ever. I'm so, so sorry."

She must recognize my sincerity—and immense remorse—because her face softens. "Dude. Dial it down. It's not like we just got married and you cheated on me on our honeymoon."

I spit out a weak laugh. "No, but this is a dick move."

"It is. I won't deny that." She runs a hand through her dark hair. "Can't say I'm not disappointed, either. I was looking forward to this all week."

"I'm sorry," I repeat through a lump of guilt.

"You're lucky you have a rep for being a good guy. I know you don't pull this shit with women."

"I don't," I moan. "I don't think I've ever felt this bad in my life. I can't apologize enough."

Nicole fiddles with the sleeve of her tight top. "I'm really embarrassed," she admits.

"Please don't be. This is all on me."

"Well, obviously. But that doesn't change the fact that I just walked in on—you know what, it's fine. Let's just forget it."

I search her expression. "Are we good?"

"Yeah, we're good." Sighing, she steps closer and gives me a little pat on the shoulder. "But I think you owe her an apology too. And I should probably let you get to that."

I still feel like shit as I walk Nicole to her car. Once she drives off, I glance toward Cassie's front porch. I don't want to go and ring the doorbell because I'm not sure if her mom and grandmother are home. But I also don't want to climb up to her window for fear she'll push me to my death.

Dismissing both options, I go back inside to get my phone.

Me: *Meet me out back so we can talk? Please?*

Part of me expects radio silence, but Cassie responds.

Cassie: *Date #2 is over already? Does someone have a stamina problem?*

And people say you can't discern tone over text.

Me: *It's really not what you think. Please. Just come outside?*
Cassie: *Fine.*

She meets me on the dock. Arms crossed, eyes apoplectic. She's wearing her dress, and now that I know what's underneath it I want to kick myself harder for forgetting to cancel with Nicole, because there's no way I'm seeing a single thread of that lingerie again tonight. Even if we do make up, the moment has passed.

"I made the date with her on Sunday," I explain. "After you and I . . . you know. Window sex."

Cassie nods, mouth flattening. "I think that might make it worse."

"I was trying to avoid temptation. I thought maybe if I found a distraction, I'd be able to see you again without being tempted to blow up our friendship. So when Nicole asked me out, I said yes. And then I got home that night and overheard you and your mom, and, well, you know what that led to." I gnaw on the inside of my cheek. "I screwed up. You and I have been hooking up all week, and I've been swamped with work, and I honestly just forgot to let her know the date was off."

"That is *such* a dick move. Especially to her."

"Trust me, I know. I just spent the past ten minutes begging her forgiveness. And now I'm begging yours." I meet Cassie's eyes. I know she hears the heartfelt note in my voice. "I don't juggle women. I might sleep with a lot of them, but never at the same time. Ask anyone who knows me—I don't play games. That's not who I am. You *know* that's not who I am, Cassie. I'm a Boy Scout. I'm the one who asked to get grounded. My parents raised me to treat women with respect. That's why I was afraid I'd be taking advantage of your inexperience."

She bites her lip in hesitation. "If you didn't want to be exclusive, you could've just told me."

"That's not it at all." I frown. "It didn't even cross my mind to not be exclusive. I assumed we were."

"Really?"

"I told you, I don't date more than one person."

"*Are* we dating?"

"Flinging. Hooking up. Whatever you want to call it."

My body is tight with frustration, because I can't quite explain how any of this makes me feel. All I know is the sheer panic, the helplessness that was squeezing my throat when Cassie stormed out and I thought I might never see her again.

"I like you," I say gruffly. "I have a great time with you. I'm wildly attracted to you. And I don't want to ever do anything that makes you look at me like that again. Like I was total slime."

She draws a breath. "When I thought you had another date . . . another girl lined up, or maybe even a whole roster of them . . . it upset me."

"I know. I'm sorry. I promise I'm not seeing anyone but you." I drag a hand through my hair, offering a rueful smile. "I had a whole thing planned for tomorrow. For you, I mean."

"You did?" Her forehead creases. "You never mentioned anything."

"I was planning on asking you tonight. You know how Gil told me I can use the Lightning? I thought . . ." I shift awkwardly. I don't think I've ever been so tongue-tied around a chick before. "I thought we could go out on the boat. Maybe anchor at Kearny's Cove. You wouldn't think it, but there's a roomy cabin below deck. It's cozy. We could do an overnight . . . ?"

The implication hangs in the air.

Cassie visibly swallows. We both know what will happen if we spend the night alone together in one bed.

"That sounds nice," she finally says, a soft smile tugging on her lips. "I'm in."

I almost sag over in relief. "Perfect. So it's a date."

"Just one date, Tate. Your *only* date of the evening." The humor dancing in her eyes tells me we're good again.

"My only date. Scout's honor."

* * *

"You ready?" I ask the following day, jumping on board the Lightning. I hold my hand out to Cassie. It's late afternoon and we're supposed to be leaving for our overnight, but she remains standing on the dock. Her gaze is focused on the gray and black life vests I set down on the copilot's seat.

"Do we need to wear those the whole time?" she asks warily.

"Only when she's moving. And it's only a precaution."

"Okay, now I'm kind of scared. Just how fast do you plan to go?"

"Fast." I'm practically shaking with excitement. "Gil says she can do 125, 130 miles per hour." I shudder happily. "I'm gonna come in my pants, ginger."

"Should I be jealous? Of the boat, I mean?"

"Probably."

That gets me a laugh. "Fine. Let's go."

I grip her hand to help her in. While she dons her life vest, I stash the cooler below deck, but grab two bottles of water out of it to throw into the cupholders. Once we're seated, I gently steer us away from the dock. Don't want to go all speed demon right from the jump. A bit farther out, I give her more juice. The boat comes to life. Anticipation coils in my gut as I ease the stick forward. When the Lightning's bow rises, Cassie jumps in alarm.

"It's fine," I assure her, and the bow settles. Oh man. This is nuts. Only cruising speed, and she's still going faster than any speedboat I've ever been on.

"Why are we going out so far?" Cassie looks worried the more miles I put between us and land.

"This is a no-wake zone. We need to go just past there, beyond the speed restrictions." I slice forward, cutting around the bend in the bay. Once we're far enough, I slow to a crawl, then idle for a minute. The Lightning gently bobs on the waves. I do a quick assessment. Wind is light, providing no resistance at all. Waves are decent, not too choppy.

I turn to Cassie with a grin. "All right. I'm gonna give it all I've got. All she's got. You ready?"

Cassie takes a breath. "Okay. Do it before I change my mind."

I accelerate and the Lightning takes off.

Cassie yelps, holding on for dear life. And we're not even going that fast yet. Maybe eighty, ninety miles per hour. It's incredible how much the Lightning still has left in her. Adrenaline surges through my blood as I speed up. The wind rushes past our faces, slicking my hair back. Cassie's ponytail hovers in the air like the tail of a kite, sticking straight out. Yet the Lightning is stable. So stable you'd never guess how fast we were going.

Like a little kid, I let out a loud whoop, and turn to see Cassie grinning at me. Then she throws her hands up and whoops too, and we surrender to the speed, the exhilaration. We're about a hundred miles an hour now, but I want more. Just a little bit more. I adjust the trim, play with the throttle, and then we're flying. One hundred and twenty miles an hour, and I'm on another plane of existence. We barely feel the chop. We're fucking soaring, so fast it feels like slow motion. It's unbelievable.

I let her fly for several more miles before slowing. My heartbeat takes a while to regulate. I look over and Cassie's still smiling. Her face is red, cheeks slightly windburned. The hull rocks as I bring us to a not-so-ass-puckering speed.

"That was incredible," I say, still breathing hard.

"You look like you just had an orgasm."

"I feel like I did. I've never piloted anything like her." She's a dream to handle. Tight turns, responsive.

"You should buy one."

I bark out a laugh. "Um, no. This is a million-dollar speed-boat. And Gil got it used."

"Holy shit."

"Exactly. I'm saving up for a sailboat, anyway. That comes first. Powerboats are playthings for later in life."

"You're a plaything for later in life," she cracks.

"Nice."

As we cruise toward Kearny's Cove, she fixes her ponytail, which got messed up during the wild ride. I slow us almost to a crawl and grab my water bottle. I gulp down a much-needed swig, then offer it to Cassie, who shakes her head. She's busy examining the cockpit, running a hand over the sleek vinyl upholstery.

She glances around the deck. "How is there a cabin down there? Doesn't seem like there'd be any room on this thing."

"First of all, don't call my girlfriend a thing."

She snorts.

"And the cabin is shockingly spacious. Seriously, you're going to love it."

"Am I now?"

A heated look passes between us. My heart's beating fast again. This time it has nothing to do with the Lightning and everything to do with Cassie Soul. I'm dying to get inside her. I've been thinking about it all goddamn day.

We arrive at Kearny's Cove, a gorgeous private spot that's shel-tered by a rock wall so the wind barely touches this part of the bay. There's a beach, albeit a tiny one. A narrow strip of sand, situated between the rock face and the reeds.

"This is such a pretty spot! Is this where we're having dinner?" Cassie asks.

"Yup."

She eyes me. "How many other women have you brought here?"

"None," I answer truthfully.

"Really?"

"Really."

"Why not?"

I shrug. "I guess I've never met anyone I liked enough to bring on a romantic overnight."

"Oooooh, Gate's trying to be romantic, huh?"

"Not anymore," I grumble.

"You didn't do this kind of stuff with Alana?"

"Nope. We only ever hung out at her house. Never even went out to dinner."

I anchor us and grab the cooler from below. Then I kick off my deck shoes and hop into the water. It splashes around my knees, soaking the bottom of my shorts. I deposit the cooler on the beach, then return to help Cassie off the boat.

Dinner consists of grilled chicken, Greek salad, fruit for dessert, and a bottle of champagne that makes Cassie snicker when I pull it out. "Stole that from the club again?"

"Sure did."

I pour her a glass. We're on the blanket I laid out on the sand, lazily eating our dinner while the sun begins its descent toward the horizon light.

"Okay, this is romantic," she relents, admiring the colors streaking across the sky. Brilliant pinks, reds, and oranges. The sunset is almost as pretty as she is.

After dinner, we stick our trash in the cooler and talk over champagne about nothing in particular. Cassie's birthday is next weekend. I offer to take her to dinner, but she has plans both days; dad on Saturday, mom on Sunday. She seems more enthused about the former, but I get the sense she and her stepmother have an awkward relationship, which puts a damper on most family occasions.

Cassie confirms that by adding, "Honestly, I don't think Nia likes me very much. I'm just a reminder of my mother. Aka, her husband's nasty ex-wife."

"Where did you say she was from again? The Dominican?"

"Haiti."

"Oh cool. Does that mean she speaks French? Wait, or is it Creole?"

"French, but according to Nia there's a perceivable difference between Haitian French and French French. She says it's in the intonation. Not that I would ever hear the difference. She's really nice," Cassie admits. "Dad found himself a good one."

Eventually, darkness falls over us, so we wade back to the boat. We kick off our shoes and go below deck where Cassie's eyes widen.

"See," I say smugly. "It's huge."

The cabin is more than just roomy—it offers plenty of amenities for an overnight in the cove. Built-in closets for storage, a pull-out refrigerator, a portable head. The center table converts into a bed, which I'd already set up before we left the dock.

"It even has air conditioning?" She gapes.

"Yup. Told you, this gal ain't cheap."

Cassie flops cross-legged in the center of the bed. "Do you think you'll accept Gil Jackson's offer? To sail to New Zealand?"

I'd mentioned it over dinner but didn't linger too long on the subject. It's been gnawing at the back of my brain since Gil's phone call. "I don't know. I'm still thinking about it."

"That's nuts that he has all these boats. His own fleet. Or is it an armada? What do you call a bunch of boats?" She wrinkles her nose. "A bushel?"

"Yes, baby, a bushel of boats. You nailed it."

"I sense sarcasm."

"You sense right."

Her indignant expression dissolves into a smile. "I will forgive that because you called me *baby* and that kind of turned me on."

"Oh, did it?"

Just like that, we're eye-fucking each other. And suddenly my entire body clenches in anticipation at the knowledge that it won't be long before we're real fucking.

"Come here." Her voice is throaty.

I join her on the bed. Try to sit at first, but she promptly pushes me onto my back. I land with a thump, smiling up at her. She looks so good right now. Eyes shining. Cheeks red. Windblown hair—copper, not ginger, although I won't give her the satisfaction of letting her know she's right about that. In her seated position, her shorts have ridden up her thighs. I reach out, unable to stop myself from stroking her smooth flesh.

She bites her lip. "Are you starting something here, Gate?"

"I don't know . . . you want me to?"

Rather than answer, she bends down to kiss me.

I kiss her back, sliding my fingers through her hair, giving a gentle tug to pull her closer. She's on top of me now, those delectable tits crushed against my chest, nipples puckered tight. I reach between us and give her left nipple a teasing pinch, knowing how sensitive her breasts are. As if on cue, she lets out a moan, and I smile. I love every single sound she makes when we're fooling around. None more than that soft, breathy whimper right before she's about to come. But we're not there yet, not even close to hearing that particular whimper. And I'm not bothered. It's not always about the destination. Sometimes it's all about the journey.

Rolling us over, I start off slow, kissing her neck and enjoying the way she shivers. Her hands idly run up and down between my shoulder blades, stroke the back of my head, tangle in my hair. It's fucking glorious. I grip the bottom of her tank top and drag it upward, my lips following the trail of exposed skin until they reach her collarbone and collide with the fabric of her top. I tug on it.

"Off," I order.

Laughing, she rises off the bed to pull the shirt off, along with her bikini top.

I touch her shorts then give the side of her ass a little smack. "Up," I growl.

"I love your monosyllabic caveman talk."

"Damn right you do."

She lifts her ass and I yank on her shorts and underwear, tossing them away. It suddenly occurs to me this is the first time I've seen her fully naked. I can't even believe that. I prop up on one elbow to admire her, my hand gliding over her perfect, naked flesh. Aside from her chest, she's kind of small everywhere else. I skim her rib cage, feeling the protrusions beneath my fingertips. The sharp jut of her hip bone.

She's watching me as I touch her. "You're teasing."

"No. Just enjoying." My fingers dance over one knee before sliding toward the juncture of her thighs. Licking my lips, I drag my knuckles over her slit.

Her breath catches. "That feels so good."

"I've barely gotten started." Grinning, I take off my shirt, but keep my shorts on. I don't need that temptation yet. Then I grip her ankles and start dragging her to the foot of the bed. There isn't a lot of space up there, so I kneel on the ground in front of her, bring her ass to the end of the mattress, and lower my face between her legs.

We both moan when my tongue makes contact. This is my favorite thing in the world. I don't think Cassie believed me when I told her that, but it's the truth. Nothing gets me harder than going down on a woman. Making her moan and squirm. Her gasps for air. Her thighs squeezing around my head, desperate to keep me right where she needs me. It's the pinnacle of sexual excitement. So fucking good.

As my erection strains against my zipper, I work her with my tongue, my fingers, until finally I hear it—my favorite noise. I groan happily, and know she feels that low, husky response on her clit. Her hips start moving. She grinds herself against my face, taking all the pleasure I have to offer, and it's not until she goes completely still that I abandon my post and kiss my way up her body.

She welcomes my kiss and I love that. Doesn't care that her taste is still on my tongue. She practically eats my face off, her nails digging into my shoulders as one hand fumbles for my zipper.

"Why are these still on?" she demands. "This vexes me."

"Oh, it vexes you?"

"Yes, it vexes me. I've very vexed."

I let her roll me onto my back. She's clawing at my shorts, wrenching them down my hips. My dick springs out, hard and eager.

Cassie gives an amused look. "Somebody's excited."

"Damn right I am." I suck a breath in when she takes me in her hand and starts to lower her head. Oh Christ. "No," I say, pulling her off me.

She looks offended. "What do you mean *no*?"

"No blowjobs."

"Ever?"

"No, not ever. Just now. I want to be able to last more than three strokes."

Her eyes twinkle. "You should have jerked off before we left. I read some guys do that to take the edge off."

"I did jerk off before we left," I growl, and she bursts out laughing.

"And you're still that close to ruining this experience for me? Jeez."

I know she's joking, yet I can't fight a self-conscious pang. "Damn, Cass. Don't say that. Now I'm going to have that in the back of my mind the whole time."

"No, don't." She launches herself at me again, our naked bodies colliding. Cupping my face, she looks into my eyes. "There's nothing to ruin. Even if we don't have sex right now, this is still one of the best days of my life. Honestly."

"Mine too," I confess. My first ride on a Fountain Lightning and I had Cassie by my side? Whatever happens between us in the future, I'll never forget that moment. And I'll never forget *this*. I squeeze one full, perfect breast. Sweep my thumb over her beaded nipple. When I bring my hand between her legs I find her wet and ready for me.

Yeah. I won't forget anything about tonight.

She's trying to reach for me again, and once again I intercept her fingers. "Hold that thought," I say and bend over the bed for the overnight bag. I unzip the side pocket for the condoms I stashed there.

Once I'm suited up, I ease my body on top of hers. Lightly touch her hip and lower my lips to kiss her nipple. Then I raise my head and meet her eyes. "You good?"

"I'm great," she says and guides me between her legs.

I only make it about an inch before we're both sweating. The sensation of her clamped so tightly around me short-circuits my brain. I forget how to fuck. Like, I actually do. I just lie there, my tip lodged inside, and it isn't until she groans impatiently that I snap out of it.

"Ready?" I whisper.

"Mmm-hmm."

I push myself inside her, past the resistance, kissing her to swallow the soft yelp of pain. "You okay?" I murmur against her lips.

"Uh-huh. Just give me one second."

I go still again, surrounded by her snug, warm heat. It's the greatest feeling in the world. Ever so slowly, she starts to move. Canting her hips. Digging her nails into my shoulder. It's torture. And I don't know if she's doing it on purpose, but her pussy is rippling around me, squeezing tight, releasing, then squeezing me in again. I clench my ass cheeks because I'm scared if I move I'm going to start pounding into her.

She squeezes me again, and my hips snap forward, hard and deep, summoning a startled sound from Cassie. I choke out a curse. I'm not going to survive this.

"All right," I mumble. "Here's what's going to happen."

A smile dances across her lips. "Yes, please share."

"I'm rolling us over and you're going to ride me. You're going to set the pace, okay? I'm trying so damn hard to go slow right now, but my body isn't going to let me in this position."

A moment later she's astride me. I shove a pillow under my head and soak in the sight of her. Flushed cheeks. Lust-drenched eyes. She hesitates, looking a bit uncertain.

"Take what you need," I say softly. I gaze up at her, completely at her mercy. "Every part of me is yours."

Cassie smiles. Slowly, she begins to ride me. Her palms flatten on my chest. Her lips part. She leans forward and her hair falls over us like a curtain, tickling my pecs. She kisses me, then makes a breathy sound.

"Oh, I like that."

"What?" I ask thickly.

"Kissing you while you're inside me." Her breathing quickens. So does the tempo, sending a bolt of pleasure through my body.

My balls tingle. Ass clenches again. I realize my fingers are curled over her hip, digging into her flesh. I loosen them. Force myself to relax.

She stops again. Dismayed. "What if I can't finish this way?"

"Then I'll go down on you again." I sigh happily. "All night, preferably."

"You really wouldn't care?"

"I really wouldn't care. Why should I, as long as this feels good for you?"

"It does," she assures me, leaning in to kiss me again.

I tug her so that she's draped over my chest. Then I lift my hips in a teasing, upward thrust at the same time I slide my tongue in her mouth.

Her eyes pop open and she gasps.

"What is it?" I ask, freezing.

"Oh. This position," she says, her voice dreamy. "It's rubbing the right spot." She rotates her hips, moving her lower body over mine. "This is the one."

Suddenly she's grinding her clit against me while I'm buried inside her, and I know she's found her rhythm. Her spot. Then I hear it, the telltale whimper, and my body fails me. With her nipples scraping my pecs, her ass filling my hands, her body gripping me tight, I can't fight it any longer.

"Cass, I'm gonna come. I can't stop it."

She mumbles, "It's okay," and I go off like a rocket. The pleasure is just starting to abate when Cassie reaches the place she needs to be. Her orgasm elicits another rush of heat in my body, like the aftershocks following an earthquake, tiny ripples after the initial blast.

Once our breathing is back to normal, she settles at my side, her head resting on my shoulder.

"So?" I say hoarsely. "Did I ruin it for you?"

"Definitely," she whispers. "It was so bad."

"So bad."

She giggles, her soft breath tickling my flesh. Silence falls over us. As we lie there in the dark, a sensation of pure serenity washes over me.

"I'm sleepy," she murmurs.

"Then close your eyes." I close mine too. Listening to the wind whistling beyond the cabin. Feeling the rocking of the hull on the calm water. The warmth of Cassie's naked body against mine.

I can't think of a better way to fall asleep.

CHAPTER 23

CASSIE

August

Only thirty minutes in to the twins' birthday party, and I'm second-guessing my desire to have children. I thought *two* six-year-olds were loud. Fifteen of them? It's one endless shriek that doesn't let up. The kind of unceasing noise that worms its way into your soul.

Dad and Nia rented a bouncy castle that takes up nearly half the backyard and currently contains eight little girls who are jumping up and down screaming at the tops of their lungs. It sounds like they're getting murdered in there, but I think they're having fun? The remaining seven girls are seated around the crafts table, where one of the counselors from the twins' day camp helps everyone construct their own sparkly tiaras. Dad hired the teenager for the afternoon, and she's a big hit so far.

Speaking of Dad, this is the fourth time he's hurried inside to "get something." Took me a while, but I'm starting to think he's not actually getting something, because he keeps returning empty-handed. On to him, I sneak away from the party and follow him inside. Sure enough, he's leaning against the kitchen counter, scrolling through his phone.

"You're not getting anything," I accuse.

He looks up, eyes dancing behind his glasses. "Sure I am. I'm getting peace and quiet."

I wander toward the other side of the counter and admire the girls' birthday cake, courtesy of Nia's bakery buddy Chandra, who ratted out Dad the day we were turtle browsing. Chandra and her daughter Sava are here today, the former chatting outside with Nia, the latter one of the kids getting murdered in the bouncy castle.

"Do you think the twins suspect?" I ask him. "About the turtle."

"Not in the slightest," he replies. "Last night Roxy was complaining again about having to wait till next year for a pet."

"Is everything all set up? The tank? The water? The—what did that Joel kid call it? UV light?"

"UVB," Dad corrects. "And it's all done. Even decorated the little dude's new digs with this waterlogged cypress tree decoration. It has all these branches he can perch on. I gotta admit, he's cute."

"Uh-huh. And what does Nia think about your new roommate?"

"She's still not thrilled about it, but she's just glad it's not a dog. As far as pets go, this one is low maintenance if you ignore the fact that it lives for a thousand years."

I snort.

"I'm glad you're here," Dad adds. "And I know I've already said it a bunch of times today, but happy birthday."

He comes up to wrap his arms around me in a warm hug. It's rare to receive any physical affection from my father, and I lean into his touch. I might not see him as often as I'd like, but when I do, I'm happy to be around him. It's so much easier with him than Mom. With her it's a minefield; I never know when I'll set off the next verbal attack.

As if reading my mind, Dad releases me with a light, "How's it been with your mom in town? You two getting along?"

"You know, the usual." And then, also as per usual, I change the subject. "I wish I hadn't wrapped the *Kit 'n McKenna* book already. I'm dying to show you how it turned out." I hesitate, feeling myself blush. "And you'll be happy to know I spoke to Robb about trying to publish it."

Dad's eyes light up. "You did? Excellent."

"His boss at the design studio has some contacts in the agent world. Talent agents, literary, that kind of thing. He's going to give Robb a few names of people who might want to rep us." I shrug. "Who knows—maybe this is the career path I'll end up on." When Dad brightens again, I raise my hand in warning. "Don't get your hopes up. Publishers might hate the concept."

"They won't," he says confidently. "And I can't wait to see it. I don't know what the girls are going to love more—the turtle or your book."

"The turtle, Dad." I roll my eyes.

A couple hours later, after all the birthday cake has been devoured and all the horrible shrieking children are gone, the remaining five of us gather in the living room for the grand unveiling. We decided to wait until their friends were gone, because as Joel the Pothead Turtle Whisperer had warned, turtles are highly sensitive. We didn't want to give the poor thing a heart attack when he swam out of his cypress tree and found fifteen screaming girls in his face.

A thirty-gallon tank now resides against the back wall of the living room, hidden by the black tablecloth Dad temporarily draped over it.

"What's happening?" Roxy demands, perpetually mistrustful. "What is that?"

"Why don't you go and look?" Dad beams at her. Even Nia looks like she's fighting a smile.

Wearing identical expressions of suspicion, the twins approach the covered tank.

"Pull the tablecloth off," Dad encourages.

Surprisingly, Roxy hesitates, and so it's Mo who ends up tugging on the cloth to reveal the turtle tank beneath.

Even more surprising, the girls stay deathly silent. Not a shriek to be heard.

"Girls?" Dad prompts.

They turn toward their parents, wide-eyed.

"Is . . . is it for us?" Monique whispers.

"He sure is." Nia's smile breaks free. It's hard not to smile when the girls are trembling with quiet excitement.

"Come," Dad says, urging them closer. "Come see him."

I step forward too. I also want to see the little dude. I peer at the tank and search the artificial rocks, branches, and little log that serves as a basking spot. That's where I find him. Dad's right—he's kind of cute. Small, maybe four inches max, with a mottled black shell and distinct stripes on his head.

"What's his name?" Roxy whispers.

"He doesn't have one yet," Dad says.

Not entirely true. I think this one was LL Cool J. But I don't blame Dad for wanting to rename him.

"I was thinking, though . . . maybe we can let your mama name him?" Dad tips his head as he awaits an answer.

Nia looks startled. "Me?"

He winks at his wife. "You. We all know Mama had her doubts about him, but she fell in love with him the moment she met him. So I think she should name him."

"Name him, Mama," Mo pleads.

Nia eyes the turtle for several long beats. Then she says, "Pierre."

I swallow a laugh. "Excellent choice."

"Pierre," Roxy echoes solemnly, pressing her nose to the tank.

"I will love him forever," Mo breathes. She's got both hands on the glass and is staring at him in adoration.

"Can I hold him?" Roxy begs.

"No, me first!"

Dad shakes his head. "We're going to go easy on the holding thing. At least for a little while. Pierre's experiencing a real culture shock right now."

"And," Nia adds, donning a stern look, "we need to have a serious talk about how to take care of Pierre, and what your responsibilities will be. *Oui?*"

"*Oui,*" the twins promise.

"We'll do that tomorrow. Tonight, we still have a birthday dinner to eat," Dad says cheerfully. "And your sister has a present for you too . . ." he trails off enticingly.

My sisters spin toward me. "What is it?" Roxy demands.

I give her an innocent smile. "I don't know . . ." I walk into the hall to grab the wrapped present I left on the credenza, then return to offer it to Roxanne. "Why don't you two sit on the couch and open it?"

Unlike the awed silence Pierre received, my gift garners actual shrieks.

"It's Kit!" Mo shouts, trying to grab the hardcover out of her sister's hands. "Let me look!"

"We're looking together!" Roxy flips to the first page and stares at the drawing. "This is a real storybook!"

"It is," I confirm.

She scrunches up her forehead. "But it's *your* story."

"It is my story," I agree. "And I wrote it down and put it in a book for you. And . . ." I join them on the couch, settling in between them. "Look." I flip back to the intro page. "Can you read that for me?"

The twins are going into the first grade in September, but they've been at an advanced reading level for a while now. They squint at the page, eyes widening when they recognize their names.

"*To Roxanne . . . and . . . Monique,*" Roxy reads in stilted pauses. "*The best . . . sisters . . . in the word.* I mean, *world.*" She gazes at me, mouth gaping open. Then she screeches with joy. "I'm in the book!" she shouts. "Momo, you're in the book too!"

"We're in the book!" Mo jumps up and starts bouncing on the cushions.

"Monique," Nia chides, instantly plucking her off the couch and setting her on the floor. "We don't climb on the furniture, remember?"

Guilt pricks into me as I'm reminded of the last time she scaled the furniture. Under my watch, when a cabinet almost felt on her head and crushed my sister to death. At least Nia doesn't seem to be holding a grudge about it.

"Can you read it to us?" Roxy asks, hugging my arm.

"Please?" Mo launches herself at me, trying to climb into my lap.

"Why don't you girls do that now while your mama and I start fixing dinner?" Dad suggests. He's wearing a soft smile as he sweeps his gaze over the three of us.

He and Nia disappear into the kitchen, and I settle in to read my sisters a story.

* * *

Over dinner, Dad pours a glass of champagne and hands it to me. When I raise an eyebrow, he raises one back. "You're legal now," he says. "And I'm going to pretend this is your first glass of champagne."

"It is," I say innocently. "Never drank a single drop until this very moment."

That draws a genuine laugh from Nia.

Dad clinks his glass with mine. "Happy birthday, Cass."

"Happy birthday, Cassie," my sisters echo.

"Happy birthday, Cassandra," Nia adds in.

Dinner is tasty, as it always is when Nia cooks. Afterward, Dad hands me an envelope that serves as my birthday present. Inside is a gift card, which is pretty much what I expected. It's always a gift card.

"Figured this way you could go and pick something out for yourself," Dad tells me. Which is what he says every year.

"It's perfect. Thank you." But it's hard to ignore the pang of unhappiness that tugs at my insides. I know it's far easier to please first-graders than your college-senior daughter, but sometimes it would be nice if Dad made an actual effort.

The girls beg me to spend the night, and although I hadn't been planning on it, I can't say no to those faces. I text Tate to let him know I won't be coming by later.

Tate: *No birthday sex??!!*
Me: *Sadly not. My sisters don't want me to leave.*
Tate: *I'll allow it, but I'm not happy.*

I know he's kidding, which is confirmed when he sends a follow-up.

Tate: *Have fun. See you tomorrow?*
Me: *For sure.*

Hell, now I'm almost regretting agreeing to spend the night here, because just seeing his name on my phone gets me going. Sexually. Because that's what my world has been reduced to. Sex.

And sex. And then more sex. I'm voracious about it now. I crave it all the damn time.

I freaking love sex.

Or maybe it's Tate.

Of course it's Tate. You're falling for him.

Wait, what? Where the hell did that come from? I chide my mind for even suggesting such blasphemy. I can't, under any circumstances, allow myself to fall in love with the guy. I'm leaving in three weeks. He's staying behind. Not only that, but we agreed to a fling. We even discussed the terms. Therefore, I'm not allowed to engage my heart in this. Only my body.

Luckily, my body is very much in love with Tate's.

"Let me help you with those," I say when I spot Nia carrying in plates from the dining room.

"*Non, non.* It's fine."

"You cooked dinner for me," I protest. "The least I can do is help with the cleanup."

Nia once again dismisses me. "Go spend time with the girls. Their bedtime is soon."

I press my lips together, fighting a wave of irritation. Despite my best effort, the words biting at my tongue cannot be reined in.

"Why don't you like me?"

Her expression turns to shock. "What?"

"Why don't you like me?" I repeat.

"Cassandra . . ." She places the dirty dishes in the sink and slowly steps toward me. She rubs the bridge of her nose. Uneasy. "I—"

"Cass!" Dad calls from the living room. "Come check this out!"

"Pierre is swimming!" yells Roxy.

Relief sweeps through me. I'm immensely grateful for the interruption, because voicing the question made me realize I don't want to know the answer.

Why do we do that, anyway? Ask questions with glaringly obvious answers. Painful answers. I guess human beings really are gluttons for punishment. It's like Peyton, whenever she gets ghosted by a guy. She always wants to know the reason. Wants to know why. And I always counter with, *Why does it matter? Either way he's not interested in you.* But still she persists, *Yes, but I want to know WHY.*

Nia doesn't like me. That much is clear.

So, really, the *why* doesn't matter.

* * *

Tate: *Make sure not to throw out the newspaper today.*

The message comes in as I'm pulling into Grandma's driveway the next morning. Okay. Intriguing.

I hop out of the Rover and head into the house to have a look. Grandma wakes up ungodly early in the mornings, and if she'd already gone out to grab the newspaper, she would've tossed the *Avalon Bee* on the hall table and only brought her paper of choice—*The Wall Street Journal*—into the kitchen with her.

Sure enough, in the hall I find the abandoned Saturday edition of the *Bee*. Curious, I unfold it, then burst out laughing. Oh my God. This is incredible.

"Cassie?" comes my mother's voice.

Still giggling over the paper, I carry it into the kitchen, where Mom is drinking her coffee at the table.

She gives me a wry smile. "What's so funny?"

"This." I hold up the newspaper to show her the front page, which features a half-page photograph of the Bartlett family. Gavin, Gemma, and Tate (missed opportunity for *Gate*) pose in front of Bartlett Marine, with Gavin in the middle, his broad grin flying off the page. Tate's dad is definitely larger than life, and the headline reflects this:

MR. CONGENIALITY OF THE BAY

Mom leans forward to study the article, her eyes instantly narrowing. "What's this?"

"Tate's dad." Another giggle pops out. "The *Bee* did a profile on him. It was all he could talk about the first time I met him. He's so proud of it."

My phone buzzes in my other hand.

Tate: *He already has TWO framed copies. One for the dealership, one for his home office. He thinks he's a celebrity now. He just called me asking if he should schedule a press conference.*
Me: *Let the man have his moment in the sun, Gate!*

Laughing, I leave my phone on the counter and head for the fridge. At the table, Mom is scanning the article, still looking displeased. Well, of course. Someone other than her is getting attention. The nerve!

"Your grandmother tried to convince me the other day that you were dating that boy, but I didn't believe her." Raising one eyebrow, Mom pushes the newspaper away and picks up her coffee cup. "It appears I was wrong."

"Tate and I aren't dating." I stick my head in the fridge hoping the chill might cool down my suddenly warm cheeks.

"No? Because also according to your grandmother, the land-scaper says it looks like someone's been trampling the rose garden beneath the lattice at the side of the house. The one that leads right to your window."

Damn it. I poke my head out, my hand emerging with a con-tainer of yogurt. "It's not a big deal," I say, going to grab a bowl. "We're just hanging out."

Mom shakes her head in amusement. "It's not like I don't know exactly what that means, sweetie."

I shrug. "It's just a casual thing. We're parting ways at the end of the summer, so it's not going to lead to anything."

"I see. Well, I suppose so long as you're having fun."

"We are."

"And so long as you're taking precautions." Mom offers a pointed look.

My cheeks are scorching again. "We are."

"Then I guess I don't have anything to worry about," she fin-ishes.

I'm confused as to why she was worried in the first place. Mom's never paid much attention to my love life, other than to criticize me for not having one.

She changes the subject, watching me as she sips her coffee. "How is your father?"

I brace myself. Waiting for the . . . *and his nurse?*

But it doesn't come.

"He's good. We had a nice time. The girls loved their gift."

"Speaking of gifts." Mom finishes her coffee and walks to the counter, and it's then that I notice the neatly wrapped gift near the knife block. A crisp lavender envelope sits atop it. "I decided I'd wait until today to give you this, since you were so busy yes-terday."

Her tone lacks bite, but that had to be sarcasm, right? Some kind of resentful subtext, like, *You were so busy yesterday . . . because your father and his nurse kept you away from me all day long.*

Only, I see none of that on her face. Not an ounce of hostility.

"Yesterday was super busy," I agree.

I open the envelope first and pull out a card with a delicate purple flower pressed onto the front. Inside, the card is blank save for my mother's uber-concise handwritten message: *Happy birthday, Cassie. Love, Mom.* And there's a check for five thousand dollars.

"Some spending money for your senior year," she explains.

"Thanks." Gift card. Check. Both my parents enjoy taking the easy way out, apparently.

"Now here's your real present," she says, sliding the gift box toward me. Her tone is light, joking even, but it's belied by the anxiety in her eyes.

Okay. This is weird. Why does she look so anxious for me to open this?

I study the narrow box, which is around the size of a sheet of paper and not too thick. Clothing, I realize, when I lift the lid and glimpse fabric beneath the white tissue paper. I part the paper.

It's a crop top.

I steel myself. This must be some kind of attack, right?

"I had Joy pick it out," Mom says. A nervous look darts across her face.

Holy shit, this is not a joke. I repeat, this is not a joke.

It's a sincere gesture.

"Oh," I say in surprise.

I run my fingers over the ribbed material. I saw this top in one of the boutiques on the strip when Joy and I were shopping a few weeks ago. I'd picked it up, admiring it, asking Joy if emerald green was my color. I didn't end up buying it, only because I didn't feel like dropping two hundred dollars on a strip of fabric.

"I know I was out of line," Mom starts.

The shocks just keep coming.

"Last week when we spoke on the patio," she clarifies. "You'd just returned from dinner and I remarked on your outfit. I may have been a tad rude about it."

May have? A tad?

"Just a tad," I say lightly.

"I'm sorry. I was in a very bad mood that night, and I'm afraid I took it out on you." She laughs, and it sounds genuinely sheepish. "I don't think you're a bimbo. Obviously I don't think that. Like I said, I was in a bad mood. I apologize."

I can't get over the feeling that somehow, someway, this is an inexplicable ruse. A trick with an end game I don't know yet. It's difficult to trust my mother. You can't trust a person who's spent years making you feel unworthy.

Mom isn't done. "I spoke with your grandmother about it when we were in Charleston, and she pointed out that when I was your age, I was also insecure about my looks. And those insecurities aren't helped by someone sharing their negative opinion about your wardrobe choices. Also, if you do choose to have a breast reduction—"

I brace myself again.

"—I will happily accompany you to the consultation. But if you choose not to, that is also okay." She reaches out and touches the soft material of the crop top. "Either way, I'm sure you're going to look wonderful in this. Why don't you wear it today? Pair it with that long skirt we bought last week, the khaki one with the gold flowers? That might be a nice outfit for our day in Charleston." Mom pauses. "That's still the plan, right? Birthday Sunday in the city?"

"For sure. I just need to shower and change and then I'm ready to go." I clutch the top a little tighter, surprised by the lump of emotion that forms in my throat. "Thank you for this. I love it."

For once, I'm not lying.

CHAPTER 24

CASSIE

A few days after my birthday, Mom takes me and Tate out to dinner on the boardwalk. That in itself is a shocking development, but she continues to surprise me once we're seated at the Italian place and she generously hands over the leather-bound wine menu to Tate.

"Why don't you pick the wine, Tate?" It's a big honor coming from Mom, and I can tell he's fighting his amusement over the ceremonial tone with which she makes the offer.

I'm equally surprised Tate agreed to this dinner at all, considering he hasn't been my mother's biggest fan since the night she bimbo-shamed me. But Mom's been badgering me about it for the past couple days. I suspect a part of her still doesn't believe Tate and I are seeing each other and she wants visual proof.

I don't entirely blame her. I mean, let's not kid ourselves—Tate is probably the best-looking guy I've ever been in the same room as, and I've been surrounded by cute college boys for the last three years, so that says a lot. He surpasses them in looks. The perfect golden boy with his perfect face and perfect body. Even Mom can't stop checking him out. It's both creepy and validating, two things I didn't think could coexist in my mind. But I like knowing I'm not just some foolish girl blinded by a crush. That he's actually as hot as I think he is.

"I'm not a big wine drinker," Tate tells her. "You'd be doing yourself a disservice if you put me on wine-picking duty for the night." He hands the menu back. "But if you're interested in beer, then I'm your man."

Mom proceeds to do another shocking thing. "You know what? Let's have beer tonight."

My jaw drops. "You're going to drink beer? Here?" This is one of the nicest restaurants in the Bay. Normally she wouldn't be caught dead drinking anything other than the most expensive wine in the restaurant's cellar.

There's something different about her. Even her outfit gives off a different vibe. She's clad in an expensive sleeveless dress, a sky blue that complements her red hair, which she's uncharacteristically wearing down. She doesn't seem so uptight tonight. She'd even complimented my dress when Tate and I met her outside the restaurant.

And don't get me started on *that* perplexing exchange. Mom had greeted Tate with a warm smile and said, "Nice to see you again, Tate," and he'd responded with, "Nice to see you again too, Tori."

Tori.

My eyebrows almost jumped off my face as I turned to Mom to clarify. I don't think I've ever heard anyone call my mother Tori. Dad called her Vic sometimes, but mostly Victoria. Even Grandma always uses her entire name.

"All my friends call me that," Mom had responded, rolling her eyes at me. "Where have you been, Cass?"

To be fair, I always kept a safe distance whenever she had a friend over to the penthouse. It was much easier than putting on the whole mother/daughter act, the one she's so skilled at. When new friends, acquaintances, or strangers are around, she pretends we're the bestest of friends. We're Lorelai and Rory from *Gilmore*

Girls, giggling together in our pajamas and casually chatting about our crushes.

Which has never happened, nor will it ever.

But I guess we're pretending again tonight. Me and Tori. Best buds. Luckily, I know Tate can see through it.

When the waiter arrives, Tate orders an obscure-sounding beer, which he explains is locally brewed. Mom tells the server to make it two, but I beg off when he looks toward me. Instead, I order a Diet Coke. I need to keep a clear head. I don't know why the three of us are here and it still feels like a trap.

"This is nice," Mom remarks, only deepening my suspicions. What is she up to? "So, Tate. Cassie said you're a sailor?"

"Not professionally, but yes, I love to sail. Used to compete in high school." While he talks, he plays with the edge of his napkin, and I watch the way his long fingers move.

Heat tickles my core when I remember the feel of those fingers moving over *me.* Stroking my body. Biting into my ass, my hips, as I rode him.

Oh no. *Don't blush,* I tell myself.

He catches my eye and grins. Damn it. I'm blushing.

"I don't compete as much I'd like to anymore," he continues, while reaching for my hand.

He links our fingers together and I try not to smile. Holding hands during dinner? He's making a statement, and I notice Mom gazing on in approval. Now *that's* a rare look on her.

"Too busy these days with work," he says.

"You work at the Manor?" she prompts.

"Part-time, weekends mostly. The rest of the time I'm at the family business."

"And what would that be?"

"Bartlett Marine. Dad and I run it. It's a dealership, but we handle rentals and charters too."

I just listen to the conversation. Mom can be very charismatic when she wants to be. Disarming. I used to have friends from high school come over and look at me like I was crazy for even insinuating that my mother could be a raging narcissistic bitch. They all thought she was fabulous. I can't entirely gauge Tate's opinion of her. He was a bit reserved when we first sat down, but he seems to be warming up to her.

"Cassie showed me the newspaper article about your father," Mom says, smiling. "Sounds like you hail from a family of celebrities."

"Man, do not tell my dad that," Tate replies with a groan. "He's already walking around the dealership thinking he's hot stuff because they ran a profile on him. Like, dude, it's the *Avalon Bee,* not *GQ.*"

As Mom laughs, I come to poor Gavin's defense. "Have *you* ever been featured on the front page of a newspaper? Any newspaper, for that matter?"

"Uh, yeah," he shoots back. "I'm in the picture on the front page of the *Bee,* in case you forgot."

"For an article about your *dad.* Jeez. Get your own achievements." I give him a taunting smile. "You can't complain about his excitement until you've experienced your own fifteen minutes of fame. You'd probably be even worse, too. Accepting fake Oscars in front of the mirror every morning."

"Cassie," Mom chides, but her eyes twinkle with humor.

"What?" I protest. "Look at him. He looks like the guy who delivers fake speeches in the mirror. Don't deny it."

He snickers. "I would never."

Mom's gaze shifts toward him, assessing. Lingers a little too long, but when she turns back to me, her expression still contains humor. "He does seem like the type," she agrees.

I can't believe my mother and I sided on something. And even crazier, that I'm genuinely enjoying myself. At dinner. With my mother present. People in hell must be wearing parkas right about now.

Whether or not she's putting on an act remains undecided. But I'm still relaxed, my guard down. I end up ordering a cocktail. And now that I'm twenty-one, I can do that without stressing that someone is going to ask for my ID.

Dinner is excellent, which is to be expected from the most expensive restaurant in town. This place gets the freshest lobster and the best cuts of meat in the Bay. As we eat, Tate tells us funny stories about working at the yacht club. Seems like during every lesson, something ridiculous happens.

"Couples are the worst," he insists. "Any time we take out a sailboat that's bigger than thirty feet, at least one half of the couple demands to act out the king of the world scene from *Titanic*. Then I have to stand there taking pictures, like, a thousand of them, because the first nine hundred and ninety-nine are apparently never good enough for the 'gram."

"Oh dear," Mom says, giggling into her beer. She just shocked me by ordering a second one. "You poor thing."

I suppose I can overlook the way she's blatantly flirting with my sort-of boyfriend if it means she's not frowning at my outfit or talking about breast reductions. Over dessert, she even shares some stories about her own days at the country club.

"There was this golf instructor—Lorenzo." She sighs dreamily. "I had the biggest crush on him. Almost fainted with excitement when he asked me on a date. I think I was twenty-one, maybe? It was right before I met your father, Cass."

I almost spit out my drink. "Mom! You dated Lorenzo? The immortal Italian vampire?"

Tate snickers into his beer.

"I don't even know what that means," she says.

"It means he's worked at the Manor for five hundred years because he never ages." I suddenly feel the color draining from my face. "Oh my God, he could have been my father." I glare at her, aghast. "You almost got me sired by *Lorenzo.*"

"No chance," she replies, lips pressed tight together as if she's fighting an onslaught of giggles. "Let's just say Lorenzo had some . . . performance issues."

I gasp.

Tate groans. "No. Why did you have to tell me that? Now I'll never be able to look him in the eye again."

When the bill arrives, he tries to reach for it, but Mom firmly divests him of that notion. "It's on me. I'm just glad you were able to join us. I wanted to meet the boy who's been sneaking into my daughter's window this summer."

He winks at me before answering her. "No comment."

"I'm glad you two are spending time together. It's so nice to see you with a boyfriend," Mom says to me, and I don't think she's mocking me.

What planet is this? Are we in another dimension? Either that, or I've snagged a guy so hot and perfect that even Mom can't find fault in him.

"Thank you. This was great," Tate tells her. "We should do it again while you're in town."

"Of course." She takes the black AmEx the waiter returns to her, quickly signing the check. "And you'll be accompanying Cassie to the Beacon's grand reopening in a few weeks?"

He glances at me. "We haven't really talked about it. I was planning on going, though." He flashes an awkward smile. A little bashful. "Wanna go together?"

I feel my cheeks reddening. "Sure."

"Excellent." Mom pushes her chair back and stands. "I assume your parents will be there too? According to my mother, the Cabot girl invited nearly half the town."

"I'm not sure," he replies, helping me out of my seat. "I don't know if there's an official guest list. I'll ask Mackenzie."

Mom waves a hand. "Your parents are welcome to come as our guests. The Beacon was in the Tanner family for decades." She winks. "We still have a bit of clout left."

We reach the door, Tate once again thanking her for dinner before we part ways. He and I have plans to go to the Hartleys' house, and Mom sashays off toward the Mercedes parked across the street.

Uneasiness swims inside me as I watch her drive away.

"You okay?" Tate asks, interlacing his fingers with mine.

"Yeah. I'm just . . . baffled."

"Baffled."

"Yes. Like, what the hell was that?" I gesture toward her disappearing taillights.

"I don't know. I thought it went pretty well. I was expecting a lot worse, but it ended up being kind of fun."

"Exactly. That's the baffling part. My mother is never this nice. Something's going on here. First she apologizes to me and buys me a crop top, and now this? This pleasant, condemnation-free dinner without a whiff of tension or a shred of criticism? No. I don't trust it."

He grins at me. "Aren't you the silver-lining girl?"

"This doesn't qualify as a silver-lining situation. This has never happened before. I told you, she's not this nice. Especially to me."

"You're saying there hasn't been a single genuine moment between you two in your entire life?" He sounds dubious.

I stubbornly shake my head. "There's always an ulterior motive with her. An agenda. The last time she buddied up to me this hard, she was going through her divorce with Stu and it turned out she wanted me to sign a written statement from her lawyer claiming Stu emotionally abused her throughout their marriage and she therefore deserved to have their prenup dissolved. Then when I refused, she told me Stu had never even liked me."

"Damn. Seriously?"

"Seriously. My stepbrother assured me that wasn't true. But still. That's why this—" I vaguely motion toward the street and the restaurant. "I don't get it."

He goes quiet for a moment. "Have you considered the possibility it's genuine this time?"

"Fool me once . . ."

"I get that. And I'm not saying you should blindly trust it. But . . ." He hesitates. "Maybe she's realized that having a combative relationship with her daughter isn't ideal."

"And when did she have this epiphany?"

He shrugs. "Who knows. Could be because you guys are selling your grandmother's house, the family business. It's the end of something, and endings make people nostalgic. Even narcissists. Sometimes it causes them to look inward and take stock of themselves. Triggers self-awareness they may have been lacking before."

"Maybe." I'm still not convinced.

"Look, we never truly know our parents. They lived entire lives before we ever came along, you know? All those experiences shaped them, made them who they are, and sometimes people become set in their ways and their personality defects, and it takes something major to jar them into making a change. Who knows what triggered your mother, but maybe she's ready for that change."

We start walking down the sidewalk, which is crammed with tourists even on a Wednesday night. It's so busy we had to park nearly a mile away.

"I think you should give her a shot," he says. "Be open to the possibility this olive branch is sincere."

I bite my lip. The problem with Tate is, he doesn't understand toxic parents. His family is perfect. As a couple, Gavin and Gemma are madly in love. As parents, they've always been there for him. He's the only guy I know who can proudly say that his mom is his best friend. And his dad too! If anyone has a *Gilmore Girls* relationship, it's Tate. He's Rory, and *both* his parents are frickin' Lorelai.

I envy him. Truly. I'd love having that sort of relationship with my parents. Hell, even just one of them. But I don't.

Tonight was nice, though. I can't deny that. My guard was nonexistent, and Mom didn't strike. I'm unscathed. Happy, even.

"I had a lot of fun tonight," I confess, albeit reluctantly.

"Then you should give her a chance. It's never too late to repair a relationship with somebody. To try and build the kind of relationship you want with them."

"You really believe that?"

"I do." His hand tightens around mine. It's comforting at first, but then he rubs the inside of my palm with his thumb, and the tone instantly shifts.

"You did a sexy thing," I accuse.

He nods in agreement. "I did a sexy thing."

We reach the parking lot, where he does another sexy thing by moistening his lips with his tongue.

"So." He licks at the corner of his mouth. "I know you lost your virginity less than two weeks ago, and, well, I don't want to throw everything at you all at once, but . . . how do you feel about car sex?"

"Yes," I say instantly and tug his hand toward the Jeep.

CHAPTER 25

CASSIE

On Friday morning, I stop by the Hartley house on my way to town to drop off a stack of photographs for Mackenzie. Since we're selling the house soon, I've been helping Grandma sift through the attic this week, digging through old boxes and decades' worth of treasures. I found a box of photographs of the Beacon Hotel throughout the years, and after we scanned them so Grandma could have a digital record, she suggested choosing a few of the originals to give to Mackenzie. When I called Mac about it, she'd been over the moon. She plans to frame and hang them at the hotel, along with an original map of Avalon Bay she somehow got her hands on. The map itself is so old the paper is virtually disintegrating and they need to keep it behind protective glass, away from any moisture.

While I'm at the house, Mac and Genevieve, who has the day off, drag me to the back deck so we can go over our plans for Beach Games, which commence tomorrow. It's a two-day affair that's bound to get ugly if the deadly determination on my teammates' faces is any indication.

"According to this," Mac says, reading from her phone, "the only events that require all four team members on the field of play at the same time are sandcastles, volleyball, and the water balloon toss. The others are either two-man only, or two-man heats."

"This is confusing," I inform her. "And so is that scoring system on the second page of the pdf. Who the hell organized this, a ten-year-old?"

Gen snickers. "Beach Games is spearheaded by Debra Dooley. She's the president of the Avalon Bay Tourism Board."

"*Debra Dooley* sounds like a cartoon character," Mac retorts.

"Trust me, that's not far off. Deb has the energy levels of thirty preschoolers. Just wait." Gen checks her own phone. "I'm down for the windsurfing and the swim. But I'd rather die than give Evan the satisfaction of watching me fall off the tightrope."

"Oh, I'll do that one," I volunteer. "I know you wouldn't think it because of these things—" I gesture to my boobs—"but somehow they aid my balance instead of toppling me over."

Mac snickers. "I can do the tightrope. But I'm not doing the tug-of-war. Rope burn sucks."

We look over the rest of the events, tentatively assigning players to each one. "I'll text Zale the assignments and see if he wants to make any changes," Mac says when we're done. I've yet to meet this Zale, Mac's new activities director, but from the way she describes him, he sounds like a blast.

"Tate and Danny will take any water sports easily," Gen says, still looking at the list. "But if good fortune is upon us, Evan will be the one windsurfing. He's a disaster, so there's no way Hartley and Sons will score."

"Speaking of Tate," Mac says, turning to eye me. "Coop said you two are dating."

"You needed Cooper to tell you that?" Gen demands before I can answer. She snorts loudly. "You mean the fact that they couldn't keep their hands off each other when they were here the other night and then left early with those guilty expressions— that didn't tip you off?"

I can't help but laugh. "She's got a point there."

Mac rolls her eyes. "Well, obviously I suspected at that point. But this is my first chance to be alone with Cassie. I wanted confirmation." She lifts one delicate eyebrow. "It's true, then?"

"We're not dating, per se. It's more of a fling."

"Flings never stay flings," Gen informs me. "They either turn into relationships, or someone gets their heart broken."

I shrug. "I'm not too worried. We live in different states, so it will have to end regardless. We're just having fun. And don't worry, my heart's still intact."

Because I refuse to engage it. I had one slip, one minor setback the other day at my dad's house, when my heart insinuated itself into what was supposed to be a summer of passion. *You're falling for him*. Okay, well, I heard you out, heart. And I've decided to ignore you.

Since then, I've been making a conscious effort to not get emotionally attached. And to temper my expectations. Luckily, I'm very proficient at not expecting too much out of people.

Whatever's happening between Tate and I, it's better if phrases like *falling for him* don't enter the equation.

Mac sets down her phone. "Want to stick around for a while? Take the dog for a walk on the beach?"

"I would," I say regretfully, "but I have to go. I'm meeting my mother at a salon in town. We're getting manicures."

"Must be nice to have a mom to do that kind of stuff with," Genevieve says, her voice surprisingly wistful.

"You're not close with your mother?"

"Well, she just died this past spring—"

"Oh gosh, I'm so sorry."

"It's all good." Gen shrugs. "Even when she was alive, Mom and I weren't close."

"Oh, this manicure doesn't mean we're close. Trust me. We've always had a very strained relationship. But she's been making an effort since she got to town, so I've decided to meet her halfway."

Because the silver lining to this, the best-case scenario, is that we manage to repair the relationship and have something better going forward. Worst case? She goes back to being a raging narcissist, which I've dealt with my whole life anyway, so there'd be nothing new there.

I bid the girls goodbye and drive into town. The salon is situated on a street parallel to Main Street, making it easier to find parking. It's a quiet location, sandwiched between a massage therapy clinic and a chiropractor's office.

Mom is already there when I walk in, seated at one of the manicure stations. "Cass!" she calls, waving me over.

"Hey," I greet her, while taking in the familiar surroundings. "I totally forgot about this place. Grandma used to bring me here when I was younger, remember? I'd always come home with neon pink nails."

"And then you'd shriek bloody murder when your father and I tried removing the nail polish once it started chipping."

"Because God forbid your six-year-old go outside with chipped nails," I say dryly.

That gets me a genuine laugh.

"Would you like to pick your color?" my manicurist asks while I settle at the table next to Mom.

"Oh, no color," I answer. "Just French tip."

"No color?" Mom frowns. "That won't look good for the grand opening."

It's the only critical remark she's made in a while, so I let it slide.

"I'll need to get another manicure before then, anyway. I have Beach Games this weekend," I remind her. "I'll be digging in sand and playing volleyball, so there's no point doing anything too fancy today."

She relaxes. "That's right. I forgot. You're competing for the Beacon."

"Yes. Really looking forward to it, too. It's going to be a blast."

"Maybe I can convince your grandmother to come watch some of the events," Mom suggests. "Or at least to attend the winners' ceremony."

"I honestly can't envision us placing, let alone winning." There's some stiff competition this year. The dudes from Jessup's Garage. The local fire station. Tate and the yacht club guys. The Hartleys. We'll be lucky if we win one event.

We settle in to be pampered as our nails are washed, buffed, and painted. My manicurist is a quiet teenager with long black hair, while Mom's is a super chatty woman in her thirties. She's visibly pregnant, informing us she's eight months along with her fifth child.

"Lord, you have four already? I could barely handle one," Mom jokes, nodding toward me. I make a face at her. "And now five? You deserve a medal of valor."

The woman laughs. "It sure is challenging at times. My boys are both under the age of six, and my girls are entering their tweens and becoming real handfuls, I tell ya."

Once our color is done, we're ushered to the drying area where we're ordered to sit for twenty minutes.

"Five kids?" I whisper when we're alone. "That sounds like a nightmare."

"Five is too many," Mom agrees.

A question bites at my tongue. It's one I'd never have dreamed of asking in the past, but we've been getting along so well lately, and my curiosity gets the better of me.

"Did you and Dad ever want more children?"

She looks startled. "Well. I suppose so. Your father did, certainly. He wanted at least three." A flare of bitterness darkens her expression. "And he got his three, so . . ."

"What about you?" I swiftly steer the subject away from Dad, partly because I've been enjoying our noncombative interactions, but mostly because we're stuck with our hands in these heaters which means I'm effectively trapped here with no escape.

"I didn't, no," she finally admits. "I was happy with just one child. You know I don't enjoy chaos. And growing up with three older siblings was very chaotic, especially having two older brothers who played sports. Your uncles were always tormenting me and Jacqueline. So, yes, I was content with one child." She hesitates again, for much longer this time. "With that said, I can't deny I was elated when I got pregnant for a second time."

I can't stop my loud gasp. "You were pregnant again after me?"

Mom's eyes flick across the room. The manicurists are chattering away with other clients, oblivious to our conversation.

"Yes." Her voice becomes very soft, as if she doesn't want to be overheard. Or maybe the subject is too emotional for her. Mom's not a fan of feelings. "I got pregnant when you were ten."

"How come I never knew this?"

"Your father and I didn't want to tell you yet. We were already having problems in the marriage, and then I lost the baby at nine weeks." She sighs. "They advise you not to announce the news to the world too early. Wait until the end of the first trimester to see if it sticks. And it didn't stick."

My heart squeezes. There isn't an ounce of emotion in her voice, but her eyes tell a different story. I don't think I've ever seen my mother appear this vulnerable.

"I'm sorry. I wish I'd known."

"No, I'm glad you didn't. You would have gotten your hopes up for a sibling and then been devastated when it didn't happen."

"You could have told me after the fact," I point out. "Once I was older."

"There was no point. The baby was gone, and then your father and I got divorced." Something in her tone changes, a sliver of regret slicing through it. "Although it may have contributed to why I fought for full custody of you."

She voices the confession then pulls her hand from the dryer and casually examines her nails, as if she hadn't just dropped a major truth bomb.

"What do you mean?" I push.

"Maybe it wasn't fair to your father, but after losing the baby, I clung to you a little tighter than I should have." She pauses. "Perhaps that wasn't the right thing to do, but . . . well, you can't change the past, can you?"

She quickly adopts a cavalier expression, unruffled by the fact that she just shattered my entire world view. Or at the very least, altered my view of *her*. I'd always believed she insisted on full custody to be spiteful, to get back at Dad, but this potential new motive provides another glimpse into my mother. A softer side I didn't know existed.

I reach over and touch her arm. "I'm really sorry, Mom. That must have been tough to go through. A divorce and a miscarriage around the same time."

"It's fine, sweetheart." She jerks away from my touch. Not in a rude way, but it's clear I made her uncomfortable. Physical comfort—any comfort, really—isn't something we typically offer each other. Maybe I was overreaching by going for that consolatory pat.

The main lesson I've taken from this conversation, though, is that Tate was right.

We never truly know our parents.

CHAPTER 26

CASSIE

I never gave much thought to pep talks. In school, I didn't play sports or belong to a team. But I'm fairly certain a pep talk is supposed to pump your teammates up, not make them fear you. The Hartley twins never got that memo.

"Let's hear it again," yells Evan. "Louder this time! What are we gonna do?"

"Murder," the two non-Hartley team members recite. Thoroughly unenthused.

"And who are we gonna murder?" shouts Cooper.

"Your girlfriends."

"Hey, assholes," Genevieve calls. "We're right here, you know."

Evan turns with an expression of the utmost innocence. "Baby, hey. Didn't see you there."

She just snorts.

Mac, meanwhile, seeks out the authorities. "Hey, Deb," she says, waving a hand. "Any chance we can switch sandcastle stations? Our neighbors are obnoxious."

"Tattletale," Cooper taunts.

Debra Dooley waves back. "No, siree! We're about to start!" Our Beach Games host looks exactly like her name sounds. Short, plump, with a helmet of brown hair and bangs slashing a straight line across her forehead. She's wearing khaki shorts, a white polo, and a pink adventure hat that would make my dad drool.

Looks like we're stuck next to Hartley and Sons. To our other side, huddled about six feet away, are the women from the Soapery, the store on the boardwalk that Grandma loves so much. Their team consists of the owner, Felice, her manager, and two employees. To be honest, I'm more worried about them than the Hartleys. They hand-carve all their soaps. A sandcastle should be easy for them.

Deb Dooley and her team of volunteers from the tourism office wrote up a practical event schedule for our two-day competition. The more labor-intensive events are taking place in the morning when it isn't too hot. Once the sun starts scorching us around noon, we'll be switching to water events. The teams arrived at nine, and I've been told we're done by one thirty. We also get an hour for lunch.

"All right," Gen says while the tourism people discuss some last-minute details among themselves. She lowers her voice. "Are we still doing a fish?"

"We *must*," insists Zale, who became my all-time favorite person within three seconds of meeting him. "We agreed to be ambitious."

"I know, but it'll be tough," Gen argues. "Especially the scales. How are we going to make them look all detailed?"

"Oh, my sweet talentless flower," Zale chirps, "leave the artistic endeavors to the designers. You and Cassie are the muscle. The pail bearers. Mac and I will handle our fish friend."

Gen rolls her eyes. "Did you just call me *talentless*?"

"'Fraid so." He flashes his bright white teeth, which he informed me he had professionally whitened just for this occasion. In the twenty or so minutes I've known Zale, I've become privy to his beauty routine, his family history, and the reasons he broke up with his last three boyfriends, two of whom were named Brian. With his tall, lanky frame, dazzling smile, and wild Afro held back by a navy bandana, Zale is larger than life. His exuberance is downright contagious.

A crowd has already gathered at the boardwalk. Deb and her army of volunteers roped off the sandcastle-building area from the public, and I smile when I catch sight of my dad and sisters. The girls insisted on showing up for the "opening ceremonies" to cheer me on.

"Go, Cassie!" Roxy shouts when Dad hoists her onto his shoulders.

I look over and wave, then scan the beach for Tate's team. I didn't see where Deb placed them. On the other side of Hartley and Sons are the mechanics. Beyond them is the team from the bakery—Nia's friend Chandra catches my eye and waves. I finally spot Tate's team about fifty feet away. They're huddled together, talking strategy. Last night I kept bugging Tate to tell me what they planned on building, to which he declared he would drown himself before sharing trade secrets with the enemy. And I thought I was overdramatic.

"Ladies and gentlemen, the twentieth annual Avalon Beach Games are about to commence!"

Damn, where did Deb get a microphone? And did she say *twentieth*?

"Twenty years they've been doing this shit?" Zale says. He's not from the Bay, only moved here this summer after Mackenzie's headhunter poached him from a golf resort in California. "Damn. You southern peeps have too much time on your hands."

Gen snickers.

"My name is Debra Dooley, and I'll be your host for this year's competition." Deb is bouncing around with excitement. "I'm the president of Avalon Bay's Tourism Board, and that means I love this town! I love it hard, folks!"

I smother a grin.

"The Bay is home not only to some very extraordinary people, but to the greatest, most unique businesses on the eastern seaboard! And we have a group of brave and beautiful participants for this summer's Games, including a team from the newly renovated Beacon Hotel, which is reopening at the end of the month."

"Whooo!" Genevieve shouts, jumping up and down. Since she's in tiny shorts and a black string bikini, her antics draw the eyes of nearly every male on the beach. My eyes aren't idle, either. She has great boobs. Perfectly proportioned.

"I know what you're doing," her fiancé warns from beside us.

"What?" she says innocently.

"You want to distract all the dudes into thinking about your tits instead of their sandcastles. Well, it ain't gonna work, Fred," he declares, using that completely random nickname he has for her that they both refuse to explain.

"Too late," his teammate Spencer says. "All I'm thinking about is her rack now."

Evan glowers at him. "That's the mother of my future children, asshole."

"The mother of your future children has a great rack."

"Our first event requires all four team members," Deb says into her mic. "The rules are simple—just build something! Anything! It could be a castle, it could be a flower, it could a self-portrait! You're allowed to use your hands and any of the tools provided. Shovels, pails, spatulas. Go nuts, everyone! You can also take advantage of any natural objects you find on the beach. Driftwood, shells, seaweed, and rocks are all fair game. What isn't allowed is anything man-made. If we see any food coloring or cement—"

"Who the fuck brought their own cement?" I hear Cooper mutter, and our respective teams shudder with laughter.

"—you will be disqualified." Deb claps her hands. "All right, everybody, get those sculpting hands ready! You have ninety minutes to wow the judges with the most impressive sand structure ever made. May I remind you that last year's winners, the beautiful ladies from the Soapery—"

I knew it. They're definitely our biggest competitors in this event.

"—constructed a five-foot sand interpretation of Cinderella's castle. That will be a tough one to top, ladies, but I believe in you."

"Someone's playing favorites," Mackenzie grumbles.

"For real. Dooley better not be one of the judges," Cooper growls.

"I think we found the competitive couple on the beach," I whisper to Gen, who giggles.

"Ready, set, sculpt!"

Anyone who thinks building something out of sand is easy is dead wrong. It's hard. And my only task so far is carting plastic pails from the ocean to our build site. It's nine o'clock and the sun's rays aren't even that strong, yet Genevieve and I are sweating profusely as we toil to replenish our team's water supply. After each trip, though, each sharp order from Mac and Zale to pat this, tamp this down, build this up, I'm starting to see a method to their madness. Gradually, our fish comes alive. It's about six feet long and three feet wide, its curved tail slashing a semicircle in the sand, scales intricately carved by Zale's spatula.

By the time our ninety minutes are up, I'm genuinely impressed by Team Beacon's creation.

"Not half bad," Gen says, admiring our handiwork.

"Not half bad?" Zale echoes. "It's exquisite."

"I wouldn't go that far—"

"Yes. You would. And you should." His tone brooks no argument, and Gen wisely shuts up.

I check out the Hartley team's creation, my eyebrows soaring when I notice it's not half bad either. They constructed a lion, complete with a wavy mane, thick paws, and an open mouth brandishing a set of lethal-looking teeth.

"Dammit," Mackenzie mutters, sidling up to Genevieve. They're surreptitiously studying their boyfriends' work. "It's pretty good."

"Ours is better," I assure them.

Zale agrees. "There's no structural integrity in that lion's mouth. One gust of wind and those teeth are falling off." He grins. "And my weather app has just informed me we should be expecting a lil' bit of wind."

Turns out he's a prophet. By the time the judges are nearing our section of the beach, the wind has picked up. They approach the Hartley lion just as half its face crumbles off.

"Son of a bitch," Cooper curses.

Mackenzie looks over with a sweet smile. "Better luck next time, sweetie."

This couple is vicious.

The three volunteer judges scribble something on their clipboards, then walk over to inspect our fish. I hear a couple *oohs,* which bodes well. Zale links his arm through mine, whispering, "We got this in the bag."

But there's no contest, not when the Soapery created a sprawling sand replica of Santorini, Greece. Even if I hadn't been told what it was, I could have easily guessed. Santorini's trademark staggered, dome-shaped buildings crop out of the sand, topped by colored shells the ladies scavenged from the beach. They've somehow managed to create blue accents. White walkways made of crushed shells. It's goddamn breathtaking.

The *oohs* and *ahhs* get louder. The judges furiously scribble and take pictures. Nobody is at all surprised when Felice and her team are declared the winners.

Team Soapery now leads the scoreboard with three points. The bakers, no surprise, come in second with their four-foot-tall sand cake, earning Team Bakery two points. And to my delight, our fish places third, which grants us one point.

"We're in this," Mackenzie exclaims, pumping her fist.

"Unlike *some* people," Genevieve says loudly.

I love my teammates.

*　*　*

The next few hours are some of the most fun I've ever had. Due to the windy conditions, the windsurfing race ends up being the most competitive. It's split into two heats, which means two scoring opportunities. Tate and Danny compete for the club; Mac and Gen for the Beacon. And Gen, who practically grew up on the water, causes an upset when she beats Danny. He crosses the finish line a mere second later, stunned to find himself in second. Zale and I cheer like maniacs from the shore, because Gen's win just earned our team three points. Mac, sadly, doesn't even place. Tate takes that heat easily, with Team Mechanics finishing second, and another upset occurs when Team Bakery steals third place from Team Firefighters.

I'm frankly shocked by all the upsets. There are eight teams in total, the participants ranging in age and skill level, but some of the competitors come out of left field. Like when the tiny waitress from Sharkey's Sports Bar defeats a gigantic mechanic in the footrace to take third. Or when one of the firefighters, who's two hundred and twenty pounds with tree trunks for legs, nimbly dances across the tightrope as if he were raised in the circus, winning first place.

After his windsurfing win, Tate strides down the sand, shaking water droplets from his golden hair. He smiles as he passes me.

"Nice win," I say grudgingly.

"Thanks, ginger." He winks before rejoining his team.

"Why does he call you *ginger*?" Zale asks blankly. "Your hair is clearly copper."

Gasping, I throw my arms around my teammate's neck. "THANK YOU!"

To cool off after the last water event, Debra Dooley announces it's time for tug-of-war.

Zale and I are representing Team Beacon. He's lean but muscular, and, as I told Mackenzie during our strategy session, I'm freakishly strong.

"All right, Cass, you ready for this?" Gen encourages. "Let's see you use that boob power!"

I roll my eyes at her. Normally I might bristle at the big-boobs joke, but that one was actually kind of funny. "I'll do my best," I promise.

Since Deb's scoring system makes very little sense to me, I struggle to understand as she explains how the tug-of-war event will work. It seems to be a bracket setup, four teams narrowed to two, narrowed to one winner. But you also get one point for every round you win along the way. And then the usual first-, second-, and third-place scores. Whatever. Just pull the rope, right?

Zale and I face off against the Soapery ladies: Felice and her manager, Nora. I feel like a sadist at the notion of destroying two fifty-year-old women, but they surprise us with their fortitude.

"Dig in!" Zale shouts. He's our anchor in the back. I'm in the front. "Dig your heels in, Cassie! We got this."

I hold on to the rope for dear life, while our teammates scream their encouragement from the sidelines. Inch by inch, we manage to drag our opponents closer to the red line. Sweat drips down my forehead. I see Felice's forearms straining. A red vein in Nora's forehead pulsating. They're losing steam. Giving up. Zale and I give a final tug and Team Soapery is out.

"One point for Team Beacon," Deb declares after blowing her whistle. "You guys are moving on to the next round."

Of the other three matchups, I'm not shocked that the teams with the biggest dudes make it through. The Hartley twins, the firefighters, and the yacht club guys.

We're facing the firefighters next, and I'm not optimistic.

"We can take them," Zale assures me.

We're huddled together several feet from the battle area. Deb's given each team a couple minutes to talk strategy, but the firefighters don't bother utilizing their allotted time. They're already in position, rope in hand. Cocky assholes.

Rightfully so, however. "Zale. There's no way. That big dude is, like, two hundred pounds."

He disagrees, his voice low and confident. "You saw what they did against the mechanics, right? They placed the short guy in the front, big one anchoring. Now look what they're doing."

I discreetly peek over. Interesting. The big dude is up front now.

"See?" Zale says knowingly. "Bad strategy. They think because you're in the front, he'll be able to single-handedly wrench you over the line."

"So I should go to the back this time?"

"No. Let's not talk crazy now. You need me to anchor. But you, my special goddess warrior, won't let him move you. You're not gonna budge, because we're gonna what?"

"Dig our heels in," I answer dutifully.

"Exactly. Dig those heels in. You're a stone, Cassie. Immovable. You're a statue. You're Stonehenge."

Now that's a pep talk.

"Now rub sand on your hands to dry them off," he orders. "A dry rope is a winning rope."

As we're getting in position, I notice Tate grinning at me. "Come on, ginger," he calls. "Let's see what you got."

Deb blows the whistle and the round begins. Somehow, against all odds, Zale's strategy works. We're statues. We don't move. Don't budge. I don't think the firefighters know what hit them, and they expend all their energy attempting to dislodge our heels, which are dug in so deep we're part of the sand now. Our opponents are dripping with sweat, but we're Stonehenge. We're immovable. Standing our ground.

"Now," Zale orders, and we make our move, yanking hard. The shorter guy can't control the rope and the two men go flying forward, landing face first in the sand.

"Another point for the Beacon!"

"Holy shit," I exclaim, dazed. "We're in the top two!"

Zale screams and lifts me off my feet to spin me around.

The Hartleys face off against Tate and his partner next, the latter team beating the twins after a competitive battle involving many an expletive. Then Tate's sauntering up to me with a shit-eating grin.

"Ohhhh, look what the cat dragged in," he taunts.

"You're the one who dragged yourself over to me, dumbass," I point out. I kneel down to stick my hands in the sand. They're sweaty, and I need them dry. As Zale says, *a dry rope is a winning rope.* That's not a real phrase, but hey, it got us to the finals.

Where, I suspect, our luck is about to run out. Tate's six-one and has those strong sailing hands. His partner Luke is six-five and also happens to have strong sailing hands. The two of them have dominated their matchups. But Zale and I did manage to beat the firefighters, so maybe there's a shred of hope for us.

"Don't look so worried," Tate tells me. "It'll be okay. I'll help you up after your face hits the sand."

"That's so romantic," I say. I look at Zale. "Isn't he so romantic?"

"You guys dating?" Zale asks, his gaze shifting between us.

I answer, "Sort of," at the same time Tate responds, "Just a little."

We look at each other and grin.

Then I drag my fingers across my throat and warn, "You're going down."

"Oh, I *am* going down. On you later tonight."

Zale lets out a howl.

"Is that supposed to be a threat?" I demand. "Because it sounds fun."

Tate winks. "More like a promise."

Then the whistle blows and we get our asses handed to us. The round lasts about four seconds, and I do indeed get sand in my face after I collapse. I'm pretty sure Luke was capable of taking us down all on his own.

Like the gentleman he is, Tate keeps his promise and helps me to my feet. "You okay?"

"I'm good. Nice win."

Although we lost, our efforts in the tug-of-war event awarded Team Beacon with four points. Mackenzie does some quick math and looks concerned when she realizes the Hartleys are closing in on the lead we accrued thanks to our windsurfing upset.

"It's fine," Gen reassures her. "We're still ahead by a lot."

Except suddenly we're not. Team Hartley embarks on a winning streak that makes Mac and Gen see red. They crush it in beach volleyball. Then Evan and Alex dominate their swimming heats, each coming in first. By the time one thirty rolls around, Team Hartley has added nine points to their total score.

Everyone's tired and ready to go, but we're stuck there for Deb Dooley's final speech.

"All right, everybody! How much fun did we have today? I think this was peak fun for me! And I'm looking forward to seeing all of you again tomorrow, bright and early! We'll be starting the obstacle course at eight forty-five sharp—the rest of tomorrow's events are listed on the schedule we emailed to you this week. We'll be wrapping up around one thirty P.M., with the winners' ceremony starting at two. Today's standings are being posted outside the tourism center as we speak, so make sure to take a peek before you head home for the day!"

The moment she finishes speaking, it's as if everyone on the beach has transformed from adult to child. A mob of us hurries across the street toward the tourism center, a little blue building that stands at the entrance to the boardwalk. Near the door, an easel holds a huge chalkboard with the scoreboard written on it. Genevieve practically hurls herself at it. She studies it, then threads her way through the other teams back toward us.

"We're in third place overall," she says flatly.

"That's great!" I counter. "Why do you look so pissed?"

"Hartley and Sons are in second place."

"Damn it," growls Mackenzie.

First place is currently held by the firefighters, with the yacht club in fourth. When I see Tate wandering my way, I stick out my tongue at him like an immature ass. "We're beating you."

He slaps his chest as if struck by a bullet. "Oh no. My ego can't handle it. I might need a blowjob to make me feel better."

I snicker, and he slings an arm around me and leans down

to plant a kiss on my lips. My heart skips a beat, because I still can't get used to the reality that Tate Bartlett just goes around kissing me.

"That was fun," he says.

"It really was. Did you compete last year?"

He nods. "We came in second overall. Third the year before."

"Look at you, collecting trophies left and right."

"Baby, don't even talk to me about trophies. My dad's kept every single trophy I've ever won in my life, since I was, like, five years old. They're collecting dust all over the house."

"What trophies were you winning at age five?" I challenge.

"You kidding me? I was five when I won my first dinghy race. Damn trophy was taller than I was." He grins. "Pretty sure Dad has a framed photo of it at the house. Tiny me struggling to hold up a monster trophy."

"I need to see that picture. Get on that."

"I'll see if my dad still has it prominently displayed in his office," Tate promises with a laugh.

"Hey," Evan interrupts, elbowing Tate in the arm. "Bonfire at our place later." He winks at me. "Gotta celebrate our lead."

I look at Gen, who's standing next to Evan. "Fraternizing with the enemy, are we?" I say, raising a brow.

"I mean, we live together."

"Fair. I'll allow it. Do you want to go?" I ask Tate.

"Like, a date?" He feigns uncertainty. "I don't know. That's a big commitment."

"Fine. I'll go alone."

"Nah, I'll go with you. I'm stopping in to see my folks for dinner, but I can come grab you after."

He removes his arm from my shoulder but doesn't release me completely—his hand instantly seeks out mine. As Tate laces our fingers together, I don't miss the amused gleam in Evan's eyes.

"So this is a thing now, eh?" Evan says.

Once again, Tate and I answer at the same time.

"Sort of."

"Just a little."

CHAPTER 27

TATE

Before I even turn the knob on the front door, I hear the explosion of noise behind it. The kids always know when someone's home. Especially when it's their papa. Sure enough, the moment I step inside, two tornadoes slam into me.

"Hey, guys." I drop to my knees to show them some love. "Aww, I missed you so much."

Fudge, our chocolate lab, has both paws around my neck. He's a hugger. Polly, our shepherd, waits her turn like the proper lady she is. She always plays it coy. Sits there looking pretty until I can't resist.

"Oh, you pretty girl, c'mere," I tell her, and soon she's trying to climb into my lap because these two always forget how big they are. Ninety-pound lapdogs. We used to have a third, a border collie named Jack, but he died this past winter. I miss the old guy.

As I rub behind her ears, Polly's tongue flops out happily. She collapses on the hardwood and offers me her belly. Fudge does the same, and suddenly I've got eight paws sticking straight up in the air and two bellies demanding to be rubbed.

Which is how my mom finds me. "Am I interrupting?" she asks dryly.

At the sound of her voice, the dogs jump to their feet, instantly bored of their prodigal papa's return. Their toenails click on the floor as they dash off to who knows where. I'm but a speck in their proverbial dust.

"Damn. And I thought they missed me," I remark, watching their disappearing tails.

"Speaking of missing. Hey, kiddo." Mom laughs and flings her arms around me. "I hate this housesitting gig of yours."

"No, you don't. You love the alone time with Dad."

"Well, duh. But I still miss my son."

"We text every day."

"Still miss you. Are you hungry? Dinner's almost ready."

"Famished. Where's Dad?"

"Upstairs in his office. He forgot to fill out some paperwork at work earlier, so he's taking care of a few things before dinner."

"Cool. I'm gonna go up and say hi to him. I need something from his office."

In the upstairs hall, I find Dad's door ajar. I approach and give it a light knock. "Dad?"

"Yeah, come in, kid." He greets me with a big smile. "How goes it? How was Beach Games?"

"Intense. We're currently in fourth place."

"Who's in first?"

"Frickin' dudes from the fire station. They always dominate." I walk toward the glass cabinet that spans one wall of the office.

It's pretty much a shrine to our family, containing all the accomplishments we've amassed over the years. Dad's baseball trophies and photos from his time in St. Louis. His and Mom's wedding pictures. All my childhood trophies and first-place ribbons. And there, sandwiched between Mom's framed college diploma and a copy of the deed to Bartlett Marine, is the photograph I was telling Cassie about. Me, posing after the first sailing race I ever entered, holding the first trophy I ever won. Or rather,

300 • ELLE KENNEDY

trying to hold it. My teeth-gritting expression reveals I'm struggling not to let the thing flatten me.

"Do you mind if I take this out so I can snap a picture of it?" I point to the photo.

"Go for it." He chuckles. "Taking a walk down memory lane?"

"No, I was just telling Cassie about this earlier. Thought she'd get a kick out of seeing it." I open the cabinet and carefully remove the frame, then place it on the edge of Dad's desk and fuck with my phone camera until I'm not seeing any glare.

"Man, I was a cute kid," I remark.

Dad snorts. "And so humble too."

I take a pic of the pic, then return it to the cabinet. As I'm shutting the door, my gaze snags on another framed photo, this one featuring a younger version of my father hanging off the mast of a shiny white yacht. He's grinning from ear to ear, loving life.

"Was this your Hawaii-to-Australia sail?" I ask, glancing over my shoulder. "The one that took you a month?"

"Thirty-two days," he confirms. "Man, what an adventure. I almost died in Hurricane Erma."

"Sounds fun." My smile falters when I suddenly think about Gil Jackson's offer. It's constantly been on my mind, nagging at me, but I haven't made any decisions yet. It would be a huge commitment, leaving the Bay. And sure, I can do it in sixty days, but who knows if or when I'd get an opportunity like that again. If I accept the gig, I want to maximize my time on the *Surely Perfect*. That means four months. Four months and the adventure of a lifetime.

"Uh-oh, you've gone serious on me." Dad spins around in his chair, propping his hands behind his head. "What's going on, kid?"

"Gil asked me to deliver the *Surely Perfect* to him in New Zealand."

His eyebrows shoot up. "Really?"

"I know, right?" I lean against the bookshelf. Hesitant, because I value my father's opinion. But I also know he won't want me taking so much time off. "They bought a house in Auckland and plan to live there half the year. They'd need her there by New Year's Day. They'd pay me, obviously."

Dad is startled now. "You're considering this?"

"Of course I am. Why? You think I shouldn't?"

His casual pose changes, arms dropping, hands clasping together in his lap. His expression grows serious as he considers the question. "What's the starting point? California?"

"Florida. It'll take a couple days to sail from Charleston to the port in Miami. I'd stock up there. Prep the boat. And then I'd set sail to Auckland."

A frown mars his lips. "This is a transatlantic crossing, Tate. No. It's too much for you."

"I'd take it easy. Gil said he'll help me chart a manageable route."

"Easy? Manageable?" Dad shakes his head in disbelief. "We're talking about crossing the North Atlantic, the South Atlantic. Indian Ocean. Then you've got the gulfs, the Tasman Sea."

"It's a lot," I agree.

"It's too much," he repeats. "And he needs her there by the first of January? That puts you in hurricane season."

"The tail end of it," I argue. "It adds some risk, yes, but the tough sailing starts later in the journey. By November the season will have passed. Any developing hurricanes are likely to be west, right?"

"That's not the only concern, kid. The trades will be difficult. You'd be looking at fifteen, twenty knots. Not to mention squalls. I did an Atlantic crossing before you born, nothing too intensive, just to the Canaries. And even that was tough." He sounds unhappy.

"You gotta pay attention to what's happening north when you tackle a voyage like this. Those long trailing cold fronts from the North Atlantic can fuck with the trade winds."

"I'd adjust for all that."

"A friend of mine did an Atlantic crossing in winter once. Said it was the worst sailing of his life." Dad's eyes flicker with concern now. "Waters could get rough."

"I can handle it."

He rubs the bridge of his nose. "Look. I mean, part of me thinks, yeah, you can. I've never seen anyone handle a boat the way you do. But it's a big undertaking for your first solo, you know?"

"I know," I say, nodding.

"If it's something you're seriously considering, maybe wait until spring, then? And start off a little less ambitious, maybe only a week or two? Chart a course from here to, I don't know, the Virgin Islands. Yeah, BVI would be good. You could take the Beneteau 49 if she's not booked for a charter—"

She's not a Hallberg-Rassy, I almost blurt out, but bite my tongue.

"—and give yourself a small taste of the solo journey. Know what I mean?"

"Yeah, I guess." We can both hear my lack of enthusiasm for his alternate proposal.

"If you accepted Gil's offer, you'd be gone, what, two, three months?"

"About that. Longer if I take the scenic route," I joke.

Dad doesn't crack a smile. "That's a long time to be away from home. I need you at Bartlett Marine, kid. I can't handle it by myself."

I want to point out that he handled it by himself for years before I started taking on more responsibility. But it's clear what he thinks of this plan.

Sensing my unhappiness, he sighs. "I built this business for our family. For you, so that one day you would take it over. I thought that's what we were working toward these past few years. Teaching you how to run it."

"We are. But if I'm ever going to do a major solo voyage, shouldn't I do it now? Before I have even more responsibility?"

Dad is silent for several long beats. "I truly don't think you're ready for it," he finally says. "And I need you here, at the dealership. But if you want to go . . ."

I swallow my disappointment. "No," I say. "It's fine." He's probably right, anyway. It's a crazy idea. Dangerous. "I'll tell Gil to hire a more experienced captain."

"I think that's a smart idea. And if you did want to plan something for the spring, I'd be happy to sit down with you and—"

"Dinner's ready!" Mom's faint voice calls from below.

"Shit," Dad says with a pained look. "I still need to send this email. Tell your mother I'll be right down?"

"Sure thing."

Downstairs, I help Mom set the table, hoping she doesn't notice I'm feeling subdued. But she's a mom, so of course she notices.

"Everything okay?" she asks. "What were you talking to your father about?"

"All good. We were just going over some sailing stuff. And I needed to take a picture of Dad's trophy shrine to show something to Cassie. I'm meeting her after this."

Mom smiles and hands me a stack of silverware from the utensil drawer. "Which picture?"

"The one of me after my first dinghy race."

"Oh boy, I remember that day," she says with a laugh. "Standing there at the marina, worrying my five-year-old son was going to drown. Gavin assured me you could handle it, and what do you know—he was right. You won. Your dad was practically bursting with pride." She's quiet for a beat, then says, "You're spending a lot of time with Cassie."

I lay down the silverware on the table. "Yeah. I guess."

"Is it serious?"

I lift my head to see her fighting a smile. "Not really. It's going to end when she goes back to school in September."

"Do you want it to end?"

That gives me pause. "To be honest, I hadn't considered the alternative."

"But you like her."

I do like her. I like her a lot. In fact, I'm getting impatient for dinner to start, because the sooner it starts, the sooner it ends and I can go pick Cassie up for the bonfire. I saw her all day and I'm already dying to see her again.

"Yes. I like her."

"Then why does it have to end?" Mom asks.

For the life of me, I can't think of a good answer to that.

* * *

Later, at the bonfire, I'm still thinking about my mother's question.

Why does it have to end?

I mean . . . does it? Cassie and I agreed to a summer fling, but sometimes flings . . . evolve. My biggest fear was that I'd end up hurting her because of my need to keep things purely physical, but that need seems to have . . . evolved. We go out on the boat. We have dinner when I get home from work. Hell, I've gone for dinner with her and her *mother*. Somehow, without noticing it, I allowed all this to happen. And I don't even care. I *like* it.

Fuck.

Whatever we have going on these days, it's a lot more than physical.

I gaze across the fire where Cassie's sitting with Genevieve and Heidi. She and Heidi are laughing about something, which is a bit shocking because Heidi isn't the chatty, giggly type. She's the type who eats her own young. That's why she and Alana are such good friends. Stone hearts, those two.

Speaking of Alana, when I go to the coolers to grab another beer, my former flame sidles up to me. She looks gorgeous as always, and yet I'm startled to discover I'm not attracted to her anymore. She's gone back to being the Alana I first met in junior high, just another one of the awesome girls in my platonic friend group, someone it wouldn't even occur to me to sleep with.

"Hey," she says.

"Hey." I twist open a fresh beer.

"You've been avoiding me."

I glance over. "Not at all."

"Oh really? So it just happens that we used to see each other all the time and now I haven't seen you since . . ." Alana thinks it over. "Damn, since the last time we were here together."

"Shit, really? That was more than a month ago."

"Exactly."

"I promise, I'm not avoiding you," I assure her. "I've been slammed at work this entire summer. I haven't really hung out with anyone other than Cassie."

"Ah," she says knowingly. "The other redhead."

"Purely coincidental," I reply with a grin, although I do find it funny.

"So you're not avoiding me."

"No."

Those sharp eyes continue to study me. "I don't think you're lying."

"I'm not. I've been at the dealership, the yacht club, chilling with Cassie. This weekend is Beach Games. Lots going on. I've gone out with Evan for a couple drinks, but that's about it. And I'm housesitting for the Jacksons, so I've been away from the regular 'hood."

"Oh yes, you're lapping it up in the land of clone luxury."

"Pretty much. How've you been?"

"I'm good. Got a job as an au pair."

"You hate kids," I remind her, grinning.

"These ones aren't too bad. And the pay is great. I swear those clones like to throw their cash around like their entire life is one long strip club visit."

I think about how much Gil offered me to sail the *Surely Perfect* and I have to agree. "You dating anybody?" I raise a brow.

"I am not . . . unlike some people." Alana laughs. "It's weird seeing you with a girlfriend."

"She's not my girlfriend."

"Uh-huh, that's what they all say." With that, Alana saunters off.

Beer in hand, I wander to the fire and grab a chair, dragging it next to Evan's. Heidi's gone, and Gen and Cassie are now near the deck in an intense huddle with Mackenzie and their Beach Games teammate Zale. When Cooper passes their huddle, Mac lifts her head and all but hisses at him like a feral cat. He holds his hands up in surrender and keeps walking, rolling his eyes when he approaches us.

"I just got accused of espionage for walking by their team," Coop says cheerfully.

I snicker. My eyes remain on Cassie, who's laughing at something Gen said.

"Gen really likes your girl," Evan remarks, following my gaze. "And Gen hates most people."

"It's hard not to like Cassie," I admit.

Cooper's brows jerk up. Then he chuckles. "Interesting."

"What?"

"Nothing."

"You sound like my mother. She was just grilling me about Cass."

"I mean, you're acting very boyfriendly," Evan pipes up, sounding amused. "So if that's not the path you want to take," he warns, "you should probably course correct right about now."

I take a swig of beer. "Boyfriendly how?"

"Every time I turn around you're holding her hand."

"So?"

"You never held Alana's hand," Cooper points out.

"Alana would bite a dude's dick off before she let him hold her hand."

"Did you even try?" challenges Evan.

I pause. "No."

"Why not?" His smug smirk tells me he already knows the answer to that.

And he's right. I never felt that sort of tenderness toward Alana. We both kept an emotional distance because we knew it was never going anywhere.

But there's no distance with Cassie. She's always within my reach. She melts into me when I come to her. She doesn't keep me at arm's length. Doesn't play games. I'm happy when I'm with her. And as I think about all the ways she and I just fit, that question once again surfaces in the forefront of my mind.

Why does it have to end?

CHAPTER 28

CASSIE

"This is it. What we've trained our entire lives for. And by entire lives I mean the last two days. And by trained I mean we randomly decided who would compete in what event. I mean, I didn't train—did you?" Zale glances around the huddle.

"I swam some laps in my pool," I tell them. "Does that count?"

"Now that's dedication to the team," Mackenzie teases.

"The Beacon is forever indebted to you," Genevieve says solemnly.

I snicker. I had a lot of fun with my teammates this weekend, and I'm sad to see it end. Alas, only one event remains in the twentieth-annual Avalon Beach Games: the water balloon toss.

It's been a frustrating day thus far for Team Beacon. We didn't place in either of the obstacle course heats this morning. Team Yacht Club won both, which had Tate strutting around like a self-righteous peacock. We also lost out on third place in the bucket relay to those damn firefighters. We made up for it by placing third in the three-legged race, thanks to Mackenzie and Zale. Unfortunately, "the stupid twins because they have the same stupid size legs," as Mackenzie had poetically framed it, won that race to give Team Hartley three points.

As it stands now for Mac and Gen's side bet, their boyfriends are beating us by one measly point. In the scope of the actual competition, I think our teams are vying for third place overall. But since my teammates are more concerned with their side hustle, they proceed to torture my brain with a bunch of math that makes no sense.

"All right," Mac is saying. "They're up by one, so that means we need to place third in order to tie—"

"What's the tiebreaker?" Zale interjects.

"No idea. We didn't anticipate a tie. We'll have to come up with something. But if we place second, that becomes moot, because then we get two points and we win. First place, we get three points and we win. *But*—we only win if *they* don't place."

"Wait, what if they place third and we place first?" Gen points out. She squints as she does some mental math. "Then they get one point, which puts them up by two. But we get three points, which puts us up by one. We win."

"Right. But . . . damn it, if we win and they come in second, we tie again. So—"

"Stop," I wail, covering my ears. "I can't listen to this anymore."

"For real," Zale moans, his face scrunched in sheer pain. "This is too complicated. You sound like my brothers droning on about their dumbass fantasy football standings, trying to figure out if they made the playoffs."

"All right, everyone!" Debra Dooley yells into her microphone. I swear, she brought that thing from home. None of the other volunteers have mics. "We're about to start!"

A few yards away, Evan calls out to his fiancée. "Hey, Fred, what size should I order your French maid costume in?"

"In your dreams," Gen shoots back.

"Every night," he promises.

Mackenzie's gaze travels to Cooper, and she cocks her head at him. "Well? I'm waiting. Where's *your* smartass comment?"

Cooper smirks. "I don't heckle the downtrodden."

"Heckle this," she retorts, flipping him the bird.

I smother a laugh. It's funny seeing each of them interact. Gen and Evan are chemistry personified, every word exchanged practically oozing sex. Cooper and Mac are more adversarial, yet when they look at each other, their connection is unmistakable.

I look over at Tate, remembering the way he held my hand last night at the bonfire. His fingers laced through mine feels so natural, and I wonder how on earth I'm going to say goodbye to him in two weeks. My flight to Boston leaves three days after the Beacon's reopening, and a part of me is already thinking, well, I *do* get a week off for midterms in October. And I *do* get Thanksgiving off. And Christmas. New Year's.

Maybe we can make something work. Not a relationship or anything; I'm still doing my best to keep my heart disengaged. But who says we can't keep sleeping together? Hooking up when we have the opportunity? We're not sick of each other yet, so doesn't it make sense to keep the fling going until we are? That is, if Tate's even interested in extending the fling.

For some reason, though, I get the feeling he is.

"We'll do a random draw to determine the order for the toss," Deb says, and a volunteer rushes over with a baseball cap containing slips of paper with our team names. "Up first will be . . . the handsome sailors from the Manor!"

The rest of the names are pulled from the hat, and we're gratified to hear we'll be going last. Gives us an opportunity to watch the other teams and learn from their mistakes.

As Tate and his team come forward, Deb quickly goes over the rules again. The water balloon toss requires all four members to stand in a line, starting at about two feet apart. The balloon is thrown down the line from one person to the next, and after each completed leg, the team members must take a step back. The distance between each person gets bigger and bigger, and the team that makes it the farthest distance without popping their balloon wins those coveted three points.

"Ready?" Deb shouts. "Annnd toss!"

This is it. Do or die.

Team Yacht Club makes it to a distance of fifteen feet separating each member before the balloon hits Luke in the face and explodes, soaking him. Tate shoots me a wry look as they return to the sidelines, as if to say, *you win some, you lose some.* He takes everything in stride. I love that about him.

"Fifteen feet is the distance to beat!" announces Deb.

The bakers and mechanics are up next, finishing with an impressive twenty-two feet for the former and a dismal twelve for the latter. The firefighters finish with twenty feet. The Sharkey's staff with nine.

Then it's Team Soapery, working together like a well-oiled machine. Each time Deb shouts, "Annnd step!" the four ladies take a step to widen the distance. Deb shouts, "Annnd toss!" and the balloon exchanges hands.

Three minutes in, and they're already twenty feet apart.

"Whoa," Zale marvels.

"It's the underhand throw," Mac whispers to our team. "We need to go underhand."

Team Soapery makes it a spectacular twenty-nine feet before Felice catches the balloon wrong and it bursts in her outstretched hands. Still, the ladies know they kicked ass, grinning from ear to ear as they head for the sidelines. They've got a good seven feet on the best team, the bakers.

"Hartley and Sons, you're up!"

Cooper smirks at his girlfriend as he saunters by. "You're saying all we have to do is beat twenty feet and we're guaranteed to place? Oh no! So hard!"

Mackenzie and Genevieve simultaneously throw up their middle fingers, sparking a burst of laughter from the gathering crowd. When I glance toward the onlookers, I'm alarmed to spot my dad's face. He's with Nia and the twins, and they all smile and wave when they notice me looking. Shit. I didn't know they were coming back today. Mom and Grandma are supposed to show up too. For the winners' ceremony.

Panic flares inside me, while I strain to remember the last time Mom and Dad were in the same vicinity.

The saving grace here is that Mom and Grandma haven't arrived yet. That means I have time to warn Dad off before they get here. But first, we need to murder this water balloon event.

On the field of play, the Team Hartley line moves with swift precision. They nail their five-foot throws. Ten. Fifteen.

At nineteen feet, the biggest upset of today's Beach Games occurs.

Spencer, their day laborer, tosses the balloon to Evan. His hand slips on the release, just slightly, but it's enough to alter the trajectory. The balloon veers toward Evan's right, forcing him to take an abrupt step, and his body isn't quite in position as he attempts the catch.

Splat.

The water explodes in Evan's hand.

"Man down!" Deb crows into the mic, and the firefighters cheer loudly, maintaining their current third-place score of twenty feet.

"Oh baby, why are you all wet?" Genevieve coos when Evan stomps back. She pretends to be confused. "What happened? I wasn't looking. Did it pop?"

"Use that little-girl voice again"—he narrows his eyes—"and it better be tonight. In bed."

Mac winks at Cooper as he passes. "I'm pretty sure that wasn't twenty feet . . ."

He snorts. "You haven't placed yet, princess. And right now we're still beating you by one point."

Finally, it's our turn. I can't even believe how nerve-wracking this is. How is this low-stakes, small-town beach competition making me sweat this much?

"We got this," Zale says.

"We got this," Gen echoes.

"Annnd toss!" Deb yells once we're in position.

Team Beacon makes fast work of it. Five feet. Ten. Fifteen. Those are the easy ones. Now come the scary little one-footers between fifteen and twenty. If we hit twenty, though, we only tie with the Hartleys, and we can't have that. We want the win. Which means we need to beat not only the firefighters but also the bakers in order to move to second place.

At eighteen feet, my palms are so clammy I have to bend down and wipe them off in the sand.

At nineteen feet, I can't feel my legs anymore.

The pressure is monumental. We're tossing for twenty now. If we make it, we've tied the firefighters.

We make it.

"Annnd step!"

We take another step. If we succeed in this next sequence, we've knocked the firefighters out.

"Annnd toss!"

Zale tosses. I make the first catch.

I look at Genevieve. "Ready?"

She wipes her hands on the front of her denim shorts. "Ready."

Very methodically, I throw underhanded in a perfect straight line. The balloon floats like a weightless feather into her waiting palms. She catches it, and a collective breath of relief travels through the crowd.

Gen turns to face Mac, features creased with deep concentration. She tosses.

Mackenzie makes the catch.

"Twenty-one feet!" Deb declares.

"Holy shit!" Zale screams. "We did it! We did it!" He starts jumping around, thrusting up both arms and punching the air.

I choke out a laugh. "We're not done!" I remind him. "We're still playing."

"Oh, right."

"We have an actual shot at second place here," Gen marvels.

And we do it. We make it to twenty-three feet before my balloon explodes at Gen's feet. Doesn't matter, though. We successfully edged out the bakers to finish second place in this final event.

We've beaten the Hartleys at Beach Games.

By *one* point.

That was really fucking close.

"What size thong do you need?" a smirking Gen asks the twins once our team celebration dies down. Her gaze shifts to Evan's groin. "I don't know if they make it in extra small, sweetie."

"Extra large, you mean." Growling, he lifts Gen off her feet as if he's going to toss her, but instead brings her close. She wraps her legs around him and they start making out.

Rolling my eyes, I wander over to my dad, who now stands alone on the boardwalk. "Nice job!" he exclaims, giving me a quick side hug.

"Thanks. Where are the girls?" I ask, glancing around.

"They got bored of watching you throw balloons, so Nia took them to get ice cream."

I nod. "Hey, so I should probably warn you—Mom and Grandma are going to be here any minute. They're coming for the winners' ceremony."

"Really? Your mother?" He lifts a brow.

THE SUMMER GIRL • 315

I smile ruefully. "I know, right? But . . . I haven't said anything to you about this, mostly because I didn't trust it at first, but Mom really has been making an effort since she got to town."

"Has she?" I can't quite discern his tone.

"She has. It's been fun, actually."

Dad is taken aback by that. I don't blame him. I've never used the word *fun* in relation to my mother.

"Oh. Well. That's great, Cass. I'm glad to hear you're enjoying yourself and that she's putting in the effort."

This time, I easily pick up on the skepticism lining his voice.

"Like I said, I didn't entirely trust it. But she's been good lately. Attentive. Funny. Forthcoming . . ." I hesitate for a beat. This probably isn't the most appropriate time to take the conversation deeper, but I also suspect we likely won't get another opportunity to discuss my mother, and so the words just slip out. "She told me about the miscarriage."

Dad lurches as if I struck him. "She did?"

"Yes." My palms are sweaty again. Dad and I rarely discuss anything this sensitive, so I'm unsure how to navigate it. "I'm glad she did. It made me understand her better, you know? Why she fought you so hard for custody. I thought she was trying to keep you away from me, but I guess she was trying to keep me close after her loss. So . . . yeah. I'm grateful that she told me."

"Yes. Well." His expression shutters, but not before I glimpse a flash of anger.

"Cassie!"

I turn in time to see my sisters racing toward me. Nia trails after them, wearing brown sandals and a loose-fitting sleeveless dress.

"Wanna know what Pierre did today?" Roxy exclaims. "He farted!"

The girls proceed to double over in high-pitched laughter, while their mother grimaces.

"It was very unpleasant," Nia says stiffly.

I glance at Dad. "You didn't warn them about the whole stink-pot thing?"

"*Clayton?*" growls his wife.

"Thanks, Cass. Thanks a lot."

I snicker. "Hey, you knew going into this purchase that if they handled him too roughly he'd unleash a fart attack."

"Fart attack!" Mo squeals, and the girls start skipping around shouting those two words over and over again. A resigned Nia offers an apologetic smile to all the people who turn to stare at us.

"Attention, Avalon Bay!"

A voice suddenly blasts out of the boardwalk's PA system. Deb, of course. I've heard Debra Dooley scream into microphones so many times these past two days that I could now pick her voice out of a lineup.

"The winners of the twentieth-annual Avalon Beach Games are about to be announced. Please make your way over to the Tourism Center."

"Did you win?" Mo asks me, wide-eyed.

"I don't think so. But if my teammate's math is right, we may have come in third. I'll see you guys later, okay? Gotta find my team."

"We're heading out now," Dad says, which tells me he took my warning seriously. "But I'll call you later. Good job today."

"Thanks, Dad."

There's a large crowd gathered at the tourism hut when I arrive. I search the sea of faces until I spot Zale's familiar Afro. "Cass!" he shouts. "Over here!"

I join my team, and we wait impatiently while Deb delivers another one of her speeches about how much she loves this town. She stands atop a low stage that barely holds two people, let alone a team of four. The winning teams select one member to go up and accept their trophy.

The firefighters win first place, while the yacht club takes second. And for the Beacon's long-awaited return to the world of Beach Games, our team comes in third.

We break out in cheers as Gen hops on to the small stage to accept our third-place trophy from a beaming Deb Dooley. It's about ten inches tall with a copper finish and gold accents around the beach ball figurine at the top. The brown wooden base just has a generic THIRD PLACE engraved on it.

Gen flashes the Hartleys a smile as she saunters past them holding our trophy. "Aww, they don't give these out for fourth?" Gen asks sweetly. "Look how cute it is."

"A third-place trophy, Genevieve?" Cooper shoots back. "Grow the fuck up. If you don't win, you lose."

Mac offers a brisk nod of agreement. "He's not wrong."

"You two psychos are made for each other," Evan mutters.

"Hey, Cassie," Mac says, turning to smile at me. "Thanks so much for being on our team—this was such a blast. Will you come back next year?"

"Really? Even though I don't work at the hotel?"

"What do you mean? The Beacon was in the Tanner family for fifty years. You'll always have a place here."

I'm so touched, my eyes start to sting. I didn't expect to form genuine connections this summer, but I'm so glad I did. Stupid Grandma was right. It is nice being part of a group.

Speaking of Grandma, I suddenly spot her in the crowd, a frown staining my lips when I notice she's alone. I excuse myself and make my way toward her. She greets me with a smile, but it's clearly strained.

"Hey," I say, leading her toward a less busy section of the boardwalk. "Where's Mom?"

"Well . . ." Grandma presses her lips together.

"What's wrong?"

"Nothing's wrong. But . . . perhaps a little hiccup. We just ran into your father and his family in the parking lot." Grandma pauses. "Your mother stopped to speak to Clayton."

Shit.

"Damn it," I mutter. Then I force a smile so Grandma doesn't worry. "Are you cool waiting here for a minute? I want to go and make sure nobody's been killed."

I race off in the direction of the little gravel lot behind the tourism center. This situation needs handling ASAP. Last thing I need is for Evil Mom to make a reappearance when we still have a week left in the Bay. Which means I need to defuse any bombs that might blow the rest of my summer to smithereens.

I catch sight of them immediately, gratified that it's just the two of them. Nia and the girls must be in the car already. Silver lining, I guess.

Hurrying toward them, I manage to catch the tail end of Dad's incensed accusation.

"Using the miscarriage to turn our kid against me? Trying to make yourself look like some sort of martyr? That's low, Vic, even for you. You fought for custody because you're a selfish—" He stops abruptly. "Cassie, hey. Hi, sweetheart."

Mom whirls around. Her brown eyes blaze with anger. Not directed at me, though. She's still wholly focused on my father.

"Guys," I beg. "Please. I don't want you two to fight."

"Neither do I, Cassandra. But I'm not the one fighting, am I, Clayton?" Mom says coldly.

Dad frowns. "Victoria . . ." I don't know if it's a warning or an appeal.

"No, I think this conversation is over. Why don't you go now? Your nurse and her children are waiting in the car."

"*My* children," he growls.

I reach for Mom's arm. "Come on," I urge. "Tate's taking us to lunch. He and Grandma are waiting."

Her thunderous expression doesn't change, but she also doesn't object when I start leading her away. I glance over my shoulder at Dad, whose face is bright red, his movements jerky as he repositions his glasses on the bridge of his nose.

"I'll see you this weekend," I tell him. "We're still doing dinner, right?"

"Yes, of course. See you then, sweetheart."

And then Dad stalks off and Mom is still fuming, and I feel like I just fought off a pack of rabid dogs. *This* is why confrontations should be avoided at all costs. They never lead to anything but misery.

CHAPTER 29

TATE

"That was so brutal today," Cassie moans against my shoulder, her breath tickling my skin. We're lying together on the dock. Sharing one lounge chair, which means we're practically on top of each other. Not that I'm complaining. I welcome any opportunity to have her delectable body pressed up against me.

"You're still thinking about it?" I say gently.

"How can I not? I don't even want to know what would've happened if I hadn't been able to drag Mom away. They looked like they were going to murder each other."

"That's rough."

"I mean, it's par for the course with them."

It's difficult for me to relate to that. My parents rarely fight. They bicker, sure. They've gone through a rough patch or two, but I've never seen them treat each other with anything close to the level of vitriol that Cassie describes with her parents. Their confrontation really affected her today, and the lunch that followed wasn't much of a palate cleanser. Tori was plainly in a bad mood, and I was glad when the check finally arrived.

I spent the rest of the day trying to distract Cassie from her parents' argument. We passed the afternoon swimming, barbecuing, and hanging out on the dock. At sunset we took the Lightning out for a ride again, which in turn got me so hot I couldn't even wait to find a bed when we returned to the house. We had sex on the dock, which, I won't deny, is a bit risky. But Tori and Lydia had gone out for dinner, and we tried to be quiet, mindful of the other houses along the water. Not sure if we succeeded. I can be loud when I come.

Now, we're still in our bathing suits, cozied up on the lounger, while the night breeze floats along the bay and I absentmindedly stroke her soft hair.

Cassie snuggles closer, and a sense of pure contentment washes over me. Even now, a solid hour postcoital, I'm still recovering from the sex. I swear it only gets better with this woman. I forget myself when I'm inside her. The entire world disappears and it's just me and her. Her warmth. Her pussy. Her smile. It's perfection. And the more I think about it, the more I don't want this to end. I'm already thinking about the holidays, the possibility of flying to Boston to see her.

Or, even better, accepting Gil Jackson's offer and asking Cassie to join me on the *Surely Perfect*. For a weekend. A week, a month. As long as she wanted. A horde of images suddenly swarms my mind. Cassie and I on the open water. Her hair blowing in the wind as she helps me sail. Having sex on the deck. Falling asleep in the cabin. Cooking together in the galley—

Jesus. What the hell is my brain doing right now?

None of that is ever going to happen, least of which because I already decided not to go. I promised Dad I wouldn't.

"Are you going to talk to your dad about the argument?" I ask, my gaze focusing on the darkening sky.

"God no."

"Why not?"

"Because clearly it's a sore subject for him."

"As it should be. She had a miscarriage. She fought for sole custody of you instead of agreeing to joint custody like he wanted." I lightly stroke Cassie's arm. "Don't you want to know more about that? His perspective about the miscarriage and everything that followed it?" Now I find myself frowning. "Don't you want to talk to him about *real* shit?"

"We do," she protests. "Sometimes. Sporadically." She sighs. "All right, fine. We don't talk about anything deep. I hold a lot of it back, but—"

"But there's a silver lining?" I guess with a dry chuckle. "Okay, let's hear it."

"I have him in my life," she says simply.

I furrow my brow. "And he'd go away if you shared your feelings?"

"He might. I . . ." Her voice cracks. "I don't want to be a burden on him. He already has his hands full, raising two little kids. He doesn't need his grown-ass daughter whining about her feelings and demanding to know why he never fought for custody. Telling him how much it hurts that he gave her childhood bedroom away, how awful it is to feel like I've been replaced. How fucking jealous I am of his new family."

I take a breath, tightening my arm around her. "Man. I didn't realize you felt any of that."

"Yeah. I do." Her hand trembles against my abdomen. "Right after the twins were born, when Dad suddenly had even less time for me, I used to listen to this one song all the time. It was called 'Jealous,' and I'd lie in my bedroom in Boston and listen to it on repeat because it just encapsulated everything I felt. How jealous I was that Dad had this new life I was no longer a part of."

Damn. I remember the lyrics to that song, and they're heartbreaking. Soul crushing. The idea of Cassie feeling that way brings a hot clench of emotion to my chest.

"And don't get me wrong—I treasure my sisters, I do. And I

like Nia. But I can't tell you how many times I used to lie there crying about it. Sometimes, I'd fantasize that Dad would randomly show up in Boston and come get me. He'd push past my mother and announce he was bringing me home because he was miserable without me. Like in the song." Cassie lets out a shaky breath, a flimsy laugh. "It's stupid, I know. But I was fifteen. Angst was my middle name."

My vision goes a little blurry, and I'm startled to realize there's moisture clinging to my eyelashes. I blink rapidly, but that proves to be a mistake. One tear slips out and plops onto the cheek Cassie has pressed on my shoulder.

"Oh my God, Tate. Are you crying?"

Someone goddamn kill me.

I swallow hard. My throat is so tight it hurts.

"You are," she says in amazement, rising on her elbow to peer at me. "I'm sorry. I didn't mean to bum you out."

I lift my fist to my face and scrub it over my eyes. "Sorry. It's just so fucking sad, Cassie." I hold her closer and she's so soft and warm, and suddenly I'm hit with the vision of a ten-year-old Cassie being forced to leave Avalon Bay and her father behind, whisked away to live with her shitty mother.

My eyes feel like they're burning again, and I gulp down the lump obstructing my throat.

Christ.

"This is the sweetest thing ever," she whispers, burying her face in my neck. "Nobody has ever cried on my behalf before."

Hell, *I've* never cried on anyone's behalf before. But this is Cassie. She's the kindest soul I've ever met. The funniest, sexiest, most compelling woman I've ever been with, and I feel—

I take a sharp inhale as understanding strikes me.

I feel it.

The elusive *it*.

Whatever the hell it is that makes my parents look at each other the way they do. The feeling I'd been waiting for but could never find with any of the girls who've crossed my path over the years.

I feel it now.

The irony of this doesn't escape me. I almost didn't get involved with her because I was worried *she'd* catch feelings. Meanwhile, my feelings for *her* hit me out of nowhere and knocked me on my damn ass.

But what does that mean for us? She lives in Boston, and I can't leave the Bay for the time being. Long-distance relationships are hard to maintain, but maybe we could manage it. She graduates this year anyway. Maybe she'd consider moving back here. This was where she was born. Where her father lives. And it's evident she loves him deeply.

"You have to talk to him," I say. "To your dad. Hell, and your mother too. She should know how much her words have hurt you. Don't you want parents you can be honest with, instead of sweeping everything important under the rug? Just be honest, Cass. With both of them."

"Sort of like how you're honest with your father about how badly you want to sail to New Zealand?"

"I mean, it's not like I *didn't* tell him about it. I did. I just can't go."

"Sure you can. Your contract ends soon. You have all of autumn and winter off."

"I already promised Dad I'd work full-time at Bartlett Marine."

"The dealership will be waiting for you when you get back," Cassie says softly. She sits up, watching me, her eyes shining with encouragement. "It's only a few months. Bartlett Marine isn't going to implode if you're gone for three months."

I chew on the inside of my cheek. "I know. I just . . . I don't want to let him down."

That earns me a gentle smile. "See?"

"See what?"

"We both do it. Hold back our own feelings because we don't want to disappoint our parents or make any waves."

She's right.

She's right about everything.

If I go, Bartlett Marine will still be there when I get back. If I don't go, I'm letting the opportunity of a lifetime slip away. I might never get another chance to sail a goddamn Hallberg-Rassy halfway across the goddamn world. I'm twenty-three years old, for fuck's sake. I have the rest of my life to stay in one place and work a nine-to-five job. Three months will pass in the blink of an eye. My father will survive it.

"You know what? You're right. I think I need to practice what I preach. I'll make you a deal," I announce, a smile tickling my lips. "How about this? You talk to your dad and tell him every-thing you just told me. Talk to your mom and tell her how she's hurt you. And I'll talk to my dad and tell him I'm going to New Zealand. Deal?"

Cassie purses her lips, thinking it over. "Only if it's after the Beacon's reopening."

"You're stalling," I tease.

"No, just being practical. Any conversation with my mother creates the potential for sheer and utter catastrophe, and I still have to live with her for the next week."

"Fair. Then we'll schedule our respective conversations for the day after the reopening." I lift a brow. "Deal?"

She shakes my hand. "Deal."

My chest feels surprisingly light at the notion of telling my father I'm going to accept Gil's offer. Or maybe that feeling of ease has more to do with the other confession I plan to make.

Because after I tell Dad about the trip, I'm going to tell Cassie I'm in love with her.

CHAPTER 30

CASSIE

Last time I was in this ballroom, it was a year after the hurricane and my grandparents were giving me a walk-through of the damage. By then, the sea had done its worst, leaving behind a gaping space that could've doubled as the setting of a ghost ship in a horror movie. Everything needed to be ripped out. The drywall, the flooring. Gutted right to the studs.

Now, after all of Mackenzie's hard work, the ballroom has been completely restored. The old wallpaper and gilded wall ornaments are gone, replaced by cream paint and white panels with intricate detailing. Brand-new hardwood flooring gleams beneath our feet. The most impressive change, however, is the ceiling. It still soars impossibly high, only now there are skylights, glass panels that open up the room and provide a dazzling view of the inky sky streaked with a dusting of stars.

On the stage, a ten-piece jazz band performs an up-tempo number that makes me feel like I've stepped into another time. Everything about this ballroom feels both modern and vintage at the same time, and I watch Grandma's face as she takes it all in.

"Incredible," she says under her breath, and I see the relief in Mackenzie's green eyes.

"You did an amazing job," I tell Mac.

"It was a team effort." She links her arm with Cooper, who looks gorgeous in his tux. With his tattoos covered and his face clean-shaven, he resembles a preppy boy from Garnet College. I would never tell him that, though. I feel like it would ruin his entire night.

Mac introduces my grandmother to Cooper. As Grandma shakes his hand, she's still gazing around the room, marveling over it. Her attention lands on the chandelier. "Is that the same—"

"No, it's a replica," Mac cuts in. Her smile is hopeful. "It looks the same, though, right? I asked the designer to copy it from a photograph."

"It's breathtaking," Grandma assures her. "All of it."

The two of them wander off, Mac pointing out other updates to the ballroom. Meanwhile, I notice several familiar faces entering through the arched doorway. It's only eight o'clock, so people are still trickling in. The hotel itself isn't open for business until tomorrow morning, when guests from near and far will be checking in at the newly christened Beacon Hotel. Mackenzie says they're booked to capacity, and Genevieve has been stressing about it all week, grumbling about how she'd been promised a soft opening. I guess Mac's original plan was to only book half capacity for opening weekend, just to "dip her toe in," but Cooper talked her out of it, convincing her to make a big splash instead.

"Cass!" My cousin Liv breaks away from the crowd and hurries over to hug me.

"Hey! You look incredible."

Liv is eighteen and about to start her freshman year at Yale. She's Uncle Will's daughter, and the only cousin close to my age. The others are all thirteen or under, with Aunt Jacqueline's late-in-life baby Mariah being the youngest at five. My aunt had her at forty-four.

"Hi, squirt," I greet the little girl who waddles up beside Liv. Mariah looks adorable in a white tutu dress and shiny silver barrettes. She reminds me of my sisters, which makes me wish they were here tonight. But Dad and Co. weren't invited, and even if they had been, I'm sure Nia would rather be caught dead than interact with my mother. Not that I blame her.

I greet my aunt and uncles, who flew in last night from Massachusetts and Connecticut.

"It's a family reunion!" Uncle Max gives me a kiss on the cheek and then ruffles Mariah's hair. "Where's Victoria?" he asks me.

"I don't know. She arrived with us but then disappeared. I think she went to the ladies' room." I scan the ballroom, which isn't super crowded yet. Still, there's a fair number of people milling around, in an array of beautiful gowns and tailored suits and tuxedos. "Oh, there she is."

Mom saunters over. I can't deny she looks stunning in her form-fitting black gown, red-soled Louboutins, and elegant updo. She's forty-five and honestly looks ten years younger. Genetically, that bodes well for me.

I'm quite pleased with my own dress too. It's emerald green, with a halter-style bodice that covers my boobs nicely and a pleated skirt that swirls around my ankles. Picked for me courtesy of Joy, who's looking gorgeous herself in a white minidress and impossibly high stilettos. Isaiah is her plus-one, but from the way they've been bickering since they got here, I have a feeling this latest reconciliation won't stick.

Mom's gaze sweeps around the room, resting on the lively band, before she turns back and grudgingly admits, "This is lovely."

"Isn't it?" Aunt Jacqueline says. "Almost makes me wish we held on to this place."

Mom is quick with a reprimand. "Don't you say that, Jacqueline. We had to sell."

Uncle Will chimes in agreement. "It was time to say goodbye. Remember Mom and Dad with this place? It was their entire life. They didn't have any time for themselves."

"The world revolved around the Beacon," Uncle Max concurs.

"I know," my aunt says sullenly. "I guess I'm just sad to see it go."

Mackenzie returns to give us a private tour. Just the family, and everyone is suitably impressed by what she's done with the hotel. The tour ends on the top floor, where Mac strides down the carpeted hallway looking like a supermodel in her black satin gown and silver heels. She leads us to a pair of double doors at the very end of the hall.

"The presidential suite," she says. Eyes twinkling, she steps aside to show us the plaque on the wall.

THE TANNER SUITE.

Grandma looks like she might cry. "Oh, Mackenzie, dear. You didn't have to do that."

"No, I did." Mac's expression becomes serious, her voice thick with emotion. "If it wasn't for you, the Beacon wouldn't have stood on this boardwalk for fifty years. It's your legacy, Lydia."

The suite is as posh as you would expect. Even has a grand piano. Afterward, we return to the ballroom, and I'm surprised to witness some genuine nostalgia swimming in Mom's eyes.

"Aww, you're sad to see it go too," I accuse, my smile telling her I'm teasing. "After all the grumbling about how you didn't want it . . ."

"Oh stop," she says, patting me good-naturedly. She looks around the ballroom that's slowly filling up. The band is now playing a jazzy rendition of a Taylor Swift song, which is sort of cool. "Where is your boyfriend tonight?"

"Um . . ." I pull my phone out of my clutch and check the screen. Tate was supposed to let me know when he was coming

THE SUMMER GIRL • 331

inside. Last time we texted, he was in the parking lot waiting for his parents. "Oh, perfect. His parents just got here. They're walking in now."

A server appears brandishing an array of champagne flutes, and Mom plucks two of them off the tray. With a broad smile, she hands me one.

I eye her in amusement.

"What?" she says. "We're celebrating. Let's make a toast." She raises the delicate flute. "To our family."

"To our family." We tap our glasses. I don't know why her spirits are suddenly so high, but hey, I'll take it.

We weave our way through the ballroom, stopping to say hello to several people Mom knows. Then I turn my head and see Tate entering.

My throat instantly turns into an arid wasteland. I thought Tate in a suit was nice. Tate in a tux? It's a sight to behold. Although of course, Tate in nothing at all would be my ultimate preference. Any time we're naked together, I forget my own name. And it's not just the sex that turns my mind to mush. It's everything. His laughter. The way his blue eyes become so animated when he talks about something he's passionate about. How he's far more sensitive than he lets on. He tries to hide that under the guise of surfer-boy man-whore, but he's not fooling me. Not anymore.

I'm still floored by what happened last week. Tate shedding real tears when I spoke of my fragile relationship with my father. I plan on sticking to my end of the deal—I'm going to talk to both my parents about our relationships. But I think I'm adding Tate to that list, because it's getting harder and harder to deny my feelings for him.

I tried not to get attached and I failed.

My heart is officially engaged.

It was supposed to be a summer fling, but I don't want it to end. I don't think he wants it to end either. I wish he'd be the one to bring it up, to suggest we continue seeing other, but so far he hasn't. A part of me wonders if he's waiting for me to take the lead. I was the one who wanted the fling. I insisted I didn't want a relationship to come of it. And Tate's the kind of guy who isn't going to push the issue. If I want more, I need to ask for it. Vocalize my needs and all that fun stuff.

I take another sip, then touch Mom's arm. "Tate's here. Let's say hi."

"Of course." She sips her own champagne as she follows me toward the tuxedo-clad golden god who stole my virginity and my heart.

"Who invited *you*?" I mock glare when we reach him.

"I know, right?" Tate's appreciative gaze eats me up. "You look incredible."

"You clean up nice too." I smile and rise on my tiptoes to kiss his cheek.

His parents are standing nearby, talking to Cooper's uncle Levi, but Gemma breaks away when she notices me.

"Cassie. You look beautiful." Gemma gives me a warm hug.

"Thank you. So do you." She's wearing a yellow dress, her fair hair arranged in an updo with wavy strands framing her face. A small diamond pendant is nestled in her cleavage.

I greet Tate's dad, who's less boisterous than usual as he leans in to kiss my cheek. Maybe he's toning himself down because this is such a classy event, but when he speaks, his demeanor feels more polite than lively. "Cassie. Good to see you."

"Good to see you too. This is my mom, Victoria. Mom, this is Gemma, and this is—"

"Gavin," Mom finishes, greeting him with a tight smile. She barely acknowledges Tate's mother, offering a brisk nod in lieu of hello. "It's been a long time."

"It has." Gavin looks ill at ease, fidgeting with his bowtie. "Nice to see you again, Tori."

I blink in surprise. "Oh, you two know each other?"

"Oh yes, we're well acquainted." Mom takes another sip of champagne.

I wait for her to continue, perhaps even, you know, *explain*.

But she doesn't, and neither does Gavin.

Tate appears as befuddled as I am. We exchange a mystified look, as if to say, *what are we missing?*

Grandma chooses that moment to approach, and I try to transmit to her with my eyes that maybe now is not the time. Something's brewing here. Like the way I know whenever a storm is coming. I can smell it, feel it in the air.

"How long has it been, Gavin?" Mom asks, studying him over the top of her glass. She sips again. "Eleven years?"

"About that," he says, not quite meeting her eyes.

I notice Tate's mom shooting him a questioning look. Okay. At least Tate and I aren't the only ones who are out of the loop. And whatever this loop is, it's beginning to trigger all my internal alarms.

Grandma reaches us, her expression one of concern. "Is everything all right?" she murmurs to me.

"I have no idea," I murmur back. Then I slather on a bright smile and make a last-ditch attempt to ward off the impending storm. "Hey, Mom, I think Aunt Jacqueline is waving us over—"

"The last time I saw you . . ." she muses to Gavin, effectively ignoring me. "It was the month of August, I remember that much. And I believe we met . . . here, actually. At this bar." She absently waves her arm toward the ballroom doors. "Before it was that café out there. It was the lobby bar, remember?"

Tate's dad doesn't answer. Either I'm imagining it, or his forehead has taken on a sheen of sweat.

"Refresh my memory? I can't recall exactly when we last saw

each other . . ." With a smile that's more a baring of teeth than anything resembling amity, Mom locks eyes with Gavin Bartlett. "Oh, silly me! I remember now. It was the night you ordered me to abort our baby."

CHAPTER 31

CASSIE

What in actual tarnation . . .

I stare at my mother. I'm not the only one.

Everyone has been stunned to silence.

Well, not everyone. All around us, other people are still enjoying themselves. They're laughing and chatting. They're nibbling on hors d'œuvres and drinking their champagne. Even the band is still playing. I long to be one of those blissfully oblivious people. I miss my old life, the one from five seconds ago before I heard my mother utter those inexplicable words in that ice-cold yet oddly smug tone.

Her shocking admission hangs like a cloud in the air, lingering, refusing to dissipate.

I'm the first one to find my voice, though it comes out hoarse and unstable.

"Mom." I shake my head a few times, unable to formulate any more words.

"What?" She is completely unbothered, cheerful even, as she drains the rest of her glass before signaling a passing server for another.

Is she fucking drunk?

I look at Gavin and Gemma. Tate's dad is paler than the crisp linen napkins being handed out with the hors d'œuvres. Gemma, on the other hand, is flushed, her cheeks stained a deep, dark red. Whether from anger or humiliation, I don't know.

Mom's amused gaze flicks my way. "Weren't you the one who was so curious about my past the other day?" she reminds me. A mocking note colors her tone. "And now, not a single question?" She *tsks*. "Really, Cass?"

"Victoria." Grandma's sharp voice slices the air.

"Oh, Mother, don't look at me like that. You knew about it."

My gaze flies to Grandma, flashing a hundred different questions at her. She says nothing to remedy my bewilderment. Does nothing to assuage my distress. Her shuttered expression is vexing and it's all I can do not to growl at her.

"Okay, what is *happening* right now?" I finally shout, and this time we draw some attention. Several startled gazes. Curious eyes.

Mom takes another sip.

Gavin, who hasn't uttered a single word yet, doesn't meet my gaze. His jaw is stiff, a muscle twitching.

"Gavin?" The distrustful voice belongs to Tate's mother. And it succeeds in getting a reaction from him. His blue eyes shift, locking on to his wife. I see nothing of note in his expression, but Gemma must, because her cheeks turn redder. Lips tightening.

"Her?" she demands in disbelief. "That's who it was?"

Tate stares at his parents, his face darkening. "Seriously, what the hell is going on? What baby is she talking about?"

My stomach begins to churn. An eddy of disgust and shame. I'm looking at my mother and I realize she's enjoying this. She stands there smirking, unruffled, sipping her drink. She doesn't care to expound on this tale. She's not purposely delaying the payoff to keep everyone on the edge of their seats. That wasn't her intention. All she wanted, I realize, as she aims her satisfied smirk

THE SUMMER GIRL • 337

at a visibly sweating Gavin Bartlett—was *that*. She wanted to make Tate's father squirm. Wanted to put him in this position of having to explain himself to his family.

Without addressing his son's question, Gavin touches Gemma's arm. "Why don't we go speak privately, darlin'?"

My mother doesn't like that one bit. Whatever her original plan, I see the moment she mentally adjusts it.

With a harsh laugh, she says, "What's the matter, Gavin? You don't want to take a trip down memory lane among friends? Why on earth not?" She pretends to think it over. She's the star of this sick movie and she's relishing every second. "Is it because you don't want your son and your wife and the good people of Avalon Bay to know the kind of man you really are?"

Anger twists and cuts at my insides. "Stop it," I snap. "That's enough, Mom. Time to go."

I plan on getting this whole story, damn right I do, but not now. Not here, in a ballroom full of people. I notice Mackenzie starting to make her way toward us, Cooper at her heels. But they stop when I give a slight shake of my head.

"No, we can't have that, can we?" Mom doesn't heed my warning. She's laughing again. Cold and punishing. "You're Mr. Congeniality of the Bay. Mr. Perfect who can do no wrong. Perfect Gavin who can have an affair, screw another woman behind his wife's back, knock that woman up, and still smile to all those people who walk into his place of business and talk about how much he *loves* his boats and *let me tell you about the time I sailed to Hawaii!* Right, Gavin?" Scorn drips like tar from her every word. "Well, I'm sorry, you don't get that luxury anymore. You don't get to pretend anymore."

"Victoria." It's Grandma again. She touches Mom's elbow. "This is neither the time nor the place."

"Why not?" Mom flashes a mocking look. "This is the last time I'll ever be in this fucking town, so why *not* now?"

I flinch at the expletive. Mom is usually a lot classier than this. There's nothing classy about her now. The contemptuous smile. Those gleaming eyes, aimed at Tate's parents. It's insidious. Everything about this is fucking insidious.

And Tate. God, I can't even look at Tate. I see him in my periphery and I'm diligently trying not to let our eyes meet. I don't want to know his expression. Nobody wants to see what their sort-of boyfriend's face looks like after you both find out your parents had an affair. Allegedly. I'm still not certain what the whole story is here, but it's evident they were involved in some way.

"Mr. Perfect has nothing to say?" Mom seems almost disappointed that Tate's dad isn't taking her bait.

The man hasn't even acknowledged her since she dropped her bomb. And that's a problem. Narcissists can't handle being ignored. That's usually when they go for the jugular. And Mom is no exception.

"Perfect Gavin Bartlett, who has his cake and eats it too. Who flashes a huge smile to the world and then sits down and offers to pay for the abortion."

Someone needs to stop this. But nobody is. Grandma has gone deathly silent. Tate is motionless. Gavin just stands there taking it. And I'm too stunned, my heart pounding too fast. Too loud. I can barely hear my own thoughts, let alone string some together and verbalize them. I feel nauseous, bile burning like acid in my throat.

The person who finally puts an end to our collective torture is Tate's mom.

It's a testament to her southern upbringing, the way Gemma Bartlett wipes her palms on the front of her dress before taking a breath and stepping closer to my grandmother.

"Avalon Bay will be sad to see you go, Lydia. I've enjoyed running into you around town and chatting with you, and I do wish we'd gotten to know each other better over the years. I hope Boston treats you well." With a soft smile, Gemma clasps Grandma's hand, then releases it. "Now, I'm afraid I must take my leave. I'm feeling a wee bit under the weather."

Without sparing a glance at my mother, Gemma drops the proverbial mic like a fucking rock star and walks away.

It's chaos after that. Not the kind of chaos where people are screaming and running and making a scene. A quiet chaos, where everyone disappears in the blink of an eye. Tate's father goes after Gemma. A stricken Tate follows Gavin. My mother drains her glass and hands it to a waiter, then calmly saunters toward the arched doorway.

I stare at her retreating back, the casual sway of her hips in that black cocktail gown. I remain frozen for a moment. Before the rage propels me into action.

Heart rate dangerously high, I hurry after my mother. She's walking at a fast clip, and I don't catch up to her until she's gliding through the lobby doors to step outside.

"Are you *kidding* me?" I grab her arm before she can approach the valet. "No way. You're not going anywhere."

"Don't speak to me in that tone." Mom flings my hand off.

"Me? You're unhappy with the way *I'm* speaking to *you*? How about the way you spoke to everyone in there? *What the hell was that?*"

My voice is shaking wildly. A leaf in a hurricane. My palms feel numb, pulse racing. And through my blood surges the kind of rage that produces tears. That makes you sob like a helpless child because the ferocity of the fury is too strong for even an adult to handle.

As my throat tightens to the point of pain, I snatch Mom's hand and drag her away from the valet station.

"Cassie! Let me go."

"No," I snap.

"Cassie," she says sharply as she stumbles on her heels.

I slow down to allow her to regain her balance, but I don't stop moving until we're well out of earshot of the Beacon.

"You had an affair with Gavin Bartlett?" I demand.

She looks amused by the question.

"Don't smile at me like that." I clench my teeth. "Are you getting pleasure out of this?"

"A little bit, yes." She chuckles. "I don't think I've ever seen you so angry. You can relax. It was a long time ago."

I gape at her. "You want me to relax? You cheated on Dad."

"We were already separated." She pauses. Mulling. Then she amends that. "Talking about separation, anyway."

"But you weren't separated." I drag a tired hand over my eyes, willing myself not to cry. "When did this happen? The year before the divorce?"

"Yes. I was trading in your grandfather's boat and dealt with Gavin at the dealership. And, well . . ." She shrugs. "You've met the man. He's charming. Not to mention gorgeous."

My head is spinning. I don't want to know the details, and yet I do. "Who initiated it?" I ask warily.

"He did."

For some reason that surprises me. I pictured Mom as the instigator, strutting into the dealership in a tight dress, set on ruining a man's life.

"And it took a lot of persuasion on his end. I'd never cheated on your father in all the years we were married. If we hadn't already been having problems, I'm sure I would have remained faithful."

I feel sick again. "How long did it go on for?"

"Four months. Then I got pregnant." The humor and indifference finally abandon her, replaced by bitterness. Dark and acute. It fills her eyes, burning hot. "The thrill of an affair fades awfully fast when real life creeps in. He asked—no, he demanded—that I get rid of the baby. Said he couldn't do that to his family." She shakes her head angrily. "It was perfectly acceptable for him to be sleeping around on his wife, hurting her every single day by betraying the vows he took. Getting his rocks off in hotel rooms on his lunch break and then going home acting as if he was the perfect husband and father. So long as *he* was having a good time, then I was useful to him. And then, when his perfect little bubble burst, I became an inconvenience." Mom laughs without a shred of humor. "Victoria Tanner is nobody's inconvenience."

"So, what, you were going to keep his baby out of spite?" Oh my God. I want to throw up.

"No, I was keeping it because it was *mine*." She sounds offended I'd even voice that question, yet doesn't realize her answer is equally disturbing. As always, she talks about people, including an unborn child, like they're possessions. Tools for her to use whichever way she wants.

My eyes well up again. I feel the tears on my lashes and when I blink, a streak of moisture slides down my cheeks.

"Cassie. Stop it. You're acting like a child."

"I'm acting like a child?" I start to laugh. I'm so fucking astounded. I'm astonished that I'm related to this woman. "I shouldn't cry when I find out my mother cheated on my father? Got pregnant by another man. Decided to keep that baby. Did you really have a miscarriage?"

"Yes," she says stiffly.

"And Dad knew."

"He did, yes."

"He knew it wasn't his?" I challenge.

"Would've been hard for him not to guess when we hadn't been intimate in months by that point."

"And Grandma knew too?" I ask, remembering the way Mom snapped at her in the ballroom. "That you had an affair?"

"She only found out after the divorce. She and I weren't seeing eye to eye on something, and it came out during an argument."

Of course it did, because apparently my mother doesn't behave like a normal human being. She saves up all her ammunition and shoots it at you when it suits her. When she wants to hurt you, or needs some sort of validation.

Grandma's ears must have been burning because she appears then. Her gait is slower than usual, exhaustion lining her eyes. But her features sharpen when she reaches us, her shoulders straightening as if fortifying her for a fight.

"Not now, Mother," Mom snaps. "I really don't need your input at the moment."

"You're right, Victoria. You don't need my input. You don't need anyone's input, do you? Because you're always right." Grandma focuses on me, all but dismissing her own daughter. "Are you okay, dear?"

"Not really," I admit. "I just hope Tate and his parents are all right—"

Mom practically growls at me. "There is absolutely no reason for you to worry about Gavin and his family. He made his own bed. You don't get to cheat on your wife and lie about it for years, go on with your life as if nothing ever happened. He doesn't get that, and you shouldn't feel sorry for that man."

"I don't feel sorry for him," I say sadly. "I feel sorry for *you*."

She rears back. "Excuse me?"

"You heard me. You've been a selfish, manipulative jerk my entire life. Nothing is ever good enough for you. The way I look, the way I act, the guys I date—" I stop in horror. "Wait, is this why you've been so nice to me lately? Because I was going out with Tate? You knew he was Gavin's son."

"Of course I knew. I figured it out the moment I saw him outside the Jackson place. He's the spitting image of his father."

"So you were just pretending to be nice to me—"

"Stop being so dramatic, Cassie!" she interrupts, blowing out an exasperated breath. "Nobody was pretending. I'm your mother. I enjoy spending time with you."

"I don't think I believe that." I swallow my bitterness. "But now I get it." Shaking my head, disappointment embedded deep inside me, I meet her eyes and ask, "Was this some big plan to get Gavin in public and humiliate his family?"

"No," she scoffs. "I'm not a psychopath. But as I've always told you, if an opportunity presents itself, you take it. Tonight, an opportunity presented itself."

"Really," I say dubiously. "You didn't plan it. And you had no ulterior motives for constantly inviting Tate to join us for dinner."

"Of course not. I enjoy Tate's company too. It's completely incidental that it also gave me insight into what his family's been up to in the years since his father's indiscretion."

Incidental, my ass.

"And, I will admit, it annoyed me. Hearing about Gavin's life. How everyone in town still adores him. Getting articles written about him in the paper, photographed with his oblivious wife and perfect son. Maybe I was a bit out of line in there," she nods toward the hotel behind us, "but this town needed to know what kind of man he is."

I stare at her and see someone I don't recognize. Someone I don't want to know. I see a bitter, miserable woman who hates herself so much she lashes out at everyone around her. A woman who couldn't stand seeing the man she had an affair with living a

344 • ELLE KENNEDY

seemingly happy life and thus felt the need to humiliate him and his wife. In public. In front of their son.

I see a woman I don't want in my life anymore, and I feel a profound sense of loss.

And no matter what she says, I no longer believe the story she fed me about fighting for sole custody because she was feeling *vulnerable* and longed to keep her daughter close after the miscarriage. She did it to hurt my father, plain and simple. I was a possession to her, something she could use against him and keep from him to make him suffer.

"You're sick," I tell her. "You have an actual sickness, Mom. And I'm done."

"Cassie—"

"No. Stop. Don't tell me I'm being dramatic. Don't blast me for not taking your side or whatever else you want to bitch about. You just humiliated my boyfriend and his family at a public event that was supposed to honor *our* family—" I cut myself off, because she's not worth it. Not worth the energy I'm expending by even saying any of these futile words. This entire time we've been out here, she hasn't once apologized for her actions. In her mind, she did nothing wrong tonight.

I jerk when I feel Grandma's hand on my arm. "I think it's time to go."

"I think so too," I say, nodding.

My grandmother glances at Mom. "And I think it's better if you stay in a hotel tonight, Victoria." With a look of irony, Grandma gestures to the Beacon. "There's one right there, dear. Perhaps Ms. Cabot will comp you a room."

"Mother. Seriously."

"Yes, seriously. I'm done listening to you tonight. You destroy everything you touch. You always have. I tried to instill the right values in you, to teach you the importance of being compassionate, humble. It appears I failed." Grandma shakes her head sadly. "I'll have Adelaide's husband deliver your bags tomorrow morning to wherever you choose to stay. But for tonight, and for the rest of the visit, Cassie and I would like to be alone. Isn't that right, Cassie?"

"Yes. It is."

Arms linked tightly together, Grandma and I walk away.

CHAPTER 32

CASSIE

Me: *You okay?*
Me: *Tonight was brutal.*
Me: *I don't even know what to say.*

I stop texting after the trifecta, because no matter how upset I am, I refuse to become a person who texts in one-liners.

My heart jumps when I see Tate typing back. I've been dying to talk to him since I got home, but he had his own shit to deal with. His own parental confrontations. I would've killed to be a fly on the wall when Tate spoke to his parents, especially his dad. I need to know Gavin's side of the sordid story, because I don't trust a damn word my mother says.

As I wait for Tate's message to appear, I stare up at the ceiling, wishing he were here with me. It's eleven o'clock and I doubt I'll be getting so much as a wink of sleep. My brain keeps running over every word that was uttered tonight. Every horrible, horrible word. I could use the distraction. But Tate is home with his parents, and I assume he'll be spending the night there.

Tate: *Yeah, that was rough. How are you doing?*

He was typing for so long, I expected more. But I guess it's better than nothing.

> Me: *I don't even know. Is your mom okay?*
> Tate: *Not really. She hasn't said much since we got home. Just been quiet. We're about to take the dogs for a walk.*
> Me: *This late?*
> Tate: *She doesn't feel like going to bed yet.*

There's a beat. Then another message.

> Tate: *Dad's crashing on a friend's couch.*

Fuck. Guilt lodges in my throat like a wad of gum. I know that I, personally, didn't do this to his family, but I feel responsible, complicit in my mother's actions.

Gavin cheated too . . .

Right. I have to acknowledge that too. Not all the blame can be placed on my mother; Tate's father was equally responsible. And I doubt I'll ever know the real story about who initiated the affair, because cheaters tend to twist the truth to portray themselves in the best possible light. I'm not sure I envision Gavin as the seductive rogue who wooed my mother into his bed. But I can't entirely picture her seducing him either. Mom might be charming, but she's never been a flirt or a, well, bimbo.

I suspect as with most situations the truth is somewhere in the middle.

Either way, tonight left hurricane-scale damage on both our families. Grandma and I sat together in the kitchen for more than an hour after we got home. She was candid with me, admitting how disappointed she'd always been in her youngest daughter. Mom hadn't experienced any traumatic events in her childhood that made her this way—she was just spoiled. She was the baby, the youngest of four. Grandma didn't explicitly blame Grandpa Wally—she would never speak an ill word about him—but after our talk tonight, I get the sense he was the one who did most of the spoiling.

But spoiling your kid isn't a reason for someone to become as callous and entitled as my mother, not reason alone anyway. Some people are just born assholes, I guess.

Grandma said we'd talk about it more tomorrow, but really, what is left to say? I want nothing to do with my mother. For the time being, and possibly longer. The way she was smirking over her champagne tonight as she destroyed another woman's marriage was despicable. One of the cruelest things I've ever witnessed.

Tate: *I wish I was in bed with you right now.*
Me: *Me too. Will I see you tomorrow?*
Tate: *Yeah. Gil and Shirley return on Sunday so I gotta head back and clean the house from top to bottom.*

I can't believe the summer's over. I leave for Boston on Monday. And my relationship with Tate still hangs in the balance, unresolved. Except, now I realize there might never be a resolution. Whether we keep seeing each other or not, our families are now intrinsically intertwined. Forever.

But we're not our parents, I remind myself. We're not. I would never judge Tate for his father's actions, and I know he wouldn't judge me for what my mother's done. I'm hoping this doesn't change us. If it does, I can't be certain my heart will survive.

Tate: *I'll call you in the morning. Night, Cass.*
Me: *Night.*

I set the phone on the nightstand and crawl under the covers, but sleep eludes me. It simply won't come. My thoughts are running and running around in my head in an unceasing loop.

Mom got pregnant by Tate's dad.

And my father knew it wasn't his baby, which raises so many more questions. Did Dad know it was Gavin Bartlett's or think it was some anonymous man? And does it matter? Either way, Dad knew she was having an affair. He knew what kind of shitty person she was. And he still let me go live with her. He let me be alone with her from the age of ten to eighteen. Eight years of her attention solely focused on me. Her verbal punching bag. How could he do that?

I'm suddenly hit by a gust of anger. Sleep is all but forgotten. It all spills out, all the things I want to say to him, all the questions plaguing my mind, and it pushes me out of bed, because you know what? I'm done. I'm done bottling it up. Done not voicing my feelings. Vocalizing my needs, as Tate likes to say. I'm fucking done.

I don't bother changing, just head downstairs in my plaid shorts and gray T-shirt. As quietly as I can, I walk to the front hall and stick my feet in a pair of Grandma's gardening Crocs. Then I grab her keys and go out to the car.

It's 12:10 when I pull into the driveway of my childhood home. I stare at it through the Rover's windshield, my throat closing up. I love this house. I grew up here. My dad was here. And although I know the affair wasn't the sole reason for the divorce—they were already discussing separation by then—my mother was still the cause. The way she treated people, the way she treated him, that's what ended their marriage. But it didn't have to end my relationship with him. He didn't have to passively stand by and let her take me.

He could have fought for me.

I fling open the car door and jump out, heart pounding as I march toward the porch and then—

And then nothing. I halt, suddenly furious again. At *myself.* Because what the hell am I doing? There are two sleeping six-year-olds in there. It's midnight. If I storm in and start making demands on my dad right now, I'm no better than my mother causing a scene at the Beacon Hotel's grand reopening. Making it all about herself.

Swallowing the lump in my throat, I slowly turn and walk back to the Rover. I'll come back in the morning. It's what I should have done in the first place.

When I reach the car, I hear a soft voice say my name.

"Cassandra?"

It's Nia.

My stomach drops. Fucking hell. No. Not her. I can't do this right now. I just can't.

But she's already striding toward me, wearing white slippers and a red robe, the sash tied haphazardly around her midsection. Her tight curls are loose around her face, and there's no mistaking the concern that fills her dark eyes when she notices my tear-streaked face.

"Are you all right?" Nia frets, and for some reason the question unleashes a fresh onslaught of tears.

"*No,*" I moan and then I throw myself into her arms.

They weren't outstretched, weren't inviting me in, but the moment I'm there she wraps them around me, hugging me without hesitation. I shudder in her arms, crying uncontrollably. Gasping for air and feeling like my entire world has just crumbled around me, like I'm ten years old again and my parents are getting divorced and Daddy is telling me I can't live with him anymore but *don't worry I'll see you all the time, Cass.*

"He lied," I choke out, as the tears continue to fall. "He didn't see me all the time."

"What?" Nia says in confusion.

"He let her have me. After the divorce. He promised nothing would change and everything changed." If I had the ability to think coherent thoughts right now, I know I would be mortified. But I'm too distraught, sobbing in her arms as we stand there in the driveway. As Nia, the stepmother who doesn't even like me, provides me with the comfort that neither of my parents have been capable of giving me my entire life.

"I had to live with that woman, and he knows what it was like living with her. But he got rid of her, he got to leave. I didn't have that luxury, did I? I had to keep living with her, keep listening to all the ways I wasn't fucking good enough. And meanwhile he gets to stay here in *my* house," I spit out. It's a half growl, half sob. "With his new kids and their mother. Their perfect fucking mother."

I bury my face against her bosom and shake from my tears. She holds me tighter and runs her hand over my back, strokes my hair, and that only makes it worse because it's what a mother is supposed to do. And that makes me cry harder.

Somehow, I manage to lift my head even though it feels like it weighs a thousand pounds.

"I wish you were my mom," I tell her, my voice barely above a whisper.

And then it finally happens—the mortification kicks in, in the form of a panic attack that knocks me off my feet. It all bubbles over and I can't breathe. I've never had a panic attack before, the kind where you're hyperventilating. Suddenly I'm on the ground, the gravel biting into my bare knees. I gulp for air, crying and panting and avoiding Nia's worried eyes because I can't believe I just said that to her.

She's kneeling beside me now. "Breathe," she orders. "Breathe, Cassandra. Look at me."

I look at her.

"Do what I'm doing. Take a very deep breath. Inhale. Ready?"
I inhale.

"Good. Now exhale."
I exhale.

For the next couple of minutes, she helps me remember how to breathe. In and out, in and out, until my heartbeat has regulated and my hands are no longer numb.

"I'm so sorry," I croak. I glance toward the house, realizing the porch light is on. I catch a glimpse of movement in the living room window. Was that my father? "Did I wake up the whole house?"

"*Non, non,* you didn't."

"How did you know I was outside?"

"The doorbell camera sends an alert to my phone. It woke me up, but your father was still asleep."

"I'm sorry. I didn't mean to barge in. Something just happened tonight, and . . ." I trail off.

"Is everything all right? Your grandmother?"

"It's fine. She's fine." I inhale again. "We were at the grand reopening of our family hotel, and . . ." I shake my head, a bitter laugh sliding out. "Well, long story short, my mother decided to announce to the entire ballroom that she had an affair with my boyfriend's father when I was ten."

Nia's eyes widen. "Oh."

"According to her, Dad knew about the affair." I study my stepmother's face. "Did he tell you about it?"

After a beat, she nods. "He told me, yes. But I don't believe he knew who the other man was."

"I don't think he knew. Tate's mom didn't know about my mom." God. This is such a twisted mess. "It was so embarrassing, you have no idea. I was looking at Mom and she was this total stranger to me. Getting enjoyment out of it. My whole life, I've just wanted a mom. And tonight I realized that's never going to happen. Not with her." I give Nia a sad smile. "I'm sorry. I know I'm not your kid. You don't need to be sitting out here in the middle of the night comforting me."

Nia's tone becomes stern. "I may not have birthed you, Cassandra, but I certainly view you as a daughter."

"Bullshit." Then I wince. "Sorry, I didn't mean to swear."

She laughs quietly. "Don't worry, every day the word *merde* gets spoken in this house more times than I can count. And it's not bullshit. I admit, I've kept my distance over the years. Not because I didn't consider you a part of the family or didn't love you." She hesitates. "Your mother is . . . difficult."

"No, really?"

We both laugh.

"I figured that's what it was," I admit. "That you kept your distance because of her. But I'm not her. And I'm not *like* her. At all."

"You're not," Nia confirms. "But there is much you don't know, *chérie*. When your father and I became lovers—"

I choke on another laugh. "Please don't say it like that."

"What should I say then?"

"Say . . . *got together*."

Her eyes sparkle. "When your father and I got together, your mother was very unhappy. She didn't have nice things to say to me, or about me, at the beginning. There were many warnings, including what would happen if I tried to take her daughter from her or speak badly of her when you were around. There was a meeting with the judge—"

Shock slams into me.

"She was threatening to take away your father's visitation."

Nia sighs. "You were twelve when Clayton and I got together, and she told the judge she didn't want her ex-husband's bimbo—I had to look up that word in the dictionary—she didn't want me brainwashing her daughter into hating her. There was a mediation session, and for the first year I wasn't even allowed to be alone with you."

I gasp. What in the actual fuck? "I had no idea."

"I know. We didn't tell you. And keeping a distance became a habit for me, I suppose. But I've been watching you grow up all these years, and I think you are a wonderful young woman. So creative, with your stories, and your humor. I'm very proud of you."

"Then why don't you want me around my sisters?" The wounded question slips out before I can stop it.

She looks alarmed. "Why do you say that?"

"You've always been so protective of them when I'm around. Like you don't trust me to be around them. Last month, after Monique fell, you looked so furious and—"

"I was very furious," Nia interrupts. "With Monique!" She's flustered now. "That girl knows better than to climb on furniture! I told you before we left that night how much it was upsetting me."

She did tell me. But, I suddenly realize, when you think someone doesn't like you, everything they say becomes warped. Every look becomes distorted. Her eyes might transmit aggravation with Monique's disobedience, but my eyes see condemnation. Her tone might convey concern, but I hear accusation. I made it all about myself, and I'm ashamed when I realize that's something my mother would do.

"I thought you didn't want me around. Dad too."

"Your father? Never. Your father loves you, Cassandra. You're all he ever talks about."

A lump forms in my throat. "Really?"

"There isn't a day that goes by in this house where your name isn't spoken," Nia says. "He loves you very much."

"He never tells me that."

"Do you ever tell him how *you* feel?"

"No, but is it just my responsibility?"

"No," she agrees. "And this is why we will go inside now, so you can speak to him."

"You said he was asleep."

"When I got up, yes. But he's awake now." She nods toward the kitchen window. "I signaled for him to give us a minute when he came outside."

"He came outside?"

"Yes. When you were . . . being sad."

Being sad. Understatement of the year.

"I suspect he's preparing the tea you like. And I would like you to say to him all the things you just said to me. Why don't we go inside and do that?"

I hesitate.

She brushes driveway gravel off her knees and gets to her feet. "Cassandra?" She extends her hand.

I take it and let her help me up. But the doubts are returning, the old insecurities whipping up and making me bite my lip. "If you like me, why do you always call me Cassandra?"

"That's your name, *oui*?"

"*Oui*—I mean, yes. But . . . everyone else calls me Cassie or Cass and you never do. I thought it meant something. Like maybe you were being intentionally formal because you didn't like me."

Her lips curve with humor. "Not at all. I just think it's a beautiful name. Cas-san-dra. I enjoy the way it rolls off my tongue."

I swallow my laughter. Of course she does.

The human brain is so ridiculous sometimes. It creates these elaborate intentions for people, attributes motives, when at the end of the day, she just likes how my name rolls off her tongue.

CHAPTER 33

TATE

I walk into the kitchen the next morning to find my father at the table, drinking his coffee and reading the Saturday edition of the *Avalon Bee* while Mom scrambles eggs at the stove. I do an honest-to-God double take. I have to blink several times to convince myself I'm not imagining this charade of domestic bliss.

Dad crashed at his friend Kurt's house last night and now he's in our kitchen. He must have woken up and come straight home, and instead of slamming the door in his face, Mom allowed him in and is goddamn serving him breakfast.

I stand in the doorway, staring. They don't notice me, too caught up in their mundane activities. Mom's sticking two slices of bread in the toaster. Dad's reading the paper, no care in the world after blowing our family apart.

"What the hell is he doing here?"

They both look over in shock.

When my eyes lock with Dad's, his fill with shame. Good. He fucking better be ashamed. Since the second Cassie's mother dropped that bomb, the events of last night have been running on a loop in my head. When Mom and I got home, she refused to even discuss what happened. I've never been so frustrated in my life, but hey, I thought, it's not just my life that got completely upended. This is her marriage. So I kept my mouth shut despite all the questions burning at my tongue. I didn't push her. We walked the dogs and then she bid me good night and went up to bed.

Now she's cooking breakfast for my cheating father as if nothing happened?

"Tate," Dad starts. Cautious. "Sit down. We should probably talk about last night."

"First of all, *probably*?" I'm equal doses dumbfounded and enraged. "And second, why are you here? Why are you sitting there drinking coffee? You should be upstairs packing a fucking bag."

He recoils.

Even as I spit out the words, a bolt of hot agony rips a hole in my chest. Packing a bag. Christ, the idea of my father leaving, my parents divorcing . . . I scrape a hand through my hair, wanting to tear it out by the roots.

My father had an affair. He slept with another woman. And not just any other woman—Cassie's mother. I'm still reeling from that. I'm sure Cassie is equally horrified. I'll talk to her about it later when I see her, but, fuck, I don't even know what there is to say. Yes, this mess was caused by our parents, not us. But everything about this situation just feels fucking wrong. As wrong as Mom carrying two plates of eggs and toast to the table as if our world is unchanged. The dogs trail after her, Fudge settling at her feet and staring longingly at their plates as if he hasn't had a bite of food in forty-five years. Polly keeps a respectable distance because she has better manners.

I gape at my parents. "Why is he here?" I ask Mom. Without letting her respond, I turn to glower at him. "You couldn't even give her twenty-four hours?"

Disdain drips from my tone and he flinches. His eyes widen and I realize I've never spoken to him this way before. But I've also never been this furious.

"You couldn't even give her a full day to absorb that bomb-shell? Try to deal with—"

"We dealt with it eleven years ago." That comes from Mom. Calm and resigned.

I swivel my head toward her. "What do you mean?"

"I mean, we dealt with it eleven years ago. Granted, I didn't know it was Victoria Tanner." She gives a rueful look at Dad. "I know, I know, I was insistent about you not telling me who it was. But—"

"You knew he had an affair?" I interject.

But I don't need to see her nod to know the truth. Of course she knew. I'd been so caught up in my own shock over Victoria Tanner's bombshell that I'd overlooked *Mom's* reaction to it. When I think back to last night, I realize she hadn't acted as shocked and horrified as she should have.

"I did, yes," she says.

I turn back to Dad. This time, he won't meet my gaze. Of course not. That was the one thing Victoria—sorry, *Tori*—had gotten right last night. Mr. Perfect always needs to look good to the world.

Another rush of anger burns a fiery path up my spine. All these years, he's been acting like the model of virtue. Preaching about how family is so important, it always come first. *Never forget that, Tate.* And Gavin Bartlett does everything for his family.

Where was his family when he was banging somebody else?

Dad sees it all in my eyes, every thought I'm thinking, and it deepens the cloud of shame that darkens his face, sags his shoulders. He deserves to feel like shit after what he's done.

What's more shocking is that Mom knew all along. I think back to eleven years ago. I would have been twelve, turning thirteen. It was right when we moved to Avalon Bay. The memories surface. The arguments around the house, always behind closed doors. They made sure I wouldn't overhear them, but I knew something was up. When I asked Mom about it, she just said they were going through a rough patch and not to worry. So I didn't worry, because my entire life my parents never gave me any reasons to.

Turns out, they were arguing about the fact that he can't keep his dick in his pants.

"Tate, sit down. Please," Dad begs.

"No." I stalk over to the counter and pour myself a cup of coffee. I gulp down the scalding liquid, wishing I could just fucking disappear.

"The affair happened when we moved here from Georgia," Mom says quietly, seeking out my gaze. The total lack of anger or betrayal on her face only pisses me off more, though. "Your dad just opened a new business. I couldn't find a job. We were arguing—"

"And that gives him a free pass to cheat?"

"Of course not," she says. "I'm just providing the context—"

"It's okay, darlin'," Dad interjects, his voice gentle. "This is for me to fix." With a ragged breath, he finally meets my eyes. "I fucked up, kid. Eleven years ago, I committed a very selfish act—"

"Several selfish acts," I remind him coldly. "Because it sure doesn't sound like it was a one-time thing."

"No, it wasn't. It lasted for four months. And I hated myself for it every single day."

I snort. "If you expect me to have any sympathy—"

"I don't. I don't expect sympathy. I know what I did. Your mother knows what I did. And yes, it took me four months to come clean to her."

I narrow my eyes. "You told her yourself?" For some reason I imagined Mom breaking into his phone or stumbling across a hotel receipt in his pocket.

"Yes, I did," he says, and there's a sliver of pride in his tone that triggers a fresh rush of anger.

"Sure, Dad, pat yourself on the back there."

"Tate." He looks hurt.

"So you came clean, big deal. It doesn't change the fact that you slept with somebody else."

"We were struggling with the new business. We were low on money. My ego was in the gutter."

"All I'm hearing is more excuses."

"No, you're hearing the truth. And like your mother said, it's context. People aren't black-and-white creatures. Sure, we know what right and wrong ought to be. But sometimes the line between those is a bit gray. Life clouds your judgment and you cross lines you never thought you'd cross. People do stupid things. *I* did a stupid thing, and for eleven years I've woken up every single day with the intention of showing your mother that I recognize the pain and suffering I caused her, and that I consider each day she continues to stay with me the greatest gift of my life."

At the table, I notice Mom's eyes welling up with tears.

I don't know how I feel about this. To me, cheating is unforgivable. I don't know how she forgave him. But she must have, because I haven't picked up on any bitterness or resentment in our home since then. No closed-door arguments. No hostility. As far as I know, they're open with each other. They seem as in love today as they have been my entire life.

"I don't expect you to understand." Dad shrugs. "And I'm not asking for your forgiveness."

I laugh harshly. "Gee, thanks."

"The person I hurt already forgave me," he says simply.

I scoff at him. "You don't think you hurt me?"

"Has your life been different this past decade?" he asks. "Have we loved you less? Have I treated you worse?"

"No, but . . ." I'm mad again, because . . . yes, he's been a good father. No, it didn't affect me then. But it's affecting me *now,* goddamn it. A growl escapes my throat. "You fucked my girlfriend's mom."

Dad flinches.

Mom goes pale.

"So, please, don't sit there and act like that's cool. I don't care if Mom didn't want to know the name of your mistress. You should've said something the moment I started dating Cassie—"

"I didn't even know she was Victoria's daughter. I had no idea!"

That gives me pause. When I think on it, I realize he might be telling the truth. I told them Cassie was a neighbor, but I didn't specifically say which house. I don't think I even mentioned her last name . . . I shake myself out of it. Fuck that. I'm not getting hung up on minor details.

"You've spent my whole life harping about family," I mutter. *"Family is the most important thing, Tate.* Team family! And then you almost blow up our family. And she was right about how hard you try to present yourself as this good guy. Some selfless, perfect saint. But you were selfish when you cheated, and you're selfish when you go on about the dealership and how you built it for me—"

"Tate—" he tries to interject, looking alarmed.

"Because it's not about me. It's about *your* selfish needs. You want me at the dealership so you have someone to look at boat pictures with. You want to have someone there so you can take Mom on vacation. It's not about me." I slam my cup down. Liquid sloshes over the rim and splashes the cedar island.

Mom stands up. "Tate," she says sharply. "I understand that this is a big shock for you, but we're still your parents. You can't speak to your father like that."

I just stare at her. Then I snort and stalk out the back door.

I don't know where the hell I'm going. I'm barefoot, clad in plaid pajama pants and an old yacht club T-shirt. I just round the side of the house and walk down the street. This street on which I've lived since I was twelve. The town I fell in love with the moment we got here. My first day of school, I met the twins, Wyatt, Chase. I met Steph and Heidi and Genevieve, and immediately had this big friend group. I was swept away, so caught up in this new awesome life of mine that I wasn't paying attention to my parents' lives. I was vaguely aware of "the rough patch" and then it passed, and I never even stopped to consider what it meant.

And now I'm stalking down the street on bare feet, trying to figure out why I'm so angry, and that's when it hits me.

I'm mad because he's fallen off the pedestal. Not that I intentionally placed him on one, but I had always looked up to my dad. I admired him. I never wanted to let him down. He was the strongest, kindest person I knew. He could do no wrong, and now here I am, discovering that at the end of the day, he's perfectly capable of being a selfish prick.

I mean, I should've known. Everyone's capable of that. But I guess you never really expect it of your parents.

I end up at the small park at the end of our street. It's only seven o'clock on a Saturday morning, so the park is empty. I spot a mother pushing a stroller along the path about a hundred yards away, and that's about it.

I find a bench and sit down, burying my face in my hands. I regret snapping at my mother. My father, not so much.

They worked through it. I get it. They had eleven years to do that. I had eleven fucking minutes.

I smother a sigh when I hear his footsteps. I know it's him and not Mom because I know my mother, and she would want us to mend our relationship first. Which just makes me angrier.

"She always puts you first," I accuse.

"I know." His voice shakes.

I look over. His eyes are wet, rimmed with red.

"Always," he repeats as he sits down beside me. "Because that's your mom. She's the best person I know, and I don't deserve her. I don't know where she found the strength to forgive me. Trust me, I thank the Lord every day that she did. I never take that gift for granted."

"I can't believe you cheated on her."

"Me too," he admits. "Never thought I was capable of hurting someone like that. I'm not proud of it. I carry that shame with me every day."

We stare for a moment at the swings that begin swaying in the sudden breeze. As if invisible children are making them move. It invokes images of me in this park, hanging out with my friends. I was so happy to move to Avalon Bay. I didn't realize that move was the precipitating factor in almost losing my family.

"Did you really demand she get an abortion?" Bile coats my throat.

"I didn't demand it. I just said we should." Dad looks as sick as I feel. "I was planning on breaking it off with Victoria that night at the Beacon. The guilt had been eating me alive and I came clean to your mother the day before. Begged her to give me another chance. So I went to meet Tori to tell her it was over, and that's when she told me about the baby. I said I'd support her either way, but that I loved your mother and would never leave her. And, yeah, I told her I thought it would be best, for both of us, if she didn't keep the baby. I was selfish. I didn't want a child with her." He blows out a breath. "But you're wrong, kid. After the affair almost cost me everything I hold dear, I made a vow to never be selfish again. These past eleven years haven't been an act. I devoted my life to your mom and to you."

"I didn't ask you to do that."

"Of course not, but you're my kid, my blood. I *was* trying to leave you a legacy. I know you don't believe me, though, so if it means canceling a vacation or writing you out of my will, then so be it." He shrugs. "Nobody's perfect. Least of all me. We're all just human. Good, bad, and everything in between. Luckily, I found a woman who shares my belief that one mistake doesn't have to define a person. I'm not perfect," he repeats, then pauses for a moment. "With that said, I think you should accept Gil's offer."

The sudden change of subject makes my head spin. "What?"

"Take that voyage, Tate. I shouldn't have talked you out of it."

I stare at my feet. "You didn't. I'm going. I was planning on telling you today, actually."

He laughs under his breath. "Of course you're going." Another chuckle, before he goes serious again. "Tate. The reason I didn't want you to go isn't because I need you at work. To be honest, that sounded better than saying I'm fucking terrified."

I lift my head. "What do you mean?"

"It's a dangerous crossing. I don't know if your mother and I would survive if anything happened to you. But we've never sheltered you. We've let you make your own mistakes, and you're pretty good at recognizing them. And we need to let you take your own risks too, so if your heart is telling you to go, and I know it is, because—" He laughs again. "—my heart did the same damn thing when I was your age. You should go."

I nod slowly. "I will."

"And I know I said I didn't need your forgiveness, but I'm going to ask for it anyway."

Dragging my hand through my hair, I glance over with a rueful smile. "If Mom can get past it, then so can I. Just give me a little time."

"You got it, kid." He claps me on the shoulder. "Why don't we head back to the house before your mom sends Fudge and Polly on a rescue mission. I don't like making her worry."

And she must have been *really* worried, because her entire body sags with relief when we trudge into the house five minutes later. She was standing vigil at the front door, the dogs sitting at her feet, like some weird oil painting. I flash her a smile of assurance, and then Fudge rips a dog fart and we all snicker.

"Everything okay with my boys?" Mom prompts, studying our faces.

I shrug. "Getting there."

A faint smile touches her lips.

"Hope you don't mind if I skip breakfast," I tell her. "I'm just gonna go upstairs and change, then head back to the Jackson house. Gotta start cleaning."

"No problem, sweetie."

Up in my room, I shuck my pajama pants and grab a pair of faded jeans from my dresser. I shove them up my hips, then grab my keys and phone off the nightstand.

There's a knock, and I look up to see Mom lightly rapping her knuckles against my half-open door. "Hey. Got a second for me before you leave?"

"Always. What do you need?"

She walks in and sits at the edge of my bed. After a beat, I sit beside her. And then she begins to talk.

CHAPTER 34

CASSIE

"Hey."

My head lifts at Tate's approach. "Hey."

It's nine in the morning and he's back from his parents' house. I was up in my bedroom when I heard his Jeep pull in, and a moment later his text popped up, asking me to meet him down on the Jacksons' dock.

He looks tired as he lowers his body next to me, dangling those long legs over the edge of the dock.

"Did you get any sleep last night?" I ask.

"What do you think?" he says wryly. "You?"

"What do you think?" I mimic. I let out a sigh. "My mom's gone."

He's startled. "Gone how?"

"Oh, I mean she left. Caught a flight to Boston last night. Grandma told her not to come home, to stay at a hotel. I guess her pride wouldn't allow her to do that. She sent Grandma a message this morning asking to have her bags shipped to Boston."

"Did you two talk at all?"

"Oh, we did." The memory of the confrontation outside the Beacon is going to stay with me for a very long time. Hell, the events of that one night alone will take ten years' worth of therapy to unpack.

"She had her excuses. Claimed she didn't plan on ambushing them at the party."

Tate snorts. "Bullshit."

"That's what I said. It doesn't matter, though. What's done is done."

He studies my face. "So where did you leave it, you and her?"

"It's over," I say flatly. My heart clenches, a ripple of pain moving through me. "The relationship is irrevocably broken."

"Cass . . ."

"It is. And now I feel . . . free. No longer feel trapped by it. I always told myself I *had* to be in this relationship. I *had* to take the abuse because, well, it's my mother. That's what people always say, right? *It's your mother.* They can't fathom cutting a parent out of their lives."

I lean closer to him, resting my head on his shoulder. After a beat, he puts his arm around me. His fingertips stroke my bare shoulder. A part of me feared he would show up this morning and announce he wanted nothing to do with me after my mother's nauseating actions. But he's here and he has his arm around me, and I'm weak with relief.

"I don't need to be in that relationship, Tate. Maybe one day, if she has that moment of self-reflection you were talking about. But that's not happening anytime soon. And in the meantime, I need to live my own life. Without her in it."

"And you're okay with that?"

"I am. I mean, it hurts. But having her in my life hurts more."

"I guess that's the silver lining?" He runs his palm over my shoulder again, a comforting gesture.

"Oh. No. The silver lining would be that if I hadn't had a complete breakdown after confronting my mom, then I wouldn't have gone over to my *dad's*—where I had another complete breakdown. I was very busy." I can't help but laugh. "But enough about me. How did it go with *your* parents?"

"It went." His answering laugh is dry. "But you can't just leave me hanging like that. What happened at your dad's?"

I peek up at Tate with a self-deprecating grin. "Well, I went to confront him and ended up curled in a fetal position of tears on their front lawn. Nia came outside and we had a moment. A good one, actually. Then I went inside and talked to my dad. I did what you told me. Shared my feelings. Vocalized my needs and all that crap."

Tate snickers.

"I told him I want a relationship that involves more than light-hearted banter and turtle shopping. That I want to be able to come to him when I need him and not worry he'll push me away. It went well. I feel very grown up now." I tip my head, smiling again. "You've changed me."

Those chiseled features soften. "How did I do that?"

"You taught me how to stand up for myself. How to be honest with the people around me. I used to be a real chickenshit. But you make me feel strong and—"

He kisses me.

It comes out of nowhere. Dare I say, reminiscent of the old Aaron days, but at least Tate's tongue is still in his mouth. He presses his lips to mine in a soft caress before pulling back.

I run my fingertips over the stubble rising on his jaw. "You okay?"

"Just kiss me again," he says, and our mouths collide. Now his tongue slides through my parted lips, bordering on desperate. His fingers are in my hair and he's groaning against my lips. There's an urgency there, a thick thread of emotion wrapping around the two of us, and I realize both our hearts are engaged.

I pull back and the words just slip out.

"I love you."

His eyelids pop open. "What?"

"I know I said a lot of things before. That I didn't want a relationship. This would end in September. There was no pressure. I know I said all those things. But something's changed. I don't know how, but it just has, and now I'm in love with you." I gulp, staring at my hands. They're trembling. "You told me to talk about my feelings. Those are my feelings. I love you."

"I love you too."

My gaze flies to his. "You do?"

"I do. I've known for a while. Just didn't have the balls to tell you."

"Wait, so I'm suddenly dropping feelings bombs and you're holding them in? Is that what you're saying? We've switched places?"

"Something like that." With an indecipherable look, Tate strokes my cheek. Then he brings my face toward him, and his lips touch mine in an infinitely gentle kiss.

But this kiss . . .

It doesn't feel right.

A drop of moisture splashes the tip of my nose and I look up in confusion. Tate's blinking rapidly. He drags the side of his thumb over his eye.

"What's going on?" I ask uneasily.

"I don't want it to end either," he confesses, emotion creasing his features.

Joy flickers through me. "Okay, good—"

"—but it has to," he finishes, his voice a scant whisper.

My heart sinks like a stone to the pit of my stomach. "W-why?" I stammer.

"You asked how it went with my parents." He lets out a breath.

"They worked through the affair. Mom forgave him a long time ago. All these years of being disgustingly in love, it wasn't fake. They are in love. They love each other a lot, in fact."

"That's good, no?"

"It's great. And I understand my dad's reasons for what he did. That's not to say I condone his actions. He was wrong. He did a shitty thing and he hurt her. But she forgave him. Their marriage is rock solid."

"This is all good, Tate . . ."

"Dad and I had a moment alone and talked about our own stuff, too. Worked through some shit. I'm going to sail to New Zealand."

I nod, the dots suddenly connecting in my head. "I see. And you think it has to end with us because you're leaving for three months—"

"No, that's not it."

I rub the bridge of my nose. I'm so confused. "I don't get what's happening right now."

"I spoke to my mother alone too."

"Okay . . ." None of this is making sense yet.

"She forgave him," Tate reiterates, his voice breaking slightly, "but that doesn't mean she needs to be reminded of it every single day."

A sick sensation crawls into my stomach and wraps around my intestines. "And I'm a reminder of it," I whisper.

He nods. Agony flashing in his eyes.

"We talked for a while. Mom never wanted to know who he had the affair with, but she knows now. She knows it's your mother. She admitted it'll be hard to see you if you and I were together, if we were a couple."

I feel the tears coming. I briefly close my eyes, hoping to ward off the onslaught. I can't even blame Gemma for this. That's the worst part. I *understand*. Of course she doesn't want this reminder. Every time her son brings his girlfriend home, she has to be reminded that her husband cheated on her? With the girlfriend's mother?

"I can't do that to my mom," Tate says hoarsely. "I love you, Cass. I do. But I wouldn't be able to live with myself knowing I was hurting my own mother. I can't do that to her."

His jaw is working. Throat squeezing as he swallows repeatedly. He looks so upset.

I reach for his hand, lacing our fingers together. "It's okay. I understand."

"I'm so sorry." Sheer misery hangs from every word.

"You can't bring home the girl whose mother almost destroyed their marriage. It's going to be a dark cloud over our entire relationship going forward, especially if your mother can't get past it. There's no silver lining." My bottom lip starts quivering. I bite hard on it. I don't want to cry. "So I guess this is goodbye."

"Guess so." His voice cracks again, and so does a piece of my heart.

"I had a good summer," I tell him.

"Best summer of my life."

I smile. His eyes are looking a little misty again. Mine are rapidly following suit. I can barely see him now, my vision is so blurry. We're both weepy, and I know if I sit here any longer, I'll break.

"I'm glad I met you, ginger."

"Glad I met you too, Gate."

I leave him there on the dock. I don't know how my legs manage to carry me all the way into the house. But somehow I make it. Even in my bedroom I continue to fight the tears, because what if he's in *his* room now and we pass our windows at the same time, so I step into the bathroom and sit on the edge of the tub. And only then do I cry.

CHAPTER 35

CASSIE

November

"We did it!" Tate's flushed face fills my laptop screen. He rakes a hand through his wind-kissed golden hair, beaming from ear to ear. Relief jolts through me. I've been in a constant state of worry since he set sail, and every time I see him, safe and sound, I want to weep with joy. "I mean, it was touch and go a couple times. Definitely almost pissed myself during that squall last month—"

I shiver. That was a bad one. I saw the video he shot of the deck after the squall and it still haunts my dreams.

"—and I'm never going to stop apologizing for subjecting you to my a cappella version of 'Poker Face' the night I killed that bottle of Jack."

I giggle.

"—but the voyage has officially come to an end. Sort of. I'm going to stick around here till my girlfriend's parents steal her back from me." He lovingly sweeps those blue eyes over the *Surely Perfect*'s topsail. "Spend the next month sailing around Australia. See what the fuss is all about. So, stay tuned, folks. Journey's not over yet. Talk soon. Cheers."

The video ends.

I start to cry.

It's a weekly routine now. Every Monday, when Tate posts his travel vlog, I sit on my bed, open the laptop, and subject myself to thirty or forty minutes of Tate recapping his week. I'm not sure what editing software he's using, but his videos are excellent. Photo overlays, date cards to show when certain footage is from. Some footage is fixed, when Tate sets the camera somewhere and just lets it film. My heart always soars when I watch those capable hands hoisting a sail, tying a rope. But my favorite part of his videos is *this*—when it's just him, sitting on the deck, or at the table in the galley, talking to me. Well, to everyone. But I like to think he's talking to me.

Peyton says I'm torturing myself. Joy has threatened to fly in from Manhattan and stage an intervention. They think I need to move on. I'm sure they're right. There's nothing helpful about this, nothing to be gained from staring at Tate's handsome face week after week for three months straight. All it did was make me miss him more.

This semester has dragged. I can't concentrate on school. Can't be bothered to see friends or attend any parties. I haven't gone full recluse yet—I still shower. Still wash my hair and eat food. I clean my dorm room and text people. I even respond to emails from my new literary agent Danna Hargrove, who sold the Kit 'n McKenna series for us in a five-book deal. It was a modest advance, but Danna's excited for the potential. She thinks the series will take off. She's already talking about TV adaptations and merch.

I, as always, am tempering my expectations. But I'm hopeful. Robb's on board as illustrator, and the first book, the one I gave to my sisters, releases next fall. The deadline for the second book is in the new year, so luckily I don't need to force myself to be creative right now.

I'm not feeling creative. Not feeling anything, really, least of all happiness. But now it's Thanksgiving, and my spirits are slightly elevated. I'm looking forward to seeing my family. Since the night I showed up at Dad's house and cried in Nia's arms, things have been really good. Dad's been making an effort to check in about how I'm feeling, and Nia and I even started texting.

With my mother, it's the opposite. I haven't spoken to her since that night. I have no interest. She's texted several times, calls frequently, and though I can't bring myself to block her, I don't take her calls. According to Grandma, it's driving my mother crazy. I'm discovering that narcissists don't like the no-contact method. Every now and then I worry she'll show up on campus and try to wrest a reconciliation out of my stubborn hands, but so far, she's kept her distance. Who knows how long that will last.

I shut my laptop, leaving it on the bed as I head downstairs to rejoin my family. Nia's prepping dinner, while Dad pretends to watch football in the den when everyone knows he can't name even one player on any of the teams playing today. In the living room, my sisters are sitting in front of Pierre's tank, showing him the drawings they made of him.

I walk over to them and peer at the glass. Pierre's chilling on his cypress tree. I give him a wave. "Hey, little dude." I look at Mo. "Any fart attacks lately?"

"*No*," she complains, and Roxy heaves a disappointed sigh.

Snickering, I wander into the kitchen where I find Nia at the counter glaring at her cutting board.

"Um. Everything okay?" I eye the pile of diced onions she's amassed, trying to figure out what the problem is.

"I ran out of onions," she grumbles.

"You, Nia Soul, ran out of an ingredient? Didn't you just give me a whole braggy speech when I was here at midterms? The one about your fancy sixth sense that allows you to always purchase the *exact* amount of potatoes required?"

"Yes. *Potatoes*." She's gritting her teeth. "These are onions." Nia curses under her breath, a mixture of English and French expletives that make me grin. "*Merde*. I don't have time to go look for a store that's open right now. I have too much to do—"

"I'll go," I offer. "I'm pretty sure Franny's Market is open till four today. They're always open on holidays."

Relief loosens her shoulders. "Are you sure you don't mind?"

"Yeah, it's no problem at all." I grab Dad's keys off the counter. "I'll go now. How many do you need?"

"Two. So get four."

I snicker. "Four it is."

"Thanks, Cassandra."

I leave the house and get into Dad's truck. It's so strange not to be driving Grandma's Rover. Or staying at her house. But Grandma doesn't live in the Bay anymore. She's in Boston now, residing in the same building as Aunt Jacqueline and Uncle Charlie and loving her quality time with the grandkids. Our house in Avalon Bay belongs to another family now. Some venture capitalist, his much younger wife, and their three children. Grandma says they seemed like a nice family. I hope they enjoy the house. It holds a lot of good memories for me.

At the market, I bypass the carts and march toward the produce aisles. I pick out four large onions, managing to stack two in each hand, then turn around—and slam right into Tate's mother.

"Gemma," I squeak. "Hi."

"Cassie." She's equally startled. "Hello."

Then silence falls.

Oh boy. This is awkward.

I stand there, trying to figure out what to say. I haven't seen her since that awful night at the Beacon. Do I bring it up? Ask how she's doing? Apologize on behalf of my mother?

Now we're both fidgeting with whatever's in our hands. In my case, unfortunately, it's onions. And then I *forget* that it's onions, and stupidly raise one hand to rub the bridge of my nose. My fingers, now covered in the onion curse, trigger a reflexive rush of tears. Shit.

Gemma takes one look at my face and bursts into tears too.

"Oh, no, no," I assure her, trying to wipe my eyes with my elbow. "I'm not crying. It's the onions."

"Well, *I'm* crying," she blubbers. "And it's not because of onions."

"Oh."

Our gazes lock.

Sniffling, she rubs her eyes with her sleeve, then gives me a sad smile. "Do you have a minute to talk? I know it's Thanksgiving, but . . ."

"Sure. Let me just pay for these. I'll meet you outside."

A few minutes later, we reconvene in the small parking lot. The market is the only store open in the plaza, but the café at the end of the row has an outdoor patio. I gesture toward it.

"Let's sit," I suggest.

She nods. We walk to the patio, where I flip over two of the chairs and set them on the ground.

We sit across from each other. I watch her, sorrow tightening my belly. "How are you doing?" I finally ask. "We haven't spoken since the night . . . you know, the night."

"The night," she echoes wryly.

"Just so you know—I had no idea what my mother was going to do. She took me by surprise, same as she did everyone else."

Gemma's eyes widen. "Oh. No. I never for a moment thought you were involved."

"Ah, okay. Good."

Another silence falls.

"I've been watching all of Tate's videos," I say. "That was some voyage, huh?"

"Took ten years off my life." She shudders. "He could have died in that squall. Lord! And then when his GPS broke!" She's now swallowing repeatedly, appearing nauseous. "Never have kids, Cassie. You're constantly living in fear they might die."

"Nah, when the GPS broke, that's when I was the *least* concerned about him."

"Really? Because I was picturing my boy lost in the middle of the Indian Ocean."

I shake my head. "Tate will never get lost, not as long as the stars are still in the sky."

My heart suddenly swells with emotion. I miss him so much. I think about him all the time. Sometimes I dream that I'm on the *Surely Perfect* with him. We're lying on a blanket on the gleaming teak deck and gazing up at the stars. He points out all the different constellations and tells me where the fuck we are.

Gemma must see the raw pain in my eyes because hers fill with tears again. "Can you ever forgive me?" she blurts out.

I blink in surprise. "What?"

Rather than clarify, she seems to change the subject. Her face takes on a faraway look. "His videos, Cassie . . . he's happy, yes. He's always happy when he's sailing. But I know my son. He's not at peace. His eyes are troubled."

I never saw any indication of that, but she's his mother. She knows him better. She's probably catalogued every last expression on Tate's face. Every flicker of emotion.

"We've spoken three times," she tells me. "Once a month. He calls from the satellite phone. It's expensive, so he keeps the calls short. But I hear it in his voice. He's sad."

A sob rises in my throat. I hastily swallow it down. *I'm sad too,* I want to say. But I don't. Because I understand the reason we broke up—she's sitting right in front of me. And I don't blame her for it, not one bit.

"I asked him to break up with you," Gemma confesses. "I told him I couldn't stand to have you around."

"I know. I get it. Honestly, I do."

"I was wrong."

I frown at her. "What?"

"I was wrong," she repeats with a firm shake of the head. "Gavin cheated on me, but I took him back. That's all that matters."

"But my mother . . ." I furrow my brow.

"I don't care about your mother. The affair was never about your mother. It was about my husband. It was about his own insecurities, his perceived inadequacies. And he's worked so hard on himself over the years. I'm proud of him. And I'm ashamed of myself for putting my own needs ahead of my child's."

"Gemma, come on. You're being too hard on yourself."

"No." She shakes her head. "Tate comes first. Always. Forever."

I gulp down another lump of emotion at the proof that they exist—good mothers. The proof is in Nia, and how fiercely she loves her girls. In Gemma, and how fiercely she loves her son. I might not have that, but it makes me happy to know others do.

"He loves you. You're the first girl he's ever felt that way about. I've watched him over the years." She sighs. "I know my boy. He was always a player—that's what we say these days, right? A player?"

Mmm. Not quite. I believe the term is *fuckboy*. But I keep that to myself. Besides, that's not what Tate is. It's not who he is. He's the best man I've ever known. Wise beyond his years. More sensitive than he lets on.

And, fine, he's great in bed.

"Then this summer, he met you and fell in love, and his own mother took that away from him. I'm ashamed."

"Gemma. Stop."

"So, please, can you ever forgive me?"

"There's nothing to forgive."

I reach over and take her hand. She clasps it with both of hers. "I miss him," I confess.

"I know. So do I." She smiles. "I put together a care package for him last night. I need to send it to Auckland before he sets sail for his Australian adventure. Do you know how much it costs to ship something to New Zealand? Gavin almost choked on his tongue."

I laugh. "Well, I mean, it's literally at the bottom of the world. It's bound to be expensive." Then I bite my lip, as something nags at the back of my mind. It starts as a tiny seed, then grows into a full-fledged idea that has me squeezing Gemma's hand. "But if you need a delivery person . . ."

CHAPTER 36

TATE

December

I exit the tiny grocery store three miles from the marina, muttering a string of curses under my breath. The kid that loaded these bags overfilled this one. And it's a paper bag. A delicate fucking creature. As I feel the bottom about to give out, I execute a swift maneuver, readjusting my grip at the same time I heave the danger bag on top of the meat bag. I swear, if this thing bursts and all my carefully hand-picked fruit rolls away? And then my apples go rolling on the dirt and I have to chase after them like an asshole—

"Tate."

I stop. Frowning.

Weird. I swear I heard Cassie's voice saying my name. I snap myself out of such insanity and keep walking.

"Tate! I know you heard me! Are you running away from me?"

Now it's Cassie's *outraged* voice.

Wait, is this actually real?

I spin around. Unfortunately forgetting the delicate paper-bag pyramid in my hands. I manage to hold on for dear life, but the fruit bag is in great peril, and Cassie runs over to grab it out of my hands.

"You okay there?" she teases.

All I can do is stand and gawk.

"Tate?"

Finally, I find my voice. "What are you doing here?"

"Oh, I asked the guy at the marina where you were, and he said you came here to buy groceries, so my cab driver brought me—"

"No, I mean *here*. In New Zealand. You realize you're in New Zealand, right?"

"No! Really? I thought I was on a beach in Miami!"

A smile springs to my lips. Goddamn. I missed her. And I can't stop staring at her. Her red hair is twisted in a loose knot on top of her head. She's wearing jean shorts and a blue T-shirt. White sneakers. Her eyes are shining and her cheeks are flushed, but the latter might be because of the sun beating down on us. It's hot as hell here in the winter. Or rather, their summer.

"I'm still trying to figure out if you're real." I blink. Blink again. But she's still standing in front of me.

Cassie smiles. "I'm real."

"And you're in Auckland."

"I'm in Auckland."

"Because . . . ?"

"Oh. Right." She brightens. "I'm dropping off a care package from your mother. It's kind of bulky, so I left it at the office in the marina. We can grab it when we get there."

I stare at her again. "Now you're just talking gibberish."

Cassie starts to laugh. "No, I really did bring a care package from Gemma. I ran into her last week when I was home for Thanksgiving."

I narrow my eyes. "I spoke to her the day after Thanksgiving. She didn't mention seeing you."

"I asked her not to. I wanted this to be a surprise. But I had to write a couple final papers before I could get away."

"Cass."

"Yes?"

"I am not complaining that you're here. Not one bit. But what is happening right now? Why did you come?"

"I came because . . ." She bites her lip, suddenly bashful. "Because I missed you."

My pulse quickens. "I missed you too," I say hoarsely.

More than she'll ever know. These last few months have been the most challenging of my entire life. Me against the elements. Singled-handedly sailing some of the toughest waters I've ever navigated. I'm not gonna lie—I was scared. Terrified I wouldn't even reach my destination. But I persevered, and one of the reasons I did was Cassie. Whenever I thought, *fuck, I might actually not make it,* I heard her voice in my head, making some smartass remark. You can do it, Gate.

Now she's right here, and while I don't have a proper explanation yet, I can't help myself. I set the grocery bags on the ground and pull her into my arms. She squeaks in surprise, but I just tighten my grip and let out a ragged breath. "Just let me hold you for a minute."

And she melts into me. I bury my face in her hair, inhaling the sweet scent of her shampoo. The soft strands tickle my chin. Her arms wrap around my waist.

"I really fucking missed you." My voice is still so hoarse. Thick with gravel. I force myself to release her, searching her enigmatic expression. "What exactly did my mom say to you?"

"She said she wants her son to be happy."

My chest clenches. The notion of hurting Mom is still so soul crushing. But these past three months without Cassie have also been pretty fucking awful.

"And she asked me to forgive her," Cassie says. She meets my eyes. "I think that means she's okay if I'm your girlfriend."

Heart racing, I put on a cocky grin. "Girlfriend, eh? That's rather presumptuous of you. Who says I want you as my girlfriend?"

"Sweetie. I think you kind of ceded the upper hand when you smelled my hair and told me how much you missed me."

She has a point. My smile widens so big I feel like it'll crack my face in half. The sun is almost blinding, but I don't slide my aviators on because I want her to see my eyes. To see the sincerity in them when I say, "I love you."

Happiness warms her gaze. "I love you too."

"Are you really here?" I ask.

"I'm really here. And you have me for three weeks. I need to go home for Christmas," she says regretfully.

Three weeks. Damned if my dick doesn't twitch hearing that. It's been three months since I've seen her. Kissed her. Touched her.

"Three weeks, you say?" I cock a brow.

"I have to warn you, though . . . I might need to put in some work on my next children's book while I'm here."

My jaw drops. "No."

"Oh yeah. Five-book deal, baby. The first book in the Kit 'n McKenna series debuts next fall. They love it so much they want to rush it out."

"You're a fucking rock star."

I tug her into my arms again and then my lips are devouring hers. Hot. Desperate. Because three months' worth of pent-up lust is now bubbling inside me.

"I want you naked so bad right now," I growl.

Cassie grins. "Then let's go get naked."

I lead her toward the dusty black Jeep parked a few yards away. Yup, I traveled to the ends of the earth and they give me another Jeep. I wanted something cooler, like a Humvee. But this was all the rental place had.

We load the bags in the back and hop in. Cassie is beaming. Her lips are curved in a smile. Cheeks flushed with excitement. Everything about her sends joy rippling through me.

"Wait, let me get my sunglasses." She twists toward the back seat to rummage in her purse. And I can't help copping a feel of one delectable tit.

"Save it for the boat," she teases. When she turns back, shades in hand, she suddenly makes a happy noise. "Look at the silver lining."

I glance over, grinning. "All right, let's hear it."

"No, I mean, *look* at it." A brilliant smile fills her face as she points to the sky.

I follow her gaze and realize she's right. Backlit by the sun, today's clouds have very distinct edges.

"I've never actually seen clouds with silver linings before," Cassie marvels. "It's beautiful."

I lean over and place a kiss on the corner of her jaw. "Beautiful," I agree, and I'm not looking at the clouds.

EPILOGUE

CASSIE

March

"I'm worried about Pierre."

One might expect to hear that from my sisters.

Or my father.

Or maybe even Tate, who's developed a close relationship with my little sisters' turtle over these past few months. Dad is constantly texting pictures of Pierre to my boyfriend.

But no, the worry-laced remark comes from none other than Nia, who walks up and slides into the booth next to Dad. The three of us are still finishing up our coffee and dessert; across the restaurant, Tate and the girls are crowded around one of those toy machines where you have to maneuver a claw hand to try and capture one of the plushies in the glass box. Roxy demanded he win them the stuffed turtle, and I'm discovering that Tate is incapable of walking away from a challenge.

"Why?" Dad asks his wife, his forehead creasing. "What's wrong? What did Joel say?" Nia had just stepped out to answer a call from their turtle sitter, and has returned looking quite distraught.

"I asked him how Pierre is and he kept saying LL Cool J is

fine." She sounds flustered. "I told you we should have asked Chandra instead. That boy's brain is jumbled from the ganja."

"*Jumbled from the ganja*," I howl into my coffee. "I love it. Title of my next book."

Dad snickers. "Nice," he tells me, before putting a reassuring arm around Nia. "Don't worry. Joel's not in some stoned stupor—well, he probably is, but not about this. LL Cool J was Pierre's former name."

"Oh. I see." She relaxes.

"And trust me," I add, "nobody will take better care of that turtle than Joel. He's the turtle whisperer."

Although they may need to spray the house down with air freshener when they get back to the Bay tomorrow, because I guarantee Joel smoked pot in there while he was housesitting.

Dad, Nia, and the girls flew to Boston over March break to visit me. Technically, I live in Hastings, the small town an hour from the city that houses the Briar University campus, but I drove into Boston to spend the weekend with my family. And Tate, who heard about the visit and insisted on tagging along.

He and I have seen each other twice since our Australia adventure. A weekend at the end of January, and another one during my February break, but Tate bemoans it's not enough. He's right. I miss him every second we're not together, and I'm counting the days till graduation. I've already booked my flight to Avalon Bay. I'm going to stay with my family, but lately Tate's been dropping hints that we should find a place together for the fall.

"Cassie! Look!"

I grin when I glimpse my sisters racing toward the booth. Both their hands are clasped around the stuffed turtle, which they're holding up in a victory pose. Behind them, Tate struts over with a smug look.

"And you doubted me," he accuses. He glances at my sisters. "Remember how she doubted me?"

Roxy nods sternly. "She did. I remember."

"I remember too," Mo says.

I roll my eyes at all of them. "Of course I doubted. That machine is rigged. Nobody ever wins."

"Oh really?" Tate points at the turtle. "Does that look rigged? I don't think so, ginger."

"Don't think so, ginger," Roxy echoes, while Nia and Dad laugh into their coffees.

I glare at Tate. "You're a bad influence on them."

"Nah."

"Nah," Mo mimics.

I sigh and take the last bite of my lemon cake.

Tate sits beside me, slinging one sculpted arm around my shoulders. "I think you're just jealous, babe. Want me to win something for you? There's a lobster in there that's almost the same shade of red as your face."

"You're *so* funny." I glower at him, but he just winks. Besides, we both know I'm not actually mad. If anything, I'm so happy he's here with me right now.

We're happy.

Like, disgustingly happy.

The last thing I expected from my summer fling was to get a boyfriend out of the deal. All I wanted was passion. Fun. Maybe a little bit of romance.

But I got so much more than what I bargained for. I found true love with the greatest, funniest, sweetest man I've ever met in my life. A man who taught me how to express my feelings, even when they suck. And thanks to him, I got my dad back. I was finally able to free myself from my mother's clutches and end a relationship that was hurting me. I made a genuine connection with my stepmother. Hell, I even got to see Australia—from the deck of a yacht piloted by the hottest captain on the planet.

"It's cold!" Mo complains, burrowing closer to our dad. A group had just entered the restaurant, and since our table is near the door, a gust of cold March wind cools the air.

"Seriously," Dad grumbles. "Isn't it supposed to be spring? I don't know how you survive living up here in the Arctic."

I grin at him. "The northeast is not the Arctic. And I don't mind the weather. Especially in winter. The snow is so pretty."

"Winter sucks," Roxy informs me.

"Totally sucks," Tate agrees, before planting a kiss on my cheek. "Summer's my favorite season."

I meet his playful blue eyes. "Yeah? Why's that?"

"You know. All those cute summer girls rolling into town . . ."

"*All* of them?" I accuse.

"Well, just one." He finds my hand under the table. "And this summer is going to be even better than the last."

I lace our fingers together. "I can't wait."

ACKNOWLEDGMENTS

Every time I return to the world of Avalon Bay, there's a smile on my face from the words *Chapter One* all the way until *The End*. This little beach town is so much fun to immerse myself in, and I'm so grateful that I get to spend my days losing myself in fictional worlds. Even more, I'm grateful to the people who allow me to do that:

My editor, Eileen Rothschild, who let me lean into my silly side with this book and write about Keanu Reeves turtles and whatever other random things came to mind.

The Griffin all-stars: Lisa Bonvissuto, Alyssa Gammello, and Alexis Neuville, for their support and cheerleading for this series, and Jonathan Bush, for another amazing cover.

My agent, Kimberly Brower, for finding such a good home for this series.

Assistants Natasha and Nicole, who keep me on task when I'd rather be binge-watching TV shows.

Ann-Marie and Lori at Get Red PR for helping spread the word about the Avalon Bay series.

And as always: every reader, reviewer, blogger, Instagrammer, Tweeter, BookTokker, and supporter of my books. Your continued love and enthusiasm is what makes this job worthwhile!

ABOUT THE AUTHOR

Amanda Niccle White

A *New York Times, USA Today,* and *Wall Street Journal* bestselling author, ELLE KENNEDY grew up in the suburbs of Toronto, Ontario, and is the author of more than forty romantic suspense and contemporary romance novels, including the international bestselling Off-Campus series and Briar U series.